DRAGONSEERS AND BLOODLINES

SECICAO BLIGHT BOOK TWO

CHRIS BEHRSIN

Cover design layout by Miblart

To my father, for all the fascinating talks.

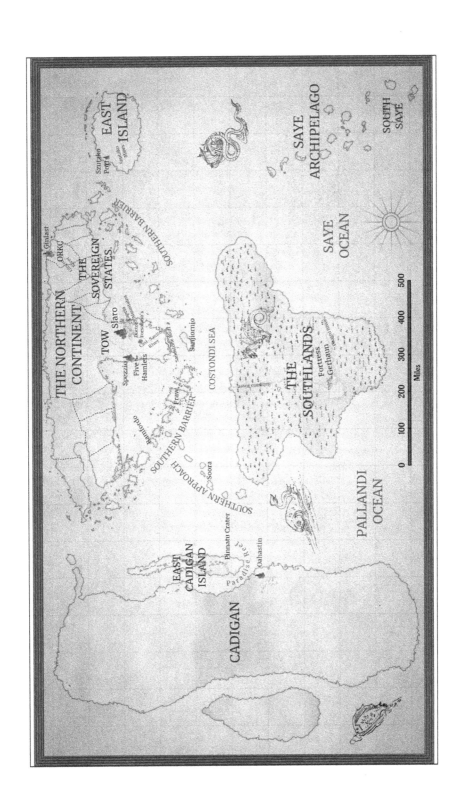

CONTENTS

PART I

TAKA

"What adult doesn't look back into their past and wish at least something had been different about their childhood?"

— TAKA SAKO

1

The training dummy attacked me with the fury of a possessed scarecrow.

Okay, so in all honesty, it wasn't the dummy that attacked me but me who sent a misaimed kick at the dummy's wooden stump. And that was all it took for the thing to come tumbling upon me – a mass of sand and skin of reinforced burlap so tough, you couldn't cut it with a knife.

And all I had to defend me were two sharp knives – crafted just like Sukina's – and my feminine form, stronger than it used to be, due to training so hard for the last two years. But still, I couldn't get the strokes right. I just didn't have the grace that Sukina used to.

The thing sent me flat on my back and pinned me to the ground underneath its weight. I softened the fall as much as possible, and then I lay there, defeated, as I gathered the strength to shift the thing off me.

This is how it had been since Sukina had died. I was the last of a kind, the only remaining dragonseer, save for Taka who in many ways was also one. But dragonseers had to be female, and Taka was now male, due to a magical drug forced on him by King Cini III. Thing is, Taka was only a ten-year-old kid.

I lay still a moment, as I watched something pass overhead through the brown, roiling secicao clouds. A flying form, as dark as a crow, though much larger. *"Charth,"* I said inside my mind, reaching out to the dragon through the collective unconscious. *"Is that you?"*

One of the dragonmen had been visiting us every day, ever since Sukina's funeral. After we'd said our goodbyes to Sukina, Gerhaun had had a conversation with Charth, asking him not to come again. Charth was too dangerous, Gerhaun had told me. He had the spirit of Finesia inside him, and it was only a matter of time before he turned on us.

Since then we'd never seen him resting on the ramparts, but always flying overhead, as if in defiance. But he never responded in the collective unconscious, no matter how much we reached out.

Dragonseers, men and women who could turn into dragons (known as dragonmen), and dragon queens could telepathically speak through a medium known as the collective unconscious. We only needed a strong enough source of it, and the resident dragon queen, Gerhaun Forsi, was the source here in Fortress Gerhaun. Here, that is, in the middle of the Southlands – a barren continent infested with a plant known as secicao with an ambition of taking over the world. The collective unconscious served other purposes as well, like keeping the noxious clouds from the secicao away and allowing us to at least breathe in this place.

I watched Charth pass by, hoping at least for some response from him. For Sukina's long lost love to reach out and acknowledge that life goes on. And perhaps tell me that Francoiso – his brother and a lost affair of my own – was still alive. That he hadn't had his throat ripped out by Alsie Fioreletta, when both of them were fighting in dragon form. But we live as we dream, alone.

I sighed and then pushed the training dummy off me. I propped it back into the ground, filled in the sand around the stump to secure it, and walked back into position to attack again. I pulled back one knife and glared at the two red circles that I'd drawn in red wax to emulate eyes.

"This time," I said. "I will take you." I studied the spot on the ground just in front of it. Two stabs and then a cartwheel kick to the head. That was how Sukina used to do it.

"Auntie Pontopa. Auntie Pontopa." Taka came running through the double doors at the edge of the sparring ground. In the corner of my eye, I saw he was carrying something metallic that glistened in what low light came through the clouds.

"Not now, Taka," I said, and I lowered myself ready to charge. Lieutenant Wiggea, my trainer, would admonish me for this, telling me never to choreograph my intentions, whether in melee or ranged combat. But he wasn't here, and I wanted to communicate to Taka that I was busy. How many times had I told him not to distract me during training sessions?

"But look what I've found, Auntie Pontopa? I went exploring…"

I wasn't going to grace him with the pleasure of looking. The boy had to learn that he'd only get my attention when it was due. He had my parents to look after him and he didn't need me. Anyway, it was time for me to show him how awesome a fighter his dragonseer auntie could be.

The muscles on my face tightened and I charged with the same kind of fury the training dummy had attacked me with moments before. I kept my eyes focused on the scuff mark where my hands would hit, a little further back than my previous attempt.

I dug the side of my foot into that spot to halt the momentum of the charge, which I transferred towards my right hand for the first knife lunge. The second lunge came from my other hand, below the first. It hit the training dummy in its stomach. Then I took a step back with my left foot and prepared myself to launch the cartwheel.

But I stepped back so far that my foot slipped on the sand. To stop myself doing the splits in front of Taka, I tumbled into a forward roll. And I ended up barrelling right into the training dummy, hitting it with my head, and knocking it to the ground.

It took a short moment for my senses to return to me, and what I heard first was Taka's laughter. "You're funny, Auntie Pontopa. You should work in a circus."

I grunted and spat some sand out of my mouth and stood up to look at him. His cheeks had filled out a little since I'd first met him at the palace, and before that when I'd seen so many pictures of him on the front pages of the magazines. But while he had favoured ornate clothes back then, now he wore loose cotton trousers, a leather jerkin and a simple frilly white shirt with bits of sand trapped between the creases. His hair also had a sandy colour – very different to Sukina's rich black – but he did have his mother's and grandfather's dark almond eyes.

"You can be my token monkey," I said. Quite fitting, really.

This got him laughing again. "I've always wanted to be a monkey, Auntie Pontopa. Look at me, I'm a monkey." He puffed out his cheeks. "Ooh ooh ooh. What do you say? Do I make a good monkey?"

"Much better than I could do myself. Anyway, what have you got there? Is that one of your father's automatons?"

He had his arms cradled around something, his hands cupped over it so I couldn't see it properly. But eight spindly legs dangled from it, and I guessed it to be some kind of spider.

"No," he replied. "Papo never lets me touch any of his work. 'When I'm old enough, I'll show you how secicao power works,' he says. So, I went looking for some automatons of my own."

I shook my head and sighed. I guess Taka had come pestering Faso before he came looking for me. And, given Faso was his biological father, you'd think he should be the one looking after him. My parents instead had taken on the job of nanny, but probably today they'd decided to have a bit of a rest. "So where did you get it?" I asked. Then it dawned on me. "Dragonheats Taka, did you?"

"There was this room," Taka said. "And I saw something in the wall and I managed to open it. And this is what I found."

Blood started to rush to my cheeks. I raised my voice. "Taka, Gerhaun told you never to go near that room." It was meant to be reserved for his training.

"But there's nothing inside, Auntie. Just this stupid spider, which I can't seem to power on."

It was there to teach him how to calm his mind so he could control his thoughts and not reveal anything of value to foes listening in on the collective unconscious. But he'd need someone to train him well enough to do that, and I still had a lot to learn before I was ready to take on the role of his mentor. Wellies, I was pretty new at all this myself. Added to the fact, he was still so young that a spider automaton crawling over him in the dark would probably traumatise him for life.

I snatched the automaton out of Taka's hands. "You should do as Gerhaun says. She sets these rules to protect you, and you know full well where you can play and where you can't."

He looked at me in shock. Clearly, he'd expected me to be impressed by his trophy. "Gerhaun never said anything about not picking up any spider automatons. What does it do anyway?"

"It was meant to be a secret. And it will remain that way until you're ready."

"Fine," Taka said. "I don't need your stupid automatons anyway. I can look after myself." And he turned on his heel and stormed off out the door.

Just a moment later, a terrible piercing sensation stabbed in my head. The pain was so sharp, it caused me to clutch my hands to my temples. Dragonheats, Taka had let off his scream again. I'd thought we'd drilled into him that if he did that there'd be consequences, and he'd just have woken Gerhaun from one week of sleep as well.

My vision went blurry and I sat down on the floor and closed my eyes a moment to recover. When I finally got around to opening them again, I saw Mamo and Papo enter the courtyard through the doorway. Mamo opened her mouth, rushed over to me, and put a hand on my shoulder. Through the blurs and the stars, I could just make out her flowing curls, the same as mine, although hers now had greyed. "Darling. Are you alright? What have we told you about training too hard?"

I shook my head. "This wasn't the training, which I can handle, by the way. It was Taka."

Papo stepped forwards and scratched his salt-and-pepper beard. "Taka did this? How? He's just a child."

"His scream, Papo. Did you see where he went? I thought you were meant to be looking after him."

"He wanted to spend his birthday with his father. So, I took him to the workshop." Mamo grimaced. "I guess he didn't last too long there."

When I heard my mother mention the word birthday, my heart jumped in my chest. "Wellies! His birthday... I'm sorry, Mamo, I forgot... I've just had so much on that..." I glanced at the scuff mark in the ground in front of the training dummy and gritted my teeth. "If I'm going to face off against Cini and Alsie again, I have to be ready."

Mamo sighed. "I'll go and find Taka. Cipao, you stay there."

"But..."

"You know what the doctor said. Keep it steady." My father had taken a bullet back home in the Five Hamlets, just after King Cini had burnt our cottage to the ground and Sukina, Faso and I had flown in to rescue my parents. Papo had thus spent quite a while recovering at old-family friend's Doctor Forsolano's. After we'd rescued Taka from the palace and Sukina had passed away in Forsolano's sickbed, I had to leave my parents at his place for a while. That had given my father plenty of time to recover.

But during the extraction mission six months ago to get my parents out of there, Papo's injury had relapsed. Fortunately, Doctor Forsolano had opted to come south with his old-time friends, so he could give my father advice not to rush into things. And running after Taka wouldn't be good for him right then, I was sure.

Papo folded his arms over his chest. "Fine," he said. "I'll just sit here and watch my daughter train then." He placed himself on the stone bench by the side of the door.

"I'll be back soon," Mamo said, and she reached down to kiss me on the cheek. "Pontopa, you look exhausted, you should rest."

"Just one more pass," I said. And I stood up and brushed off the dust.

Mamo shook her head. "We'll talk later." She rushed out the door.

My head had stopped spinning. I squinted and tried to muster some energy to attack the dummy again, but having my father staring at me was a little offputting. I turned to him.

"Don't mind me," he said. "Attack and all that... I want to see what you have in you."

"But you wish it could be you who could be fighting."

"Oh, all those punches and dropkicks, I never had it in me. They trained me to use firearms during the Dragonheats and that was it. We were never meant to do close combat."

I smiled. "When fighting some of these people, the only chance you get is close combat." I was thinking of Alsie Fioreletta in particular, the king's right-hand woman who could turn into a dragon herself. Alsie Fioreletta who killed Sukina. Then, there was King Cini as well, whose secicao hardened his skin so much that no bullet could harm him. But a blade across the throat could.

"And I wish it could be someone else. Not my dear daughter," Papo said.

Although, ironically, I wasn't really his daughter by blood. And my mother only half-so, all thanks to Doctor Forsolano's prenatal technology and my mother donating her womb for me to grow in after my first mother had died with me inside her.

"You know there's no other way," I said. "It's either I fight, or this world becomes destroyed by secicao."

"I know, I know," Papo said. "And I hope soon that I'll be able to fully recover and join the battle."

I shook my head. "Papo, you're fighting no one," I said. Then when I saw the scorn on his face, I let off a meek smile. "Okay you can watch, but just don't distract me."

"I'll try," he replied with a shrug, and he took out a magazine from the front pocket of his dungarees. This time, he read The Fortress Digest – a tiny magazine compared to the Tow Observer he used to be so fond of. There was just so little news here worth publishing. But this came with the territory in a barren land in the middle of nowhere, with the only life outside being a plant that wished to choke up the planet.

I gritted my teeth and charged at the training dummy again. I didn't even stop this time to register the point on the ground where my right foot would stop me. And in a way, that kind of helped. I scuffed at the dust as I pushed the side of my foot into the ground. Then I lunged with a quick one-two with my knives, angled the blades outwards so I wouldn't injure myself and launched myself into a cartwheel. I felt a sense of oneness as my feet followed a graceful arc. And then, a hard thud twisted my ankle, causing me to yelp out in pain. I landed on the other foot and collapsed on the floor. I rubbed at my ankle as the training dummy toppled to the ground.

Papo rushed over to me. "Pontopa, are you okay?" He clutched at his chest as he lumbered forward.

"Papo, what did Doctor Forsolano say? No sudden movements."

"Wellies, what am I meant to do when my daughter goes and injures herself all the time. Here, let me have a look."

He crouched down and felt at the skin on my ankle. I clenched my teeth and tried not to make a sound. "It's swelling fast, you better take it to Doctor Forsolano."

"I'll be fine. One small bruise isn't going to stop me."

"Pontopa, you're taking this too far. It's time for you to rest, and you know that." Quite fitting advice really, given he'd do the exact same thing were he in my situation.

"I need to get stronger. The bruises will heal, but Sukina won't. I need to fight for what she fought for, Papo."

"But you won't get there overnight," Papo said. "It will take time."

"We don't have time. Cini's forces are strengthening every day. You've read what's happening." I pointed at Papo's magazine. "The king's automatons are getting even more powerful, as he improves them with secicao power. It could be weeks before the next dragonheats and the troops and dragons of Fortress Gerhaun will need a strong leader behind them."

"They need a strong heart, not physical strength. You can only give them what you have."

"No, Papo. I must give them more."

My father put down his magazine and folded his arms. "You'll kill yourself, Pontopa." And with those words, a wave of grief rose up inside my chest. The memories flooded back to me. Sukina clashing blades with King Cini, in a brilliant display of knives against sword.

Alsie letting out her Banshee's scream to disable us all and stop Sukina killing Cini. The dart burying itself in Sukina's throat, thrown by Alsie's fair hand. And watching Sukina die in Forsolano's sickbed. Feeling completely lost after that about what to do next. Now, I had responsibility. I couldn't let Sukina down.

"Sometimes," I said. "We have to risk our lives... For a good cause."

The features on Papo's rugged face sank. He opened his mouth to say something, but I raised my hand to stop him.

"Papo, you know I have to do this."

And he sighed and then returned to reading his magazine.

Meanwhile, despite the pain in my ankle, I continued to practice attacking the training dummy. In a way, I realised, in the heat of battle, I couldn't let minor injuries get in the way. So, I tried to conceal my pain from my father, keeping as straight a face as possible as I dived and darted and lunged and stabbed at my target.

And I got into the flow of things too. I don't know how much time passed before I was interrupted mid-swing by a commotion coming from the doorway.

Lieutenant Wiggea – not just my trainer but also my most trusted (and handsomest) dragonelite guard and the most likely to get the next promotion – stormed through. He had slick brown hair and wore an olive coloured uniform with a neatly ironed shirt and cotton trousers. He had a parchment in his hand and three other guards followed foot behind him.

"Dragonseer Wells. Dragonseer Wells, I knew I'd find you here."

"What is it, Lieutenant?" I asked.

"It's Taka... He's missing."

"What? How did he get out?"

"He just walked up to a Grey, sang to it, leapt on, and then he was gone. We tried to catch up, Maam, but his song kept his dragon flying so fast, and he slowed down our own as well. We lost him into the clouds after that."

My heart was beating hard in my chest. I kind of promised Sukina I'd look after Taka. "Lost him? Have you any idea where he might have gone?"

"That's not all, Maam. We went searching and got ambushed by automatons. We took out four Greys in the search party and lost three of them. Only I got out alive."

This wasn't good. "Wiggea, tell me everything. And fast..."

He tugged on the collar of his shirt. "There's not much to tell, Maam. We encountered an airship, with guns on it and ten or so war-automatons on the ground. Taka had already weakened our dragons. And we found his dragon dead. We're guessing the airship got away with Taka."

I furrowed my eyebrows. "Did the airship have an insignia on it?"

"No, Maam."

I looked up at the sky. *"Charth, please don't tell me it was you..."* I reached out and said this in the collective unconscious, just in case he could hear. But Charth wouldn't, surely. Not after how much he'd risked getting Taka out of the palace in the first place.

As I thought about it more, I started to feel sick. Sukina had died so that we could rescue her son. Now, two years later, we'd lost him once again. And we didn't even know who had taken him.

I clenched my fists at my sides. "Cini must have a play in this. And probably Alsie Fioreletta too."

Then, I reached out again in the collective unconscious. Gerhaun, it seemed, was now awake. I was right, she hadn't been able to sleep through Taka's scream. *"What should I do, Gerhaun?"* I was really at a loss.

Despite the urgency of the situation, Gerhaun's old and tired voice sounded completely calm inside my head. *"What do you think you should do, Dragonseer Wells? If you want to be the leader, you need to make decisions like this for yourself."*

"I need to investigate," I said, though I hated the idea. *"I need to see what happened first-hand, look for clues."*

"Taka didn't go far, it seems," Gerhaun said. *"I already sent some more dragons to scout the location. Perhaps someone even enticed him out there."*

It occurred to me then. How could we have been so stupid? Maybe it wasn't Charth but Alsie flying overhead all this time. She could have been using her powers to try and convince Taka to leave Fortress Gerhaun's walls, despite us instructing the boy not to.

"There's no way of knowing," Gerhaun said. *"But whoever it was, you have to make haste. We might be able to catch up with them if we make the right decisions."*

"Right." I stormed towards the door.

But Gerhaun had already read my intentions. Not always, did I remember to mask my thoughts. *"Don't go alone, Pontopa. Take a team with you. Oh, and take Faso as well. It's time he realised the consequences of not stepping up to the plate as Taka's father."*

"Right." I turned to Wiggea. He stood to attention and saluted.

"Your orders, Maam?" he asked.

"Get a team of twenty men and twenty Greys together. We're going to go and see what happened."

"And you'll take Velos I presume." Velos, by the way, was my own personal dragon who I'd grown up with since I was seven years old.

"Yes, but first I'm going to go and find Faso. That buffoon is coming with us, whether he's busy or not." I had a bone to pick with the inventor. While I'd genuinely forgotten Taka's birthday, he had deemed it as unessential and shunned Taka away.

"Papo," I said. "I need to go a while."

"Let me come," he said. And he leaned forward, clutching at his chest as he stood up again.

I raised an eyebrow. "No, you should stay. You know what the doctor said. I'm only going out to investigate and will be back soon."

Mamo then came wheeling through the door. "Pontopa, I can't find Taka anywhere," she said. Then she saw the concern on Wiggea's face. "Oh my…"

"Papo will explain," I said, and I hurried out the door.

2

Faso wasn't inside his workshop but in the section of Fortress Gerhaun's courtyard that he'd cordoned off to construct his dragon automaton. He didn't turn to look at me when I approached, and instead was busy tightening up a plate the size of his hand with a wrench. Faso's six-legged pet ferret automaton, Ratter, sat on his shoulder, watching the inventor's every move as if supervising the whole operation.

The air had a slight chill to it, a little more than usual. Sometimes, the wind came from the ocean to the west and then passed through this land which saw very little light through its thick gloomy clouds. It brought with it the smell of secicao – a faint eggy tang that took some getting used to, I have to admit.

"Faso, you buffoon," I said. "Why did you turn your son away on his birthday?"

"Not now, Pontopa. I'm busy." That was the problem with Faso – he never seemed to care about anything but science.

I put my hands on my hips. "Do you really think that your stupid automaton is the most important thing in the world right now, Faso?" He had the thing splayed out across the floor, a flat brass carpet, looking especially unimpressive.

Faso looked up at me, bemusement stretched across his eyebrows. "This 'stupid automaton' is going to save many human and dragon lives. Much like the armour I developed for Velos saved yours, if you remember. While you're whacking training dummies all day, I'm creating something of value."

I snorted. "Something of value? Well, I'll have you know that because you just shunned Taka away, he's gone and run off and got himself kidnapped."

Faso jerked his head up towards me and his eyes widened. As if startled, Ratter darted down Faso's arm and buried itself in the sleeve of the inventor's pinstripe suit. This sleeve was flared out a little more on the left and seemed to be one of Ratter's favourite hiding places.

"What? When? Who took him?"

"Wouldn't you like to know? But if you'd have looked after him when he wanted you to, none of this would ever have happened."

Faso shrugged. "I offered to have him help out in my workshop. But he said it was too boring and would rather go train with his favourite auntie."

"So, you just let him go?"

"Yes, what else should I have done?"

"You could have offered to do something that involves actually focusing on spending time with your son rather than your machines. Maybe you could have even accompanied Taka to the training grounds."

Faso exhaled, puffing out his cheeks. "I can't abandon my work. Anyway, we could argue about this all day, but we should go out and get Taka back, right? Whoever took him, Velos and his armour will shoot them down. It's been a while since I used the dragon armour..."

"We don't have a clue where Taka went," I said. "Lieutenant Wiggea sent out a task force, and they were ambushed not far from here. Only Wiggea managed to retreat and come back with the news."

"Then you wanted to investigate the last place he was seen, right? I'm sure having me along would help you find some clues."

"And help you appease the guilt you should be feeling for abandoning Taka?"

"It sounded like you abandoned him, Pontopa," Faso said. "He went straight to find you. And now you're just screaming at me to make you feel better."

"You're right. I should just push you out of the sky and leave you injured on the floor. See how you like to be left alone."

Faso sighed. "The number of times you've made that threat and never acted on it. You know I'm far too valuable to Gerhaun."

"Fortunately for you. Otherwise, I'd have left you rotting in Gerhaun's prison a long time ago."

"Surely that's Gerhaun's call, not yours."

"Whatever. Now, leave that damn machine alone for a while and get moving."

"Pronto," Faso said. And he carefully slotted a metal part into place on the dragon automaton, then he stood up sharp.

I stormed through the long corridors of Fortress Gerhaun, far enough ahead that Faso couldn't walk alongside me. I didn't want any of his nattering right now. Together, we went through the winding corridors, passing hanging tapestries depicting dragons in battle against King Cini's war automatons. A young girl and an even younger boy waltzed passed us and I almost bumped into them.

"Watch it," I said. And the girl looked up at me and then ran away giggling. These children should have been Taka's playmates, but they tended to stay away from him. Taka had told me numerous times they were scared of him because they found him somehow different.

Which was why he spent so much time around the adults.

My dragon, Velos, no longer had to stay in the courtyard, since we'd managed to build him his own stable on the outer perimeter of the fortress, just inside the castle's walls. With the exception of a little shelter in the west part, the stable was open at the top, which made it much quicker to get out into the Southlands when we needed to take him out on missions. And, I admit, these missions had been few and far between over the last year. Still, I made sure to take Velos out at least once a day, although it had been a long time since I'd left the Southlands.

After a few sharp turns down the fortress' musty corridors, we reached his stable, and I opened the wooden door into a wide-open area. Since Velos was much larger than the other dragons and wasn't used to confined spaces, we'd decided to knock down two walls to create a stable three times the size of a usual Grey's.

Velos deserved it – he was a VIP around here, as a coloured dragon, which made him the only creature in the whole fortress who could mate with Gerhaun to create eggs. Together, Gerhaun and Velos had produced five eggs now, but all of them had hatched as male dragons and all of them Greys, meaning they were infertile. You could tell the type as soon as the egg was laid, as it would be the same colour as the dragon inside. Dragon queen's eggs would therefore be a shiny gold colour and an egg like that hadn't been birthed for hundreds of years.

Coloured male dragons were also much rarer than Greys. If Gerhaun birthed one of those, once hatched we'd have to send it out of the Southlands so the secicao fumes didn't end up turning it into a Grey. Rarest of all were dragon queens, and Velos felt continuously anxious that he hadn't birthed one yet. Every man and dragon alike knew that Gerhaun Forsi was getting old and would soon leave this world. If she didn't have another queen to replace her, then an entire lineage would become wiped out in the next few hundred years, making it a lot easier for Cini and his successors to dominate the Southlands and for secicao to destroy the planet.

This put a lot of pressure on Velos, and I kind of felt for him.

Velos sensed my anxiety as I entered his stables. In response, he raised his head to the sky and roared, sending a stone tumbling off the top of the stable wall. Then, he lowered his head to me and crooned as I stroked the blue leathery skin at his muzzle. Meanwhile, Faso didn't waste any time climbing up the ladder on the armour that Velos wore on his back. The inventor took his position on the rear seat. "My, my. I forgot for a while what a marvellous creation this armour is. It's funny how you lose sight of your earlier genius when you're working on loftier things."

Indeed, his armour was a veritable war machine, complete with cogs, Gatling guns on each flank, and these huge soft bladders that contained the secicao oil needed to power the device and augment Velos' speed and accuracy.

"I still think he'd be better off without it," I replied. Although, I said it more to temper Faso's ego than to communicate what I truly believed. I didn't like the armour aesthetically, but it had saved our lives several times, one of the few things about Faso I was grateful for.

I sang a song to Velos to placate him a little. Dragonsongs were strange in that they didn't sound like songs as such, but rather like orchestral harmonies. Lacking melody but still having an innate sense of beauty about them. To listen to one would be more like listening to a waterfall than listening to a traditional tune. But still, they had powers that could command legions of dragons. And only dragon-seers could sing them.

The song not only calmed Velos' mind but also my own. We were both kind of one, anyway. I'd grown up with Velos since birth and he'd looked after me as much as I'd looked after him. Once I came of age, I spent a while working for King Cini, harvesting secicao for his military operations against dragons, until my favourite author and (it turned out) fellow dragonseer, Sukina Sako, came to visit and illuminated me on how nefarious these operations were.

I climbed up on Velos' back and took my position just behind his steering fin. "We need to go out and get Taka back, Velos," I said.

The dragon growled in agreement. He didn't understand my words, spoken in the native language of Tow, but he always understood the sentiment behind them.

Some warmth rose up from beneath my feet and, underneath them, Velos' armour began to glow green. Faint pulses of light weaved through the network of veins in the metal, set between cogs and other intricacies. I turned to Faso, who was just bringing himself back up from the spigot that he'd turned to send the secicao through the armour.

"Are we ready?" I asked.

"Breathing apparatus," Faso pointed out.

"I know..."

There was a compartment underneath the seat, and I took out my bit-and-clip breathing device, much like what divers used. This would give me oxygen when I entered the secicao clouds. Most would prefer a traditional gas mask, and there was also one inside the compartment, but I hated the stuffy feeling underneath such masks. I also checked that my pistol and golden hip flask were secured in my belt that I'd threaded through my leather jerkin.

The flask contained secicao oil – a drug that we used in the military to augment soldiers in superhuman ways. The effect depended on the blend, and I'd mixed mine with the kind Sukina used to use. This would give myself the ability to see in the dark, gain dexterity and strength, and to compress time inside my head so things seemed slower than they actually were.

I kept the flask inside the armour usually, so I had it available when I flew out on missions. I'd promised Wiggea I wouldn't use secicao during training, as I needed to grow my skills without the oil. But on this assignment, we'd need the extra strength and speed, particularly if we were going up against Alsie and whatever ruthless automatons King Cini had sent with her.

Faso's secicao had different abilities than mine, raising his mental acuity rather than focusing on brute physical speed and strength. That helped him, he'd pointed out many times, to make snap decisions as he fiddled with the armour's complex controls at the back. Although, strangely, his secicao also gave him the ability to leap great heights.

"You're not forgetting about me, Maam?" Lieutenant Rastano Wiggea's voice came from the floor just below Velos' ladder. I looked down into his soft hazel eyes. Although Wiggea worked me hard during training sessions, outside of the ring he was the kindest man you'd ever meet. And, as he had been before to Sukina, he was as loyal as a dog to me. My most trusted dragonelite guard employed by Gerhaun Forsi to protect me until death. He wore a similar olive coloured uniform to the other guards around Fortress Gerhaun, but he also had a few chevrons on each shoulder to denote his rank, and a golden dragon broach pinned to his breast pocket that depicted his special status.

"Of course not," I said. "Hop on, Lieutenant."

Lieutenant Wiggea saluted and then climbed up the ladder. Once he was seated and seatbelted in, I turned around and I nodded to Faso. Then, I pulled down on Velos' steering fin to launch him into the roiling brown-grey clouds. As I did, I sang a song to the other twenty Greys that Wiggea had also assembled in the courtyard, instructing them to launch.

Soon, we were in formation, speeding towards the ambush site.

3

I felt the dragons in the collective unconscious before I saw them through the thick brown secicao clouds. A couple of them still had some life left in them. Not entirely dead, but the last threads of their souls being sucked away into the thorny secicao that entangled them. They were far too gone for rescue and I could feel their anguish in my mind.

I sang a song to thank them for being brave. To tell them that it's okay to go now. If I could see images, or hear their words, then they'd perhaps be able to tell me exactly what happened – who took Taka and where they were heading now. But I could only feel emotions. A sense of having failed. I added a slight lilt to my song to tell them that they'd done their best. To communicate my gratitude even more for them fighting to the end.

We'd entered a particularly thick area of cloud cover, reducing visibility for anything but a few metres. Usually, we'd be able to see up to around a hundred yards or so, but there were days that the clouds became especially thick.

Then we saw them. Three dragons lying on the ground, their riders strewn across the dusty earth, not far away from the dragons. Bodies of both humans and dragons mutilated as if their bones had broken when they crashed into the ground. Stout brown thorns were plunged into them as if feeding off them and their clothing and grey scales had become stained with coagulated blood.

"Brace yourself for landing," I called back to Faso and Wiggea. And I sang out to the other twenty Greys to instruct them to do the same. It had been difficult at first to enunciate words with a clip on my nose and my teeth clenched around a bit, but I now had the skill down to an art.

Soon after, a shot came from the dense cloud cover. The bullet clinked off Velos' armour sending out a spark.

"Dragonheats," Faso shouted. "We've got company." His voice was muffled through his mask.

My heart jumped in my chest. In all honesty, I hadn't expected for the automatons to still be there. It was a good thing we'd assembled a large force. The air became filled with a brief silence as I thought about what to do next. Then, another shot sounded, but it didn't make contact with anything.

I looked over my shoulder to see Wiggea with his rifle poised, watching the horizon. He was one of the best shots in Gerhaun's forces and there was a good chance he'd shoot down any threat before the Gatling guns on Velos' armour latched onto it.

I didn't hesitate to change my song with harsh notes that instructed the dragons to circle around and gain height. I held my breath, removed the bit from my mouth for a brief moment.

"Augment," I shouted. I took a swig of secicao oil and glanced over my shoulder quickly to check Wiggea and Faso were doing the same.

The world ghosted green and, in the distance, I could make out the outlines of the automatons on the ground. I recognised them from the history textbooks. Their spindly chicken legs had been perfectly engineered to balance two machine guns, and a thick brass plate formed their armoured heads. They had bright spots at their eyes, now green but what would have been red if not for my augmented vision.

There were about ten of them, a fair match for twenty dragons. I pulled Velos upwards and continued my song to choreograph our side of the battle. These songs came naturally to me as I'd known them since birth and had always heard them in my dreams.

But this song didn't stop one of the dragons roaring to the sky in pain because of the bullet that had lanced his shoulder. My heart sank as I watched him plummet to the floor, the rider letting out a shot from his rifle at the automatons on his way down.

We were close enough to the automatons now that I probably didn't need augmented sight to see them. But the secicao still gave me augmented strength and reflexes, enough to duck out of the way of close flying bullets. Meanwhile, the armour pumped secicao through Velos, giving him extra agility to help avoid injury.

The war-automatons charged forwards in a single line, strafing the sky with bullets. Clearly, they had just arrived and hadn't had time to enter a more defensive formation. That gave us an opportunity. I pushed down on Velos' steering fin and entered him into a sharp curve, so we approached the line from the automaton's backhand side. Following that, the Gatling guns on Velos' flanks surged into action, causing the armour to vibrate underfoot. The shots sent up plumes of dust around the automatons, forming such dense cover that it was hard to see if they were hit. That was until we passed the end of the line and saw the dust settle a bit. Two of the automatons had collapsed onto the floor, but the rest were standing strong and glowing green in my augmented field of view.

"Dragonheats, someone's reinforced their armour," Faso called. "And they're using my secicao technology." Faso had initially developed the technology to power automatons with secicao, and so he complained every time he saw the king had stolen his ideas.

I clenched my teeth. I wasn't so worried about that. Whoever had placed these automatons had known what they were doing. And they'd come prepared to shoot us down. Which meant that there would likely be more automatons close by.

And my suspicions were confirmed, when I peered through the clouds to see a swarm of flying automatons speeding towards us, all of them spherical and darting around each other like wasps. "Hummingbirds," I said.

"Dragonheats," Faso said. "Retreat, damn it!"

But, instead, I'd already turned Velos towards the swarm, and I sang a song to instruct the following greys to follow the leader.

"No," I muttered under my breath. "We're going in." Whoever was orchestrating this wanted us to flee so the Hummingbirds could follow on our tail and gun us down during retreat. A better strategy seemed to fly out of range of the war automatons and lure the Hummingbirds into the sky where we'd be on an even keel.

I pulled down on Velos' steering fin and we soared upwards. On the way, I felt a tug on my heartstrings, as another three dragons got shot down by the war automatons, taking our force down to fifteen. One rider tumbled off his dragon, screaming out as he fell towards the ground.

The secicao clouds extended high above The Southlands. So, it was impossible to get above them. But further up, the air would still thin, and the rotary blades on the Hummingbirds wouldn't, in theory, be able to carry the automatons high enough. Yet, as expected, they still followed us from below. Once you'd encountered enough swarms of Hummingbirds, you kind of knew how they'd been programmed to behave.

"Pontopa," Faso called out. "What are you doing? The secicao power will allow them to get higher."

I looked down at the green cloud of secicao gas pulsing around them. "If we fled, they'd outrun us on retreat," I pointed out.

"Not with my armour."

"And what about the other dragons?"

"You need to think about our value here. You're a dragonseer and I'm the best scientist Gerhaun has. The other dragons and men are expendable."

But I wasn't going to let that idiot sway me. Faso was useful for working the dragon armour, but he was also an annoying backseat driver. So, I ignored his protests and charged at the Hummingbirds, letting out a song to instruct the other dragons to keep their distance. The Greys had no armour and so had no chance up close against the

Hummingbirds. But their riders could still snipe the Hummingbirds down from afar.

Faso screamed out something as we cut through the clouds of Hummingbirds and then Velos' Gatling guns sprayed bullets through the swarm as we barrelled right through it. The Hummingbirds reacted by trying to close in, shooting out sparks from their central guns. But they only connected with the armour, which wasn't enough to shock Velos out of the sky.

And soon, we were clear of the Hummingbirds, and a wave of trepidation washed over me. Something was wrong. This had been too easy, and the Hummingbirds hadn't followed us. They weren't trying hard enough and clearly they weren't powered up to full. But why?

Soon enough, an airship came into sight, providing an answer. It had no flag, so it was impossible to see who was orchestrating this assault. Alsie Fioreletta perhaps, the dragonwoman? Maybe she was here working for Cini, or even worse the mythical Empress Finesia who apparently inhabited her mind. The airship balloon had no markings on it, and instead took on a cloudy brown colour, which I could see more clearly now the effects of the secicao oil were fading.

A man stood upon the deck of the airship. A pirate, it seemed, in no particular uniform like the rest of his crew. Like the others on his airship, he sported a gas mask. He also wore a white shirt that blew in the wind, loose baggy trousers, and long grey hair.

I pushed down on Velos' steering fin to still him into a hover. Behind us, the Hummingbirds had also stopped in position, as if to wait to see what would happen next. I sang a song to warn the dragon riders to hold fire. There was a system – I relayed a message to the dragons and they picked up my commands with their acute hearing, and then they made gestures with their heads and wings which told their riders what to do next.

"Pontopa Wells," the man called out. He had quite a distinguished accent for a pirate. "You are to surrender and to follow us, and I'll let the rest of the forces live."

I looked back at Faso in astonishment. "After what happened to the rest of the Greys down there, I highly doubt that," I told him.

Faso's face had lost all its colour and his bottom lip was trembling. "Shouldn't you find out what he wants?"

I sighed. "Remind me next time we go on one of these excursions to bring a loudspeaker."

"I'll bear that in mind... If we live through the end of this."

I pushed down on Velos' steering fin to edge him forwards, and he let off a roar to tell me that he didn't want to go. So, I sang a song of harsh notes as a rebuke. Velos shuddered a little and the armour shook underfoot.

"What are you doing, Pontopa?" Faso asked.

"Just talking to Velos. He's not in the best of moods. But you have a seatbelt, you're quite safe."

"I mean are you going to talk to the captain?"

I nodded, then I sang some more notes, this time to calm down Velos' anxiety. He roared again, then pushed forward. A couple of Gatling guns placed on the side of the airship tracked us as we approached. Meanwhile, the pirate lifted the loud-speaker and spoke through the mouthpiece. His voice was kind of tinny through his mask, but it was clear enough to understand what he was saying. "I warn you, try anything and we'll shoot you down."

I wasn't going to try projecting my voice several hundred yards. Humans didn't have the acute hearing that dragons had. So, instead, I raised my hands in surrender. I wasn't going to give up, of course. But I didn't want to get shot out of the sky.

Then, I turned Velos to the right a little, so we could approach the airship from the side. I took hold of a pistol from my belt and kept it low, in case I'd have to use it. It wouldn't have been much use though, the pirate now had three crew members on board, in various baggy attire, and all with Pattersoni rifles trained on us.

I halted Velos at a point several hundred yards from the airship's deck. And, before we levelled out, I took another swig from my hipflask flaring up my abilities.

"Who are you, what do you want and where's Taka?" I asked. Straight to the point.

Though the reflection on his mask concealed a lot of it, I could see the pirate had a layer of full growth stubble on his face. "I've been ordered not to give you any information until you cooperate with us."

Absolutely useless. "Then why should we trust you? You've killed without warning. Kidnapped a dragonseer child. And as soon as you take us, there's nothing to stop you shooting our men and dragons out of the sky."

The man scratched at his neck and turned his gaze down towards the ground a moment where our men and dragons lay dead. "All I can give you is my word," the man said again looking at me. "I'm a man of great respect in my land and I won't go against my promises."

"Your land which is?"

"Lady Wells, I'm not going to give you information yet, as I've said. You must come with us and see for yourselves."

I turned to Faso. Before only his lips were shaking. But now his hands were gripped right on the supports in front of his seat, the white of his knuckles showing. "What choice do we have? We have three rifles pointed at us for wellies sake."

I gestured over at the Gatling guns with my eyes, suggesting that Faso might be able to pump some more secicao through Velos' armour so it can gun the airship down.

But he wasn't having any of it. "Are you crazy? These people don't look like idiots." Faso turned to the airship captain and addressed him himself. "Don't worry, we're not going to show any aggression. Lady Wells here will cooperate. Won't you, Pontopa?"

Before I could answer, a roar came from somewhere behind the airship, loud as thunder. I couldn't see what was happening beyond the clouds, but more men ran up on deck and pointed out at something in the distance. They readied their rifles.

"Looks like you could do with some help, Dragonseer Wells," a voice came in my head. It sounded dour, lacking emotion…

"Charth," I said. *"What are you doing here?"*

The guards turned towards Charth and let off some shots. But it wouldn't have done any good even if they hit him as, excepting the weak spot at his throat, Charth was immortal once in dragon form.

His blackened scaly body speared through the sky and right into the captain. He swept the man away in his claws and disappeared into the clouds. *"Looks like we now have a prisoner,"* he said in the collective unconscious.

Back on the airship deck, the man with the smartest looking attire shouted out something to his comrades. More men came over to his side of the airship and we had more rifles pointed at us.

"You're not going to shoot us," I said, noticing the uncertainty in the senior guard's eyes. "Because we now have your man of high esteem."

"Release him," the pirate guard said. "That's an order."

I couldn't help but laugh. "You don't give orders to the other side," I said. I kept the channel open in my mind as I spoke, so at least Charth could hear my thoughts as they formed themselves.

The guard's eyebrows furrowed. Clearly, he didn't like taking no for an answer. "You will obey, or you will die, Miss Wells."

"Conversely, I think you would rather not have your captain lose his life by tumbling out of our friend's claws. It seems quite fitting that we'll just fly away, with your leader as a prisoner."

"You're a fool. Our Hummingbirds will take you down before you reach your base." He had a point; it would be no good if Charth returned with the prisoner alone.

"Ah," Charth said. *"I almost forgot. Brace yourself Pontopa, I've been practising."*

And before I had a chance to ask what he was talking about, a nauseating ear-splitting scream came in my ears, numbing my senses and blocking off the channel from Charth. I clutched my hands to my temples and tried to shake off the pain. I couldn't see the Humming-birds behind me, but I knew from experience that the scream was enough to disable them.

Despite the fact my head was spinning, I tried to keep my composure. Even though, all I wanted to do right now was throw up. "We'll be going now," I said.

"Pontopa, what are you doing?" Faso's voice sounded muffled behind me. He had no connection to the collective unconscious, and so he had no way of knowing what Charth had done.

I pushed down on Velos' steering fin, to turn him so sharply that the guards' shots missed their target. "Gatling guns, Faso," I said. "We're getting out of here."

"But the Hummingbirds."

"They're disabled. Now, do as I say."

I didn't turn around to check that he followed my orders. But I didn't need to. Soon enough, the Gatling guns came to life, laying into the bottom of the gondola as we turned away from it.

My head was still spinning so much that I couldn't form a channel to Charth to ask what his plans were. I just hoped that he would deliver the prisoner to Fortress Gerhaun as, otherwise, we'd have no way of knowing where Taka had gone.

We approached a wall of disabled Hummingbirds, all of them lifeless. One by one, they fell out of the sky as we passed through. My senses had begun to return a little then, enough to sing a song and order the remaining dragons to retreat.

We had some work to do at Fortress Gerhaun, and I knew already it was going to be a busy day.

PART II

GENERAL SAKO

"I said it once and I'll say it again. Blunders and dragonheats!"

— GENERAL ORGATI SAKO

4

Two men were waiting for us in Velos' stable when we arrived back at Fortress Gerhaun. The first was my father, pacing around anxiously. The other was Sukina's father, General Sako. A trail of green smoke rose up from the secicao pipe hanging from his lips. He had the same almond upturned eyes as his daughter, complimented by a bushy handlebar moustache and round, ruddy face.

Both men stood by the stable door, and I touched Velos down a good twenty or so feet away from them. Velos lowered his head so I could dismount as quickly as possible via his neck. General Sako approached me as soon as my feet touched the ground.

"Blunders and dragonheats," he said. "What happened to my granddaughter, Pontopa? I thought you were meant to be looking after her?" During moments of stress, he sometimes forgot that Taka was now a boy.

"I'm sorry, General," I said. "He ran away without me knowing about it."

Faso had dismounted a little slower. He approached the general, keeping a wise distance from him. "We couldn't find him."

General Sako turned to him and pointed a finger. "You, young man, should have been keeping an eye on him. You're his father, for wellies sake."

"I'm sorry, I had work to do. Creating technology that saves lives. You know how important that is, right?"

General Sako's nostrils flared and I decided to step in before he thumped Faso. "General, there's no time. A prisoner... Did Charth come here?"

"Yes... I ordered to have him shot down, and so he flew off pretty quickly."

I opened my mouth wide. "Shot?" Really, shooting Charth would do no good when he was in dragon form unless someone happened to hit him in the throat. But really, it was the intention behind the action that bothered me. "General, Charth had a valuable prisoner. He's the only lead we have for where Taka might have been taken."

And I had so many other questions for the dragonman as well. Like how he'd known to coincidentally turn up just in the nick of time. And why could he, all of a sudden, use Alsie and Taka's trade-marked scream.

Now, General Sako's face was turning a shade of red. "Of course, I wanted him bloody well shot down for wellies sake. If it weren't for him and his infernal father, Colas, none of this would have happened. King Cini would never have stolen Taka off us, and Sukina would still be alive."

My own father was loitering in the background against the wall, watching the exchange with interest. Though he and General Sako had bonded quite well in the last several months, he knew to stay back whenever the general's temper flared up like this.

I walked over to Papo, so he could stop looking meek and become part of the conversation. As soon as I approached, he opened his arms and embraced me in a big hug.

"Pontopa, what Charth said... I thought we'd lost you."

"You mean he had time to explain himself?" I glared at the general. I was pretty furious with him, to be honest. Yes, I know that Charth and General Sako had their history. But Charth had redeemed himself by helping us escape in the palace two years ago.

He was our ally now, even if he had the spirit of Finesia living inside of him.

"He left the prisoner down here," Papo said. "The good old general got something out of this before Charth flew away."

General Sako had now walked over to cut into the exchange. He clearly hadn't liked me blanking him like that, even though he'd deserved it. "One day, I'll hunt that dragonman and his father down and kill them both. What they did cannot be forgiven."

"But we have the prisoner," I said.

"Yes, in the cells. Though my men can't get a word out of him. We'll let him rot there without food until he gives us some valuable intel."

I shook my head. "It might be a long time. He wouldn't tell me who he worked for either."

A channel opened in my mind. *"Dragonseer Wells, did you learn anything?"* Gerhaun Forsi asked me in the collective unconscious.

"Not yet. The pirate captain wouldn't tell me who he was. Did you have a chance to talk to Charth?"

"I did," Gerhaun said. *"Though, like the general, I'm not entirely sure I trust him. Sukina might have had feelings for Charth once upon a time, but now you can't know whether his intentions are Finesia's or his own."* It had taken me quite a while to accept that the mad god Finesia lived within the spirit of secicao. During my childhood, everyone had drunk secicao warmed in cups in a form that wasn't as strong as oil, but still lifted human ability slightly. But once I'd learned how destructive the stuff was, I'd stopped drinking it.

"Charth seemed to be on our side, this time." I said back to Gerhaun. Much as he had when he'd helped Sukina, Taka, and I escape from Cini's palace. Meanwhile, his brother, Francoiso, whom I married, had sacrificed himself to aid our escape. *"Anyway, what did you learn?"*

"Just as much as you know," Gerhaun said. *"That the captain tried to take you hostage. But the prisoner doesn't want to reveal anything more."*

"Is Charth nearby?" I asked. Even though Gerhaun had banished him from Fortress Gerhaun, I guessed the situation would cause him to hang around.

"He said he needed to leave. He seemed concerned that there were rumours Alsie was coming to the Southlands to supervise a harvesting operation and he wanted to investigate."

That didn't sound good. But if Alsie was here then it would have made sense for her to try to kidnap Taka and return him to the king. If, that was, she knew where to find him.

"We need to interrogate the prisoner."

"I agree", Gerhaun said. "Maybe you'll find a way to get information out of him."

I smiled. "You know, I think I might have another plan."

General Sako, my father and Faso were all watching me. They'd learned to wait patiently whenever I zoned out so I could have a conversation in the collective unconscious. I focused on General Sako. "Come on, general, let's go and talk to the prisoner."

General Sako snorted. "You really think you'll make a better interrogator than my best-trained guards."

"No," I said. "Not me. Papo, Faso, you stay here."

Faso nodded, seeming to like that idea. But Papo shifted awkwardly on his feet. "Let me come. I want to have a word with that man myself. No one sends war automatons against my daughter without a good telling off." He cupped his fist in his hand.

"No, Papo," I said. "This is work, and as Doctor Forsolano says, you shouldn't be moving around too much, which includes swinging punches at rogue airship captains."

"Fine." Papo crossed his arms. "I'll just twiddle my thumbs here then."

And, without him, General Sako accompanied me to the cells.

As far as cells went, Gerhaun's were a luxury that I didn't feel this pirate, or whoever he was, deserved. Each had a bathroom en suite with a toilet and sink. The cells were placed underground near the outer castle walls, with windows at the top that brought in a little light. We found the pirate captain down there, lying on the bed and staring up at the ceiling, looking as if he'd rather take his own life (if we'd given him the means to do it) than reveal anything to us. Much to my amusement, someone had removed the mattress, and so he lay down on hard planks of wood.

He didn't even seem to notice we were there until I tapped my foot against the stone. It was loud enough to cause him to jolt upright and then turn towards us with a scornful look on his face.

Before I spoke, I opened a channel in my mind so Gerhaun could hear what I said.

"Well, well," I said. "It looks like the tables have turned. Who's the one who needs to follow orders this time?"

The man glared at me but still said nothing. Though it was cold down here, a bead of perspiration trickled down his face. He had a purple welt on one cheek, probably where General Sako had punched him.

"At least tell me your name," I said. Still not a word.

"Blunders and dragonheats." General Sako turned to the guard at the cell door. "Give me the key."

The guard in olive uniform nodded.

"Wait," I said. "General, this isn't a time for violence. Let me go in there."

"But he's dangerous."

"He's handcuffed for wellies sake. Please, my father's protective enough. I don't need this from you as well." I turned to the guard. "You come with me. But, if I can request, general, please stay outside."

"Fine," General Sako said and folded his arms.

I nodded and then unlocked the door and went inside the cell. I tapped my foot against the stone and waited for the man to do something. But he didn't react in any way.

I sneered at him. "Look, you have two options right now. Either you give us the information we need or you get interrogated by a dragon queen. I know which I'd prefer."

But the pirate completely stonewalled me, his gaze vacant and his eyes focused on a point on the wall behind me.

"At least tell me your first name. That's not so difficult, is it?"

I waited a moment and let the silence wash over us both. Eventually, the man decided to at least say something. "You can call me Grea." Unfortunately, that name didn't identify him by location. It wasn't a real name, but a diminutive form used in many countries. Though it was still possible that he was Greandio from my homeland in Tow.

"Right, Grea. So, you know what we need. Tell us what happened to Taka Sako and who you work for. After that, we can come to some agreement, I'm sure."

At that, the man looked at me straight in the eyes. Though his expression remained blank. "If I tell you who I work for, then he'll do a lot worse to me than you possibly can down here."

"Ah, so it's a he." I smirked. Getting somewhere, at least. That meant the boss wasn't Alsie. "King Cini, I presume?"

"I'm saying nothing."

"What if we agree to shelter you here? You'll be quite safe."

That caused him to let off a sharp, dry laugh. "In a fortress of over a thousand troops, you don't think you have at least one spy? The assassins will come for me soon enough if I'm lucky. More likely, I'll be given a lifetime of torture. And my family are already dead."

That caused me to feel for this man a little. "You didn't choose this life?"

"I've already said too much," he said. And he tightened his lips as if to communicate that he'd let out no more.

I asked more questions but couldn't get another word out of him. Eventually, I left the room and turned to General Sako.

"My men will continue to work on him," he said. "We'll get answers soon enough."

I sighed, then turned to the guard. "Take him to Gerhaun," I said.

"Blunders and dragonheats," General Sako said. "I can handle this myself."

"Look, you know full well that Gerhaun is the most terrifying creature in this fortress. She has the most chance of getting something of value out of this man."

"But I hate violence," Gerhaun said in the collective unconscious. Clearly, she'd been listening in the channel I'd opened to her.

"*Gerhaun, with all due respect,*" I said." *Each minute we lose here is a minute that anything could be happening to Taka.*"

"*You're right,*" she replied. "*I'll do what I can.*"

And I watched the guard jostle the pirate out of the room. And Grea went without resistance as if resigned to his fate. Then I took one glance at General Sako who stood there staring at the bed in the cell. I had nothing more to say to him, and so I went upstairs to pass some time.

5

I figured that Gerhaun would be a while, so I went to pay my respects to Sukina. There were two places I could have done so. The first, the catacombs where a beautiful blue marble statue perfectly represented Sukina's chiselled face. But it always felt so cold down there, and the stone lifelessness of the statue creeped me out a little. So instead, I often found myself in the shrine that Faso had created.

After Sukina's death, Faso had taken hold of Sukina's bedroom for quite a few months. He'd created painting after painting of her in warm hues that expressed how much he'd cared about her, even though he'd spent most of his life away from her. It turned out that Faso Gordoni was quite a talented artist underneath it all.

The bedroom lay behind a single wooden door, and a cleaner swept three times a day to keep this room free of dust, on Faso's request, to preserve the life of the paintings. Inside the tiny boxy room, once barebones, images of Sukina gazed out like a saint from wall to wall, some of them also resting on the woollen blanket on Sukina's single bed, in front of which rested hardback editions of her published novels. Sometimes I imagined I could hear her voice in my head, talking to me like she used to in the collective unconscious. She helped me understand what it was to live in this strange dragonseer world.

I turned to one of the paintings and addressed her in my mind. As I did, a tear ran down my cheek. I let it fall to the floor without wiping it away.

"*I'm sorry, Sukina,*" I said. I kept this channel closed so even Gerhaun wouldn't be able to hear. This was the most private of conversations. "*I promised you I'd look after Taka, and I failed. I'm a failure...*"

I calmed my mind and waited for a response. I never knew when I might hear her voice and it always came like an echo at the back of my mind. The kind of voice you might hear just before dozing off to sleep. But this time, nothing came.

"*You have to understand, Sukina. I want to help Taka. I want to see him grow into a strong man. And though he's male, I do believe he'll become a fine dragonseer one day.*"

Still nothing. I often wondered if this was madness talking to Sukina like this. She existed, Gerhaun had said, in the collective unconscious. But she wouldn't be able to talk to me anymore. Once she was gone, she was gone.

"*But often I feel that I'll never be good enough. You were the strongest person, the most amazing fighter, an insightful author who inspired thousands... Everything about you was perfect. And now Fortress Gerhaun needs a leader like you and I can't live up to your name. How can I look after Taka, and get strong enough to fight, and lead, and save the world all at once? I wish you were here, Sukina... I wish you could tell me what to do.*"

Another tear emerged at the corner of my eye and I wiped it away with the back of my hand. This wasn't doing me any good. I had to quell the anxiety. Still my mind as Sukina instructed me. And I remembered her words then. She'd said it to me once, just before I'd gone into that quiet, pitch-black room and sat on the floor while the spider automaton crawled over me. The same spider automaton that Taka had brought to me before he ran away.

"Let your worries drift away," Sukina had said. "And focus only on what you can control."

But it was hard when I had so much responsibility and so many things I could control and no time to address them. Not while the world was slowly falling apart. How could I ever know what to do next?

I felt someone trying to contact me in my mind. Not Gerhaun, someone else. I wiped the tears out of my eyes and opened the channel.

"Dragonseer Wells." It was Charth's dour voice that came resonating through the collective unconscious. *"I tried contacting Gerhaun, but she seemed otherwise engaged. But there's something you should know."*

"Charth," I said. *"What is it?"*

"Alsie Fioreletta, she's in the area, supervising a harvesting operation. I spotted her thirty miles or so to the northeast."

"Dragonheats! Mammoths?"

"Five of them and coming close."

"Does she have Taka?"

"I don't know. I couldn't get close enough to tell. If I reveal myself to Alsie than she'd kill me, and what use would I be to you then?"

A wave of panic rose up in my chest. I tried opening up a channel to Gerhaun Forsi. *"Gerhaun,"* I said. *"Gerhaun!"* But she didn't respond. You just couldn't distract her while sleeping or concentrating on something with anything short of banshee's scream. *"I can't reach her, Charth. What should I do?"*

"Assemble a force. I'll accompany you into battle. But you need to act now."

He was right. Two years ago, the first time I'd visited Fortress Gerhaun, we'd had to react quickly because one of these 'Mammoth' harvester automatons had ventured close to us. If such a machine accidentally stumbled upon Fortress Gerhaun, then word would get back to the king. That would cause Cini to send in more automatons, ultimately resulting in a war. And given how quickly King Cini was advancing his technology, I doubted we'd be able to win.

"I'll go and find General Sako," I said.

"Send my regards."

"I'm not sure he wants them, Charth," I said. *"You're not exactly in his good books."*

"I wish I could change that..." And given the way Charth said it, I knew he meant those words.

"If only we could change the past," I said. *"Now, keep your distance, and I'll let you know when we're ready."*

And I felt Charth break the channel in the collective unconscious.

Then, I stood up, wiped the tears from my eyes and I went off to find General Sako.

6

W hile I preferred to visit Sukina's shrine, General Sako would never go anywhere near it when he wanted to pay his respects to Sukina. Faso had created the shrine, who the general didn't feel knew Sukina particularly well at all, despite the inventor having been in a relationship with her for five years. So instead, I found General Sako in the crypt, gazing up at Sukina's lifeless marble statue, so tall it towered up to the high ceiling and lit by one hundred torches. She had an urn containing her ashes cupped in her hands.

"General Sako," I said.

He turned to me and shock registered in his wide eyes. No one expects to be jostled out of mourning their most dear departed.

"I'm sorry to disturb you like this, but this is urgent. Five Mammoth automatons have been spotted near the fortress. Thirty miles to the northeast. We need to assemble a large team, at once."

The general shook his head hard. "What? Why didn't my men report this to me if it was so urgent? How did you find out before me?"

"The automatons weren't discovered by our troops, and Alsie Fioreletta's accompanying them. Taka might be somewhere nearby."

"But if not by our troops, then who did find them? It's not like the maids go out in The Southlands for afternoon strolls."

"There's no time to explain," I said. If I mentioned Charth then I'd also have to justify that he wasn't a traitor leading us into a trap. "Time is of the essence."

General Sako's moustache twitched. "Right," he said, and he picked up a talkie from his belt. "Lieutenant Candiorno. Call an emergency briefing. It looks like we're going out to battle. And we're going to require a large force."

"General?" came a tinny voice on the other end, charged with a little static.

"Do as I say, for wellies sake," General Sako said. "Oh, and send scouts to the northeast to return on the first sign of sighting anything. They're looking for Mammoth automatons, you hear?"

"Aye aye, general." And the voice fizzled out.

General Sako turned to me. "Well, well. Two missions in one day. I just hope you find Taka so I can give him his birthday present."

"I'm glad someone remembered," I said.

The general's gaze drifted off into space. "How could I forget?"

THE COURTYARD WAS ALREADY PREPARED for a briefing. Once General Sako gave orders, his troops would scurry into action, and so the guards were just putting up the last of the foldable seats, most of them already sitting down, facing the large screen at the front. Ratter stood on a table at the back with a projection device in his mouth. This let out a beam of light that displayed a picture of a Mammoth automaton on the screen.

I'd seen one of these automatons up close in person. They were great hulking beasts with Gatling guns arrayed all around them. Though heavily armed and armoured, their principal function wasn't to kill. Instead, they'd been created to churn up vast strands of secicao within their whirring blades at their mouths, tossed in through two massive tusks which rose and lowered as the machines trundled along. And, Mammoths were highly impervious to damage.

I walked to the front row, passing Faso who had placed himself at the back. He sat next to Winda – the chief engineer, who seemed to be quite taken with Faso. I'd spoken with her about him recently, and she said that Faso had seemed a little aloof since Sukina's death. I reassured her then that he only needed a little time, although I was unsure if anyone could really teach Faso how to be kind to people. I sat down next to Wiggea, and he gave me a warm smile.

General Sako stormed to the front of the room and stood by the projector. "Come on, come on," he bawled out. "We don't employ you all so you can sleep all day. Candiorno did you send out the scouts?"

The officer on duty was sitting on the second row. He stood up and saluted. "Already on their way, sir. Three Greys with riders, accompanied by Hummingbird scouts on Mr Gordoni's request."

"Hummingbird scouts. Blunders and dragonheats. Gordoni, what's the meaning of this? Stand up, boy, so I can see you."

I turned around to see Faso tugging at the collar on his shirt. "Sir, I managed to use Sukina's blend of secicao for science. Now, these automatons can see a much wider blend of electromagnetic radiation than our regular automatons. They'll be able to see much further than our enemy, sir."

"Hah, further than a dragonman?" He was referring to Alsie Fioreletta, who was technically a dragonwoman. But I doubted General Sako cared.

"I don't know," Faso said. "I don't really have much data on her right now. We need more people who can turn into dragons. Do you have access to any, sir, who I can use for some experiments?" And he put an extra sarcastic emphasis on the 'sir'.

General Sako's eyes widened. "Blunders and dragonheats, Gordoni. This isn't a time for joking. Or do you want to spend some time in the cells?"

"I don't think Gerhaun would allow that in the heat of battle." Faso was getting a little more ballsy around the general, on occasion, now he had some prestige around the fortress.

Perhaps it was because he had a woman nearby he wanted to impress. So, maybe things might develop between him and Winda after all. Faso had apparently given up on me, after deciding – as he said to my face – that I'd be too high maintenance. Little did that man realise how much maintenance he was himself.

"Just try me…" General Sako said, his face puce.

"Actually, I think you might be interested in hearing about my new technology. I think this would give us the winning edge."

General Sako cast Faso a hard gaze, turned to the picture of the automaton of the screen, and then looked at an officer in the front row – specifically at the pistol at the man's hip. "Faso Gordoni," he said. "Circumvent my authority like that again and I'll have you hung from the ramparts. Now sit down."

"Don't you want to hear what I have to offer?"

"Winda can do that quite well, don't you think?"

Asinal Winda stood up, cast Faso an abashed look, pushed him down by the shoulders and then walked towards the screen at the front. Once she reached it, she pointed a remote control at Ratter. The projector in the ferret automaton's mouth cast a new image on the screen at the front. And my jaw dropped in horror at what I saw.

It was a painting of Velos, with this huge cannon thing underneath his belly, almost as long as his tail. Out of it, came this intense beam of white light, cast against a war automaton where it erupted in this brilliant display of energy.

"Faso Gordoni and *I*," Asinal Winda said, putting extra emphasis on the last word, "have been working on the ultimate weapon. A pure tunnel of brass lined on the inside with microscopically woven carbon fibres. The weapon's source, a highly compressed chamber of secicao oil, ignited at 1,300 degrees Celsius. A wonder of nature and mathematics, because that number also happens to be two to the power of fifteen."

General Sako let off a loud cough. "Mumbo jumbo, Asinal Winda. Please, get to the point. We want to know what it does."

"Well, it takes around a minute to charge, from its own secicao reserves inside an inbuilt tank, detached from the armour. The cannon's load must then be released immediately after charging, and there's enough power in there for three shots. If it hits its mark, it can punch a hole in any automaton armour, right to its central control system and out the other side. A shot from this will fell a mammoth in one burst."

I could just about make out the smile underneath General Sako's moustache. "Indeed, it's remarkable. You've truly exceeded yourself Winda. Congratulations."

Winda looked awkwardly towards Faso. "Well, it wasn't…"

"Nonsense. I know who does the work and who just busies himself barking orders in your laboratory."

And all the while this exchange was going on, anxiety was beginning to rise in my chest. I stood up. "Winda," I said. "I'm guessing you can't put this on any dragon."

"No. Just dragon armour for now."

"So why not develop more armour for the other dragons?" General Sako said.

Faso stood up again at the back of the crowd and shouted out, "because the need for dragon armour will soon be rendered obsolete by the introduction of my dragon automaton."

"Exactly," I said. "I can imagine the cannon suiting dragon automatons. But you've got to be kidding me if you think you're going to put that cannon on Velos. He won't be able to sit down or run around. And how will he have the space to breathe?"

Winda scratched her ear. "With all due respect, Dragonseer Wells, this weapon is only intended to be used when airborne. It has foldable wheels on its base and hinges for easy installation and removal. It's also possible to install it in flight, providing Velos flies absolutely straight. Then, all Velos needs to do is land in a specially constructed frame and the cannon will detach itself."

"But Velos would hate this thing."

"Dragonseer Wells, this could win us the war," General Sako pointed out. "You may want to protect your dragon, but so long as he can handle the weight."

"We've made modifications to lighten the cannon, and the use of carbon fibres makes this as portable as it can possibly be," Winda said.

"And the best thing is," Faso said, glee evident in his voice. "Our team of engineers are installing this as we speak."

"What?" I said. "Faso, you... You didn't have my permission, you swine."

"Oh, relax," Faso said. He showed me his talkie. "I've already heard reports that Velos quite enjoys the extra accessory. We've made him look even meaner than he looked with the armour alone."

"Dragonheats," I muttered under my breath. And I was already up and getting ready to rush to the stables. "If you excuse me, General. Continue the briefing and I'll be back promptly. I need to sort this one out."

"Dragonseer Wells," he said. But I was already storming through the doors at the back of the courtyard. The tapestries and torches whizzed past me, and my head was spinning with rage as I remembered when Faso had installed that armour without my permission in the first place. I told him then that if he ever tried anything like that again, I'd fly Velos over his metal workshop and melt him down within his abode.

The first thing I saw as I swung open the doors to Velos' stable was the cannon, pointed right at me as if it wanted to annihilate me on the spot. Velos, admittedly, didn't seem too bothered about it and had his neck craned to the sky as if posing for a photograph. He stood on top of a brass scaffolding, his legs on platforms on either side and the cannon pointing out of the centre. Meanwhile, engineers in blue denim coveralls scurried around him, fixing cogs, tightening screws and polishing the massive gleaming gun.

But that wasn't the worst of it. Papo stood there watching the progress with his hands on his hips, spine arched backwards, and head held high. He didn't notice me come charging into the room. Instead, his gaze was fixated on the engineers and the massive gun leading out of Velos' underbelly.

"Papo!" It was kind of ironic really, My father had also helped Faso put the armour on Velos. And now, here he was supervising another one of Faso's hare-brained experiments on Velos, without my permission!

"Oh, hi, Pontopa," Papo said. "Marvellous, isn't it? I heard you're going out on a mission and Faso's ensured me that this cannon will keep you out of danger. But keep your distance from your enemies, will you? And I've decided to come too, to make sure you're safe."

He had his arm in a sling now. Obviously, he'd overdone something and I imagined the beratement that he'd later get from his old pal, Doctor Forsolano.

"Papo, will you ever learn? Faso's not to be trusted. And certainly, he shouldn't be putting things on Velos without my permission."

Papo looked at me, surprise registering in the arch of his bushy eyebrows. "Pontopa, this makes a lot of sense. Surely Faso's shown you the schematics. The cannon's easy to remove and is much mightier than the Gatling cannons and will surely get you out of a pinch. Don't worry, I made sure to ask plenty of questions."

"Don't worry," I said. "Don't worry! I'm not worried, because that thing's coming off."

Velos turned his head towards me sharply and bared his teeth.

"Whose side are you on, Velos? You can't sit down with that thing on. What happens if you need to rest?"

"I think you're on your own with this one, Pontopa," Papo said.

"And I'm the only one who's making sense. Take it off now! That's an order." Although I wasn't sure exactly who I was giving orders to at the time.

The engineers had halted there, their hands frozen as if time had suddenly stopped. There came a commotion from the doorway and Faso, Winda, General Sako, and Lieutenant Candiorno came rushing into the room.

General Sako came right up to me and pointed his finger at my nose. Really the guy was so small that he only came up to my chin. But still, he made up for that in stockiness, and many said he was as strong as an ox.

"Don't you dare circumvent my authority again, Dragonseer

Wells." He turned to the engineers. "Why have you stopped working? That cannon needs installing pronto."

I tried to imagine how Sukina would have behaved in this situation. She wouldn't take any of this kind of flak, even from her father. And so, I knocked the offending finger away. "You have no authority over me, general. You know full well that we rank the same."

"Yes, but munitions and armaments are my responsibility."

"And the well-being of the dragons is mine."

"He looks very well to me if you ask my opinion. A fine figure of war, in fact. Winda, you heard me, order your men to start working again."

Winda looked from General Sako to me and then back to General Sako as if trying to decide who it would be safer to obey. Faso had taken a spot next to my father and he looked at Papo as if asking for approval. My father smiled, and then Faso said, "Okay, I'm in charge of this operation. You can start work again as the general asks."

But I wasn't going to let them get away with things so easily. I let out a harsh song to reprimand Velos for taking the wrong side. And that caused the dragon to reach his head up to the sky and roar, sending the engineers scattering.

"Dragonseer Wells," General Sako said. "Stop that immediately."

"I agree," Gerhaun's voice came in my head. "What have I told you about keeping your calm, Pontopa? In situations like this, you can't be so headstrong."

Unsurprisingly, having a dragon queen talking in my head all of a sudden jolted me out of my senses, even though we'd spoken this way many times before. I'd been so angry that I'd forgotten to mask my thoughts from her.

"Gerhaun," I said. "I thought you were busy."

"I wanted to see how you handled this situation by yourself. But clearly, you still have a lot to learn."

"But Faso did it again. He went ahead and installed something on Velos without my permission."

"I know you have your connection to Velos, but you are responsible for *every dragon in the fortress now. I'll talk to Faso about his methods, but you have to admit, this action makes a lot of sense. At least for the time being."*

"He went behind my back. Was this what he was working on when he should have been spending time with Taka for his birthday?"

"The man works too hard, yes. That is his flaw. Yours is your inability to delegate, rather than taking everything on yourself. You need to learn the value of patience, Pontopa. Then, you will be in control."

I took a deep breath. She was right, I guess. Still, I didn't like the way that everyone had gone behind my back with this. I let off a big sigh and then centred myself. We had bigger fish to fry right now.

"How's it going with the interrogation?" I asked Gerhaun.

"Making progress," she said. *"But I've intervened all I need to and you seem to have your wits about you again. If you excuse me, I'll get back to my job, and you can get back to yours."*

Faso, General Sako and my father were standing in admiration of the cannon when I zoned back to reality. None of them needed say anything. They just had their eyes wide open with awe.

"Men," I muttered. "What is it about you and machines?"

General Sako turned his head. "What? Oh, I see you're back with us, Dragonseer Wells. Have you finished receiving your telling off from Gerhaun?"

I shook my head. "I guess this time, getting to those Mammoths is of prime importance."

"I'm glad to see you've got your head screwed back on your shoulders," General Sako replied.

Papo stepped forwards. "So, Pontopa, when do we go?"

The general turned to him and looked down at his sling. "You've got to be kidding me, Cipao Wells. You're going nowhere. Men like us are meant to stay at home and supervise."

"And don't you ever wish you were out in the battlefield? That's my daughter we're talking about."

The general's eyes became slits. "Are you forgetting, Cipao? I lost a daughter on a mission. It took me a long time to accept it but going out on missions like this is what dragonseers have to do."

Papo looked down at the floor defeated. "I'm sorry," he said.

"Oh, don't worry," Faso stepped forwards, the tail of his suit swinging behind him. "My cannon will keep Pontopa safe."

And everyone in the stable stopped and looked at Faso in astonishment.

"There's some things Faso," I said. "You just can't say."

Faso looked down at the ground abashed. General Sako stared at him a short moment, as if to rub in his stupidity. He might have agreed with Faso on the decision to install the cannon, but the general seemed to harbour great dislike for the inventor. I wondered if those two would ever get over their differences. They were both family now, after all.

"Right," General Sako said eventually. "So, now we've got this little wrinkle sorted out, we should probably get started."

"Return to the briefing?" I asked.

"Affirmative. Gordoni boy, you probably need to prepare things here. I think my troops have seen enough of your inventions now, don't you?"

Faso gave a mock salute. "Aye aye, sir," he said. "It would be good to supervise operations here and to fill the tanks in the armour."

"Then get right on it. And make sure everything's in tip-top condition."

General Sako turned on his heel and walked out the door. I took one moment to glance at Faso, who was standing on tiptoes, stretching his arms above his head, and looking smug. I snorted, shook my head, and then I followed General Sako out the door.

From behind me, out echoed a deep growl from Velos, almost as if he was happy to see me go.

PART III

ALSIE

"There is no stronger force in this world than the will of an empress."

— ALSIE FIORELETTA

7

The rest of the briefing went pretty smoothly, without incident. I sat on the front row playing with my nails, as the secicao clouds whirled overhead and General Sako droned on about battle formations and the like. I could smell the strong stench of secicao in the air that day. The scent somehow managed to permeate through the wall that the collective unconscious formed between Fortress Gerhaun and the clouds. It was almost as if Alsie Fioreletta's nearby presence infused the secicao with extra power. She, after all, had the spirit of Finesia inside her.

While the briefing was happening, I sensed Charth flying nearby, keeping vigil. So, I reached out to communicate that he could also accompany us into battle.

Charth used to be a female dragonseer before his father, Colas, converted him into a dragonman through a special drug known as Exalmpora. Eventually, as his connection to Finesia grew, Charth lost the ability to command dragons and instead gained near immortality, the ability to breathe secicao, great strength and other powers, and who knows what else. And I say near immortality, because in human form he would be just as fragile as any other human, with one exception. Dragonmen and dragonwomen didn't age.

Of course, I never told General Sako that Charth would be aiding us. Also, I doubted Charth would want to go anywhere near Alsie Fioreletta. She was around thirty per cent larger than him in dragon form, and much, much stronger.

Although, I did wonder at the time whether the sheer power of the cannon Faso had developed would be enough to bring her down. Perhaps she wasn't immortal but just extremely tough. Of course, she moved so fast that I doubted I'd ever have a chance to hit her with the cannon and test the limits of her power.

Soon enough, we got the briefing out of the way, assembled the troops and took off into the air. Instead of the bit-and-plug device, I wore one of Fortress Gerhaun's specially created gas masks. It had a hose leading from the mouthpiece to a green pouch on the back, filled with secicao oil and heated by an inbuilt burner. After turning a dial on the tube, gas would slowly infuse from the tank to the mask, meaning we constantly had a source of secicao oil and still had our hands free for other things. This made a lot of sense in the Southlands, particularly when we'd have to engage in ground combat using the Pattersoni rifles on our backs. And, because of the secicao resin on the ground, we also wore wellies just in case we had to land and wade through the stuff. Secicao resin would burn through normal shoes. Although dragon scales, fortunately, were much tougher against the stuff.

General Sako and I had assembled a team of one-hundred-and-fifty Greys, each with a dragon rider on their back. This was the largest force I'd ever led into combat, although I had managed to call a larger force to help me when I escaped from the Northern Continent with Faso and Taka after Sukina's death.

Wiggea, Faso and I rode on Velos, of course. Lieutenant Wiggea had agreed to sit on the central seat, his Pattersoni rifle at the ready. We might need the extra firepower and his sharp shooting if we were to get close to these Mammoth automatons. Faso was in his seat at the back, controlling how much oil Velos took into his armour through the spigot. He'd also installed an extra device, powered by a control panel on the handlebar in front of his seat. This told the cannon when to fire.

I couldn't help but wonder how Velos felt with that massive gun attached to his belly. I had imagined it would be pulling him down to the ground, making his flight a lot slower and a lot clumsier. But he seemed, instead, to sail along quite smoothly.

"How come he can take the weight?" I called back to Faso. "What did you do to Velos?" I kind of imagined that Faso had put some kind of extra solution into the secicao that fed Velos through the armour – something that wouldn't be good for him in the long run.

And I heard the inventor let off a cursory laugh from the back seat. "Obviously Pontopa, I can't expect a simple mind like yours to understand the basic principles of aerodynamics. This gun acts like a spear, cutting through the air so that it passes more easily over Velos' wings. His head does exactly the same thing, which is why he's shaped like he is. And I believe we're flying in a V formation right now for similar reasons."

If I didn't have Wiggea between me and him, I would have turned around to thump him right now. "I understand this stuff. I'm not stupid, you know."

"Of course. You just choose not to try to think things through, sometimes."

"I do more than you realise. If I reacted on instinct all the time, you wouldn't be sitting safely in your seat right now."

"And I'd have had had one less black eye in my lifetime." Faso was referring to the huge welt I'd caused over his eye after he'd installed the dragon armour on Velos without my permission. Really, I'd been quite proud of my strength back then.

"Anyway," Faso continued, "if you're wondering why Velos can handle the weight better, I've also added some extra strength to the secicao blend."

"You mean to tell me that he wouldn't be able to carry this cannon if it wasn't for the secicao?" Which didn't sound good. All we'd need then is for the supplies to dwindle or for there to be a leak somewhere and the cannon would drag us to the ground.

"Didn't you listen to Winda?" Faso asked. "The cannon is made of super light materials. Plus, Velos is a strong beast. Of course, the extra weight would be harder on his wings. But he can manage it and he'll get more strength for it, naturally, as he carries it more."

Two years of Faso Gordoni and he hadn't got any less annoying. I thought I'd try to get some moral support from Lieutenant Wiggea instead. After all, he was my most trusted dragonelite, so you would have thought he'd be on my side. "What do you think of the cannon, Lieutenant Wiggea?"

I turned around and saw the astonished look in his eyes. Clearly, he wasn't used to being asked his opinion on things. "What do you mean, Maam?"

"Aesthetically and practically. Do you think it works, or do you think he'd do better without it?"

"I think it does its job, Maam. Cini's forces and automatons are getting stronger and anything we can do to combat them, is to our advantage. We have to keep with the times."

"But surely we can get better physically and mentally. That's why you're training me, right? If we rely on technology to make us stronger, what will we become then?"

"I think we need to learn to live with it," Wiggea said.

I sighed and looked out into the distance. I had really hoped that Wiggea would side with me, and not having his support caused my heart to sink slightly in my chest. I guess I just wanted to be on the same wavelength as him. There was something about him that I liked... A lot.

I couldn't see Charth, the secicao clouds being so thick. But I'd kept a channel open between us so I would know he was nearby.

"How far?" I asked the dragonman in the collective unconscious.

"Not sure," Charth said. *"But I think about twenty minutes still. If I risk sensing Alsie, she might soon also be able to sense me. We need the element of surprise."*

"So how did you spot her in the first place?"

"She spotted me." Charth said. *"I reached out thinking that it was you or a dragon queen. Fortunately, I escaped, and she chose not to pursue."*

A wave of panic rose up in me as the realisation dawned on me. "*If she didn't chase you, maybe she wanted us to follow. She could be luring us into a trap.*" The airship captain had after all wanted me to follow him to his leader. He had said it wasn't a woman but a man. But maybe he was trying to lead me astray. Or maybe Cini was somewhere in an airship, overseeing this all.

After all, wherever the king's consort went, the king would surely not be far away.

"*I don't think we have a choice,*" Charth said. "*And you've assembled a large enough task force to defeat five Mammoths.*"

"*Five Mammoths, but what else is there?*"

"*Just her.*"

"*No airships?*"

"*Not that I could tell. Although, you have to understand, visibility was limited.*"

I sighed. "*I guess then we have no choice.*"

"*No, you don't.*" The dragonwoman's voice resonated through the collective unconscious, loud and clear. Alsie Fioreletta. "*You know, I've learned some new tricks since I last saw you, Dragonseer Wells. No more masking your thoughts in the collective unconscious anymore. I've found ways to break through.*"

I gritted my teeth. "*Alsie,*" I said. "*You shall soon die.*"

"*You really think you have a chance against me? You foolish woman.*"

"*One day,*" I said. "*You said it yourself. One day we shall battle, and it shall be me who wins Alsie Fioreletta, not you.*"

In a way my words surprised myself. I really don't know what part of me was talking right then. It was if someone else was talking inside my mind for me. And that person certainly wasn't Sukina.

"*Oh, Dragonseer Wells. That day is far in the future, I'm afraid. Today, I only need to remind you of the limits of your capabilities. You still have a long a way to go.*"

"*We shall see.*" I said. "*I have also got stronger.*"

"*Ah, but I haven't shown you the full extent of my new powers. You know, since Charth and Francoiso left, I've had a lot of valuable time to spend with*

Finesia. I never realised how powerful my connection to her could be. All fuelled by Exalmpora..."

Exalmpora was the potion that they forced Sukina and I to drink at Cini's palace when we'd gone in to rescue Taka, then being masqueraded around the palace as the king's nephew, Prince Artua. Enough of it would turn a dragonseer to a dragonman or dragonwoman and had caused Sukina and I to literally lose our minds. Alsie had been feeding the same stuff to Taka from a very early age and was responsible for his change in gender.

"This is the end," I said. "And you shall hand back Taka."

"Taka? I don't have him. Weren't you meant to be looking after him?"

I clenched my teeth. I wasn't going to play Alsie's games. "So, if you don't have Taka, then where is he?"

"You mean you lost him? Dearie, dearie. After all that effort you put in to rescue him and the lives you lost, you cannot even watch over him for a couple of years. I had a feeling that you and Gerhaun would be irresponsible guardians."

"Where is Taka?" I said again, refusing to let this conversation to get side-tracked.

"I don't know, I told you. And I never lie."

"Then you have no reason to live today," I said. Maybe we'd be able to use the new-fangled cannon to punch a hole in her after all.

"We shall see." Alsie said. And she cut off the channel.

She did so just as soon as the first Mammoth came into view. It looked spectral as it emerged from the secicao clouds, like the ghost of a beast from ages past. It faced us head on with its great tusks bared to the ground and its blades whipping through shreds of secicao as it swallowed them whole. It trundled on two reinforced caterpillar tracks. And, as expected, it glowed green.

"Augment," I shouted. And I turned the dial on my mask to let the secicao gas pass through the filters.

"Keep Velos steady," Faso shouted. "I'll fire up the cannon."

"Shouldn't we first see what we're up against."

"We see our first target in range, let's show these people what we can do. Scare them a little."

"It's only Alsie and some automatons, I don't think there's anyone we're capable of scaring."

"Actually," Alsie once again opened up a channel in the collective unconscious. *"I think you'll see there's nothing there."*

I blinked in surprise. As soon as she finished her sentence, the Mammoth automaton vanished from view. All I could see was the clouds ghosting faintly around it. The air then seemed to shimmer around me, and some harsh notes resonated in my mind. A tune, I'd never heard before, which grated like a thousand screeching violins.

"What's this?" I said, clutching my hands to my ears. *"How are you doing this, Alsie?"*

"Let's just say that I've learned some new songs. Dragonsongs, they've been around since the beginning of time. But there's other songs that don't just manipulate dragons, and Finesia knew always how to sing them. She once had the greatest connection to the collective unconscious than any creature that's ever lived. And still, her memories remain."

I tried to make out what was happening through the secicao clouds. But I could only see the thorny branches beneath. No hint of metal. Was the automaton actually there?

"Pontopa, what are you doing?" Faso screamed from his back seat. "Keep Velos steady. The target's right there."

"I can't see the target," I shouted back.

"What are you talking about? It's in plain sight. Have you gone blind?"

Clearly, whatever Alsie's dragonsong was, it wasn't affecting normal people. I turned back to Wiggea. "Can you see the Mammoth?" I asked.

"Yes, Maam."

I shook my head. "Faso, power down the cannon."

"What? I can't. Once it's charged, it has to release its load. Just fly in the direction, damn it."

The armour shuddered underneath me and a great beam of white light emerged from beneath Velos. It connected to a point on the ground and sent the secicao there up in flames. "You missed!" Faso screamed. "What were you thinking? It was a straight shot, and you missed!"

But I had nothing to say to that. Right now, I didn't have a clue what was going on.

"I see you've also brought the young inventor with you," Alsie said. *"You know, I took him as a boy under my wing through his late childhood. Now it saddens me to see him fighting for the wrong side."*

"He loved Sukina," I said. *"Meaning you're not exactly in his good books."*

"Such a sad story. Well, I guess it's time to give you a fighting chance."

The song cut off from my mind, and I took a deep breath as if a tight vice had just been loosened around my heart. The song had kept my breath stifled in my chest. I could see the Mammoth again, a little off to the right from the fire that burned just next to it. It had its head turned to us now, raised up in the air as if it wanted to grind up Velos within its whirring maw.

"Fortunately for us, Alsie said. *Faso isn't the only brilliant scientist to have graced Tow. The king has an equally brilliant mind working for our kingdom, as you shall soon see."*

Beneath us, the ground began to rumble, and dust started rising from around the Mammoth's feet. Molehills popped out of the grand, beneath the thorny strands of secicao, as huge metallic drills emerged from these. Soon enough, the dust settled, and we stood looking at a good two score war automatons, that had somehow concealed themselves in the ground.

"Dragonheats," I shouted. "An ambush." I turned Velos sharply off to the left as shots began to boom around us. The sky became filled with dragon roars, my comrades started getting shot out of the sky. A dozen or so must have tumbled to the ground in that first volley from the enemy. And each dragon life lost was also a strike against my own emotional endurance. With each loss of life, came a ripple in the collective unconscious, almost as if Gerhaun had lost a part of her soul.

The Gatling guns on the side of the mammoth also whirred into action, sending down more dragons. As we passed, I caught sight of the other four Mammoths behind the first. Their forms looking like huge ghost in my augmented vision and edging ever closer to us.

Beneath me, Velos' armour rumbled and took on a fluorescent green hue. His Gatling guns let out a cannonade of gunfire at the foremost Mammoth. At the back, Faso had one hand on the spigot and the other on the cannon control at the handlebar. But I couldn't see where the shots hit, and they didn't seem to do much damage. It was as if the automatons had been reinforced since we'd last seen them.

"We're outnumbered, Pontopa," Faso shouted. "We must retreat."

"You never want to stay to see these battles through," I said. "I thought you wanted to test out your cannon."

"There'll be other times for that."

"Look, if we let these Mammoths survive, then they'll stumble across the base. We'll regroup and I'll call reinforcements. These things have to go down today."

I flew away from the automatons. Charth sped in front of me, then did a loop the loop and flew underneath in the opposite direction. *"I'll scout for weaknesses,"* he said in the collective unconscious.

"Good," I said. And I bellowed a song at full vocal power out of my lungs, sending it out to Fortress Gerhaun. Gerhaun Forsi would hear this and hopefully call the entire fortress into action. She had thousands of Greys at her disposal and would surely send out a significant percentage, if not all of them.

"Well, well, I didn't expect the opportunity to eliminate your entire base today," Alsie said in response. *"But that's not what Finesia wants."*

"Then what do you want?" I said. *"I can never understand your intentions Alsie Fioreletta."*

"My intentions aren't my own but those of Finesia. She wants you and Taka to join her side. And she's been working on Taka a long, long time. And then there's your 'ally' Charth. You seem to trust him, but he's turning back to Finesia's side and it's only a matter of time. Charth, my dear, you know it won't be long until your will is Finesia's own."

"I won't let that happen," Charth said.

"You really think you have a choice? You can't draw off Finesia's gifts without her claiming something in return."

I really felt we were going off on a tangent here. I decided to get back to the important stuff. *"What do you want Alsie? You didn't answer that simple question."*

"Well, well. Let's make a list. Firstly, I wanted to show off my new powers. That way, you'll know in future not to cross me, like you intended today. At least for a while, for yes dragonseer one day we shall do battle. I've seen this in my dreams, and you will soon enough see it in yours. And only fate will decide the outcome of that battle, the decision about who will win is not your own."

"So, you don't have Taka? And you didn't come to claim him? So why exactly are you here?"

"To supervise the king's harvesting operations, of course. Now, that is, Charth and Francoiso are unavailable for the job."

"And you know full well that the presence of these harvesters puts our entire base at risk."

Alsie Fioreletta roared out into the sky. I took this, somehow, to be a dragonwoman's equivalent of a sigh. *"You remember Charth when you told the dragonseers that these Mammoths will never stumble across Fortress Gerhaun? I wish to honour that agreement, of course. Finesia doesn't yet want the king to discover you. Oh, she has far greater plans for Fortress Gerhaun."*

"She can't be trusted," Charth said.

"Oh, can't I? You should know, Charth, that Finesia always keeps her word. And you also know she also has plans for you as well."

"She may," Charth replied. *"But I'll never listen to her voice."*

"Oh, you can't resist forever my darling dragonman. She can give you the life you dreamed of as a child. Immortality. To be one of the most powerful creatures on this earth. A new race better than both man and dragon. She can help you to get revenge on your father. Isn't that want you truly want?"

Another roar boomed into the sky, this time coming from Charth flying a lot closer to us. *"No, I cannot accept that. My will is my own."*

"But you will turn eventually, Charth. No matter how much you try to resist it, Finesia will find a way through to your soul. Dragonseer Wells, he says you can't trust me, but actually this man is even more dangerous. With me, I'm always honest about where my allegiances lie."

"I am loyal to the dragons and the land, and I have been since I became a dragonseer," Charth said.

"That's right. For now..."

All this time while the exchange between Alsie and Charth was happening in the collective unconscious, I was trying to work out what to do next. Faso was screaming out his own worries from the back seat, but I wasn't listening to him too much. Wiggea was characteristically and courageously quiet, seemingly trusting that whatever action I took would be for the greater good.

"Pontopa, can you hear me?" Faso shouted. I'd zoned out a little during my conversation in the collective unconscious. But now, I decided to grace Faso with an answer.

"I can, Faso. And if we retreat, Alsie will follow us to the base and that will be the end of us. This battle needs to happen here and now." I wasn't entirely sure that Alsie would follow us, of course. But I didn't trust her one bit.

I could feel the strength of thousands of dragons from Fortress Gerhaun approaching. Gerhaun hadn't decided to accompany them. But if she had, she would have needed to leave the pirate at the base. She needed the answers out of him even more urgently than before. If Alsie and King Cini hadn't kidnapped Taka, then we needed to know who had.

"Pontopa, you're crazy," Faso said. "We fly in and they'll shoot us down for sure."

"We have a whole force at our disposal," I pointed out.

"And dragonheats knows what else that woman has in store."

"Oh dear, oh dear." Alsie's voice sucked me back into the collective unconscious again. *"I ask you to retreat and still you don't think it wise. You know, I really don't have time for this. And, I guess there's no harm in reducing the numbers in Gerhaun Forsi's forces."*

There was a shudder again and I looked over my shoulder to see a hatch opening on one of the Mammoth's backs. Out of it, came a swarm of Hummingbirds, glowing green in the low light. "Dragonheats," I said.

I turned the dial on the front of my mask to let more secicao gas through. I took a deep breath of this and alertness suddenly washed over my senses. The entire battlefield ghosted into a faint green and I could see all the automatons. Thousands of war automatons in a line. Hummingbirds, emerging not just from the back but from several compartments arranged across the Mammoths' huge hulls.

"Retreat!" I shouted out loud. And I let out the song to instruct the dragons to do the same, urgent and stochastic. Staccato notes that told them, indeed we had to act fast.

"Finally," Faso shouted.

But I kept Velos towards the back of the retreating flock. We'd need the firepower of the Gatling guns to shoot at the Hummingbirds as they attacked us from the rear. The aim was to meet up with the larger flock of reinforcements before the automatons even reached us.

The swarm of Hummingbirds approached us in swift force. Many of our dragons couldn't get ahead of them, and they were brought down to the ground. *"The scream, Charth."* I said. If he used it, he could bring them down.

"Dragonseer Wells, if I use that then... It's a gift of Finesia."

I tightened my mouth. Alsie had said that the more Charth uses Finesia's abilities, the closer it would bring Charth to the edge. *"We don't have a choice,"* I said.

"But, it's still no use. Alsie would just overpower it. And there's too many of them. Fleeing is the better option."

Meanwhile, Velos' guns started working on their targets and shooting them out of the sky. But still this was a battle I knew we couldn't win. Beneath us, on the ground, the soil crumbled beneath the secicao and more war automatons popped out like moles. Wellies knows how many of these Alsie had posted and when we'd finally leave them behind. We had no way of telling how large the size of the enemy was.

They fired as soon as they came out of the ground, felling more dragons. Strangely, none of the shots seemed directed at Velos. Almost as if they had some kind of central intelligence coordinating them all. Something had certainly changed in them, and I wondered if somehow Finesia was also within the secicao that powered these things, orchestrating the whole thing. Beneath me, Velos' dragon armour pulsed green. Did that mean Finesia could control it too?

I shuddered at the thought.

Meanwhile, more dragons fell around me. This tore at my heart, as I had a connection with each of them. Each loss of life killed a part of my soul. They were my responsibility and I'd failed them. Just as I'd failed Sukina by letting Taka go. And failed everyone by letting Sukina die all those years ago.

Fortunately, soon enough, after we'd got far enough out of range, the automatons stopped firing. They turned back towards their makers as the larger flock of dragons approached us from the front. I looked into it, and I wondered if I should turn around and order a full-scale assault. But something told me that we'd be annihilated on the spot. I certainly didn't want to have the fall of Fortress Gerhaun as part of my legacy. So, I sang the song to order all the dragons to turn around and head back to Fortress Gerhaun.

"Now you're learning," Alsie said. "Run back to safety. Oh, and if you want to know where Taka went, I suggest you start looking for Captain Colas'. I hear he expressed quite an interest in the boy when he heard he'd disappeared from the king's palace."

I shook my head. "Taka stays with us," I said. Just in case Alsie was having any bright ideas about taking him again.

"Obviously not, because you don't have him."

"And when I do, we're going to keep him. I'm not going to let this happen again."

"Big words, Dragonseer Wells. But Finesia has plans for you. You, Taka and I, together we will become a great race of immortals and part of Finesia's grand scheme."

"I will serve no mad goddess," I said.

"We shall see. Alsie said. We shall see."

And with that her voice cut off out of the collective unconscious. And when she did, it reminded me of the rift caused when Sukina had left us all.

I was left feeling strangely alone.

8

I'd caused quite a traffic jam at Fortress Gerhaun. The fortress had been designed for letting in only around twenty dragons at once. So, to orchestrate the landing of over a thousand dragons was a task within itself.

Hummingbirds were sent out to relay orders between men and the control centre, a room presently full of men and woman on typewriters deciphering information from the Hummingbirds and typing out messages to General Sako and his officers.

Of course, Velos being the celebratory dragon around here, we were allowed to land early. We pushed ahead of everyone else and, as we landed, we saw General Sako scurrying around the courtyard, sending messages to the sky with red semaphore flags. One of his guards waved us in towards the head of the golden dragon mosaic at the centre of the courtyard. A brass scaffold on wheels had been set up there so Velos could land without damaging the cannon. This was climbable, allowing Wiggea, Faso and I to quickly dismount.

Several strong looking olive-suited guards then wheeled Velos into a position besides two other Greys. Velos didn't seem so happy with the idea. Even with his celebratory status here, he couldn't quite find a connection with his own kin. He'd much rather had gone straight to his stables, I'm sure and wellies knows how long he'd have to wait in the courtyard. Still, he stood there on his two hind legs and waited patiently for more guards to come in and remove the cannon from his underbelly.

General Sako rushed over to me as soon as he saw me. "Dragonseer Wells. Gerhaun wants to meet with you at once."

"I know," I said. She'd already told me in the collective unconscious that she had news.

"Well, I just thought you might want to be quick about it. She knows of Taka's whereabouts."

"Captain Colas," I said.

General Sako furrowed his eyebrows. "Blunders and dragonheats, you've heard already? I might have known it would be my old nemesis. So he went and delivered the boy to the king for a bounty, I guess. You can't trust that old man with a piece of straw."

"I don't think the king has him," I said. Somehow, I think Alsie would have told me otherwise. I mean one thing I knew about that woman was that she never lied. "But you're right, I need to see Gerhaun."

"Let me know what you find out," General Sako said. And he rushed back to his duties beckoning Greys in to land.

Just before I walked off, Ratter scurried off Faso's shoulder and ran off towards the edge of the castle. "What's he after?" I asked Faso.

"Beats me. But I programmed into him with a little more autonomy lately, so I have more time to work on other things. He seems to be in pursuit of something."

I watched for a moment as the thing scurried up the ramparts. One of the guards noticed it and called out to it. The guard raised his rifle and Faso rushed over and pushed the man's rifle back down, shouting out his protestations. I left them arguing and darted into the corridors and towards Gerhaun's treasure chamber.

EVEN AFTER KNOWING her for a couple of years, Gerhaun's immensity still amazed me every time I saw her. People said that the Greys were towering beasts, just under three times the size of man. Velos was even bigger than them, and often struck fear into those that encountered him for the first time. But, in comparison, Gerhaun was as large as three cathedrals stacked one on top of the other, and she had had her treasure chamber built with a chimney that she could fly out of and which rose even taller than her.

She wasn't scaly like the other dragons and didn't have reptilian skin. Rather she was made out of the gold of the earth, as shiny as the treasures she guarded that funded Fortress Gerhaun's military operations. And she always looked so noble with wise eyes and an expression that commandeered both fear and respect in those that met her for the first time.

But it was clearly fear in the mind of the pirate she'd just interrogated. In fact, in this particular instance, I would describe it more like abstract terror in his expression, as if he'd just been down to the underworld and encountered all the demons that lived there. His eyes were wide, his pupils constricted, his jaw long, his skin blanched of colour. He looked as if he had lost his soul.

"What did you do to him?" I asked Gerhaun in the collective unconscious.

"Exactly what you had asked," Gerhaun said. "I found out where he had taken the boy."

"And how exactly did you manage to get out of him what General Sako and his troops couldn't?"

"My, my," Gerhaun said. "You should never ask a lady about her methods of torture."

I looked at the man, astounded. He didn't have a scratch on him. Gerhaun must have used some act of psychological torture, which I hoped one day she'd teach me herself. It could come in useful.

"So, what did you find out?" I asked.

"The man works for Captain Colas." Gerhaun said. "He's a mercenary pirate hired for gold, and the older man wanted to take Taka hostage. Apparently, a contract with Captain Colas comes with a promise that if they fail, he'll send out more mercenaries to kill the contractor and everyone in their *family. But, for success, he offers enough gold to feed a family for several generations."*

I nodded. *"Alsie expected Colas to have the boy too."*

All of a sudden, there came a rush of air from the chimney. Before I could even react, a huge blackened form shot down it and landed on the ground. A dragon, black except for the oily rainbow sheen which ran across its body, now stood right next to Gerhaun.

The giant dragon queen turned her head, ready to bite it to pieces. I also readied the rifle on my back, worried this was Alsie Fioreletta come down to exact her revenge. Not that a rifle would do much good, unless I was an excellent shot.

Meanwhile, a cloud of black dust rose up from the dragon's position. Out of sight behind the dust cloud, the dragon began to morph into human form.

"If you excuse me," Charth's voice came in the collective unconscious. *"It's about time you started to let me into these private conversations."*

Charth sounded much more cavalier than I'd remembered him in the palace. More like his deceased brother and less like his former, dour self.

"Charth," Gerhaun said. *"You know that you've been banished. You're not welcome here. If the men see you... if General Sako gets a hold of you."*

"I'll be out of here before they even ready their rifles," Charth said. *"But I wanted to talk to this pirate man myself."*

The dust cloud had now settled, and I could see a ferocity in this man's eyes. Really, Charth looked even scarier than General Sako right now. And I could tell he had a thirst for revenge. When Charth spoke in the collective unconscious, his voice had much more timbre than was usual. Certainly, something within him was starting to change.

Charth in human form had blonde hair swept back and greying slightly. He wore a grey cardigan and corduroy trousers as well, kind of old-fashioned looking and almost matching the colour of his hair. Remarkably, a dragonman's or dragonwoman's clothes never got lost during transformation, and I sometimes wondered where they disappeared to.

"Very well," Gerhaun replied to him. *"If you must..."*

"He worked for my father," Charth said. *"And I've wanted to know for a long time where he is. I have debt to pay to him."*

"Charth. I've told you before, vengeance is never the answer. Sukina had to learn that the hard way and you must too." And I could sense intense concern in Gerhaun's voice.

"But if my father hadn't betrayed us in the first place and snatched Taka away, Sukina would still be alive."

"Colas wasn't the one that killed Sukina."

"Still, he deserves to die."

My jaw had dropped incredibly low by this point in the conversation. I certainly hadn't expected to hear so much anger and hate in this flat, emotionless man.

"Do you know where Colas is now?" I asked Charth. *"Or Gerhaun, maybe you managed to get that information out of the pirate?"*

Charth shook his head and I looked up to see Gerhaun do the same.

"My father worked for the king for a long time," Charth said. *"But he only did so for a lot of cash. I thought I might find him in his manor estate in Spezzio. After what happened to Sukina I wanted to deliver my wishes. But I arrived and the whole place had been deserted. Clearly, he'd packed his bags and all his inventions and flew off to live somewhere else."*

I walked over to the pirate, who looked up at me wide-eyed as if an orphaned child found in the streets and starved of food. "Where is he?" I asked the pirate.

But as before, he said nothing.

"He doesn't know," Gerhaun said. *"I got him to speak the truth through my own methods, and I'm pretty sure he's told us everything he can. He made his deal with one of the old man's liaison in a bar on the Southern Approach and he never even met Colas."*

"Who does know?" Charth asked. *"And what the hell would the old man want with Taka?"*

"So many questions which I wish we had the answer to," Gerhaun replied. *"But for now, we only can act on the information that we have."*

Charth walked over to the man. He looked him up and down, and then lifted him up by his shirt collar. "You better be telling us everything you know. Because whatever you're scared of, I can do a lot worse to you, I'm sure." I was slightly off to the side of Charth and I saw the features morph on his face into dragon form. He let off a snarl, displaying razor sharp teeth, before his face went back to normal.

"*Leave him, Charth,*" Gerhaun snapped in the collective unconscious. And Charth sighed and dropped him to the floor, where the pirate collapsed into a heap.

We hadn't noticed Faso enter the room, who stood by the double doors with a small piece of paper in his hand. "Well, well," he said once I turned to him. "I wanted to pass over the news, but this is quite entertaining. Say, aren't you Charth Lamford the dragonman? We've met before, right, in the secicao jungle? Pontopa, you do know he works for the enemy…"

"He works for us now. He helped our escape from Cini's palace, remember?"

Faso clearly knew nothing about the brief love affair that Sukina had had with Charth, after she'd broken off his relationship with Faso. Nor did he know anything about the forced marriage between Sukina and Charth that had happened at the palace two years ago, nor consequently the marriage between me and Charth's brother. Nor did I intend telling Faso about any of this anytime soon.

"Well, I've never got my head around all the allegiances around here. But wellies, man, look at you. You could do with some fashion advice, for sure."

Charth rose his head high in the air. "I'll bear that in mind next time I'm wading through secicao resin."

"Well, it doesn't matter. I don't care so much what you wear. Although you might be pleased to hear that I know of Taka's location."

I put my hands on my hips. "Captain Colas has him, we know that already."

"Ah," Faso smirked. "But do you know where?"

"Let me guess, you've got some information from the office and wanted to rush ahead of the messenger and claim credit?"

"What, no. This didn't come from the office. It came from one of Captain Colas messenger automatons. A mechanical crow flying overhead that Ratter went chasing after to disable. We have the crow in the laboratory, which Asinal Winda is dismantling to discover it's inner workings as we speak."

I walked over to Faso and snatched the piece of paper out of his hand. "Captain Colas sent a message to us? Why on earth?"

I unfolded the slip of paper, stained yellow with smears of secicao resin.

"HURRY UP SLOWPOKES!" it said. "WE'RE ALREADY MILES AHEAD OF YOU. I HAVE THE BOY AND YOU CAN FIND HIM ON EAST CADIGAN ISLAND. BRING ONLY PONTOPA WELLS, ONE DRAGON AND A COUPLE OF ESCORTS. ANY OTHERS AND THE BOY WILL DIE."

I relayed the words to Gerhaun and Charth in the collective unconscious as I read.

"He wouldn't kill Taka would he?" I asked.

Faso looked at me wide eyes and folded his arms. "Please don't tell me you want to test that. I've already lost Sukina, I don't want to lose my child too." He looked up at Gerhaun. "Gerhaun, don't send an army out there, please."

And in response, Gerhaun's spoke out in an incredibly deep voice that laced the walls of the treasure chamber. "Dragonseer Wells, call a meeting immediately. We need to act fast."

I nodded and turned towards the door.

"Then I should make my leave," Charth said. And with those words, the dragonmen stepped aside and became a cloud of black dust. He speared up through the chimney and into the secicao clouds above.

I didn't waste another second and was promptly into the corridors rushing towards the courtyard.

9

By the time I got out of Gerhaun's treasure chamber, the traffic jam had been averted and most of the dragons had been corralled back into their stables. General Sako and a few troops still milled around the courtyard and they looked absolutely exhausted. I felt a little bad that I had to call a meeting, but time was short.

"Blunders and dragonheats," General Sako said as I approached. "Not again. Another meeting? Does work here ever end?"

"It's about your grandson, general," I said. "We know exactly where Colas is."

"What? Where?"

"East Cadigan Island," I said. I didn't want to spend ages getting to the point.

"Then we must send a force at once." He turned to Candiorno who stood just besides him, almost dozing off on the spot propped up against his rifle. "You heard me, officer. Summon a team together at once."

He saluted but before he could march off, I countered with, "Wait!"

General Sako twitched his moustache. "You're not circumventing my orders again are you, Dragonseer Wells?"

"No. You just don't have all the information yet. Captain Colas said that if he sees anyone else other than me, a dragon. and two escorts, he'll kill the boy."

"Blunders and dragonheats! Candiorno cancel those orders immediately."

The man stood to attention. "Affirmative sir."

"Good." General Sako turned to me. "So what's our plan of action?"

"Gerhaun wants to call a meeting in her treasure chamber immediately. High ranking officers and scientists only."

General Sako turned to his trusted officer. "Well, Candiorno. You heard the man. Get a team together immediately."

"Affirmative sir." the officer saluted again. "Will that be all sir?"

"Yes, yes. Now go. Time is of the essence."

And the olive-coloured suited officer marched off into the corridor to prepare Gerhaun's treasure chamber for the all essential briefing.

RATTER WITH A PROJECTION device in his open mouth, and the screen were already set up in Gerhaun's trove when we arrived. Gerhaun had shuffled over to the side a little to make space for the lieutenants, captains, corporals and admiral who comprised Fortress Gerhaun's leaders. Admiral Sandao was also present, as we'd no doubt need the fleet to help us get out some of the way.

We sat in rows, much like we had for the briefing in the courtyard. Although this time the regular troops weren't allowed – there would be a more official briefing later, I was sure.

I sat at the front, next to General Sako on one side and Wiggea on the other. Faso stood in front of the screen, with a retractable pointer that he leant on as he waited for Asinal Winda to get Ratter working at the back.

Soon enough, Ratter powered up and projected images of East Cadigan Island onto the screen. The images displayed some jungle terrain, and there was some yellow text on the screen instructing us to 'wear insect repellent', and that there was 'danger of dengue fever'.

Wide trunked trees rose out of the brown ground in the pictures, leading up to a canopy of palm and massive umbrella shaped leaves. A muddy river ran into the distance and a monkey with a funny face sat in one of the branches of the tree, looking at the camera as if wondering what the wellies it was doing there.

East Cadigan island was part of the much larger continent of Cadigan that lay to the west and spanned from the world's northern icecaps to those in the south. Though Cadigan had plenty of coal, it lacked saltpetre. This had caused the continent to fall behind in its development of guns and other weaponry, which made it easy for King Cini II's forces to colonise the land during his early reign.

But while Cadigan mainland had miles upon miles of fertile plains that Towese forces could build attractive cities around, East Cadigan Island was made up of impenetrable jungle terrain. Whenever man tried to plant a farm there, the jungle would grow over it, meaning it remained largely uninhabited, or at least so I had thought.

"Why the dragonheats would Captain Colas want to take Taka to East Cadigan island?" I asked.

Faso, who stood by the projector, had something to say about this. "A jungle would be the perfect place to hide anyone. It's discreet, and King Cini would never even think about looking for him there."

"But no one lives there." I said.

"Apparently so," General Sako from behind me. "The old man's taken Taka to be adopted by monkeys."

"Actually," Faso cut in. "There are indigenous tribes that live in East Cadigan island. A fascinating race of people indeed, although quite primitive. I've visited there myself, and they have quite some rituals. Plus, there's artifacts there that date back to the beginning of mankind."

I smiled. According to myth, life had been forged by The Gods Themselves. But Faso would never believe any of that. I'd had the discussion with him many times before. Faso believed that we all came from monkeys, and that dragons had evolved from sharks. Any suggestions to the contrary, he'd dismiss as 'magic and nonsense'. Oh, and in Faso's mind the Empress Finesia could never have existed.

General Sako harrumphed from besides me, then he stood up, walked to the front of the room, and turned to face us. "So, it appears our course of action is clear. Given that the East Cadigan rainforest is virtually uninhabitable, then there's no way that Colas of all people can have any forces there. Plus, given our troops have been trained to operate in a secicao jungle, they should be able to stay concealed within another kind of jungle. We'll send ten of my commandos and ten of Sandao's marines into there to support the rescue operation. A cloak and dagger operation. Admiral Sandao, are you with me?"

"Hang on a minute," I said, and I stood up. "From what I've heard of this old man, he has riches enough to buy an entire continent. Which means he can afford mercenaries, and no doubt a host of automatons. If we don't do as he says, we might put Taka in jeopardy."

I looked up to Gerhaun who was watching the situation passively from high above us. Her wise eyes watched every move I made. She was taking a backseat again, testing how I would manage this situation. And I could see in the expression of her face that she approved.

Meanwhile, my bravado against General Sako had shocked the room into silence. Even the old general seemed quite taken aback by it. It was Faso who decided to finally speak out and support me. "Pontopa's right this time, I'm afraid to say," he said. "Captain Colas is quite an accomplished scientist. He's published hundreds of journals under different pen names in his lifetime and I've read them all. And through his trove of wealth and incredible resourcefulness, he'll be able to see your covert troops coming before they even put foot on land."

"Blunders and dragonheats, Gordoni," General Sako said. "You know full well that means Taka can be at even greater risk. We'll be sending our only dragonseer right into the firepit."

"That's why we need Admiral Sandao's help," I nodded to the meek looking well-mannered man sitting a few seats away. "He can keep a couple of dragon carriers a hundred or so leagues away, so I can call them out if we have any trouble."

I knew enough about geography to realise that there was a shallow reef known as Paradise Reef just south of East Cadigan island. Probably, Sandao's fleets wouldn't be able to get any further than that. But it should be close enough for me to call for help if I need it.

"And how do you know he won't shoot the dragons down?" General Sako said.

"How do you know he won't zap your troops on first sight of them," I replied. "If it wasn't for Charth, his mercenaries might have stumbled right across Fortress Gerhaun and killed us all before taking Taka."

"Charth..." General Sako twitched his moustache. "Please don't tell me you want him to be your third escort."

"No. Colas' instructions were clear and Charth stays." I nodded up to Gerhaun. The more I thought about what Alsie had said and Charth's recent behaviour, the more I doubted we could trust the dragonman.

"You really think you can control him," General Sako said.

"He cares about Taka; he won't do anything." Then I bit my tongue, realising what I'd just said. But he had looked after Taka in Cini's palace for most of the duration of the boy's life.

"Blunders and dragonheats. That fool doesn't care about anyone but himself. Admiral Sandao, I want to have a handful troops on each of your ships. My best shooters. Then, if we see Charth flying anywhere nearby, we'll shoot him down on sight. If we get him in the throat, I believe that will be enough."

Sandao nodded. "Very well," he said.

"And one more thing, I'm coming too. If anything goes wrong, I'll march in to East Cadigan and I'll take Colas down myself."

I looked up at Gerhaun. *"Is that okay?"* I asked in the collective unconscious. *"You're remarkably quiet up there, Gerhaun."*

She looked at me and then she lowered her head towards us. I could feel her warm breath washing over us. Instead of replying in the collective unconscious, Gerhaun Forsi chose to speak out loud.

"So, it's decided," she said. "Which is good because, I finally need some rest. Admiral Sandao, take two hundred and fifty Greys on five carriers and whatever cruisers, destroyers and battleships you feel you might need. And send back regular reports by Hummingbird. Because if anything goes wrong, I'll need to rally the dragon queens."

Admiral Sandao stood up, raised his head to Gerhaun and saluted. "Affirmative," he said.

"Good," Gerhaun said. "And General Sako. Yes, I understand your concerns. But please keep your troops off land until you're sure it's absolutely necessary to send them in. We can't afford to lose Taka and Dragonseer Wells here, and I think Mr Gordoni is right about the risk."

General Sako looked up at Gerhaun but didn't salute like the admiral. "I'll do what is necessary."

"And I'll always trust you to make the right choices," Gerhaun said. "Now, if you excuse me, this meeting is adjourned."

The officers at the back stood up first, and they left in single file. Sandao and the remaining rows followed them out. Asinal Winda then walked up to Ratter, turned off the beam, unscrewed the projection device, glanced once at Faso, and walked out the door.

Faso didn't notice Winda leave, but instead stood staring at the screen with his hands on his hips, as if ruminating over last of the images burned into his head. Ratter scurried off the table and then climbed up onto Faso's shoulder, watching everyone leave with caution. Dragonheats, I could never trust that automaton, particularly the way its red crystal eyes glowed.

Gerhaun had already turned her head away from us, and now rested it out of sight behind a pile of gems on the floor. She'd be asleep soon; I could feel her spirit drifting out of the collective unconscious. She'd been awfully tired the last few days – more than usual. I hoped everything was alright.

So, I also thought it best to set an example as it was now only me, Faso and General Sako left in the room. "Come on you two," I said. "Gerhaun needs her sleep and we should leave."

At that, Faso snorted. "Why does she get to sleep while we do all the work around here? I've never understood it."

"I would have thought you'd become quite an expert on the behavioural patterns of dragons right now."

"Exactly," Faso said. "But always in science there'll be many things that will remain unexplained. This one completely bewilders me."

I shook my head. "Faso, she's the strongest source of the collective unconscious here. I'm sure having all the thoughts of every man and dragon pass through you must be quite a tiring thing."

"But she only understands you."

"That's what you think," I said. "Just because Gerhaun doesn't talk to you doesn't mean she can't hear your thoughts."

Faso looked at me in bemusement. "No, you're pulling my leg…"

"Maybe," I said. "Although Gerhaun has secrets beyond what even I know, I'm sure. She's much, much smarter than you'll ever understand." Although, I did wonder. If there was a strong enough source of the collective unconscious, maybe regular folks would be able to hear too.

"Why, Pontopa," Gerhaun said in my head. "Thank you kindly for the compliment. Now, when are those two men, going to leave me in peace?"

I nodded. "Look Faso, Gerhaun has requested to be left alone. It's time to make your leave."

Faso glanced over at the treasure trove, then back at me. He had a look of defiance in him, as if he wanted to test Gerhaun's authority. But I held his gaze, and eventually he backed down. "Very well. I better be making preparations for the mission, anyway. You know, checking the good old cannon's in good working order." He gave me a sly smile and left the room.

General Sako was the only one left. He stood there, his arms folded behind his back, gazing into space, seemingly in a trance. I considered clicking my fingers in front of his face to snap him out of it, but then thought better of it.

"General Sako," I said instead.

He said nothing.

"General Sako?"

He turned his head slowly towards me. "Yes Sukina… I mean, yes Dragonseer Wells?"

"Gerhaun wants us to leave now."

"So soon?" He gazed off into the darkness.

"We need to prepare for our mission, General."

"Well, we better get cracking then." He made towards the doorway. Before he left, he turned back to me. "Pontopa?" he said.

"Yes?"

"I um… Blunders and dragonheats. You won't let anything happen to Taka, will you?"

I smiled. "General Sako, I know your grandson means a lot to you. And believe me, he's like a second son to me too. I'd die before letting anything happen to Taka. I promise you that. And Colas has a lot to answer for."

I saw General Sako's fists clench by his sides. "He does," he said. "It's time for that man to finally get what's coming to him."

"We'll show him, General," I said. "So now, come on, let's let Gerhaun rest." And I followed him out. Behind me the two dragonelite swung the heavy oak doors slowly shut.

I DECIDED I needed a breath of fresh air – or at least fresh as you could get when surrounded by a secicao jungle. Plus, in all honesty, I wanted a bit of alone time, away from the military, and dragons, and worried parents, and Faso Gordoni, and even (I hate to say it) Sukina. Of course, being stuck in a military base, there weren't many places a lady could get some hard-earned peace and quiet. But the courtyard was usually empty around this time and, although General Sako and Admiral Sandao would no doubt be setting it up for another briefing soon, I should have got at least fifteen minutes or so of respite while everyone sorted themselves out.

As expected, there was no one in the courtyard when I got there. All the troops would have been rushing around Fortress Gerhaun's musty corridors relaying orders from room to room that they needed to get their acts together and coordinate the briefing. Meanwhile, Faso and Winda were probably making whatever last-minute modifications they could to the technology they deemed necessary for the mission, and the only traces of them was the discarded skeleton of a dragon-automaton-in-progress lying in one corner of the courtyard floor.

I sat down on the mosaic of Gerhaun Forsi, right where her chest was. I folded one leg over the other and began to meditate. Simply letting my worries drift by, as Sukina had advised. Focusing only on what I could control. I couldn't worry this moment about how I'd failed Taka, even though I felt absolutely awful about missing his birthday and being so cruel to him. And I had to accept all the changes taking place, like Velos now sporting a huge cannon from his chest into battle and all of us having to cross the ocean to hunt down a madman I'd never before met.

I closed my eyes and watched each thought from a distance as it flickered through my mind like a firefly. Then, amidst all of it, I started to get the sense that I wasn't alone.

"You're getting better at the whole controlling your mind thing. I guess Sukina taught you well."

I opened my eyes and swung my head around to see Charth's oily dragon form sitting on the ramparts in the distance in front of me. He was in exactly the same place I'd seen him sitting just after Sukina's funeral.

"Charth..." I replied in the collective unconscious. *"I thought you said you'd stay away from this place. If General Sako or any troops see you, there'll be trouble."*

"Oh, I know well enough how to stay out of their way. You know, this is the first time in a long time you've actually noticed me sitting here."

"Except I didn't notice you," I replied.

"That's true. I guess it was I who alerted you to my presence. But it's also inconsequential. I just thought I'd inform you that I'll accompany you as the second escort to face off against my father."

I gritted my teeth. *"You'll do no such thing,"* I said. *"General Sako has ordered that if anyone sees you anywhere near Gerhaun's fleets, you're to be shot on sight."*

"How unbecoming of him," Charth said." *But I can keep my distance. Don't worry. I've crossed the Pallandi Ocean many times before."*

I took a deep breath. I wasn't going to stop Charth through threatening him. And, somehow, I believed Captain Colas would act upon his threats if he saw too many of us coming inland.

"Charth, please," I said. "*If you care about Taka, take seriously what your father said. He's claimed he'll kill the boy if he sees any less than three of us on East Cadigan Island. And we can't put Taka in danger... Please, if not for me, do it for Sukina...*"

And I felt a tear emerge in the corner of my eye.

Charth hesitated before giving me his response. "*You know he's my father. You'd think he wouldn't mind me popping in for a visit.*"

"*From what you've told me, I don't think he cares.*"

"*Probably not,*" Charth said and he raised his forelegs for a very brief moment. "*Very well, I guess I had better make the best use of my time in the Southlands.*"

I breathed a sigh of relief. I'd thought Charth was going to be a lot harder to convince to stay behind. My alternative would have been trying to convince General Sako and the rest of the troops that only Faso, Velos and I would embark on the mission. But I think that would have been even harder to pull off, as I would at least need a personal guard.

"*Charth, perhaps you could make yourself useful and track Alsie. Do you think that would be possible? I know it might be risky, but I don't trust her and would like to know what she's up to.*"

Then a sudden thought came to my head which caused me to shudder. All this could be Alsie's work. If she coerced us to vacate Fortress Gerhaun, then that would leave enough for her to destroy the place while we were away. But no, it didn't make any sense. Alsie would have destroyed us, anyway, given the number of automatons she'd had at her disposal before. Something else was going on and whatever it was, I had a feeling I wouldn't like it one bit.

"*Now I can hear your anxious thoughts again,*" Charth said. "*You better stop it, as you might wake up Gerhaun.*"

"You're right," I said. "*So, it's settled then. Faso, Wiggea and I will go and rescue Taka. While you will keep an eye on Alsie, check she's not up to anything. And please, do whatever you can to wake Gerhaun up if the fortress comes under any danger.*"

"Very well," Charth said. *"I'll do my best."*

"Promise me."

"Sorry, Dragonseer Wells. I don't make promises anymore. Not since—"

His thoughts were cut off by a commotion coming from the back of the courtyard. Two guards rushed out of the double doors there, carrying the projector screen ready for the next briefing.

I turned my head back to Charth. But, like a fleeting bird, he was already up in the air and, very shortly afterwards, out of sight.

Everything was happening so fast, I didn't have much time to say goodbye to my parents, unfortunately. But they did come to Velos' to see me off. At the time, Admiral Sandao was already preparing his fleet to enter the canal that formed both the north moat of Fortress Gerhaun, as well as a link between the massive Balmano and Phasni rivers. The boats would head west down the the Balmano and then group at river's mouth into the Pallandi Ocean.

Meanwhile, the Greys would escort them from air, just in case there were any boats or automatons waiting in ambush on the way, and then enter the dragon carriers at the meeting point. Velos would lead the aerial squad – all two hundred and fifty of them.

"You've got your hipflask," Papo said to me as we stood next to Velos and his armour.

"Of course, Papo," I said. "How many times do you have to ask?" I wanted to be kind of angry with him still for helping Faso install the cannon. But Papo would always be Papo and I'd learned to forgive him quickly about things like this.

"And Faso," my father turned to the inventor. "Everything's powered up and ready to go."

"Everything's in fine condition. We'll get in there, get the boy and get out again."

"Just make sure you look after her," he said. Then he turned to Wiggea. "And you of course, young man. Neither of you let anything happen to my daughter."

Wiggea saluted, which looked a bit silly given my father was a civilian and so wasn't a superior. "I wouldn't dream of it, sir."

And that caused a smile to stretch across my father's face. "Then I guess I'm leaving my daughter in the best possible hands."

He embraced me in a long and warm hug, and I held it for a moment not wanting to go. But I knew I had a mission ahead of me, and I wouldn't lose Taka for the world. So eventually I broke off, and I approached my mother who was standing back a little.

She also embraced me in a hug, much more delicate than my father's.

"Pontopa, dear. I know that you need to do this, but your father and I, we can't help but worry."

"I know," I said. "And I wish that this would be all over. But you know this is something I have to do."

"I wish it were different," she said. "Or at least we could come with you."

I shook my head. "It will be safer here, and I'll be back soon I promise."

I pulled myself back from my mother and saw a tear drop out of her reddened eyes. "Just don't go doing anything reckless," she said, and she took a handkerchief out of her pocket and wiped the tears away.

"Aye aye, Maam," I said, and I saluted then looked back at Wiggea who returned a sheepish smile.

My mother laughed in response.

Time, as General Sako had said, was of the essence. So I said farewell again to my parents and then climbed the ladder on Velos' armour. Faso and Wiggea mounted soon after me, and we put on our gas masks.

I pulled back on Velos' steering fin and turned him west. I then sang a dragonsong to instruct the Greys to also launch from their stables. Once they'd joined us, I looked down once more to wave goodbye to my parents, and I kept waving until they were no longer visible through the secicao clouds.

PART IV

ADMIRAL SANDAO

"King Cini may have had the best automaton technology, but it didn't matter. Because we had the best sailors in the world."

— ADMIRAL SANDAO

10

The ships that Sandao had selected weren't the largest in Gerhaun's fleet. The admiral understood that speed was of the utmost importance. And we needed smaller ships as the Balmano river, whose mouth was at The Southlands west coast, was much narrower than the Phasni river, which opened out at the continent's east coast. The dragon carriers themselves could only carry fifty dragons each and we'd sent out five of them.

Once we got to our destinations, the dragons would enter the carriers through holes leading into the hull, with hatches that could close over their heads. Other than the dragon carriers, we had about a dozen cruisers in the fleet, including the Saye Explorer, and two long-bodied destroyers. We couldn't take any battleships down the Balmano and so we had to leave them behind.

The boats travelled in a line down the river, with barely enough berth on either side for manoeuvre. Admittedly, Gerhaun's fleet didn't travel that way very often. Most of the naval battles we engaged in were against Cini's forces, south of the Southern Barrier. And the only way to get there was through the Phasni. Consequently, many of the crew found themselves navigating unchartered waters in the Pallandi Ocean.

I'd been in the Southlands so long that I'd forgotten how good the world tasted. I guess I'd been so busy training and trying to become an awesome dragonseer, I'd neglected to take Velos out here. The air of the Pallandi Ocean had the saltiness of the sea. There was a light cloud cover and through it came soft rays of light. It felt suddenly good to have sun on my skin again, and I found myself missing home. But our house and my external cottage in the Five Hamlets had been burned down by King Cini III and we wouldn't be going back there.

One thing that I knew were great hazards on this ocean were its superstorms. Merchant traders that transported coal from the Cadigan continent to Fortress Gerhaun had told me many times how they just came out of nowhere and could swallow up even the largest trawlers. The worst thing was that they approached at such a speed you didn't see them coming. The merchant captains claimed that maritime records showed no evidence of these one-hundred or so years ago and called them one of this world's biggest mysteries. I just hoped we wouldn't encounter one ourselves.

Fortunately, the land in the Southlands was mostly flat, and the Balmano's waters lacked rapids. Which meant we made it into the Pallandi Ocean pretty quickly. And not long after, we were out of the secicao clouds, and we could remove our masks and once again breathe fresh air. I sang a song to instruct the dragons to take shelter in the dragon carriers. They would need to be well rested once we got to East Cadigan Island, just in case a battle was waiting for us there.

Our destination was Paradise Reef, a stretch of water loved by merchant fishing fleets for its parrotfish and other tropical seafood. Admittedly, the dragon carriers wouldn't be able to get any further than that, although they could send out patrol boats if they needed to deploy any troops inland. And, of course, each of Sandao's carriers were equipped with them. Six, in fact.

Once the dragons had entered the carriers, I took Velos down to land on the Saye Explorer, the fleet's flagship. This was a medium-sized frigate, with a spacious enough quarterdeck to house Velos. For now, he could stay there while I supervised operations together with

General Sako and Admiral Sandao. In other words, sitting back in a deck chair and enjoying the sun against my skin.

We had been sailing for quite a few hours when I spotted the clouds looming ahead. A tropical storm swirling slowly in the distance, its eye pulling a visible spray out of the water. It was approaching fast.

The hairs on my arm began to stand on end. I was sitting in a deck chair at the time, reading a novel. Velos lay on the grooved surface next to me, hot air buffeting against my skin as he snored softly. Much of the crew was below deck, including Faso who claimed he needed to make some modifications to Ratter to prepare the automaton for humid jungle conditions.

Soon enough, the cabin doors opened below, and officers and sailors flooded out of it. They flurried into action, pointing out at the storm, shouting orders, running around ensuring all equipment was properly sealed, pulling up the patrol boats on deck with huge winches, grabbing supplies and ponchos from storage in the hull.

Admiral Sandao came rushing out after them and climbed the ladder up to the quarterdeck. "It's a superstorm," he said to me. "It came out of nowhere. You'll need to take cover. Kraken's going to hit us fast and strong."

I raised an eyebrow. "Kraken?"

"That's what our meteorologists have called this storm." He scratched at his beard. "It's like nothing we've ever seen before."

"But Velos?" It would be one of the biggest blunders in military history if we lost one of our most valuable dragons to a hurricane. "I can't leave him out here alone."

Sandao pointed at the approaching storm. "We'll hit it in four minutes. Five if we're lucky. Velos needs to take shelter in a dragon carrier. You need to get moving."

I shook my head. "Can't we just fly around it? If we use Faso's armour, maybe we can get away from it fast enough."

"You've got to be kidding." Faso came running out from the cabin behind. "I built the armour to fight battles, not hurricanes. Pontopa, I know you're not a woman of science, but this is one of your worst bloopers yet."

"I said fly around it… Not through it."

"Do you know how large a hurricane is, Pontopa? We're not talking a mere twister here, but a storm the size of several large cities."

I blushed. I didn't like being talked down to by Faso, but this time, I guess he was right. One of the dragon carriers had levelled up besides us. Admiral Sandao gestured over to it. "If I were you, I'd get Velos under deck," he said. "Rest assured you have the best sailors in the world. We'll get through this, Dragonseer Wells. Just get safe and let my men do their job."

I nodded and turned to Velos who now had lifted his head to gaze out at the storm. I'm guessing he'd never seen anything like it before, but then neither had I. A huge gust of wind came, and I had to grab the railing to keep myself on deck. The first drops of rain started to patter on the deck and splash on my skin. From behind, General Sako came barrelling out of the door to the quarterdeck cabin, Lieutenant Wiggea and Lieutenant Candiorno following in his wake.

"Blunders and dragonheats!" General Sako said. "What are you still doing up here, Dragonseer Wells? Wiggea, get her below deck immediately."

I put my hands on my hips. "We need to protect Velos."

"Then get him in a carrier. That armour won't protect him from a bloody hurricane."

I nodded and then turned to Wiggea. I honestly, couldn't think of anyone else I'd rather be stuck in a stuffy dragon carrier with during a storm, Velos excepting. "Wiggea, you can come with me. I'll need a personal guard in case anything…" I swallowed. "Anything happens."

"And what about me?" Faso said. "You're going to desert me here?"

I smiled. "You really want to be stuck in a confined dragon carrier stable, Faso?"

"No, I want to be on the bridge here studying the storm. I might learn something. As long as I can do it from somewhere safe." He glanced at the pocket watch hanging from his suit pocket. Ratter poked his head out of his sleeve and ran up onto his shoulder. The automaton turned to sniff in the direction of the storm and arched his back. He let out a hiss and scurried back inside its hiding hole in Faso's sleeve.

"Oh, you'll be fine here, Faso," I said. "Go find Asinal Winda and keep her company. She'll need a strong man to look after her, you know. It's going to be a scary time." I was teasing, of course. Faso would be showing much more fear once the storm hit than Winda, I was sure.

"Fine," Faso said. "But she can come up to the bridge to help with my studies. I'll need an extra eye to record all the data and make sure the meteorological equipment is working."

"Break a leg," I said. Another huge gust of wind came off from the ocean, bringing a soaking spray of water with it. I braced myself against it, trying to breathe. "Come on Lieutenant, let's hop on."

"Right on it, Maam," he said and saluted. Honestly, he was such a handsome man with those soft hazel eyes and hard-edged face. Often, I wondered if I anything could happen between us. But he was all about duty and would always think of me as his superior. Yet, a woman could dream.

Velos had hunched up into a ball. So, I walked around him and patted his back to instruct him to stand up straight. He raised his back, stretched his legs, turned his head in the direction of the storm and let out a roar, causing Wiggea and I to cover our ears. I grimaced and then let out a soft dragonsong to calm him.

"It will be okay," I said. "We'll be safe in the carrier. Men and dragons have been through a lot worse."

Velos lowered his head to me and I stroked him around his scaly mane. He let out a whimper, but this quickly turned into a much more reassuring croon.

The dragon turned his tail towards me. I ran up it and clambered over the two back seats before I took my position behind his steering fin. Wiggea looked up at me from the deck, saluted, and then climbed up the ladder and took position on the back seat. I buckled the harness and I turned back to Wiggea and smiled, then I pulled back on Velos' steering fin to launch him into the sky.

The wind was picking up now, and the storm approaching faster than any storm I'd ever known. Already, the hatches had closed on the dragon carrier ahead of us.

With every minute, the clouds looked even more menacing. They now were grey and cumulus overhead, swirling in abstract patterns. Velos didn't have to get far into the sky until we could feel its pull, the so-called Kraken trying to drag us into its eye, all the while roaring thunder into the main. It was hard to get Velos to fly straight, and I could feel his anxiety in my own chest as he beat his wings hard to keep us aloft.

I took my hip flask from my belt and took a swig from it as I guessed I might need the extra agility. The world turned green, and I could now see lightning striking within the mushrooming clouds. I turned back to Wiggea. "Lieutenant. Do you think you can operate the armour?" I called over the wind.

"What's that, Maam?" he bawled, and he cupped his hand over his ear and turned it towards me.

"The armour?" I pointed to the spigot and controls that Faso usually manned from the back seat. "Could you?"

Wiggea looked down at it and shrugged. "Haven't a clue, Maam."

"Never mind," I shouted. And I turned back to the weather, the wind whipping my hair every which way that it slashed like wild snakes against my face. I pushed down on Velos' steering fin, steering him away from a huge wave coming up at us from the ocean. The carrier was difficult enough to see, the sky was so grey. But I hazarded a glance over my shoulder and couldn't even see the Saye Explorer now through the murk. I'd never in my life known a storm to move so fast.

In front, the dragon carrier was being tossed up upon the waves. A stout woman stood on the wide platform, suitable for landing ten dragons at a time, and she beckoned us in.

"Hold on to your handlebar Wiggea," I called back. And I gritted my teeth and held my breath against the wind. The storm was throwing us around in a seesaw fashion, making me feel seasick enough that I couldn't imagine what it was going to be like on the boat. The platform slanted to the side at a sharp angle and the woman there went tumbling down it, stopping herself just in time by grabbing onto a pipe that jutted out from the superstructure. If it hadn't been there, she would have been swallowed whole by the sea, never to be seen again.

I tried touching Velos down on the platform. But it had lifted itself up at too sharp an angle, and his claws ended up glancing off it. I yelped, then pulled the dragon to the left slightly to stop us tumbling down as well. Fortunately, he managed to push himself back into the air. But he lost his control a little bit and we ended up spinning in a one-hundred-and-eighty-degree barrel roll off to the side. While before I could see the sky above, now I could see only churning grey water and it was approaching fast.

Blood pulsing to my temples, I pulled hard on Velos' steering fin to turn him around again. The world spun out of control for what felt like several minutes, but what must have been only a few seconds. Then, we were flying straight, looking askew at the horizon, the dragon carrier behind us. I turned back to Wiggea who now was leaning over Velos' flank, trying to find enough coordination to turn the spigot. Faso had always kept how to operate the armour as his own secret, claiming it was much too complicated for anyone but the best of minds to understand.

A column of water lashed up from the sea and whisked against my face. The saltiness stung my eyes and I squinted and yelped out in pain. No, I couldn't lose focus. We weren't going to get wiped out by a stupid storm after we'd come so far in the war against Cini and Alsie. That wouldn't be doing justice to Sukina.

I turned Velos around so we could approach the platform once again. It had levelled out relatively straight but had now started to tip in the other direction and was accelerating that way fast. If we came in too slowly, we'd miss once again. The wind was getting even stronger around us now. I found myself getting jostled around in my seat, and if it wasn't for the harness that pushed hard against my chest to keep me there, I'm sure Wiggea and I would have been eaten up by the waters.

I could feel Velos also fading. His wings were tiring. He'd never had to battle conditions like this before. "Keep it steady Velos," I said. "We can make it."

And, as if answering my call, the armour started to warm a little beneath my feet. Faint green lights began to flow through it, cutting paths through the murk, and flaring in my augmented vision. Underneath that, Velos also began to shake and a determined growl rumbled through him. I could also feel the resolve in his spirit, and with it I began to sing a song into the storm that would help clear his head.

As we approached the deck, it rose even higher on the wave. The woman there had stayed clinging on to the pipe on the superstructure, and again was waving us in. I narrowed my eyes and kept my hand firm on the steering fin, pushing it with slight micromovements to help guide Velos downwards. Meanwhile, Velos detracted his claws and readied them to clutch on to the grooves that had been drilled into the metal plates on the ship's floor to give dragons purchase when landing. But still the deck continued to rise, and the prow was now so high above us, that I had to crane my head to see the top of it.

"Brace," I shouted. And I ducked down as low as I can. Velos clunked against the metalwork of the ship and this time, dragonheats, he wasn't going to let go. I felt the pain tear into his claws, and he roared to the wind, shaking the armour and sending terror through my bones. The green light in the armour pulsed ever stronger, and I increased the volume of my song. *"Hold on, Velos,"* I thought. Because I knew he'd be able to hear the sentiment in the emotion, though not the words. Underneath us, the sea boiled like a vat of acid. It would be so easy for Velos to let go, and let the sea take us under its strong currents.

The prow continued to rise, and the boat continued to tip, and even more secicao pulsed through Velos' armour giving him the strength to hold on. And I clutched on to the handlebars with my dear life, an intense throbbing lancing in my fingertips, a result of sharing the pain tearing through Velos' claws. I felt sick, and I felt Velos wanting to give up. And I wanted to quit too. To join Sukina and not have the burden of responsibility anymore. Not to have to hold on.

But no. Fortress Gerhaun needed me... Taka needed me.

"Are you okay, Maam?" I could only barely make out Wiggea's shouting through the roar of the wind and thunder.

I didn't say anything though. I had to focus on my song, each note of the harmony giving Velos strength. His claws were slipping from the metalwork. In only moments, he'd slide off. A rope came sailing through the air behind me attached to a grappling hook. Wiggea had thrown it towards the radar. But it missed by inches and fell towards the sea.

Then, Velos lost his last ounce of strength. We began not to slide, but tumble in a sickening roly-poly down the deck that Velos had no chance to recover from. Now, we were certainly at the mercy of the laws of nature. My head glanced off the metalwork, and I screamed out as numbing pain seared through my skull. The world spun around me, and all I saw was grey metal and grey sky.

But although nature often brings bad luck, it also often brings incredible fortune. As Velos tumbled, the boat began to change direction. Despite the waves of concussion passing through my head, I could sense that we were slowing. Velos managed to dig his claws once again into the metalwork and we jerked to a halt.

"Velos," I said. Though my voice was weak.

The woman on deck had now opened a set of double doors into a room that led to a platform. Inside, was a winch hooked to a pulley. The woman rushed inside, took out the hook, and trailed it out towards us. The ship tilted against her, but still she kept low and scrambled up to us so she could attach the hook to the side of Velos' armour. The woman slipped back into the compartment and kicked a lever to activate the winch mechanism. The cogs inside clicked into life and Velos retracted his claws. We slid inside and the woman kicked shut the double doors. She proceeded to turn a crank handle on the opposite wall that lowered the platform into the hull, where fifty Grey dragons were tucked in safe and sound.

I'D NEVER BEEN INSIDE one of Gerhaun's Dragon Carriers before and had often wondered about these massive ships that could release a flock into battle so quickly. In a way, they were one of the most important weapons Gerhaun owned, since they increased the range that the dragons could attack from. Each carrier had seen many battles, particularly in skirmishes against Cini's forces at the southern barrier in an attempt to disrupt some of the larger secicao harvesting operations. And although this ship was smaller than Admiral Sandao's super-carriers, it was still quite an impressive piece of engineering.

The holding area containing the stables within the hull was surprisingly cavernous. From the outside, the carriers seemed quite flat. But the whole structure extended deep into the water with enough height to hold three coloured dragons standing on top of another. They'd designed the larger carriers not just to hold the Greys, but also in the case that they'd need to smuggle a dragon queen out of the Southlands, should one of the bases be discovered.

The manually operated elevator led down to the centre, from where a long corridor extended to each end of the ship. Each side of each end of the corridor had twelve big doors, with stables containing Grey dragons behind them and a trough full of secicao to feed them. A further stable stood at each end of the corridor, making up fifty in total. There were also four large rooms at the corners the boat, and two on each side of the elevator for stationing Sandao's marines and whoever else might be one board. Of course, there was also space in the upper superstructure for officers and sailors on duty. But now, I had no doubt that the majority of the squad was here in the hull where they'd be safest from the storm.

The woman who had saved us on deck saluted us once the elevator hit the bottom. She was one of Sandao's marines, and the epaulettes on her shoulder suggested she also had officer rank. She was older than I'd expected, with a wrinkled forehead, and a plump, ruddy face. But despite that, she still had quite a muscular build.

"This way, Maam," she said and led us towards the stable at the stern of the ship. "All of the stables are full here. But the back stable is biggest so I'm sure the Grey could make room."

I shrugged. Velos wouldn't like that one bit. But then, it would probably do him good to be in close quarters with one of the Greys. Even if they saw him as kind of different.

"Thank you," I said. "And wait."

The woman stopped in her tracks. "What can I do for you, Maam?"

The ship rocked in a sickening way and with that and the concussion from where I'd hit my head I kind of felt like throwing up. But I kept it down as this woman deserved to be commended for her courage.

"What's your name? I'll make sure to mention your brave act to Admiral Sandao."

The woman blushed. "Why, thank you. I'm most honoured. The name's Talato. Ensign Gereve Talato, Maam." And she saluted again.

She led Velos and I down the long corridor, Wiggea trailing slightly behind. At first, I sensed Velos' resistance. But it didn't last long, as he soon realised that he had nowhere better to go. It was incredibly difficult to move. With every step I took, the storm sent me stumbling against the walls. But within a few minutes, we reached the stable at the back and Ensign Telato opened the double doors to let us inside.

A Grey had secured itself against the left-hand wall. Velos bared its teeth at the Grey when we entered and the Grey whimpered and backed up against the wall. So, I sang a sharp stochastic noted song to admonish Velos. In this kind of situation, as well as in the fiercest battles, he'd have to learn to get on with his peers, no matter what grudges he held against them.

Velos whimpered and retreated to the other corner of the spacious metallic room, while the Grey turned his head defiantly away from us and rested it on the floor. There was little in the way of entertainment here. It was literally a dark holding cell with a long oil lit tube spanning the ceiling and a trough at the back of the room. The light from the ceiling reflected off the chrome walls and suffused it in a bright light. But as the ship rocked, the lights sputtered, and I wondered if at some point the bulb would twist out of the ceiling and plunge the room into darkness.

"We're here Maam," Esnsign Talato saluted again. "Now, if you don't mind, I'll join my comrades in the bunk."

I nodded. "Dismissed," I said.

"Thank you Maam. You're most welcome to join us by the way. The sickness will affect you less if you're lying down."

I looked across at Velos's head now resting low against the deck. My stomach was starting to churn a little, I admit. Although, I'd developed a little resistance to travel sickness, due to the fact I'd been riding Velos most my life (and maybe partly also due to my genes as a Dragonseer). "I'll be fine here," I said.

The ensign saluted a third time. Then, he left the stable and made her way down the corridor to the other end of the ship. And I lay down on the cold steel floor. Which wasn't the smartest thing to do, as I almost slid down to the other end of the room. But Velos put his leg over me to secure me in place.

Meanwhile, Wiggea got thrown against the other Grey dragon.

"Maam, they have harnesses to secure you in place in the bunks," he said.

"I have Velos thanks," I said. "But maybe you'd like to strap yourself into the armour and keep me company?" And unprofessional as it may have seemed, I may have added a little demure tone to my voice.

He lowered his head, sheepishly and let off a weak smile. "I think my place is with the guards, Maam."

"And leave a lady all alone with two dragons?" I think I was probably a little giddy from the concussion I'd experienced on deck. So maybe I was letting my emotions get ahead of me a little.

Wiggea's voice sounded a little stifled. "You'll be safe here, I think." And he left the room.

I lay flat on my back, listening to the breathing of Velos and the Grey for a while. It must have been the concussion, for the rest of the storm didn't bother me so much. And I soon found myself rocked vigorously to sleep.

11

When I awoke the next day, the storm had abated quite significantly. I had no idea how long I had been out. But it was light outside, I could see that, since the doors to all the stables had been left wide open, as well as the overhead hatches on the ceilings, except for the one I was in.

The elevator was at the upper level, and a couple of sailors stood at attention next to where the platform should be. The boat was also rocking a lot less, although I still felt a little nauseous, probably from not eating anything for the last however many hours it had been.

Velos began to croon as I awoke and I rubbed the scales at the front of his head, feeling his hot breath buffet over me. I stood up, walked to the doors, almost finding myself startled by Wiggea outside.

"Good morning Maam," he said. "The storm turned around rather quickly and is now heading back towards southern Cadigan mainland. Fortunately, the eye passed by our fleet by a good few dozen miles."

"Morning is it?" I rubbed my eyes. The storm had hit us late afternoon, which meant I must have been out for well through the night.

"To be honest, it's almost afternoon. But regardless, breakfast is being served in the officer's mess hall, even for the late risers. See it as a celebration meal for us all getting through the night. That was quite a storm, Maam."

"Yes, I guess we've been gifted by some good fortune. Maybe the Gods Themselves are looking over us after all."

Wiggea smiled. "I doubt that, Maam. I'd rather like to believe we make our own luck. Admiral Sandao has some of the most able-bodied sailors in the world."

"I'm sure he does," I said. "And I'd love to eat here, but surely we should be getting back to the Saye Explorer?" I no longer felt like flirting with my trainer and most dedicated dragonelite guard. It wasn't that he was any less endearing, just I had an absolutely splitting headache after the knock to my head and I wasn't really in the mood.

"I'm not sure that's a good idea, Maam. Sandao has ordered that we should rest here for the next twelve hours or so. Give Velos some time to recover and make sure that the storm doesn't change its mind and turn back towards us."

"How long until we arrive at Paradise Reef?"

"Oh, still a couple of days yet. Assuming we have favourable weather from here on, that is."

"Well, I better go up and have breakfast. Are you coming?"

"I've already eaten, Maam. But, of course, I'll accompany you."

"Very well," I said. And I made towards the elevator. Velos let out a groan once I left and the other Grey, surprisingly, joined in his lament.

"Don't worry," I said to Velos. "I'll also bring some back for you." Just because he fed primarily on secicao didn't mean he didn't like a bit of bacon every now and again. The Grey then let off a moan, and I sighed. "I guess that goes for both of you," I said. And I left hoping Velos had made a new friend.

The two sailors standing by the elevator saluted me as I approached. They wore navy blue suits and cravats. One of them turned the crank handle to lower the elevator. It let out a loud mechanical groan and then came down fast. The ship was still a little wonky and I massaged my stomach to alleviate the knot there. Soon the platform arrived and Wiggea and I stepped on it. Another sailor had manned it, who saluted and then wound another crank handle to lift us up into the open world.

THE REST of the journey was rather uneventful in comparison to what had just happened. After the last vestiges of the storm had cleared from the sky, we had uninterrupted sunshine for the rest of the way. The sailors on board still milled around their business, saluting as they passed, but not having too much time to talk otherwise. They were too busy repairing the boat from the storm damage.

This gave me plenty of time to talk with Wiggea. I'd learned a lot from him as my trainer, but otherwise he'd kept pretty much to himself so far, and I had never been able to get him to open up. But this time I decided I'd ask him directly about his personal life. And surprisingly, he turned out to be quite open about it.

"I had a wife once," he told me. We were sitting on a metal bench at the side of the ship, looking out at the dirty smoke coming out of the two funnels on the Saye Explorer. This was the morning after the storm had hit. The boat was still rocking a little, which made it much more comfortable to sit up on deck and stare out at the horizon and the endlessly churning sea, sparkles glistening on the waves like little fairies.

"In Tow?" I asked.

"No," he said. "I come from Cadigan. The south side in the city of Oahastin."

"I know of it," I said. Oahastin was one of the major colonies there, around a quarter of the size Slaro, the capital city of Tow, and growing fast. "But I've never been there."

"There's not much to shout home about, to be honest. The land is flat and the terrain around a complete desert, with some bony mountains rising above it. They built the city around a natural river coming from the mountains. But other than along the riverbanks and up in the hills, there's hardly any life around for miles."

I nodded. "So what happened to your wife? If you don't mind me asking, that is."

"King Cini…" Wiggea said. "The dragonheats."

The dragonheats? Wellies, Wiggea must have been much older than he looked. "The wars reached as far as Cadigan? I thought…"

Wiggea lowered his head towards the water. "She was a dragonseer. Or at least, her mother was. She never had a chance to meet a dragon queen and become one. King Cini's father decided to hunt her down as soon as he learned who she was."

I felt for him then. I had no idea how much he'd suffered all these years. And so, Faso wasn't the only one around who'd had a relationship with a departed dragonseer. But Wiggea was much, much more noble than Faso. Much more of a man in many ways, with a lot less tendency to complain.

"The mother?" I asked. "Who was she?"

"One of the Famous Four," Wiggea replied. "Indira."

My heart jumped in my chest as soon as he mentioned the Famous Four. These were the four dragonseers who had apparently been executed in the gas tower by King Cini II. But I later learned that three of those dragonseers survived, being later fed Exalmpora by Captain Colas until they became a different kind of creature. One that could turn into dragons and also tended to hear the voice of a mad goddess inside their heads. Alsie was one of them. Charth and Francoiso were the other two, transformed from woman to man due to Exalmpora. Just like Taka had been.

But Indira wasn't among those three. "She was the one who died?"

"Yes, the only one who actually was executed in Cini II's gas tower. But she had a daughter. Before Indira was captured by the king's forces, in Spezzio, she managed to sneak Hastina inside a merchant ship heading to Oahastin. I met the young lady later in the city, and we fell in love. Then when I heard about the Battle of Ginlast where Sukina's mother died, I vouched to protect her once the king came looking for her… But I failed…"

I put my hand on his shoulder. Wiggea was someone I never thought I'd see with a tear in his eye. "You can't blame yourself," I said.

Wiggea shook her head. "I took her to the mountains. I knew of a cave up there where no one would even think of looking. And we hid there while the king and his troops scoured the city. I'd left a note with the pastor of the church to forge her death records. That way, the king would turn around and never think to look for her again.

"Of course, he'd leave guards behind, and so instead of returning home we became nomads, roving the land on foot. This was a life Hastina, my wife by then, was okay with. So long as we both lived…

"The king never found her. But once we'd travelled far enough, the desert did. One night, I went out to hunt for food and she was taken by coyotes." He gazed out into the distance. "Even in times of war, it's nature that takes us in the end."

Wiggea was shaking by this point and I could kind of see why he didn't talk about this much. But then, at the same time, the lieutenant had given me the chance to learn about the fate of two more of this world's dragonseers. I'd always secretly wondered if there were any of us, other than myself and Taka, left.

"What did you do then?" I asked, as I sensed Wiggea had more he wanted to share.

"Oh, I did what any young fool would do. I whittled my life away in secicao and beer houses. Earning what I could on gambling and taking any menial job that would come my way. But then Sukina came looking for me and told me the truth about secicao and Fortress Gerhaun and what it was doing to the world. After what had happened to Hastina, this time I realized I couldn't let nature win."

I shook my head. "What secicao is doing. It's not nature. The blight is one of the most unnatural things on this earth." And Finesia also had some connection to it, although I hadn't quite figured out who exactly she was yet and what part she had to play in this all.

"Yes, I've learned that now," Wiggea said. "And I've grown inside since. I'm doing good now, and I'm fighting for what I feel Hastina would have fought for if she'd only had the chance. What her mother once fought for and what Dragonseer Sako fought for. What every single person on this planet should be fighting for. I found my purpose in life, and I know that you've also found yours."

I smiled. "I have. Thanks to Sukina."

Wiggea's gaze drifted off into the distance. "She did a lot for us," he said. "And I'm sure you will do too in the future, Maam."

"I hope so," I said. Although, I still had no clue how I'd live up to the legacy she'd left behind.

"Just give it time," Wiggea said. And he looked at me with an expression I could only call admiration. He held the gaze for a moment, and then he seemed to remember himself and broke it off again.

"Look, Maam, I think we're being signalled." He pointed over to where the Saye Explorer had now steered into view. A man, probably officer Candiorno, was on deck there waving an orange and white chequered flag, signalling all high-ranking officials to adjourn there immediately. At the same time, a barrage of cannon fire boomed from one side of the ship to get our attention, sending up an explosion of water from the sea.

"I guess we better be getting back to work then." I said.

Wiggea accompanied me below deck, where I sang to Velos to lead him over to the elevator and onto the carrier's elevator platform. I knew this would be the quickest way to get Velos outside, rather than finding someone to open the hatch on the ceiling.

We both mounted via the armour, Wiggea at the back and myself at the front, and then I pulled up on Velos' steering fin to get him to take off. At first, he roared out a protestation. I could feel the stiffness in his muscles from being knocked around the previous day and wellies, truth be told, I was pretty sore myself.

"We're doing this for Taka, remember," I said to him. "We can't rest forever." I let out a harmonious dragonsong to give Velos a little extra courage to carry on.

He roared again, but this roar was quieter with a flavour of appreciation. He then beat his wings and lifted us off into the air.

GENERAL SAKO, Admiral Sandao, Faso, Asinal Winda and many of the officers already had set up on the quarterdeck as we flew towards them. They were seated around a large oval metal conference table. The sun glinted off this, causing me to shield my eyes when bringing Velos in to land.

Faso stood up from his wooden director's chair as soon as we came in and walked over to examine the soft tanks on either side of the dragon armour. He didn't even give us time to dismount before he started screaming up at us, his face red.

"It's completely depleted of secicao. What in the dragonheats did you do to lose all the fuel?"

That caused rage to flare inside my chest. Trust Faso to be immediately moaning about the technology. No, 'how are you? I heard you had quite a rough ride.'

"The secicao helped us survive the storm," I replied, and I'm sure I ever so slightly had raised the volume of my voice. "If it weren't for Wiggea's quick thinking, Velos probably wouldn't have had the strength to land."

"The armour can't have possibly used it all up in such a short space of time. Even in a superstorm." Faso cast a scowl at Wiggea. "Did you leave the spigot open overnight?" Ratter stood on Faso's shoulder glaring at Wiggea, and I could swear that his eyes flared red light whenever Faso raised his voice.

"I'm sorry, Mr Gordoni," Wiggea said and tugged at his collar. "I didn't think…"

"So you should be, lieutenant. You've depleted valuable reserves. I only brought one more tankful with me, resources being limited. Now, that will have to last us the entire trip."

Now, I wasn't going to let Faso stand there and lay into Wiggea like that. Particularly after the lieutenant had helped saved mine and the dragon's life. "It's not as if you gave him clear instructions. You can't hold other people responsible for your own shortcomings."

Faso raised his head to the sky and scoffed. "I hadn't expected anyone to want to use the armour but myself. What the dragonheats did you need to use the secicao for, anyway? The carrier was only leagues away when you set off."

I put my hands on my hips. "Faso, have you ever tried to land a dragon on a carrier during a superstorm?"

"No, I've always left the piloting to you. So I can do useful things like navigate and operate the armour from the backseat. I have to do these things myself as other people tend to mess them up." He glanced over at Asinal Winda sitting at the table, as if she too was guilty of something.

"Well you're never going to get a chance in your lifetime to fly Velos," I said. "Now, you should apologise to Lieutenant Wiggea here. As usual, your behaviour is unnecessarily rude."

Wiggea put his hands up in front of him. "Dragonseer Wells, it's okay." He turned to Faso. "I'm sorry Mr Gordoni, I'll be more careful next time."

Faso didn't even offer him a glance. "See," he said to me instead. "I'm glad one of us knows his place here. Now, if you excuse me, I have to work on refuelling Velos." And he stormed off and disappeared into the quarterdeck cabin.

I turned to Wiggea. "Lieutenant, why didn't you stand up for yourself."

To which he let off a handsome smile. "I always think it's better to pick your battles. Some people just aren't worth fighting."

I shrugged. "I guess you're right," I said. "Though, somehow that man always gets under my skin."

"Only because you let him. And it looks like he feeds off that. He'd probably be much calmer if everyone just ignored him."

"And then he'd throw his weight around and start to get his own way."

"Not if people refused to cooperate. Passive resistance is quite a powerful thing."

General Sako had just stood up from his seat and walked over to us. While we were talking, Lieutenant Candiorno had laid out a map of Cadigan and East Cadigan Island on the table.

"Where's that buffoon think he's going?" General Sako said. And he indicated towards the quarterdeck door that was still swinging on its hinges.

"He said he wanted to go and refuel the armour."

"Well, that can bloody well wait," General Sako said. "Blunders and dragonheats, that man sometimes. Candiorno! Go down and tell Faso Gordoni that I've ordered him to return immediately."

Candiorno saluted. "With pleasure, General," he said, and he followed Faso into the quarterdeck cabin.

General Sako turned to me. "Dragonseer Wells, I've already heard about the trouble you had with the storm. It damaged the radio equipment on the Saye Explorer, unfortunately. So we've had to communicate by semaphore. But we managed to garner enough information to learn you had quite a rough landing."

I nodded. "The storm came around so fast."

Admiral Sandao had now walked over to join us. He nodded as he heard what I'd just said. "Superstorms are becoming an increasing problem for ships travelling to and from Cadigan. Fortress Gerhaun and its navy get their coal from there, and we've had a lot of, let's say, disrupted shipments."

"Disrupted?" I asked.

"Or, I have to admit, in the most part totally destroyed. Gerhaun thinks these superstorms are due to rise of secicao. She claims that because the blight is causing the land in the Northern Continent to become increasingly barren, there's less shelter to block gathering winds. But, anyway, you might have heard that the storm also gifted us with powerful after-currents that have sped us on our way towards Paradise Reef. We should be there must sooner than expected."

"Yes quite," General Sako glanced at his peer.

"I'm sorry, Miss Wells," Admiral Sandao said. "I wanted to get the information over to you sooner, but we got somewhat distracted." He looked down at the lower deck, where Faso walked out of a new door accompanied by Candiorno. The inventor's face was almost deep purple in colour. He must have rushed through the ship in quite a sulk, as he'd managed to walk half of it in virtually no time at all.

"I'm sure there was no rush," I said to Sandao. "So, when exactly will we arrive?"

"In five or so hours," Sandao said. "We just wanted to call a briefing and make sure everyone's well prepared."

"We don't even know where to find Colas," I pointed out.

"Yes," Sandao said. "Well, we have some extra data on that. We'll discuss this as soon as Faso gets here."

Faso walked right up to our conversation. He looked as if Candiorno hadn't been particularly respectful to him, his nostrils flared out, which admittedly caused me some satisfaction to see. Candiorno should have been the one angry having to rush after him so fast. But I guess the officer would have had to learn to deal with short-tempered people much earlier in his career.

"This better be important, General Sako," Faso said. "Because I've already seen you pin Captain Colas' location and I need to refuel the armour as quickly as possible."

"Can't you ask Winda to do it?" She was sitting at the table, talking to one of the officers sitting beside her, both of them drinking their cups of Saye Archipelago tea.

"I've not trained Winda in this task yet. And I don't want anyone to make any stupid mistakes like leaving the tap open. No, no, it's better if I handle this one myself."

"You'll have time to do that after the briefing, Gordoni," General Sako said. "But for now it's crucial that we make sure yours, Wiggea and Pontopa's operations will be aligned with those of our forces."

"What's there to discuss," Faso said. "We go in, get Taka back, and your forces sit tight here until we come back again."

General Sako walked up to Faso and put a finger to his chest. While many years ago Faso would have cowered at this, now he just looked down at it in disdain.

"Look, Gordoni boy. I don't like the way you've been talking to your superiors lately. If you're not careful, when we get back to Fortress Gerhaun, I'll have you court-martialled for insubordination. We'll see how you like sleeping on hard wooden planks and eating gruel for a week."

"I seem to remember, General..." Faso said, putting an extra sarcastic undertone on the final word, "that I'm a civilian and hence you don't have authority over me. And given I'll be travelling with Pontopa, surely it should be the dragonseer giving orders, if anyone."

I chuckled to myself. If Faso thought I'd go easier on him than the general, then he had another thing coming. "Then I order you to show some respect for all the military forces on this boat. And if you show anymore insolence, I'll make Gerhaun punish you herself."

"Hah," Faso said. "She wouldn't do anything to harm her most valuable scientist."

"Just try her," I said. "You saw what she did to the pirate captain, Faso. Gerhaun's not all smiles and roses, you know."

Faso swallowed hard and then looked over at the table. "Fine. If it's so important to you all, I'll listen to your stupid briefing. But after that, I'm straight back to refuelling."

"Very well," Admiral Sandao said. "Then let's get things underway, shall we?"

We walked over to the table and sat down. This time, Faso chose to sit on one side of me. Wiggea sat on the other. General Sako and Admiral Sandao sat at the heads of the table. A large iron pole on a magnet was placed on the map at the centre of the table, a miniature red flag waving in the breeze over it. All the maps I'd seen in the past of East Cadigan Island had lacked features, instead showing it as a massive sprawl of green land. But this map showed rivers and lakes and mountains and paths that had been cut through by tribesmen and explorers. There were even two ports on the island.

"What are those?" I asked Faso, putting my finger over one of the ports. I figured he knew as he'd already claimed himself an authority on the island.

"What?"

"The ports?"

"Oh, military outposts abandoned a long time ago by King Cini II. Apparently, he didn't see it as profitable to keep troops here. Although rumours say he had to leave because the jungle ended up swallowing his bases whole."

"It was dangerous?"

"More difficult to manage, I think. Although historical records from ages past say a great beast used to live there. Something magical, the tribesmen thought. Perhaps these superstitions rubbed off onto the soldiers a bit as well. There are records during the king's occupation of a creature with glowing red eyes that stalked the night. Complete baloney, I'm sure."

But after living with a dragon most of my life, I wasn't the kind to dismiss such things as baloney. "What kind of beast did they say it was?" I asked.

"Some kind of cat, perhaps. With the tail of a reptile. But when I visited a decade or so ago, I saw no sign of any strange, mythical creatures."

A harrumph came from the end of the table. General Sako now stood there leaning over the map. After the cough, he took a deep breath and his voice boomed out loud enough to silence everyone. "If you've please finished nattering… Thank you."

I glanced at Wiggea who smiled. He'd probably at to serve under General Sako for a period too, and I guessed he was pretty used to this kind of behaviour.

"Now, if you please," General Sako continued, "we recovered another of Colas' crow automatons during the storm. It had somehow navigated over to the Saye Explorer and carried a note in its claws. Lieutenant Candiorno, do you have it?"

Faso Gordoni perked up his ears at this. I guessed Ratter hadn't been the one to discover the note this time.

"Yes sir." Officer Candiorno stood up and saluted.

General Sako waited for a moment and the rest of the table remained silent, eyes affixed on Candiorno.

"Blunders and dragonheats, Candiorno. Can't you think for yourself sometimes? Read the note, dammit."

"Affirmative sir," and he took the note out of his pocket and began to study it, tracing a finger across the text.

"I mean out loud, Candiorno. Come on, you're not a moron."

"Yes sir," Candiorno said. Then he cleared his throat and read what the note said.

"To Admiral Sandao, General Sako, Dragonseer Wells, and all the loyal servants of Fortress Gerhaun.

"This storm was my little gift to you. To show you what happens when the powers of magic and science meet."

At that Faso let out a huge laugh from the base of his belly, causing me to almost jump out of my seat and cutting off Candiorno mid-speech.

"Have you got something to say Gordoni?" General Sako asked.

"Hah. Just that I'd never thought I'd hear such nonsense from Colas. No one on this earth can create a storm, much like they can't cause a volcano to erupt, or a meteorite to hit us from outer space."

General Sako twitched his moustache. "Of course. Now, in future, leave your opinions until after my officers have finished speaking. Please carry on, Candiorno."

The officer cleared his throat again. He seemed rather nervous. "Umm... Anyway, where were we. Yes, what happens when the powers of magic and science meet. Now, I hope that you'll keep your fleet and dragons away from my base. You may not believe it right now, but I have the technology and knowhow to fell them in one sweep. You don't know the jungle like I do. I've been building this operation for long before any of you have known me. Yes, that includes you General Sako. And this land has taken many men before you. Don't make the same mistake they did."

Candiorno paused a moment. He seemed to be putting quite an act into his reading, which he carried out in a remarkably convincing voice of an old man, even though he'd probably never met Captain Colas himself. Although I hadn't either, I'd just heard from some of the older officers here, and of course Faso, that the man was getting on a bit. Past ninety, some said, although no one in all honesty seemed to know his true age.

"Now as for you, Miss Wells. And your escorts, who expect will be Faso Gordoni, and someone else. You can meet me at Pinnatu Crater." Indeed, I then realized that the flag was placed at the crater of a volcano. "Come up to the rim. I'll be waiting for you at the peak. Oh, and you have quite a climb ahead of you, so make sure to pack plenty of water. And don't take your dragon up there, because I'll shoot him down if he comes anywhere nearby. It will remain safe at Figgaro Port, where you shall land."

Faso took a retractable pointer out of his pocket and used it to point at the easternmost outpost for the benefit of everyone involved.

Meanwhile, Candiorno paused again as everyone turned around to look at Velos. The dragon was fast asleep on the deck behind us now. I just hoped that if there was some kind of beast in the jungle that it wasn't dangerous to Velos as well.

"And I warn you," Candiorno continued. "If you disobey any of these instructions then I shall destroy you all, starting with your entire fleet. Be warned that I have much, much more up my sleeve than you've ever thought capable. Faso Gordoni, if you're hearing this, then know your technology pales in comparison."

And beside me Faso clenched his fist, which was resting on the table. Ratter emerged from his sleeve and started to let out a hiss, causing one of the officers to look over at the automaton in alarm. It seemed almost as if Faso had programmed Ratter to mirror his emotions. Goodness knows why.

"Gordoni," General Sako said. "You better keep that infernal automaton away from this mission. We have enough up our plates to not want to have to worry about an errant mechanical ferret."

"I'm sorry," Faso said. And he tapped Ratter on the back a few times and Ratter ran back up the inventor's sleeve.

General Sako nodded. "Carry on Candiorno."

"It doesn't say much else, sir. Just, 'Don't worry, Dragonseer Wells. I have a proposition for you that I'm sure you'll find quite attractive. And, of course, Taka is quite safe. Much, much safer, I assure than when that fool King Cini was looking after him.'"

I clenched my teeth. What could the man possibly want from me?

General Sako stood up and he looked absolutely furious again. "I've had enough of that buffoons empty threats. Yes, he might have more silver in his airship linings than any other man on this world, but he's bluffing. He hasn't got any power behind him at all."

"But he saw the storm coming," Faso said. "And none of your

equipment on board did. Which means he probably has quite capable technology and I can imagine some dangerous automatons. I honestly wish, by the way, I'd tested your meteorological technology myself. I'm sure we could have avoided the storm entirely had everything been set up correctly. But as for Captain Colas, we don't know yet what he's capable of. And so we're best doing as he says until we learn what he has in his arsenal."

"But you're putting the ball in his court that way," General Sako said.

I decided it was time to butt in myself. "General," I said. "This is what we discussed with Gerhaun, and with all due respect this is what we're going to do. But we're not going to hike all the way up to the crater. That's just a ridiculous demand. Velos can come up with us."

"But Pontopa," Faso said. "He might be able to shoot us down."

"You designed the armour. And I believe you said that it was the best technology around."

"Of course," Faso scratched at the back of his neck, his eyes affixed on the flag on the table. "Well, I guess that makes a lot of sense. Scout ahead before we decide what to do next. I can set Ratter to climb the mountain ahead of time and come back tell us what he finds."

"And what if Colas seizes him. We'll see more from the air than we possibly can on the ground."

"Not through tree cover," Faso said, a smug expression on his face.

"From what I can see from this map, the volcano rises above the tree cover."

"Well," General Sako said, cupping his fist in his hand. "I guess we're ready to get this mission underway."

"Good," Faso stood up. "Now, if you don't mind, I need to get back to some important stuff. Winda?"

Asinal Winda turned to him with wide astonished eyes. From the expression on her face, it looked as if they might have had some kind of argument. Which would partly explain Faso's mood. "Yes, Mr Gordoni."

"I'm going to need your help refuelling the armour. It's about time I taught you how it all works."

And he stormed back into the quarterdeck cabin, the tail on his suit swaying in the breeze behind him. This time no one stopped him from going. I turned to General Sako.

"I guess this meeting is adjourned?"

And he didn't even turn to look at me. Instead he had his narrow gaze affixed on the door of the quarterdeck cabin as if he wanted to kill the inventor who had just stepped through it.

"General…" I said.

"Yes, yes, of course. Meeting adjourned." General Sako twitched his moustache. "Blunders and dragonheats, that boy needs to learn some manners. Don't you think Dragonseer Wells?"

I smiled. "One day, we'll all learn to live with him," I said. "Now, if you excuse me, I probably better also be checking Velos is ready to go."

General Sako nodded, but didn't say anything else. I nodded back to him and then I walked over to Velos who was now fast asleep on one side of the quarterdeck.

And, just for the sake of it, I sang him a soft, reassuring song.

12

We arrived at Paradise Reef several hours later. Apparently, the currents had become even more favourable, whisking us off at speed to our required destination. I guessed from what I'd learned about Captain Colas so far, that he'd also claim these currents were his doing. In other words, that he'd want us to meet him as soon as possible.

The waters beneath us had changed in colour from deep blue to a pretty turquoise hue. When I looked over the deck railing, I could see all kinds of colourful fish swimming underneath. If I was a diver and had time, I'd gladly plunge under the surface and start exploring. But we had work to do.

Velos was wide awake on the quarterdeck now, resplendent in his brass coat. Once I used to find the dragon armour ugly, but now I secretly thought it suited him quite well. Partly this was due to the way he carried himself in it. Whenever he noticed people observing him, he'd keep his head up high, as if posing for photograph.

On either side of the armour, two soft tanks of secicao suffused the metallic surface in a faint green glow. Secicao – though it was destroying the planet, we all still relied on the stuff, including

Gerhaun's military who augmented using secicao oil so they could fight to stop the plant spreading across the world.

And I guessed that even though Faso claimed secicao power was his own invention, many of Colas' machines would also be using it. The crow automatons that had delivered the old man's messages certainly had. But still, I was confident that whatever he threw at us, my abilities as a dragonseer, Velos' sharp instinct, and Faso's technology would prevail overall.

Faso and Wiggea had already taken their positions at the back and middle seat. Which meant that it wasn't the best idea to scramble up Velos' tail as I'd have to then climb over both men to take my usual position. So, I climbed the ladder instead, and sat in place just behind Velos' steering fin. General Sako, Admiral Sandao, and several of the officers stood below watching us get ready. Once I'd mounted and harnessed myself in place, General Sako approached and stopped just beside the ladder. Meanwhile, Admiral Sandao hovered casually in the background. Given we were technically on a navy operation, seeing us off should have been the admiral's job. But the meek and well-mannered man didn't seem to mind General Sako taking control.

In his hands, the general held a clipboard, presumably with a checklist on it. He looked down at it and then cupped his hands to his mouth and hollered up to us. "Secicao flasks ready?" he shouted.

I checked that the hip flask was on my belt and I heard Wiggea and Faso jangle theirs behind me. "Check," Wiggea and I shouted back. But I don't think Faso said anything.

General Sako ticked an item off the list and then looked back up at us. "Weapons equipped?"

I reached down and felt the handles of the knives in my garters first. Then, I made sure that the pistol was secure on my hip and the Pattersoni rifle was in place on my back. "Check," I called back.

"Good," General Sako said and ticked another item off the list. "Equipment working?"

This call was for Faso and I saw him glance down at the spigot, but otherwise make no movements.

"Gordoni, answer me, boy," Sako shouted, his face red. "We do these checks for a reason."

Faso shook his head. "Of course the equipment's bloody working. What do you take me for?"

"Good, good." And General Sako swept his pen across the piece of paper once again.

"Are you all in fit condition and ready to fly?"

"Affirmative, sir," Wiggea and I said in unison. We looked at each other and smiled. Honestly, given I ranked the same as General Sako, I didn't have to call him sir. But I saw it all as part of a little game. As long as he wasn't going to do anything stupid, I was happy to at least pretend to cede power to Sukina's father sometimes. He was older than me after all.

General Sako looked up at Faso. "Gordoni, boy?" he bawled.

"What do you think?" Faso replied.

"Just answer the question, for wellies sake."

"Fine, I'm just as good as I was as when you saw me on the ground a moment ago."

The general nodded, placed another tick on his piece of paper, and then put his pen in his breast pocket.

"Very well," the general said. "Then permission to take off." He turned around and bellowed out at the top of his voice to the soldiers and sailors that stood behind him. "Clear the decks!"

Of course, this was pointless as Velos already had ample space surrounding him to launch. No one was close enough to get crushed by a rogue wing or stray claw. But General Sako was just one of those men who enjoyed his job too much. I understood this, mind. He'd lost his wife and only daughter and now had nothing left but his job. So, I personally tolerated his pompous behaviour.

I saluted, then pulled back on Velos' steering fin and launched him into the air. Just as his feet had barely left the ground, he gnashed his teeth and let out an ear-splitting roar yet playful roar. I guess he was also in the mood for a little stage play.

I clasped my hands over my ears. "Dragonheats, control yourself

Velos," I said. I still had a sore head from when I'd hit it during the storm.

And from beneath me, a rumble trilled through Velos' body, almost as if he was laughing.

"I'll remember that. Next time you have a sore head." And I sang out a staccato song as if it to admonish him. But I didn't make the notes too harsh so he'd realise I was joking around too.

Velos crooned in response. And we were soon away from the ship and sailing gently over a stunning expanse of turquoise blue.

IT TOOK us another hour before we hit the jungle proper. We sighted silver sandy beaches in the distance overshadowed by swaying palm trees, a kind of tropical paradise that I wondered why no one came here on holiday. I was sweating profusely by this point due to the heat from the sun and the humidity. It was much, much hotter here than it was in the Southlands and back in Tow. In those places, it seemed the world was getting colder – an environmental effect due to the spread of secicao and increased cloud cover. But here, you really wouldn't have noticed.

The air smelled of something different as well, of dust or burnt soil. Perhaps I could smell the ash from volcanic eruptions ages past. I'd honestly never been to a place like this before.

It wasn't long after that we caught sight of the Pinnatu volcano. A ring of cumulus clouds was haloed around it, making quite an impressive site. The mountain was a few thousand metres in height, and so wasn't high enough to be snow-capped. But still it created quite a picture, the towering beast of this land displaying its majesty over the pitiful, yet still beautiful, jungle below.

"That's our destination, I guess?" I called back to Wiggea and Faso.

"I don't see any other volcanoes around here," Faso said. "And before you ask, yes, it's dormant. The whole continent of Cadigan hasn't seen an active volcano in the last two-million years."

I sneered at Faso. I'd never liked smart-arses. But admittedly, I hadn't actually known that there wasn't any active volcanic activity in this part of the world. There wasn't much in the Southlands either, come to think of it.

But then, it wasn't as if we'd studied any of this in school. Everything was all about Tow and the Sovereign States to the east of Tow that the king claimed jurisdiction over.

We had just passed over a pristine silver beach. The volcano seemed to increase in height as we got ever closer to it. I could faintly see a hut at the top and I wondered if that was where Colas was holding Taka. It stood there alone, and I couldn't imagine there was much in terms of defences there at all. Perhaps we should send Ratter back to advise Sako and Sandao to deploy their marines and commandos after all.

"No," I thought. "*This old man probably has a few tricks up his sleeve.*"

And I would have thought after that terrible storm, we would have seen the last of bad weather in this area for a while. But that cloud that we saw around the mountain first turned grey, and then sped towards us. The next thing we knew, we were entangled in a cloying fog, with an increasing humidity that made me actually want it to rain.

"I guess this is Colas' doing too," I said with a little mirth in my voice.

"If he can truly control the weather, Maam," Lieutenant Wiggea said from behind me. "Then perhaps." His voice was so dry that I wasn't sure if he was being serious or going along with my little joke. He kind of reminded me of Charth in a way, although a little more optimistic and less of a rogue.

Speaking of Charth. I'd completely forgotten about him and hoped that he was back in The Southlands keeping an eye on Alsie. That was when, much to my chagrin, I heard him speak all of a sudden in the collective unconscious.

"*Why, hello there,*" he said. There was now a certain playfulness in his tone which didn't seem characteristic of the Charth I'd met a couple of years ago at all.

"*Charth? I thought you said you'd stay at home. You promised...*"

"I told you I didn't make promises anymore..."

"What is this, child's play?"

"You asked me to follow Alsie, didn't you? Find out what she's up to. You know, if you'd ventured a couple of hundred kilometres northeast of here, you would have run into her yourself."

"What?" I said. "What the dragonheats does she want from us?"

"I didn't dare get close enough to ask her. I kept so far away that they probably only thought me a seagull. But I thought you might want to know."

I sighed. "Charth, you know what Colas said. If there's any more than three in our party he'd shoot us down. You shouldn't be here." But I didn't tell Charth that we were also going directly against the old man's instructions by not parking Velos in the port.

"That's why I'm not going to accompany you. I'm going to make my way in alone. I have my own objectives, and getting Taka out, I'm sorry to say is secondary."

"What are you up to Charth?"

"I only came to relay the information about Alsie. Be careful, Dragonseer Wells, she has a play in this and I'm not sure quite what it is."

"At least I know she's not planning to invade Fortress Gerhaun."

"That was a given. Well, take care of yourself, and maybe I'll see you inside."

"Inside what?" I asked.

But Charth didn't respond, keeping his usual habit of being entirely mysterious. I caught sight of his black dragon form briefly passing through the fog. I hoped at least I could work out where he was heading. But he shortly disconnected from the collective unconscious and then the cloud cover was too thick to see him anymore. Even the canopy below us was now completely concealed. Although still, there was no sign of rain.

We continued onwards, Faso holding a compass at the back seat so he could correct me if I ventured Velos off course. We were still above the jungle and, as far as I was aware, as the land beneath us hadn't started climbing yet. I decided to push as close as possible to the canopy, though, so at least I could see something. And I used our distance from the massive umbrella shaped rubbery leaves below us to help keep us on course.

After a while, I noticed something strange coming from the jungle layer. There was a dot of red light that seemed to be following us, resting just next to my left foot. I tried to see through the canopy to make out where it was coming from and I caught a glimpse, just for a moment, something unnatural there made of metal. Then, the leaves rustled, and whatever it was scuttled off.

I glanced over my shoulder. "Did you see that, Wiggea?" I asked.

"I'm sorry, Maam?"

"Something below. I think we're being tracked. Keep an eye out."

"Affirmative." He leaned forwards, took the rifle off his back, and begun to scan the ground through the sights.

Behind him, Faso was also watching the ground. Ratter rested on his lap, crouched down as if ready to pounce.

"Pontopa," Faso called. "Get lower. Ratter wants to investigate something."

"You saw it too?" I shouted.

"Not sure," Faso said. "Get lower..."

I nodded then pushed up on Velos' steering fin to lower him towards the ground. I had to be careful. Visibility wasn't great here and so we could be closer to the canopy than we thought. As we descended, I felt something tugging on the hairs on my arms. Either static in the clouds from an incoming storm or something supernatural that we didn't quite understand. I was ready for both.

I glanced over my shoulder again just as Ratter leapt off Faso's lap and onto a passing branch. The mechanical ferret scurried along with us for a while at a surprising pace, before disappearing beneath the broad-leafed canopy.

Suddenly, there came a cackle from the air, causing me to jump in my seat. If it wasn't for the harness there, I might have leapt right off Velos. From nowhere, out boomed a robotic, monotone voice. Not one of a human, but one you might hear from a modified voice box.

"So, Pontopa Wells, the last dragonseer. You finally came. And you brought your dragon with you too. With ample weaponry, I see."

I looked around to try and identify the source of the voice. But I still, could only make out the grey murk and the leaves below.

"What do you want, Colas?" I shouted out as loud as I could.

"Now, I can see there's three of you," he continued as if he hadn't heard me. "And no sign of any forces on the ground. No airships to accompany you. Oh my, Dragonseer, I wasn't expecting you to be so obedient. But why, I ask you, didn't you go to the port like I expected you too? I had a loyal escort waiting for you there and he was so eager to meet you. Ah well, I guess, you still have some lessons you need to learn."

That red light flashed in my eyes. I saw it run across my chest then, and then pass over Wiggea's shoulder towards Faso's lap.

I turned to Wiggea. "Any sign of what's down there?"

"Nothing, Maam. Whatever it is, it's good at staying concealed."

"It isn't hard in this weather," I said. And I gritted my teeth and pushed Velos even closer to the canopy. Any chance we had to see what was going on, I wanted to take advantage of. We brushed against a few branches and something scratched against my bare calf. So I decided I'd probably got a bit too close and pulled Velos up a little.

A boom of thunder came from the sky. Then, another crackling static sound came from no determinate direction. And that weirdly freakish robotic voice once again filled the air. "Mr Gordoni, I found your mechanical ferret. I remember you developing it when I met you all those years ago. And how rude you were to me back then, when I was just simply teaching your girlfriend how to meditate. Well, I'm prepared to let bygones be bygones. Oh, and I've disabled your automaton. Can't have that thing sniffing around my operations."

I looked back at Faso to see an expression of scorn so heavy that he looked like he wanted to kill the man. Really, I wasn't surprised.

"But, now that armour I can see on your dragon," the voice continued. "It's quite remarkable, I must say. I see you learned a lot while working for the king, Mr Gordoni. I have to admit, when I saw you in the magazines, I often thought to myself, this man will never make a truly great scientist. You simply didn't seem to have the patience.

"Now, I'm afraid, I can't let anything like that dragon with its armour near my base, for obvious reasons. Besides, my good friends, I think a hike will do you good. Maybe you'll even meet some good friendly tribesmen on the way up."

"Dragonheats, what's that man planning," I said under my breath. Beneath us, came a rustling from the canopy and I saw that red light once more. But this time, it didn't flash, but instead pinpointed one of Velos' Gatling cannons, tracking it as he moved. The dot didn't seem to waver an inch, which I found ever so slightly disconcerting.

Next thing I knew, I was looking into some blue ball of light growing in a clearing beneath the tree line. It was attached to something brass, an automaton, but the light cast such a glow that I couldn't make out exactly what was creating it. It looked like one of those glass balls you found in science classrooms to demonstrate the principle of static electricity. Although this thing seemed to have nothing but air walling its outer perimeter.

"What the wellies is that?" I shouted.

"Dragonheats," Faso called. "It's impossible."

"What?"

"Electromagnetic pulse technology. No, I've seen prototypes, but it can't work like this. The laws of physics cannot allow it."

"Worry about that later," I said.

I swerved Velos hard to the right, hoping that Wiggea and Faso had kept their harnesses fastened. Velos responded to my hard push on his steering fin by entering into a barrel roll. Then I pulled up, to enter him into a loop the loop. If there's one thing that I'd learned fighting automatons is that you could confuse them through unpredictable aerobatics. But not this time. Just as Velos began to reach the apex of his climb, I noticed the red pinpoint spot focused on exactly the same spot of his Gatling gun, not having budged one bit.

"Blunders and dragonheats," I said under my breath. Then, instead of admonishing myself for picking up General Sako's vernacular, I pushed down on Velos' steering fin to break him out of the loop the loop manoeuvre and banked him sharply to the left.

But still, the red light remained fixed on its point.

"It's using laser light to target us," Faso said. "Dragonheats, how can the energy ball remain aerial. It's moving so slowly."

"There's no time to think about that now," I said. "Can you do anything?"

"I don't even know what it is!"

The orb was edging even closer now. It pulled at the hairs of my skin. From the sky, a few drops of water splashed on my arms. I pushed down on Velos, sending him into a stall to try and shake off this brilliant ball of energy, and the lightning that danced within it. But no matter how I hard I tried, the thing just crept closer and closer.

Sparks lashed across Velos' armour. One jumped off it and shocked me on the thigh, causing me to recoil. Velos let out a loud roar into the sky, and out of his mouth burst a torrent of green fire. This licked out at the jungle canopy, and a few trees burst into flame.

"My my," the voice came again. "I never predicted that side effect. Lucky it's about to rain, otherwise we might have a jungle fire."

And in reply, another boom of thunder called out from the sky.

I looked again at the sphere that now looked like a huge ball of bolt lightning, larger than a house. Yet it kept pushing forward, rather than just dissipating into nothingness, as lightning should.

The static from it was pulling my hair towards it now, and it hurt so much I thought the hair would tear out of my scalp. I cried out in pain, and heard Faso shouting too, although Wiggea remained stoically silent, so much I wondered if he'd been knocked out.

But I didn't turn around to check. I simply kept my eyes set on the massive globe of light as it passed over us. It caused me to shake and shudder in my seat. I couldn't move a muscle or say anything. I could only hear thunder and Colas' final words.

"I hope you have a safe landing," he said. "Enjoy the climb but take some time to recover first and enjoy the scenery. There's absolutely no rush."

And Velos roared out again, letting out another torrent of flame, before his body went limp. But his wings remained outstretched, fortunately, and so we entered into a glide.

We first hit the canopy, and bounced off it, the branches springboarding us back into the air. We dived again, and this time crashed through the canopy. Thorns and branches tore at my skin as we fell, but I was still feeling numb from the electric shock that it didn't hurt much at all. And we continued to hurtle downwards, as I kept my teeth bared and watched the ground accelerate towards us, helpless.

We hit the earth with a thud sending up a plume of volcanic ash. I jerked forward in my seat, so hard that the harness got torn out of the socket, causing a lancing pain in my shoulder. Then, I hit my head on Velos' steering fin and blacked out.

PART V

FASO

"A scientist's skill isn't measured in gizmos and gadgets, but in how much his discoveries contribute to the advancement of science."

— FASO GORDONI

13

I woke up, not in a river or on the jungle floor, as I would have expected, but in an unfamiliar bed. It felt kind of hard – even harder than the beds in fortress Gerhaun. The first thing I noticed was sunlight streaming through a low, narrow window. My vision was blurry for a while, and I could only make out I was in some kind of hut with some kind of smoke coming from somewhere, with a scent not too much unlike coriander.

As my vision got better, I had a chance to look around the room. There was a set of rickety shelves across one wall, containing an assortment of dried meats, fish, and mushrooms in jars. The lower shelves contained tall bottles full of various concoctions I didn't recognise. I took a sniff of a few of them to confirm that they contained alcohol. Some smelled like they would melt metal and others, I have to admit, not so bad.

On the other side of the room stretched a long dugout canoe with space enough for three men. It was made of a kind of rough tropical wood, and it had with elaborate carvings of creatures carved into it, including one of a panther-like beast with a long dragon flying out of its mouth. Not much like Velos, but instead the kind of dragon you see in books about mythologies from faraway places, where the dragon has no legs, the body of a snake, and flies through the air without wings, as if powered by magic.

I rubbed my head. That was twice I'd hit it in the last twenty-four hours and who knows how many brain cells I must have killed. But, strangely, I didn't feel too much of a headache this time. Either I'd been asleep for a very long time, or whoever had put me here had given me medicine to alleviate the pain. Just next to the bed, I noticed that the smokiness was emanating from a stone burner, a latticework brazier with coals mixed with blackened branches of some kind of plant burning inside.

I decided to step outside and find out whether I was a friend or prisoner here. I'd lost my clothes, and my daggers, pistol, rifle and secicao flask were also missing. Instead I wore wooden soled shoes and what could only be described as a poncho, made from a rough hemp-like fibre. The robe had the same strange creature as I'd seen on the canoe, woven onto its front – the panther with the dragon flying out of its mouth. This time, the panther was black and the dragon, was a pale blue colour.

I turned towards the door to see that same beast looking at me again on a tapestry hanging over the entranceway in place of a door. This time, it was depicted in a different art style, but still quite recognisable. Whatever this creature was, it clearly had some standing in the natives' mythology. I walked over to the tapestry, pushed it away, and stepped outside.

The air smelled musty, as if the sky had just rained out a heavy storm. The ground had a turgid muddiness to it. Brown rivulets ran in patterns along channels in the ground towards a lake. A waterfall plunged into this from up high and a rainbow rose overhead. The sun shone from even higher above. But despite it, the broad leaves of the canopy covered me in shade.

Above the waterfall, and to one side of it, towered the Pinnatu volcano, resplendent and majestic with another cover of white cloud haloed around it.

"Ah, Pontopa, you're awake." The voice came from behind me, and

I turned around to see Faso limping towards me, supporting himself on a thick tree branch as he walked.

"Faso," I said. "Where's Wiggea?"

He laughed. "Honestly, I thought the trained soldier would be up before you. He's sleeping in his cabin," Faso motioned with his makeshift cane, "over there."

I nodded. "I should go check on him. What about Velos, have you seen any sign of him?" How could I have thought about Wiggea before Velos? My handsome and most trusted dragonelite guard before my oldest friend? Part of me wanted to thump myself.

"Not yet," Faso said. "Although I'm sure he can't have gone far. He'll be hard to miss when we go searching for him. Ratter, on the other hand, I have no idea what happened to him."

A couple of years ago, I would have admonished him for putting technology over the life of a dragon, but I knew how Ratter was like a pet to Faso. Plus, in all honesty, I just didn't have the energy for getting snarky with the inventor.

"Dragonseer Wells…" I turned around to see Wiggea leaning against the doorway of his hut. "Am I really the last one up? What happened to us." He began to stumble towards us, but he also walked with a little bit of a limp.

"Haven't a clue," Faso said. "Have any of you seen our captors yet?"

I listened out for some sign of life here, but all I could hear was the roar of the waterfall, the howling of monkeys, and the cawing of exotic birds. "Faso, Wiggea and I have only just awoken," I said. "I was kind of hoping that you'd enlighten us."

"Not a whisper from anyone yet," Faso said. "And I've been awake for hours."

I remembered then how I'd encountered Charth in the collective unconscious before. I considered mentioning this fact to Faso and Wiggea, but I thought it would probably be better to keep it quiet. Yet if I could reach out to him, maybe he could let us know what was going on and tell me where Velos had got to.

"*Charth,*" I prompted in the collective unconscious. Nothing.

"Charth, are you there?" Still nothing. And I wanted to know where the wellies that dragonman had gone and what he was up to.

"Hoooooiiiiieeeehoooeee," a call interrupted us from behind. It was high pitched and came from a clearing in the jungle, just where it met the lake several hundred yards away. At first, I thought it had come from a monkey, but when I turned around, I saw a figure in a ceremonial mask, his skin dark, and his hands raised high above his head. The mask seemed to represent some kind of animal, but from this distance I couldn't see what.

"Hoooooiiiiieeehooooeeeeandalay." The call came again, and around me rustling sounds came out of the canopy. Heads emerged from up in the trees, in all directions. They belonged to more tribes-people, all of them wearing a similar looking mask.

"I guess we have met our captors," Faso said.

"I'm not sure we're even prisoners," I said. I mean, they hadn't locked us up in cells or anything. "Lieutenant, do we have any weapons?"

"Negative, Maam."

I shook my head. "Just don't do anything to provoke them. Not until we learn whether they're friend or foe."

I waited as I watched the men and women come down from their place in the branches. They had this remarkable way of climbing, not seeming to need to use branches for purchase, but instead hugging the tree with their arms and bare feet and scurrying down like super-fast sloths. Their leader, or at least the man who had called them down from their perches, waited on the ground, smoking some kind of bong with green smoke rising from it.

"Secicao," I thought. *"How the dragonheats did they get access to it here."*

The tribe had now surrounded us in a circle and started to close in on us. Wiggea, Faso and I backed up against each other. Our only chance of escape would be to fight head on. Meanwhile, the tribespeople shuffled forwards, chanting all the while, and the ring closed around us.

"Hoooieee, hoooieee, hoooieee," they screamed out in high pitched shrill voices. Then they paused and the birds from the canopy cawed a response, as if both the tribe and nature were in some kind of communion.

Both the men and women of the tribe had bare chests and feathered underpants, and none of them had an ounce of fat on them. Their wooden masks represented the same creature, I'd encountered depicted in the hut I'd woken up in. A panther with a blue dragon poking out of its mouth. But on each mask but one, the panther behind the dragon was painted in colourful patterns that seemed to swirl around as the tribespeople moved. The man I presumed to be the tribal chief had a colourless panther on his mask, painted in complete black.

When the tribespeople had reached about an arm's breadth from us, the ring stopped closing in. But the chief continued forwards and only stopped when he was right in front of me.

"Dragonseer," he said. His pronunciation was terrible, yet somehow, he seemed to know the word. "Welcome…"

"How the dragonheats does he know our language?" Faso said.

I shrugged not wanting to say anything yet. Instead I studied the movements of the tribal chief, trying to determine whether he wanted to attack us or aid us. I noticed Wiggea out of the corner of my eye doing the same. And we both had our arms slightly raised, ready to counter an attack if it came.

"Speak dragonseer," the chief said again. And he cupped his hand over his ear, cocked his head to the side, and waited.

Faso nudged me in the ribcage, and I turned around to scowl at him.

"Dragonseer, speak…" the man said again.

I sighed. "Ummm, hello," I said.

"Hoooieee," the chief called out again, raising his head to the sky like a wolf. The whole congregation around him echoed his call with an ear-splitting shrillness. Meanwhile the tribal chief backflipped backwards twice, then stepped forwards once again.

"Dragonseer speaks," he said. "It good."

I shrugged. "Thank you."

"Inventor," the chief pointed to Faso this time, who had astonishment plastered across his eyebrows. "Speak!"

"This is absolute nonsense," Faso said. "At least tell us what the dragonheats you want."

The tribal chief lowered his head and shook it, as if in shame. He walked up to Faso and prodded a finger in his chest. Faso scoffed and batted this away, and the leader backflipped away from him, almost kicking the inventor in the chin. The chief turned to the surrounding tribespeople. "Inventor no good," he said. "Hoooiiieeeeoooo."

And out echoed again, cries of, "Hoooiiieeeeoooo." Honestly, I almost wanted to join in the cries myself.

"Soldier better," he pointed to Lieutenant Wiggea. "Soldier speak!"

Wiggea nodded and stepped forward. He kept his posture straight despite his limp, and his head high. "On behalf of Gerhaun Forsi, and all the men and dragons who serve her in the Southlands, I want to extend my warm greetings."

If only I'd thought of that one, because it sent the chief backflipping and cartwheeling all around the circle in an elaborate dance. "Hoooieee, soldier best. Soldier best. Hoooieee." And whatever else he said was drowned out by the high-pitched chanting of the tribespeople.

After the commotion had finished, Faso stepped forwards. He just didn't look the same without having Ratter standing on his shoulders. It was as if not having the automaton around sapped out some of his confidence. But then part of this is because he was wearing a tribal robe instead of his usual sharply pressed pinstripe suit.

Faso seemed to want to speak to represent the three of us, even if he was the worst diplomat among us. "What the dragonheats do you want? Speak yourself and tell us what you're going to do with us."

He spoke loudly and slowly as if doing so would make him more comprehensible. But clearly none of the tribespeople understood, not even the chief. The man walked up to Faso, crouched slightly and squinted up at the inventor. "Give potion soldier, dragonseer. No potion inventor." He cartwheeled towards the edge of the ring, which opened out as he approached. The chief exited the circle, and the crowd closed back in as the sea would into a channel of sand. From the other side of the circle, several tribespeople approached with spears. They took hold of Faso by his shoulders and jostled him away.

"What are you doing?" Faso said. "Unhand me at once." But either they didn't want to listen, or they didn't understand, and probably the latter.

The ring parted to let Faso and his escorts out and then closed back in again. Then the chief came back in and examined me. He started to pad my muscles, then he ran his hands down my hips, though not in a sexual way at all. It was more as if he was testing me for something.

"Dragonseer strong," he said.

Then he moved over to Wiggea and did the same. Squeezing his biceps, pressing his hand over Wiggea's chest, running his finger along the squareness of Wiggea's jaw. "Soldier stronger," he said. It seemed that whoever had taught the chief Towese had also been kind enough to teach him comparatives.

The tribal chief came back to me, then he crouched down on one knee, almost as if proposing. He craned his neck to look up at me. I wished I could see his face, but I could only barely make out his eyes through that strange panther-dragon mask. They looked glazed as if the chief had been on drugs all his life and the irises were so dark they were almost black.

I remember Sukina had looked similar when she'd taken the Exalmpora in Cini's palace. I must have looked much the same way back then, although I don't recall examining myself in the mirror around that time.

"What do you want with us?" I asked. But it wasn't any use, because the man didn't seem to understand. Instead, he backflipped back again and cartwheeled around the whole circle. "Hoooieeee," he called. "Hooooooaaaaaaiiieeeeandallllay!"

He stopped just in front of one side of the ring, facing away from us. Then he bent over and waggled his bare-cheeked bottom at us, a feather poking out at the top. He cackled out a laugh, before standing up and motioning outwards with his arms.

The crowd parted on his instruction, revealing a flattened path leading through the grass. "Come. I show important things."

Then he turned to the men at back. "Punish inventor. Then bring back. We drink, yes."

Two bare chested women came forward from the crowd at the back, still wearing the same colourful masks. They had spears in their hands, with the tips pointed towards the sky. I decided it was better to let them take me where they wanted me to go, just in case things got violent.

The path wound around a few thick-stumped trees before opening out again into a clearing. There was a firepit set up in the centre of this, surrounded by a ring of what looked like salt in a thick pile, then a ring of stones on the inner side. A pot stood over the fire, although I couldn't yet see what was within.

It was at that point I remembered Velos. He had to be somewhere nearby and I needed to know he was safe. But I couldn't sense him right now which meant either he was sleeping, unconscious, or dead. So, just as the tribal chief turned towards me, I thought I'd try and find out if he knew anything. I stretched my arms out wide to indicate a dragon's wings, and I pushed out my front teeth. Then I let out a growl from the centre of my stomach, which probably didn't sound anything like Velos in my overtly feminine voice. I let off an obvious shrug, then I pointed around to ask where the dragon might be.

But I hadn't done a very good job, because the leader just mirrored my actions. He let out a roar much like my own, but in a much deeper and I have to admit, scarier voice. Then he clutched his hands to his belly and rolled about on the floor laughing, kicking at the ground like a madman.

The tribe had now assembled in a line, and they joined in with the tribal chief's laughter. Soon enough, more shrill cries came out from them in unison. "Hoooiiieeee, hoooiiieeee, hoooiiieee."

My heart sank for a moment and I felt a sudden wave of anxiety inside me. We really didn't have time for all this. I needed to get away from these madmen and find Velos, then we could fly into the sky, deal with Colas, and get Taka back.

But part of me wondered what the dragonheats was going on down here. Why exactly had Colas wanted us to meet these people? Maybe the old man was about to appear out of the blue and give us an anthropology lesson. I had no idea.

Then I caught a whiff of what was cooking in the pot. It had the faint eggy tang of secicao coupled with a familiar ferric smell. I recognised this immediately and found myself drawn towards the pot. It had Exalmpora within, and I wanted it.

Still, I had to show restraint. There seemed to be a ritual to whatever the tribespeople were doing, and I should try and respect that. Even though I longed for the taste of a dragon queen's blood on my tongue once more.

The leader pointed to a member of the crowd and then over to the fire pit. This was a woman, who jumped up, as if in glee, then she stepped forwards, and sat down cross legged on the ground. The chief then pointed to another woman, and also beckoned her forward towards the firepit. She displayed her appreciation with a similar gesture of glee and bounded over. The leader selected two men from the crowd in this fashion, who also pushed forwards enthusiastically. Then the ring opened, and Faso was jostled through as well.

"Unhand me," he said. "And tell me what you've done with Ratter. What is this nonsense? Don't tell me you're going to make me drink this stuff." He pointed at the green boiling liquid.

And, given he wasn't being so cooperative, his escorts had to push him down onto the floor, one of them keeping his hands secured over his shoulders while the other stood vigil with the spear in case Faso made any sudden movements.

"Come," the chief was standing beside the firepit now. The heat coming off it was almost searing and added unpleasantly to the stifling humidity. I approached cautiously and sat myself down crosslegged on the dusty ground. Wiggea did the same, although he kept an eye on the tribespeople standing near Faso as he approached.

The leader let off one last cry of, "Hooooooiiiieeeeee," before he sat down on the ground.

"What the dragonheats, is this stuff," Faso complained, "and why do you want me to drink it?"

And I looked gleefully into the solution I'd secretly craved for so long. Exalmpora, the drug that could control dragonseers. The same drug that had changed the physiology of Alsie, Charth and Francoiso and allowed them to talk to a dead empress.

"No, this can't be happening. I have to resist." I told myself. Two years ago, Sukina had helped me find clarity of mind despite the effects this drug had had on me. But she wasn't here to help me now.

And I didn't have the strength to resist it. I stared at the boiling solution, wide-eyed, and salivating. There seemed to be two streams dancing through the liquid as it boiled over the flames – one green and the other red.

Now, if I drank it, I could become strong again. I could fly into the sky as a dragonwoman, hunt down Alsie and tear out her throat. I could avenge Sukina and become the most powerful creature on the planet. Then, I could teach Taka how to be strong too. And I could control an army of my own minions and help the secicao blight spread across the earth, making this a better land. But this wasn't me thinking such thoughts. It was as if someone else existed in my head.

The tribal chief looked at me, standing stock still as he leaned against his spear and observed me for a moment. "Dragonseer. You know potion."

I nodded. Wiggea sat next to me, looking kind of anxious about something. Perhaps Sukina or Gerhaun had told him about Exalmpora. Maybe he already knew of its dangers and why I felt so drawn to it. But somehow, I doubted it.

"We all drink," the chief said. "Including you, inventor."

I turned to see Faso's blanched expression and the sheer look of disgust on his face. "Why the dragonheats would I want to drink that?" he asked and put his hand over his nose as soon as he caught a whiff of it.

"Hooooiiieee," the chief said, and he did another backflip, which resulted in much laughter from the crowd. "Tree blood. Earth blood. People blood. It good."

The tribal captain reached down to just next to the fire and took hold of a roughly textured wooden cup. He dipped this into the liquid and took out a good cupful, while avoiding touching the boiling solution with his hand. He raised the cup to his lips and took a sip. "It good," he said again. Then he pushed the cup out to Faso. "Inventor. Drink."

Faso looked down at the cup, then he glanced over at the spear that one of the tribespeople now held with the tip pointed at him. "It better not be poison," he said. And he cautiously took a sip. His expression lightened a bit, and he licked his lips. "Actually, it's not so bad..."

"Hooooiiiieee. More. Drink more."

Faso shrugged, then he tipped back his head and let the solution fall down his throat. He paused a while and looked down at the firepit. His eyes became glazed over. "I feel good. Stronger. But dizzy. What is this stuff?" And he let out a light giggle. "I haven't felt like this for years."

Exalmpora affecting non-dragonseers. Impossible. And while thinking this, I was also getting increasingly thirsty. Still, I decided to patiently wait my turn, sitting on my hands to stop myself snatching the cup off the tribal chief and taking down the whole amount of the liquid in one. He seemed to want us all to share, and I respected that.

The chief tipped the few remaining drops in the cup onto the floor. The liquid sizzled slightly as it hit the ground, and the man rubbed this into the soil with his wooden soles. He then took a cup from the liquid, handed it to Wiggea. "Soldier, drink."

Wiggea lifted an eyebrow and turned to look at me. "Dragonseer Wells," he said. "I'd rather have my head about you to protect you. I don't think this is appropriate."

I shook my head. "I don't think we have a choice, Lieutenant."

"But..."

"Just drink it Wiggea. We need to get through this."

His eyes widened in surprise. I'm sure he hadn't expected me to snap like that all of a sudden, and I felt a pang of guilt about my response. But I just as well wanted him to hurry up so my turn to have a drink would come around quicker. I was all for following etiquette and all that, as long as everyone else here did as well.

"Very well, Maam," he said. "And he tipped the cup to his lips and took the liquid down in one slow and steady stream." His eyes slowly gazed over and he entered a more relaxed slump.

"Hoooooiiiieeee," the leader said. "Soldier strong. Soldier drink." Then there came another backflip, and the chief cartwheeled around the ring once again. He returned to his place by the firepit.

"Now all drink. Dragonseer wait."

The other tribespeople who'd been selected to take part in the ritual, also moved towards the firepit and in turn dipped the wooden cup into the liquid and took down the solution in a huge gulp. The chief watched them, then he stepped forwards, this time with little ceremony and he took down a cup himself. After everyone but me had sampled the solution, he reached down, picked up another cup and lifted out the final dregs of the solution.

When he'd finished there was hardly any of it left. It was as if it had been measured out perfectly for the ceremony. And what was still in there evaporated out pretty quickly. I watched the cup with wide eyes as the funny-masked man approached with it.

"Dragonseer. Drink." He gave me the cup and I took it eagerly with both hands.

"Ready?" he said.

I nodded, and I could feel the sweat pooling in my hands. "Ready."

"You drink. You see…"

And without thinking about what he might have meant by that, I put the cup to my lips and poured it down my throat. All of a sudden, memories flooded back to me. Of the wedding with Francoiso. Throwing off my calico dress and revealing the blood red dress underneath. Then standing in Francoiso's bedchamber ready to consummate the marriage, passion thrumming through me. How much I'd wanted him then. How much I'd wanted his power and to feel the scales tear through me. How much I'd wanted to complete my transformation into a dragonwoman, an agent of Finesia.

And that had been taken away from me. Charth had knocked me

to the floor and Francoiso had pinned me down and poured the antidote down my throat to wash the effects of the Exalmpora away. All that power, just evaporating into nothingness. And all that remained was my sworn duty as a dragonseer and the chance to watch Sukina die with my own eyes.

I had no control over any of it. My destiny had been handed to me on a plate.

"You know what you want, Dragonseer Wells," a voice came in my head. It was the voice of an empress. The voice of Finesia.

"No, Pontopa. You must resist. Don't let the Exalmpora close off your mind." The second voice in my head was Sukina's. A remnant of the past resonating somewhere in the collective unconscious.

"Oh, but Exalmpora can give you everything you've ever wanted," the first voice said. *"You can become an immortal and gain the spirit of a creature you've always admired. You will never have to worry about being better than anyone else again..."*

I grinned as I thought through what this could mean.

"Hooooiiieeee," the tribal chief shouted. "Now, it's time to start the ritual. Hooooiiieeee."

I found myself joining in his call in elation. Surprisingly, I didn't find myself alarmed by the fact he could now suddenly speak my language a lot more fluently. In fact, at the time it seemed the most natural thing in the world.

He turned to the outer ring and beckoned one of the tribespeople forward, this time a man slightly broader the rest of the tribe. He carried with him a wooden stake, some kind of pipe cut in half down the cross section, and a rough clay bowl. The leader beckoned another man forward who brought with him large gourd containing what I knew to be Exalmpora and a ceramic bottle, of which I couldn't see the contents.

"Dragonseer, your blood will reveal the truth." The tribal chief said.

And I didn't even think to resist, nor did Wiggea, or Faso for that matter try to stop me. The larger man came forward with the wooden stake and pushed it into my upper arm. From it, blood started to flow, slightly blacker than my blood would be normally. It dripped down my elbow, where the man placed the wooden tube. Each drip he caught with utmost accuracy. The blood then proceeded to roll down the tube into the bowl that the man held in the other hand.

Meanwhile, the other tribespeople had poured Exalmpora and a green solution, which I presumed to be some kind of secicao oil, into the pot above the firepit. The liquid boiled in there pretty quickly and I felt myself drawn towards it once again. I leaned forward to look inside but the tribal chief put out his hand to stop me.

"Wait Dragonseer. We must share your blood."

"But I want the power."

"And you shall have it. More power than you've ever imagined." It was if the chief's voice wasn't his own, but that of another. The voice of an empress, of a goddess.

The larger man had now taken enough blood, it seemed, for the ritual. He took hold of a hemp cloth and wrapped it around my arm, squeezing it tight there to staunch the flow. He then stepped forward and handed the cup over to the chief with both hands. The chief accepted and poured the blood into the pot.

A plume of smoke arose from the solution, erupting like a volcano. I saw an image there, a woman roving a barren land with red soil. She turned to look at me, before the smoke dissipated.

"It's ready," the chief said.

The tribespeople who had been selected for the ritual then stood up and crept towards the boiling solution. This time, they took more cups from beside the firepit and handed them out so all eight of us had one, including myself. We all then waited patiently for the tribal chief to give the call, even though I wanted from the pit of my stomach what cooked inside the pot.

He had his hand held up high in the sky and he watched the firepit with intent as he waited for the last remaining drop of solution to evaporate from the pot. Then he lowered his hand as if signalling the start of the race and we all took the cup to our lips and I took the solution down in one gulp.

My mind felt clearer than it ever had before. I could hear and smell the world with such clarity. The bird songs and monkey howls from miles away. A rumbling from the volcano. Velos' soft snore, wherever in the jungle he was. And the fragrance of the leaves, the soil, the water. The air had a new freshness to it and the humidity no longer affected me.

Then, it was if everything in the world started to swirl around me. I saw nothing but patterns in the leaves, in the fire, in the clouds that passed over the canopy, and the way that the massive leaves rustled in the breeze. In those patterns, I saw a goddess roving a deserted world. And as I listened, I noticed that the world sang with a certain resonance. No people around me, only desertion. A landscape without water or sky. Without any life upon it other than myself.

And then I entered the dream, bringing me to this very present moment.

My attention drawn back to flames of the fire, the pot leaping off it and tumbling to the floor. Then the fire roaring into the sky like from a dragon's breath and the flames spewing out smoke once again. Behind them all, Empress Finesia watching me. Curling up her index finger and beckoning me forward. And I stand up wilfully and follow her within.

She points downwards, and I look into the flames. I study them with intensity until I see the spots before my eyes. And in those spots, shapes begin to form, warping and coalescing into substance. I can see myself now, naked with black oily scales lining my skin and wings protruding from my back. My hands are two massive claws and within them I grasp a claymore, staring out towards the horizon. There's another in the distance, a woman, also naked with raven hair. She tosses her head to the sky and thumps her hand down on the ground, sending out a plume of black dust around her.

Alsie Fioreletta launches into the sky in dragon form. Her skin as oily as the blackest of seas. She spears towards me, and soon lands on the ground in front of me, again sending up another dust explosion. I grit my teeth and raise the claymore into the air. The dust settles and she launches herself at me with the sword held up high, her lips a rictus of rage. Scales warp and fold in kaleidoscope patterns across her naked skin, never settling, never knowing which way to turn, undecided whether to become human or stay a dragon.

Her words enter my head. Words I've heard before. *"Not now, Dragonseer. One day you and I shall do battle and fate shall determine who wins."*

But she hasn't a chance. Because I am the most powerful being to have ever graced this planet. Finesia's favourite, her chosen one. And inside of me, the spirit of secicao lives.

I enter a crouch and lunge towards Alsie Fioreletta. She raises her claymore into the sky. Steel meets steel and her sword glances off my own, throwing her off balance. I swing the sword around again, this time in a low arc while hers slices through the air vertically like an axe chopping firewood. She jumps over my sword and I roll out of the way of hers just in the nick of time. I change to a defensive stance and watch as she puts the sword in her scabbard and then draws two knives from the sheathes at her belt.

"You cannot win this, Dragonseer," she says. "You've never had it in you."

"Ah, but I'm a dragonseer no longer. And it's you who've never been good enough. Too old for the job. Too little will to become great."

"I have much more than you've ever had and so much more."

"But fate is fate," I say. "And you know that I'm destined to claim Finesia's prize."

I raise my claymore and charge at her again. She pushes forward with her knives. I take the claymore through a vertical swing this time, aiming to cleave her head in two. But her knives are faster, and she blocks me with unbecoming strength.

She spins out of the way then and ducks underneath my sword which buries itself in the ground under its weight. A quick one two, she stabs me in the chest, and she buries her blades into me. Yet they cause no pain. I laugh out from the base of my stomach.

"You think you can hurt me. But I've prepared for this." And I kick Alsie Fioreletta in the knee. The bone cracks and she falls to the floor. I look down at the knives and pull them both out of my chest and toss them behind me. Then, I swing the claymore around in one fell swoop, spinning three-sixty degrees as I do. Alsie isn't fast enough to get out of the way – she's too weak now.

The blade slices through her neck and lops off her head, which is sent tumbling to the floor. I kick Alsie's body and it collapses to the ground. Then I walk over to the head and pick it up by the hair, examine her bloody lips.

I've prepared for this moment long in advance. And the voice of Finesia is in my head instructing me what to do. "Here is the seed where I shall plant my roots," I say. "I am immortality incarnate, and the world is my own." And I drop Alsie's head on the floor.

I push my feet into the dusty ground. The soil parts between my toes, which soon grow into roots, shredding the earth. I splay my arms apart and branches grow out of the fingers. And my shoulders tear apart as I scream out in ecstasy.

Yes, I am her, the banshee of legends, the seed of the tree immortal. My hair turns russet and takes on the texture of leaves as my roots dig further into the soil, sucking out the life of the earth. And I grow upwards and outwards, as my whole body elongates, and the scales on my skin warp into bark and knolls as old as time itself.

As my roots seep through the earth, strands of secicao plunge out of the ground, extending out as far as the eye can see. My leaves stretch further towards the sky and take on a dark green hue, before becoming black, with swirling colourful patterns inside like oil. And I grow, and I grow, until I have massive holes in my bark, out of which I birth the dragons. Hundreds and thousands of dragonmen and dragonwomen tearing up the sky, spreading to all corners of the world, bathing any life they find in liquid fire. In every continent and every sea, volcanoes spew liquid magma across the world.

Time passes, the seas dry, and the molten rock cools to acidic soil. Through this, the secicao blight spreads, and Finesia and myself as Finesia's right hand rule the earth. An army of dragonmen at our disposal, and all the secicao we'll ever need to feed on. I know now the spirit of Finesia, and it is her will to conquer the world.

"*Pontopa*," Sukina's voice says in my head. "*This isn't you, break it!*"

"No," I scream out loud. "I'm having so much fun."

"*Pontopa. Your duty. You're a dragonseer. You still have strength.*"

"I will not," I scream out. "This is my world now."

And then I hear something. The rushing of the waterfall. So strong, spraying water into a pool full of fish and ecology and life.

"No!" I scream again. But this time, I'm not refusing Sukina. I'm refusing the drug and the grasp it has on me. Not letting it touch me. I need to be strong.

It isn't beautiful. It's ugly.

The most destructive force on this world I'd ever encountered.

And that realisation brought me back to reality.

Because I knew I had to back away.

I stood up all of a sudden and turned away from the fire roaring in front of me. My eyes were blurry, and I could see nothing but hate and destruction and the need to wipe out every single creature on this planet. Yet, I could still hear the roaring of water in the distance. Purity, coming from somewhere. And it pulled me towards it.

I stumbled. Some of the secicao branches moved in to stop me, but I pushed them out of the way. There was a sharpness against my chest. A spear perhaps. Or the thorns of the secicao trying to pierce my spirit. Pierce my will.

"*Pontopa, you are stronger than this. Remember who you are Dragonseer.*" This now wasn't Sukina's voice but Gerhaun's.

"*No, Dragonseer. Turn around and claim what you want. Become immortal. This is Finesia's will.*"

I glanced back at the fire, and I saw the most beautiful shapes evolving there. My own beautiful body evolving into this magical wispy tree its leaves with a kind of dark opalescence that had all the colours of the rainbow swirling within it. The leaves dancing around the smoke in intricate patterns above the fire.

"*Pontopa,*" Sukina's voice came once again.

"*Auntie Pontopa,*" this time I heard Taka. How had he come into it? Of course, I'd sworn to protect him. That's why I was here in the first place.

I swallowed. "*I know,*" I said. And I batted the sharp object blocking my path, whatever it was, out of my way. Something tried to restrain me, but I had strength within. I bared my teeth, and then wrestled free of the thorns entangling me. And I crawled forward, almost beaten, and took a drink from the waterfall.

The pure liquid ran down my throat. I felt coldness against my hands. The chill of reality. I washed my face in the water, let my fears and desires wash away with it. Then, I braced myself, swallowed down whatever was stopping me, and I reached out and dived into the unknown.

The clarity, the hate, the lack of will left my mind and I found myself swimming through a different type of ecstasy. The feeling of being free, not so much in not having a destiny, but in choosing which destiny I undertook. In knowing that the path I was on was the right one. I saw blueness, and colourful fishes, and the water roared against my ears. And as I surfaced underneath the waterfall, I knew I was back in the real world.

I looked back towards the shore where a tribal mob awaited me, their spears pointed at me. Whatever they wanted, I had to face it.

I swam back to shore and lifted my hands, waiting for myself to be taken prisoner. The robe that I wore was now dripping wet. I looked at each of the tribespeople, trying to make out the expressions they held behind their tribal masks. But all I saw were the terrifying beasts, the panthers, dragons and lifeless glazed eyes behind them.

I put my hands on my hips and stood up straight to them. "I don't know what Colas is doing to you, and why he's doing it, but this has to stop. You need to be your own people. Don't let Colas or Finesia or any mythical beasts control your life. You're stronger than this. And if you take that drug," I pointed to where I could hear the fire roaring away, "It'll take everything away from you."

I hoped in all honesty that if they didn't understand the words, they'd at least understand the sentiment behind it. And I accompanied my speech with plenty of gestures, hoping that at least some of them would latch on to my meaning and translate it for the other tribesmen.

"Hooooooiiiieee," the cry came from behind the crowd, which

parted to let through the tribal chief. He had something in his hand, a gnarled root that had been lifted from the soil that looked disturbingly like Alsie's head. "You choose life." His eloquence that he'd been imbued with while we were on the trip had now left him.

He looked at the root in his hand, then gestured with his other for the crowd to part around him. They shuffled backwards, and the leader stepped forward and put his hand on my shoulder. Then he gave me the root. "Here," he said.

"What am I supposed to do with this?" I asked.

The tribal chief nodded and then pointed to the water. His hand extended out towards the waterfall. "Do."

I looked at him strangely, and then recognition dawned on me. I pulled back my hand and launched the root he'd given me over the water. I don't know what it was meant to signify in this ritual – perhaps Alsie's head, or my own greed for power. But I felt a sense of release wash over me as I watched it sail in a parabola and then disappear behind the waterfall.

"Feel better," the tribal chief said.

I nodded. Somehow, I did. And I also had the sense that I'd found a new ally, although I had no idea why. The chief no longer had the glazed look in his eyes that he'd worn previously. In fact, he looked a different man. Enlightened.

There came a growl from the distance. At first, I thought it to be distant thunder. But it wasn't long after that I recognised Velos' roar emanating from the jungle.

The tribal chief's eyes widened behind his mask and he turned to the source of the sound in alarm. "Hoooooiieeee. Hoooiieee." He pointed a finger into the trees. The tribespeople picked up their spears and they rushed towards Velos' location.

"No," I shouted, and I ran after them. They couldn't hurt Velos now. Not after we'd come so far.

14

The tribespeople were much faster on their feet than I. Although, to be honest, the majority of them hadn't just taken a powerful dose of a tribal narcotic. Someone had supplied them with the blood of a dragon queen and some high grade secicao oil and paid a lot of money to do it. And whatever the purpose of my own blood in the ritual was, I had no idea. Whatever Colas was doing on this island, I had a feeling it was a lot worse than I first suspected. Somehow, it seemed, he was also involved in Finesia's grand scheme.

Although the tribe had rushed ahead of me, still I ran as fast as my legs would carry me. I stumbled past Faso and Wiggea lying on the ground, not even bothering to check if they were okay. I could return to them later and I very much doubted right now that the tribe intended them any harm.

Velos, however, was another matter. The tribespeople were making all kind of shrill pitched war cry noises, batting their hands over their mouths, all the while whirling their spears above their heads as they ran. Every so often, I lost sight of them, but I could follow their sound and catch up again. Another of Velos' roars bellowed out through the forest, causing them to stop in their tracks for a moment. Then they looked at each other, pumped their spears up into the sky with a frightening ferocity, and continued to rush towards the source of the noise.

"He won't harm you," I tried shouting after them. But I couldn't raise my voice over the racket they were making. Although if Velos was threatened and Faso had accidently left the tap to his armour open when he crash-landed, then maybe the Gatling guns would annihilate them as soon as they got near.

I stopped just as the crowd had started to fan around Velos. I tried hard to push through their sweaty bodies, but they wouldn't let me. So, I clutched onto one sturdy looking man's arm and climbed up his shoulder, almost flattening him to the ground. I managed to pivot over him and landed just to see Velos gnash out at one of the tribesmen. The dragon ripped the spear out of his hand and tossed it high in the air behind him, causing the tribesman to raise a fist to the dragon in aggression as others came in with their spears.

"Velos, calm down," I shouted. Then I remembered my dragonsongs. I started singing one with soft harmonious notes to placate him.

At first, he let out a resistant growl. Dragonsongs were great, but Velos' self-preservation instinct would still prevail when in danger. "You'll be okay," I said. "These men are on our side."

Or at least I thought they were. I wasn't entirely sure. And as soon as Velos eased off a bit, they charged forwards with their spears. Velos roared again, and then he smothered the ground in front of him in orange flames. The tribespeople flanked out as they retreated, while another row waited for the flames to subside.

I had no choice. I'd kicked off my shoes automatically before I'd gone for a swim. And now the ground would be like burning coals. But still, I had to go in and stop anyone getting hurt. I rushed forward and grimaced when I stood on the smouldering patch of earth that Velos had just charred. Then I splayed out my arms in defiance. "No," I shouted at the tribesmen, gritting my teeth against the pain lancing through the soles of my feet.

But the front row continued to push forwards with their spears.

"No," I screamed out even louder. And something rose up within me. My face began tear apart for a moment, and I felt the sensation of thousands of scales trying to pierce through my skin.

"*That's it, Dragonseer,*" Finesia's voice once again came in my head. "*Claim your gift.*"

"Dragonheats," I exclaimed. It seemed the effects of the Exalmpora still resided within me from when I'd taken it all those years ago in the palace. It was in my system and that one single dose had been enough to bring everything back once again.

And the worse thing was that it felt so good. It had also helped me gain control of the tribespeople.

"No," I screamed again, and the command came out of my lungs as if they were bellows. "You shall not hurt my dragon."

"*See how good it feels,*" Finesia said in my head. "*You could have a lot more of this.*"

The crowd looked at each other again, their spears wavering in the air as if none of them knew what to do.

"Hoooiiiieeee," the call came from behind the crowd, the tribal chief again. "Hooooiiiieeee."

The tribespeople stopped stock still and then turned around and bowed to their leader with renewed reverence. They parted for him, and the chief pushed his way through. He looked up at Velos, then bowed. Then he pointed upwards towards a top of a rock. "Beast here. Our god."

I looked up to see what he might be pointing at. A catlike creature stood at the top of a large boulder, looking up at the sun emerging from the clouds. Once the sun revealed itself, the light glinted off the creature, and then I recognised it for what it was – an automaton. It bounded down the rock face and vanished into the clearing. A moment later, it was upon us. Its metal skin was mainly the colour of obsidian. But it had a blue tint to it, and green glowing veins of light flowed down it. Clearly this thing was also powered by secicao. It had a long spire coming out of its mouth, and it took me a while to realise what it was.

Soon enough, the panther automaton turned on a crowd and

something started to glow from between its sharp teeth. That same ball of brilliant energy emerged that we'd seen when we'd flown Velos over the jungle towards the volcano.

I saw then what the masks and the tapestries and wood carvings had all depicted. The age-old beast of the jungle. This terrifying panther automaton, with the dragon coming from its mouth, or in other words the glowing spire.

As soon as the tribespeople saw this terrible ball of energy begin to grow, they started murmuring to each other and backed away from the horrible beast. Then, there came a cackling from the sky and, it seemed, the god of the tribespeople spoke.

"Dragonseer Wells, I see you have met my loyal subject." The voice emanated from the sky and the ground and everywhere around me. I jerked my head around to try and identify the source, but still couldn't work it out.

Captain Colas' voice was still tinny and robotic. And soon after he spoke, the electricity in the panther's mouth died down, leaving only a open mouth containing glowing razor sharp teeth.

I turned to the panther automaton. "Colas, if you can hear me. Tell me what you want. What's the meaning of all this?"

"Oh, I just merely wanted you to meet your escorts up the mountain. Not all of them mind. And you have only about a day before you can witness the spectacle I've been preparing for a lifetime. You better get moving fast before your time runs out. Because if you delay much longer, you'll get swallowed up by it... And I'm sure you don't want that."

I looked up towards the top of the mountain, which had again begun to cloud over with a curtain of grey. The air was getting humid and tasted of rain. We'd have another downpour soon, I was sure. "We can take Velos and get up there within half an hour."

"Don't even think about it," Colas said, raising his voice slightly. "The dragon stays down here on the ground." The panther automaton turned its head sharply towards Velos and a ball of blue began to glow at the front of its mouth again. The congregation behind me started to murmur in terror.

"I really don't want to hurt him again, Dragonseer Wells," Colas said.

I clenched my fists. I got the sense that Colas was planning something big. But if we'd die if we stayed down here, did that mean Velos would also perish if we left him behind? Maybe that was why Colas had wanted us to fly him into the port. Perhaps it would have been safer for him there.

But there was no point making up theories when I didn't have much information to work with. "What are you planning?" I asked again.

"Oh, that would be telling. And I don't know about you, but I've always liked games with an element of surprise in them. So why don't you be a good girl and come up to see what I have in store?"

The ball of light within the panther's mouth once again died down. Velos turned his head towards the automaton and growled at it. And I immediately sang a calming dragonsong to make sure he didn't try attacking the thing.

"So, how do we get up there?" I said. "We'll come up and stop your stupid games. And then you'll give us Taka back."

"Ah well, first you'll need Mr Gordoni and your soldier friend. Where exactly are they now?"

I shook my head. "They haven't woken up yet."

"My, my. It must have been quite the party." Colas' voice changed in cadence from monotone to a more a high-pitched chipmunk kind of sound. He also spoke a different language, which the tribesmen latched on to, raising their heads like meerkats to listen to the fast-flowing words. Shortly after, two of the tribespeople rushed back off into the jungle.

"Don't worry," Colas said, resuming his monotone robotic tone. "Your colleagues will be here soon."

I folded my arms over my stomach and waited, tapping my foot. In a way, I wanted to ask questions, but I had a feeling that Colas wouldn't provide any conclusive answers and my uncertainty would provide him with a form of twisted entertainment. Sure enough, a minute or so later, Faso and Wiggea were jostled out of the jungle into the clearing, looking like they'd each just drunk a bottle of whiskey and then only had a few hours' sleep.

"What's the meaning of this," Faso said. His gaze fell on the panther automaton. "That thing..."

"It's what shot us out of the sky," I said. "And it's purpose seems to be to keep Velos here while we trek up the mountain."

Faso looked up at the looming clouds. "You've got to be kidding. There's no way I'm going up that thing."

"Oh, but you are," the voice came from Captain Colas even louder than before. "If you want to see your son again and show him what a responsible father you are, you will climb to the top and you'll do it without grumbling. Because, if you annoy me too much, I'll order one of my escorts to push you off a crag. And then poor Taka will become an orphan. You wouldn't want that now, would you?"

"Colas you bastard," Faso said. "Why don't you show yourself instead of hiding behind a concealed speaker system."

"Because I'm at the top of the mountain and you're not. Now get cracking pronto. Or do I need to tell my automaton to grind you into shape?"

The panther sat on the floor and let out an incredibly loud and unsettling purr.

"And what about Ratter?" Faso said. "What have you done to him."

"You won't be needing that archaic piece of technology. Why don't you try to survive without your machines for a change, Mr Gordoni? It seems you've become far too reliant on them."

Colas once again switched to his second language so he could bark out his orders. In response, a few of them had split off from the party, including the tribal chief. Others had rushed off back towards the village camp, perhaps to get supplies. By the look of things, Faso and Wiggea would need plenty of water to help them on their way. To be honest, I was surprised I wasn't nursing a hangover myself.

Soon enough, the tribespeople returned, with huge gourds carrying what I presumed to be water. The panther lay down as if basking in the sunshine, much as you'd expect a real cat to behave. I wondered for a moment if the sun powered the panther in some way. Maybe it gave it energy through warming up the secicao or something. The heat the sun emitted was much stronger here than it was in Tow or the Southlands, so it would make a lot of sense to harness it as a power source. Though how one would go about that, I had no idea. I'd leave that one up to Faso to solve, if perchance I happened to mention it to him later.

Another six tribespeople carried backpacks on their backs with supple wooden frames built over a white cloth and tied up with hemp rope. There were two women and four men, and all of them wore a similar robe to what we wore. The tribal chief had also recently put one on. I guessed that it would be a lot colder at the top of the mountain than it was here. Oddly, he also wore one of our rifles slung over his back, and I wondered if he knew how to use the thing.

The chief orchestrated everything, screaming orders and dancing around with an enigmatic display of energy. He cartwheeled from tribe member to tribe member, instructing them to place items on the floor, so others could wrap them in cloth to be placed in the rucksacks. Lots of fruit and dried meat went inside.

It wasn't long before everything was packed up and six guides stood with backpacks on them, ready to carry things up the mountain. The tribal chief then approached me and pointed up towards the mountain's peak.

The sky had become even more laden with grey by this point and gravid with humidity. A roll of thunder cracked out of thin air, to be soon accompanied by Colas' booming yet monotonous voice.

"I see you're all ready to go," he said. "Now, the faster you get here, the less chance anyone will get hurt."

I put my hands on my hips. "What's going to happen to Velos? At least give us some information."

"Oh dear, oh dear. Time is getting thinner as we speak. It's time you learned some obedience, Dragonseer." Colas then cut into the other high-pitched language, giving orders to the chief who had his ear turned to the sky and his hand cupped over it. Without saying another word to us, Colas' voice cut off, then the chief stepped forward and beckoned us onwards.

It was time to step off into the unknown.

15

By the time everything was ready, my ankles were itching profusely. I'm sure I'd had the bites for a while, but I guess I'd only just noticed, over the side-effects of the drug, that they were there. The briefing material in Fortress Gerhaun had warned us about the danger of dengue fever here. I really didn't fancy contracting this during the hike up, and so I decided before we left that we should take some insect repellent with us. I wondered then if the tribespeople had their own way of warding off mosquitoes – perhaps they had some herbal concoction more effective than our artificial repellent, or perhaps they just lived with them. I had no idea.

So, instead of climbing the mountain as the tribal chief had instructed, I took a step towards Velos, watching the panther as it growled at me again and raised itself up on its front legs. I put my hands up in the air to indicate surrender. "I need something from my dragon. He has insect repellent. And I should at least be able to say goodbye before we head on up."

I knew I wasn't talking to an automaton at this point but Captain Colas who probably had some device set up watching me. Most likely, there was a camera hidden somewhere inside the panther automaton, perhaps behind its red eyes. But there could have also been a

Hummingbird floating nearby or one of those funny lens-like devices that I'd seen Faso employ in his own workshop with propeller blades on top. Wherever it was, it was pretty well concealed, otherwise I'd be tempted to snatch a spear off one of the tribespeople, rush forward and smash the aperture open to buy us a little time.

Without asking permission, I took some further steps forward, and the panther did nothing. Velos crooned as I approached, and he lowered his head to me. I stroked the scaly skin under his neck. "It will be okay. I'll come back for you... I promise." And I sang him a song to reassure him that he'd be safe here. Even though I had no idea if he would — I didn't even know if I'd be safe myself.

He crooned again and then lifted his head away from me and turned to look at the panther automaton, who regarded me with those evil red crystalline eyes. No matter how far technology had come, devices like these hadn't grown any less menacing looking. Although, given most automatons nowadays were war machines anyway, their creators had probably factored the ferociousness into their design.

I moved around to the side of Velos and climbed up his armour via the ladder. The automaton regarded every single move I made with utmost attention. It kept itself in a crouching position as if it would leap on me and tear me to pieces if I made a single misstep. I moved to my seat and instead of sitting down on it, I unbuckled the latch there and opened the compartment underneath. Amongst the contents inside were various devices I might need including my bit and plug device for breathing, as well as a standard gas mask for harsher conditions, a spare hip flask filled with a mixture of mine and Sukina's secicao oil blends, and several aerosol cannisters containing the insect repellent I wanted.

Out of the corner of the eye, I noticed something rather strange. While the panther was watching me with intent, the tribal chief had ordered his people towards a patch not far away from where Velos' flames had scorched the ground. The tribespeople were now digging at the soil with their fingers, while the chief kept glancing over at the panther, tapping his foot impatiently.

It was obvious that he was doing something that he shouldn't be doing. But the panther automaton continued to watch me, probably not expecting any disobedience from the tribespeople. I just hoped there wasn't anything else other than the panther watching nearby.

Faso was also standing back, his hands on his hips seeming to supervise the operation. He did say he'd visited East Cadigan Island before, so maybe he had a way of communicating with the tribespeople.

Whatever they were up to over there, I decided I probably better buy them some time, and so I pretended to rummage through the compartment, even though I had found exactly what I'd been looking for. I probably wouldn't need the bit-and-plug device or gasmask as I doubted the crater was so high up that we'd have breathing problems. But I wanted that secicao flask so I could augment if I had to.

The question was, where could I conceal it without the panther noticing? The robe that the tribe had kindly donated to me didn't have any pockets. Then I had the bright idea of placing the flask under my armpit, and I could work out a better location later.

I glanced back towards the panther automaton. Then I lifted both a cannister and the hip flask together. I quickly stuffed the hipflask under my armpit, keeping it vertical to give it the best chance of concealment. If my arms had been bare, then I would have had no chance of hiding it. But because this robe was baggy, the folds of cloth concealed it well.

I threw the cannister down to the floor, causing the panther to flinch. But otherwise it displayed no threat. I reached down to get another cannister of insect repellent from the compartment. As I did, I glanced over my shoulder, to take a look what was going on. The tribespeople had already dug a hole in the earth and were now pushing the soil back into the hole again. Meanwhile, the chief was walking away from the hole, carrying a dormant device in his wide open hands.

It was Ratter, displaying no sign of life. Faso looked down at it, nodded, and then the chief stuffed it in one of the wooden-framed rucksacks already on a tribesperson's back and concealed it from view.

That confirmed my suspicions. Something about what I had done at the firepit had turned these people into our allies. Or maybe they'd been our allies all along, wanting to rid themselves of the oppression caused by Colas and his panther automaton. They'd buried Ratter for a reason, and I wished I could speak their language so I could at ask what that was.

I took hold of another cannister, and then climbed back down the ladder, making sure to keep my right arm close to my body so the hip flask didn't also drop down on the floor. Once at the bottom, I sprayed the insect repellent all over me, glad that I'd no longer have to worry about the mosquitoes, despite the slight stinging sensation it caused on my skin. I then bent down and picked the other cannister off the floor. I walked back over to the tribe and gave one can to Wiggea, who accepted it gracefully. I offered the other to Faso who just snatched the thing off me. Both men proceeded to douse themselves in repellent and then handed the cannisters to the tribespeople so they could also put them in the rucksacks.

The tribal chief then stepped forwards and he pointed up the mountain for a third time with his spear and made a beckoning sign with his free hand. Clearly, he wanted us to get moving.

We started the hike just as it once again clouded over and the first heavy drops of rain fell from the sky.

THE HIKE WAS MUCH HARDER than it looked. Admittedly, living in the Southlands for so long, I wasn't so used to ups-and-downs anymore. And we took the most direct route, it seemed, straight up with few plateaus and absolutely no descents along the way. I would have much rather flown Velos to the top and had done with it.

Once we'd hiked a little way up the mountain, a second panther emerged. While the first had been blue underneath the veins of green secicao fuel, this one instead had a red tint to it. Other than that, it looked an exact replica of the first one and equally fierce. How many of these beasts did Colas have on this island?

I wondered if Ratter would stand a chance against these seemingly stealthier, more agile, and what I presumed to be superior mechanical beasts. Of course, if I asked such a question to Faso, he'd tell me how Ratter was the best automaton ever known to man and how Colas was a lesser scientist in comparison.

But it didn't matter which automaton would beat up the other should they fight. Clearly Colas had been using these things to subject the people of the land to do his bidding. They seemed to think he was their god and I dreaded from the base of stomach what the old man was up to. The fact he was supplying the tribespeople Exalmpora had Empress Finesia's scent all over it. Which meant Alsie Fioreletta might be involved too.

I tried not to grumble too much on the way up, despite being continually out of breath and sweating out more water than I could take in. Faso, unfortunately, wasn't so stoic. He kept demanding that we should stop for a breather every hundred steps and kept complaining that if we climbed so fast then he had no time to stop and admire the view, which admittedly proved absolutely stunning once we'd got away from the rain.

"We're here to rescue your son, not to sightsee," I reminded him at least a couple of times. And each time he responded with a snarl and remained quiet for several hundred yards or so before complaining about something else.

Wiggea, on the other hand, didn't let out a single complaint on the entire hike. He kept watching over me as I walked, like a loyal guard dog. Having him there made me feel safer, even with a mechanical panther stalking us that could shred our party of ten to pieces. And Wiggea remained the perfect gentleman – catching me whenever I stumbled over a rock, or when I lost my balance again and almost went tumbling over a precipice. He brought a gourd of water close by whenever he saw I was thirsty, and he kept asking every so often if there was anything I needed. Dragonheats, if Faso took even a single a leaf out of the lieutenant's book, then the inventor would get on with people a lot better and maybe I'd respect him more.

Fortunately, though, there wasn't much rain when we got further up the mountain. An occasional drizzle here and there, but the clouds passed overhead quickly before they could dump their load on us. After quite a few hours of climbing we finally reached a plateau – the first one for what had felt like miles. Then, the ground started to rumble and Wiggea immediately moved in to protect me.

"Earthquake, Maam," he said. "Get down!"

The tribal chief looked up towards the top of the mountain and then also beckoned for our six strong guides to crouch down immediately. Faso crouched last. Wiggea held me close as I trembled in his grasp. The other six tribespeople and the tribal chief kept as far apart as possible from each other – a wise strategy in case we'd have to dodge any falling rocks.

"We're all doomed," Faso shouted out to the sky. "This is the end. A bloody earthquake and I have no technology to protect me. Colas, you're doing this to me, aren't you? You want to show me how incapable I am without technology. You've wanted to do this since you met me. You want to display me as a lesser man."

Dragonheats, the man had gone stark raving mad. Meanwhile, the ground shook underneath my feet and I half expected a chasm to tear up the earth beneath us and swallow us into the abyss. That would be ironic, after how far we'd come.

Everything was shaking so hard that even the panther looming nearby didn't seem to know what to do. One moment it was lying down on the ground trembling, the next it was trying to lift itself on two legs, and then tumbling across the plateau, the next it stood up on all fours and leaped across the ground as if trying to fly away from the earthquake. But, of course, gravity prevailed.

It was lucky we were on a plateau, really. Otherwise, I'm sure we'd all be tumbling down the mountain. But that thought gave me a little idea. Here I was cowering in Wiggea's arm and, despite how good it felt to be pushed up against a little muscle, I had an opportunity to get rid of that panther automaton.

I let the hip flask slip from under my armpit and took a swig from it. Well, I say a swig. With my jaw chattering and the world rumbling about me, I spilled much over my face. Some splashed into my eyes, stinging them. I would have thought it a huge waste, if it didn't give us a chance to dispose of our captor. But soon enough the world ghosted green, and I felt some strength and agility return to me.

I no longer felt paralysed by the rumbling ground, but instead I felt a certain synchrony with the resonance. I could feel the rhythm of the earth and I knew exactly when I could leap and when I should crouch. The panther now had also found a little more balance and through my augmented vision I could see it glowing even greener than before. A ball of light began to emerge from its mouth, but the earthquake soon knocked the panther down again, and that ball dissipated into the dust.

I got down onto all fours, knowing that I'd move faster along the shaky earth in this posture. I stalked forwards just as the panther started to get up again.

"Dragonheats, Pontopa," I heard Faso call out from behind me. "Stop it! You're going to get us killed."

Really, that man needed to learn to have more faith in ladies like me. Particularly, as I was the dragonseer here, and he'd already admitted himself to be crippled without the aid of his inventions.

So, I tried my best to ignore him as I leaped upon the back of the panther. It tossed its head to the air and let off a huge roar which sent shivers down my spine. I fastened one arm around its neck, as it tossed and bucked and tried to throw me off. Still the secicao made me strong and the added agility gave me a certain ability to sense the panther's movements ahead of time.

With my free hand, I felt around for an opening where there might be a power core. That was the way Ratter worked – Faso had installed a hatch on his back, beneath which ran an intricate array of wires and other devices I didn't understand. But even the most foolish of fools knew how to remove a power core.

The earth bucked again, sending me and the panther into a tumble. We roly-polied down the plateau, accelerating towards a massive drop. As we rolled, the sharp volcanic rock tore at my skin, causing me to yelp out in pain. But the secicao oil numbed my senses a little, which at least made the pain manageable.

The panther tossed again, and it managed to throw me off the front of it and get itself free of my grip. It darted away and then turned in a sharp circle towards me. As it leapt, it revealed two sharp claws that could have easily torn me apart. I rolled out of the way, and then turned to face it. I caught sight of a hatch on its derrière. If I could only open that, I could disable the thing. But the thing was so fast to turn around, I doubted I'd have the remotest of chances to do so.

"Hoooooiiieee," the call came from the tribal chief. The mask had been shaken off his face and so for the first time I caught sight of his pockmarked skin, dry lips, and a huge smile. He threw his spear towards me. Presumably an accomplished hunter, his aim was true. I caught the spear in mid-air and brandished it at the beast.

But the panther automaton had already launched itself off the ground towards me. This time, forward rolling underneath it would have sent me tumbling off the cliff. So instead, I ducked to the side. As the ground rocked, the panther stumbled when it landed, but it didn't fall over this time.

Before the beast could recover, I swung the haft of the spear, hoping to at least stun the thing. I hit it in the mouth hard enough to snap the spire protruding out the thing. Meanwhile, the panther automaton caught the spear in its mouth and wrenched it away from me. But surprisingly, instead of discarding the spear, it kept it clenched in its teeth. As I looked behind me, I realised why. I was right against the edge, and the spear shaft would readily knock me off it.

The beast scuffed its back paws into the ground and charged. Time dilated in my mind's eye – an effect of the secicao. As I watched the panther sprinting towards me in slow motion, I considered my options. I could try rolling under the haft or vaulting over it. But the panther had wisely kept the spear at an angle making both moves risky. Because the spear now gave the automaton additional width, I wouldn't be fast enough to run around it. I had no option but to let it knock me off the edge. Perhaps I could catch myself on the way down.

As the thing ran, it hugged the cliff face with cat-like balance, not once stumbling, even as the ground shook. In just moments I would fall to my fate and I'd never see Taka again.

A loud bang came from my right, something like the sound of a crashing boulder hitting the floor. All of a sudden, the panther tumbled to the right and started to slide down the rock. The shaft rose up as the panther fell and just missed my head by mere inches. Then, the panther plummeted down the side into the abyss.

Without even thinking, I made towards Wiggea and the rest of the party on the plateau. It took me a moment to notice that Wiggea was holding the Pattersoni rifle in his hands that the tribal chief had been carrying on his back, smoke trailing up from the barrel. The green outline in my vision was fading now, the effects of the secicao wearing off. As the sensation faded, my eyes started to sting a little too, as well as the parts of my skin that had been grazed by the sharp rocks. I rubbed my eyes with the back of my hands and looked up at Wiggea.

The ground bucked again and Wiggea stumbled to the ground. I teetered backwards and I almost went over the edge myself. I crouched down and planted the palm of my hand into the earth to stop myself falling over. Then, I pulled myself up towards Wiggea and the rest of the party. Another quake rocked the ground, and I stumbled forwards. Wiggea caught me in his arms and held me there a moment. I found myself staring into his soft hazel eyes.

"Lieutenant Wiggea," I said.

"Maam?" He cocked his head and a smile spread across his face. The rifle lay on the ground beside us now and slid across the ground as the earth shook some more. Wiggea and I crouched down together, and I buried my head in his shoulder and let the emotions come out. I don't know if I cried tears or I cried pain, but so much flooded back to me. King Cini sending soldiers to destroy my farmhouse. My father taking a bullet in the Five Hamlets to protect me. Sukina dying in her sickbed from a poison dart, all because she stayed in the palace to battle King Cini so Faso, Taka and I could make our escape. All the lives dragons and men had lost so I could live. So many sacrifices made, and I almost threw it all away by falling off a precipice.

"We did it," I said to Wiggea. "That panther hopefully won't bother us any longer."

"I hope so, Maam," Wiggea said. He hesitated for a moment. "I almost thought you were Sukina then, the way you moved."

I nodded and fought back a smile. "Thank you, Lieutenant." I guess all that training hadn't been for nothing.

The quakes were now dying down, and I was confident the earthquake would soon pass. Faso had lifted himself off the ground, no longer cowering in a foetal position. I noticed an expression of scorn on his face when he saw Wiggea holding me in his arms. Wiggea turned his head a little and then remembered himself. He let go of me, and he tugged at the collar of his robe. "I think the danger has passed now."

"I think so," I said.

But Faso looked livid. "Pontopa, there was no way of you knowing you could have defeated that thing. If it wasn't for the chief throwing the rifle to Wiggea it would have killed you and then turned on us. What were you thinking?"

I clenched my teeth and tried to not to let this buffoon get under my skin. "I saw an opportunity and I took it, Faso," I said, keeping my voice as calm as I could, even though I was seething underneath. "We need to take some risks if we're going to survive this."

"Well, you're going to need to start making more sensible decisions, Pontopa Wells. From now on, I think you need a stronger leader."

I shook my head and put my hands on my hips. "Faso, I'm still in charge of this operation. Your advice is noted, and your temper isn't appreciated right now. Pull yourself together."

A crackle came again from no determinate direction. Wellies knows how many of those speakers Colas had installed here. But now the earth had stopped growling, the old man had decided to speak in his robotic, modified voice. "What the dragonheats did you do to my panther, Dragonseer? I saw you augment, and I saw you lunge in. And now... Dragonheats, if you think you're going to climb the mountain without an escort, you're wrong. I have plenty more automatons where that came from."

The fact that he didn't seem so happy caused me to smirk a little. It also seemed to cause a little elation in the tribal chief, who had lifted himself off the ground, and began cartwheeling around while he let out waves of hysterical laughter. Colas started to speak in the tribe's own language, but the chief raised his fist to the sky and screeched out what I presumed to be an expletive with all the power of his lungs.

The realisation suddenly dawned on me that Colas could no longer hear us. Perhaps he couldn't see us either. Maybe he only had cameras within the panthers after all. And I'd also shown the tribespeople that the panther automatons could be defeated. That, if anything, had to give them hope.

"I'm sending another panther up to punish you," Colas said. "And this time, if you try anything, I'll kill one of your own."

I looked at Wiggea then Faso. "You better listen to him," Faso said. "He's a madman."

But the tribal chief was also behaving like a madman, clutching his belly while lying on the ground and kicking at the air as Colas continued to say something in the tribal language.

Once Colas had finished speaking, the leader turned to the guides who now stood with their backpacks on their shoulders. He looked up the mountain and then he motioned them along the edge of it. He started to traverse the terrain and then beckoned us onwards.

I decided it best to follow him, and as we moved, I kept an eye out for any sign of panther automatons bounding up the rockface from below. We were pretty exposed, so the automatons might be able to spot us if we didn't find a place to remain concealed. But the earthquake had kicked up a lot of volcanic ash from the ground, limiting visibility. It seemed that this time, nature had looked upon us favourably.

And so I hiked onwards with a feeling of renewed hope.

16

We traversed the mountain for a while as the dust lifted up from the earthquake settled on the ground, and the sky went from grey to red to twilight blue. Just before it then plunged into a moonless pitch-black night, the tribal chief motioned for us to halt. He and all the tribespeople with us had discarded their masks. Clearly, now they'd seen the mortality of the panther automaton, it was no longer a deity in their minds.

The chief pointed towards a cave mouth that opened up into the rock face. From it came a roaring sound and a warm draft carrying a sulphuric smell upon it, almost as if a dragon lived within.

The tribal chief and tribespeople led us down a long almost cylindrical cavern with slimy floors which got darker as we progressed inside. I found it difficult not to slip as I walked, and I half wanted to augment so at least I'd be able to see my way through here, but I resisted. I only had a small amount of secicao oil left in my flask after spilling it during the earthquake. I figured I might need this for another occasion, like if I had to fight any more panther automatons, or whatever else Colas might have in store for us at the top of the mountain.

Soon enough, the darkness transgressed into a natural red light that bounced off the walls. And as we pushed on, the heat intensified, and the roars became even louder, occurring intermittently. I expected to see a huge bonfire at the end of this, the amount of energy that was coming off the walls. But instead the passageway opened up into a brilliant display of red coming from a massive lava lake, deep enough below us fortunately that it didn't pose any apparent threat. Every so often, fire would flare out of the lake, sending out a massive boom with it and letting off a significant amount of heat.

Faso was the first to say something. "Amazing. We've just passed through a veritable lava tube into the source of the volcano itself. You know, up until now, we only knew about two accessible lava lakes in the world."

"I thought you said that this volcano was dormant?" I asked.

"So I thought," Faso replied. "So I thought..."

"Colas... Could he possibly?"

"I doubt it," Faso said. "No, this place for some reason has remained largely unexplored. Or if not, at least undocumented in the scientific journals."

"You didn't come here."

"No..." Faso looked down at the magma lake and I could see it glowing in the reflection in his eyes. "I conducted my studies much further north."

The tribal chief smiled and nodded as if he understood. I doubted he did, but he was probably instead acknowledging the expression of awe on our faces.

And I could only describe it as awesome myself, as I watched the blackened rocks bubble and melt on the lava lake's surface. Outside, the temperature had dropped quite significantly as the coolness of the evening approached. But now, I was starting to sweat again.

We traversed further along the narrow passageway that looked down over the lava lake until we reached an alcove. There, three old men stood around a firepit, and these men didn't have the dark skin of the tribespeople, but fairer skin like many of the natives of Slaro. Except they also each had hardened natural tan to them, clearly after being exposed to hours of sunshine outside. They also looked remarkably similar, like identical twins, or I guess triplets.

The firepit had a pot in the centre, but the fire wasn't lit and probably not necessary for anything but cooking due to the heat given off by the lava lake. Some tree stump stools had been arranged around the firepit, and around the walls of the alcove, a dozen or so feathered mattresses had been laid out on the floor. Above these mattresses, strange symbols had been etched into the wall. As I looked closer, I noticed them to be lit by some kind of magmatic light, almost as if they were on fire.

One of the old men turned to me as we approached. This man, unlike his brothers, had a mole that stuck out of the beard at his chin. He stepped forward and offered me his hand. "Dragonseer," he said. "Welcome to our temporary abode."

"Hooooooieeee," the tribal chief said. "Elders speak."

I looked at them in astonishment. "You speak Towese?" I asked.

The first man turned to the second of the men who'd now placed himself by the firepit and was bending down to strike a match. He threw it onto the firewood, watching it erupt into flames. He then poured some oats into the pot from a sack, followed by some water from a gourd.

Then he turned to me. This second man had a birthmark that ran diagonally across his left cheek and disappeared into his beard. "We speak many languages, Dragonseer Wells, for we are students of old with much knowledge of the world. My brother here is an anthropologist." He indicated the man standing next to me. "I'm a biologist. And our third is a linguist."

I regarded them in curiosity. "The three of you look the same," I pointed out.

The third man's grey beard had now gained a red tint, due to the light of the fire. This man's distinguishing feature was a very slightly cleft top lip. He took hold of ladle from beside the firepit and used it to stir the porridge in the pot. "We're identical triplets of the Dragonseer line," he said. "Much like you."

I opened my mouth in shock. No, this wasn't possible. "But all dragonseers are female, and they can only birth a single female offspring." Gerhaun had taught me that.

"Are you so sure about that?" The question came again from the first of the men, the anthropologist with the mole on his chin. "Can you trust your sources."

I tried to recall Gerhaun's words. It had been so long ago, but I'd relived the moment I first met her many times in my head. "A dragonseer will always have one child, no more, no less, always female," she'd said. I repeated the words exactly as I remembered them.

That caused the three elder triplets to look at each other and erupt into laughter.

"That sounds exactly like Gerhaun Forsi." This time the biologist spoke. "She was always very careful about her words. Yes, we heard she'd taken you under her wing. But notice she said will, not was. She spoke about the future, not the past. Because she plans never to let it happen again."

Faso had just joined us by the firepit. He sat down and looked at the three men in turn and then at the porridge now bubbling in the pot. "I thought I'd heard enough baloney for one day. Given the three of you are men of learning, I expected to hear something worthwhile rather than the myths and nonsense, I often hear from Pontopa here."

The linguist then turned to Faso and a sly smile stretched upon his face. He spoke with a little bit of a lisp, presumably because of his cleft lip. "I'd listen to us, Mr Gordoni. For like us you are a male component of the dragonseer line. You are more special than you might think."

That caused Faso to laugh. "Special? Of course I'm bloody special. I'm the best scientist to have ever graced this earth."

"But you don't truly believe it." The elder said.

Faso paused a moment. "What the dragonheats do you mean?"

"You say those things to mask the fact that you don't understand your true destiny. You pretend you're the best, while deep inside there's a nagging voice telling you there are people much better than you. And now you're in the realm of another scientist whose inventions are much more superior than anything you've ever dreamed of yourself."

"What nonsense," Faso said.

"Is it, Faso Gordoni?" the anthropologist said. Really, I found it kind of endearing how these three men played off each other as if they were one person. "You're the youngest male of the dragonseer line alive today, and you don't even know yourself."

"The youngest male of the dragonseer line," for a second Faso's jaw dropped. Then he looked between the men and he erupted into laughter himself. "That's a good one. I've heard a lot of mumbo jumbo from Pontopa here, but this has to be the best yet."

The biologist stood up and he looked at Faso, firelight dancing in his eyes. "And how do you know it's not true, Faso Gordoni? Did you know your grandfather on your mother's side?"

Faso shook his head. "Just because I don't know someone doesn't mean they're part of some magical, mystical heritage."

"You've seen dragons and men and women turn into dragons, and yet you have problems accepting the existence of myth."

"We all came from apes, not the dust of the earth shaped by The Gods Themselves and the wars between Finase and Honore. These myths are just nice stories we tell kids to get them to behave in school."

"So how do you explain this?" the anthropologist asked. And he turned around to indicate the writing on the wall. Now I was closer to it, I realised that the text was writing itself out slowly in pictorial representations. And my mouth and eyes opened wide in astonishment. It was as if an invisible man was sitting there and inking each new symbol using the lava of the lake.

Faso looked over at it and his eyes went wide for a moment. Then, he shook his head hard. "I'm sure there's a scientific explanation for it. I just haven't had time to study it yet."

"Well, let me tell you," the linguist said and walked over it. "This is the Wall of Prophecies. Part of a cave that writes out the destinies of people as it unfolds. Within this ancient language are the futures of the men and women who will change the world." The linguist glanced

over at me. "We believe this wall to chronicle the collective unconscious in written form."

"And I guess you're going to just tell me what will happen in my
future," Faso said. "And then you'll tell me that Pontopa and I are great
agents of good in this world who will defeat King Cini and turn the
Southlands into an absolute paradise."

"No," the linguist replied. "We're still learning to decipher it. But
making progress."

"And how the dragonheats did you find this place in the first
place?"

"It called us to it," the biologist replied. "Each of us saw it on our
dreams. So, many years ago, we abandoned our university jobs and
came right here to learn the language of the wall and the tribespeople.
Coatu here," the biologist gestured to the tribal chief, "has also been
learning Towese."

"See what I mean?" Faso turned to me as if looking for reassur-
ance. "Absolute baloney."

Now, I'd just about had enough of Faso rejecting what could have
been valuable information as mumbo jumbo. Given Faso was Taka's
father by blood, this could tell us why exactly Alsie and Captain Colas,
for that matter, wanted him so bad. I put up my hand to stop Faso
from spouting any more of his negativity and then I looked at the
three triplets in turn. "Faso might not be interested," I said, and I
glared daggers at the inventor, "but I am. How exactly, can there be a
male in the dragonseer line? I don't understand."

The linguist smiled. "You've tasted Exalmpora. Yes, I can see it in
your eyes and the lines on your face. Be careful Dragonseer, because
you're on the verge of going over the edge. Take any more and you
may become like Alsie Fioreletta yourself. The walls suggest great
dangers..."

I shook my head. This wasn't getting us anywhere. "But how is
Exalmpora related to all this?"

"Because, seven generations ago," the biologist said while he threw
a piece of firewood into the fire, "a dragonseer decided to experiment
with Exalmpora when pregnant. And it changed the makeup of the

baby within. The baby was born male and with that, the rules of drag-onseers left behind by the Gods Themselves were broken. And instead, arose the first male dragonseer heir."

I looked at him in astonishment. "And then?"

The biologist smiled, and then reached down to pick up a wooden bowl. He scooped some of the porridge into it and offered it to me. I nodded, thanked him and then tasted it. It tasted salty – just what my body needed right now.

The biologist offered a second bowl of porridge to Faso, then took another ladle of porridge for himself and sat down again. "The child was no longer a dragonseer," he continued. "But someone else. It transpired that he could have as many children as he pleased. But still he had dragonseer blood inside him, and he also became a serial womaniser with no knowledge of birth control. So he ended up sprouting many offspring. That man, Faso Gordoni, is your distant ancestor. And the male gene gifted through the Exalmpora was always dominant. Every single one of those offspring turned out to be male. And the same applied to the generation after that. And the generation after that. And the generation after that."

I put my hand to my chin. One thing still didn't make sense. "So you're saying that Faso and his ancestors and all his cousins however many times removed can only have male offspring?"

The anthropologist nodded. "I spent my life studying the ancestry of dragonseers. Commissioned, at first by Gerhaun and the other dragon queens to scour the chapel and town hall records across the globe for relevant information."

"But there's one thing I don't understand in all this. How come Taka was born a female?"

Faso smiled and stood up himself. He'd already wolfed down his porridge, and the bowl now hung limply by his side. "Aha, I was going to say the same myself. Well, Pontopa Wells, maybe you're smarter than you look."

I cast Faso another hard glare and then turned to look at anthropologist. But this time it was the biologist's turn to offer his input. "It took us a long time to dig up the records for this one, given that

Taka's birth wasn't officially registered and Cini did his best to hide this fact. But it turns out that through the entire male dragonseer bloodlines, Faso and Sukina was the only instance of a male dragonseer heir uniting with the true dragonseer line. Taka was born out of this union and it seemed the dragonseer gene once again proved dominant. And so, we presume Taka was born a dragonseer."

"You presume?" I asked.

"Yes. I personally worked for the king a while so that I could study the young child. I wished I had enough power to stop what Colas and Alsie did to him with the Exalmpora. And, unfortunately, I couldn't get enough data on Taka before the Exalmpora changed his gender."

I raised an eyebrow. "I thought the king kept Taka's origin a strict secret."

"We were commissioned by the dragon queens, remember. And they already knew who Taka was. I only worked for the king in disguise."

"And what happened to the dragonseer who birthed a male heir? There were always eight female dragonseers before Cini II started exterminating us, surely?"

"The natural order of things somehow corrected itself," the anthropologist said. "and she birthed another female dragonseer. This was the original ancestor of Alsie Fioreletta. And, since that point dragonseers, have only ever had female children, or at least as far as we can tell from our records."

Now, my head was spinning and I don't know whether this was so much from that strange Exalmpora solution I'd taken earlier that day, the knocks from when I'd battled the panther automaton, the concussion during the storm on the Saye Explorer, or the fact that all this genetics stuff was just so damn complicated.

Faso sat there scratching his chin as if he didn't believe a word of it. Over the last few days, he'd started to grow a bit of stubble, which I must say suited him a little better than that clean baby-faced look he liked to tout.

"Baloney, baloney," he said.

"But you suspect it to be true," the biologist opposite me said.

"What I know," Faso said, and he looked back at the rucksacks that the guides had propped up against the back wall of the cavern, just underneath the magical text, "is that I need to fix Ratter to give us a chance of getting out of this situation alive."

He placed his bowl on the floor walked over to the rucksacks, his posture in a little bit of a slump. He seemed to know exactly which one Ratter had been placed in, despite the fact that they all looked completely the same, or at least to me. He opened the pack, took hold of Ratter, splayed the six-legged automaton out on the floor, and then took hold of a screwdriver that he'd placed inside Ratter's hatch. With this, he started to work at fixing the automaton.

Me, the three elder men, and the tribal chief watched him while the other tribespeople stood back inspecting their fingernails and picking at the dirt underneath them with toothpicks.

"It's the dragonseer line that Faso gets his intelligence from," the man on the left told me. "The males lost their abilities to communicate with dragons, but instead gained superior intellect, and an astounding ability to focus on the most intricate of details."

I smiled. "I wouldn't tell him that. Unless you want to inflate his ego to the size of an airship's balloon."

"On the contrary," the man said. "I think it might settle him a bit to begin to accept this. The reason that he behaves the way he does is that he doesn't truly trust his abilities. Call it imposter syndrome, if you like."

"But he's always talking about how great he is."

"Because he seeks validation for that fact. If he truly believed it, he wouldn't have a need to say it to anyone."

I nodded. It made a lot of sense in a way, and it made me see the man in a new light, and perhaps even have a little sympathy for his behaviour. I mean, Faso had shown many moments of genius and had saved many lives through them. Maybe I was a little harsh on him sometimes, but he just tended to rub me up the wrong way.

My bowl was now empty, so I placed it down on the floor. "So where do I come into all this?"

"What do you mean?" the biologist replied.

"I mean, I have dragonseer blood and all that. But I wasn't born from a dragonseer's womb. So, I can never be as great as a dragonseer, right?"

"There's no evidence to suggest that. Your first set of genes were most likely dominant over those of your second."

And I thought back to my own mother, the one I'd grown up with, not the other one who had died before she could even give birth to me. If it wasn't for Doctor Forsolano's genius, and his idea to artificially plant me into Versalina Wells' womb using some proprietary technology, then I would never have been born in the first place. "So you're telling me I have no traits of my mother at all?" Surely, I at least had her curly blond hair.

"I'd need to take blood samples of both you and your mother to know exactly." The biologist said. "Maybe we could travel back together once you get Taka back and work it all out?"

I nodded. "This is a lot to take in. But yes, I'd like you to run the tests once we get out of here." And I swallowed back the thoughts that we might not. I had to believe that we would, even though I didn't have a clue what we were up against.

"Good," the biologist said. And he pointed over to one of the mattresses. "Now, you should get some rest. For we rise just before dawn to climb before the sun rises."

"You're coming with us?"

"Why not?" the linguist said and nodded over at the tribespeople. "Surely, it would be good to have someone to translate the language."

He had a point. Although I did remember how that the tribal chief had become much more eloquent after drinking Exalmpora. Or maybe that had been just my imagination. Perhaps, along with other traits, Exalmpora could traverse across languages. I felt at my skin, noticing the rougher texture than before. I'd forgotten to bring moisturiser up with me, but I wasn't sure I'd be able to use it to get rid of this scaly feel. And then, when I bent down to inspect my ankles, I noticed that the bites from earlier that day had vanished far faster than they should have done. Something was changing about my physiology, and I didn't like it one bit.

At that point, I noticed we were missing someone. Faso, the three academics, and the seven tribespeople were here, but there was no sign of Lieutenant Wiggea. I thought I'd go for a little walk to see if I could find him. And I only needed to turn the corner along the path from which we'd arrived here to find him.

He stood at the edge of the precipice, staring out at the brilliant dancing display of fire in the chasm below. I walked over to accompany him, feeling the magnificent heat rising from the lake as I approached.

"Lieutenant," I said and stood next to him.

"Maam..." He turned to look at me, a smile on his face and his expression confident and relaxed.

"You know, I just had the most fascinating conversation. You know, these three older men have worked with Gerhaun and have met her before. Oh, and there's porridge."

Wiggea looked over his shoulder towards the alcove. "Thanks, I'll get some later. And I think I remember seeing them around when I first started as a rookie soldier. Gerhaun left me instructions to leave you alone should you encounter them on your journey. She told me that they had secret knowledge that could help you learn a little more about yourself."

I raised an eyebrow. "You knew about this Wiggea? And you didn't think to tell me?"

"Gerhaun thought it unlikely that we'd encounter them, Maam. There was only a tiny chance we'd be in exactly the same location as them. East Cadigan Island is a big place."

That made me worry a little. Colas had said only to bring two escorts up, no more. "They want to accompany us. Do you think that's okay?"

"I can't imagine Captain Colas would consider them much threat, Maam. Although, in all honesty, I don't know the man. They seem to know the mountain and might be useful as extra guides, but I'm not sure they should come all the way to the top."

"But Colas is okay for the guides to accompany us?"

Wiggea shook his head. "I don't know, Maam," and he turned to look back at the raging lava below.

I looked down as well, marvelling at the patterns the flares made as they leapt across the fiery lake, like fish flopping out of water.

"You know, Maam," Wiggea said without turning around. "For a moment, with that battle with the panther, I thought we'd lost you. I'd swore to Gerhaun on my own life that I'd protect you, and you were so close to falling over the edge."

I nodded. "I'm sorry. I guess I took an uncalculated risk."

"Well, maybe the decision was rather rash. But you won in the end. I just felt... I mean, we lost Sukina, Maam. And I lost Hastina before her... I didn't want to lose you too."

I shrugged. "I guess I'm the last dragonseer."

"If we can't retrieve Taka, yes." And I was actually happy to hear that someone else believed in Taka's abilities as a dragonseer. But something told me Wiggea wasn't only just concerned about the fate of the dragonseer lineage. This seemed like something much more personal. Almost as if he'd taken a liking to me.

And to be honest, I'd taken a bit of a liking to him as well. So, I reached out, and I took his hand. I guess it was worth testing if there was anything there. He looked down, a startled expression on his face. But he didn't retract his arm. "Maam?" he said.

"Just forget about your duty for a moment, Lieutenant. Let's just admire the view."

He turned back to the lava pit. His hand was dry and warm. Meanwhile, mine must have been so clammy with the heat coming off the lava pit adding to the humidity. How was he not sweating up here? Soldier's training perhaps. But then he had said that he had grown up in a desert climate.

Wiggea said nothing, so I thought it best to break the silence. I glanced over my shoulder a moment to check Faso wasn't spying on us. I could just imagine him breaking an intimate private moment between my loyal lieutenant and I.

"You know, Lieutenant Wiggea..."

"You can call me Rastano under the circumstances, Maam."

I smiled. I'd been so caught up in the rules of Fortress Gerhaun, following military procedures, I'd never even thought to call Wiggea by his first name. "Very well. Rastano when we hold hands and Lieutenant Wiggea when we're on duty."

"Yes, Maam," he said. And he scratched the back of his neck with his other hand.

"Do you feel uncomfortable, Rastano?"

He blushed a little, still staring away from me and out at the lava. "A little. I'm sorry, I don't want to offend you. It's just, you're my..." He hesitated.

"What? Your superior."

"Yes, Maam."

"Please. If I'm going to call you Rastano, then remember I'm called Pontopa."

"Pontopa..."

"Lieut – I mean Rastano. Look at me a moment."

He turned his head towards me, a nervous tic shaking the corner of his lip.

"You're a brave man. Kind, sensitive, honest, loyal. I've admired you since the very moment we met."

"I admire you too, Maam... Everything except your sparring abilities. But you are getting better..." He had a cocky smile across his face.

I laughed. "I guess you had it tough with your sergeant too when you first started training?"

"I did, Maam, I mean Pontopa." And I found myself surprised for a moment that his first superior was her. But then I why should I be? There were plenty of women in Gerhaun's forces, many of them with high ranks.

I took hold of Wiggea's other hand, so he couldn't scratch behind his neck and continue looking nervous. Then, I gazed into his soft hazel eyes. The reflection from the lava below them swirled in them, giving them an almost menacing, powerful quality. "Rastano... Do you think in another life, where I wasn't your superior, and there weren't any wars, that perhaps we could?"

"We could what?" Although he couldn't now use his hands to make any nervous gestures, they still felt a little stiff and the corner of his mouth had that same nervous tic.

"You know what I mean…" And I was beginning to regret even asking.

"I don't know, Maam," and I could see this wasn't going anywhere.

I felt the blood rush to my cheeks, and I started to feel a little awkward. So I dropped his hands and turned away from him. "I'm sorry. I shouldn't be pushing if you don't want to."

"It's not that…" He hesitated again. "It's just…"

"I know, Lieutenant," I said. And I thought we better go back to referring to each other in military terms.

Wiggea paused for a long moment and I stood there, breathing heavily, wondering if I could push him any further. No, the elders were right, I should probably get to bed and get some rest. I began to turn around.

"Pontopa wait…" Wiggea said. He'd turned to face me.

"What is it, Lieutenant?"

He took hold of my chin then and turned my head towards me. "I'm sorry, I've never tried this since my Hastina." And he planted a kiss on my lips. Not a long one, but genuine and warm. "Maybe one day, you're right, we can try. But we need to rescue Taka first."

Now it was my turn to stand stock still in shock. Rastano Wiggea turned away from me and began to walk towards the mattresses. He stopped and looked over his shoulder. "We should get some rest, Maam."

"Yes… I guess you're right." And I followed him into the alcove where Faso was still busy fixing Ratter. The three elders were already fast asleep, as well as most of the tribesmen other than the tribal chief who watched us approach.

"Hoooiieeeee," he said. "It love, it love." And I caught a glimpse of Wiggea's face turning red.

"Don't push it," I said to the tribal chief.

"Hooooiiiieee," the chief said again and danced some cartwheels around the burning firepit. Then, he reached up to a rope that was hanging from the ceiling and gave it a tug. A huge wooden bowl that I hadn't even seen hanging there plunged down from the ceiling, completely covering the fire – flames and pot and all – and choking it out. The tribal chief then drew some thick bamboo curtains to close off the view of the magma pit. It wasn't enough to shut off the light completely, but it made the room adequately dark to sleep in.

There was a mattress on the floor to my right, and so I lay down upon it, missing the softer mattresses in Fortress Gerhaun and even more the ones I used to sleep on in the Five Hamlets.

I couldn't sleep well that night, emotions still boiling through me as if my heart was as active as the lava lake. I kept thinking first of Wiggea and that unexpected kiss he'd planted on my lips. Then I remembered two years ago, and my wedding to Francoiso Lamford, Charth's brother. How much I'd wanted him then, and I began to wonder if my feelings for Wiggea weren't my own but a side effect of the Exalmpora.

But if that were the case, surely I would have gone for Faso instead – the man with dragonseer blood. The thought of it made me shudder. No, it was more likely that I was simply attracted to Wiggea. I mean, I'd spent a lot of time with him lately, and I knew him to be a wonderful man.

And eventually, with the taste of that warm kiss lingering on my lips, a knot in my stomach, and a smile on my face, I drifted off to sleep.

PART VI

CAPTAIN COLAS

"Science happens when we begin to experiment on what we believe to be magic."

— CAPTAIN COLAS

17

"Hooooiieeee." The wakeup call came at around five in the morning, or at least that's what the pocket watch said that someone had kindly placed besides my mattress. "Hoooooiiieeee."

I turned to see a form lit red by magma light, dancing around the room in cartwheels and backflips. The fire roared out its presence from the centre of the room, its heat causing me to feel clammy underneath my robe. How it hadn't woken me, I don't know. From above the fire, a pot of boiling food sent a warm, starchy smell out across the room.

I yawned, lifted myself off the mattress and checked I was decent. I was still wearing my robe, which admittedly covered so much of me that I probably hadn't needed to check anything.

"Hooooiieee," the cry came again. And the tribal chief danced over to me and then shook my hand. "Welcome, dragonseer. You eat." He pointed at the pot that I could now see had a thin soup inside of it, containing specks of some kind of meat.

I smiled, feeling suddenly hungry, and I approached the pot and sat down on a tree trunk stool. A small bowl had been placed in front of the stool, with the soup already inside it, and so I bent down to pick it up, holding my hair back with my other hand so it didn't get caught in the flames.

Wiggea rose next with a yawn, and then he jumped straight up onto his feet like a cat, as if he'd not wanted to sleep so deeply. It must have been something about the fumes from the volcano that had sent us into such a stupor. Faso got up last out of the three of us, and as soon as he arose, Ratter darted out of his bedclothes and up onto his shoulder. The automaton watched the cooking pot adamantly, almost as if he wanted some soup himself. But he was probably just on alert because of the heat coming from the flames.

"What's all this noise about," Faso said. He had these huge bags under his eyes as if he'd been up all night. "And what time is it anyway? And where the dragonheats is my pocket watch?"

Ratter let out a hiss, scurried down Faso's arm, then his leg and onto the dusty ground. The automaton rushed over to my mattress where Faso's pocket watch rested. He picked it up within his jaw and dropped it on the floor in front of Faso.

"Ah, the culprit," Faso said, turning on me. "I know it's disturbing not being able to see the sun out here, but I have you know this is a family heirloom."

I shook my head. "How the wellies did you find that thing?"

"So you did take it?"

"No, I didn't." I folded my arms.

"Well, good for you. Once I'd fixed Ratter last night, I sent him out hunting for some of my lost belongings. And this must have been close by because Ratter managed to bring it back within a few hours."

I glanced around, wondering who might have put the watch there. Then I noticed the tribal chief pointing his finger at Ratter and sniggering. Seemed he was quite the practical joker. Although, I guess it was lucky for Faso that the chief's sense of humour didn't involve throwing his watch into the lava lake.

"If you are quite finished," the archaeologist of the three elders suddenly appeared from behind me, startling me. I hadn't seen him get up. "We have a mission to be getting on with."

"Yes, and I guess there's no one more capable of embarking on it than the last remaining male dragonseer," Faso said. He had a dry, sarcastic undertone in his voice.

"You are far from the last remaining," the elder said. "And you are not a dragonseer." He stepped forward.

"So who else is there?" Faso called after him, not letting the man leave the conversation hanging. "You're not going to tell me Captain Colas is one?"

"If he was. Then Charth Lamford would never have been a dragonseer."

"In theory," Faso said with his hands on his hips. "If your premises weren't complete baloney in the first place."

"One day, you'll realise that it is you who are assuming false axioms. Now, enough of this arguing. Mr Gordoni, you either choose to believe, or you don't."

The elder began to walk forward, and I turned in surprise to see that the guides already had their rucksacks on their backs and were ready to push onwards.

This time, I decided to lead the hike with Wiggea trailing behind and Faso behind him, Ratter staring down at the lava lake from his shoulder. They were followed by the six guides, the tribal chief, and finally the three elders. We traversed along the top of the cliff above the lava lake. The heat was even more searing that yesterday and flares roared out from the liquid rock below like angry beasts.

"This place is fascinating and certainly warrants more study," Faso said.

"Maybe it's magic," I said with a smirk on my face that Faso couldn't see.

"Pah, I would hear such things from you. And pigs secretly have wings and will one day rule this earth."

"If Cini has his way, I'm sure that prophecy will come true..."

Surprisingly, this caused a chuckle from Faso, but not from Wiggea. The lieutenant smiled when I looked around at him, but otherwise, he behaved as if nothing had happened last night. Well, I guess it was only a quick peck after all.

"Is there anything I can do to help, Maam?"

"Not yet, Lieutenant. Just keep watching the path ahead for any danger."

"As always," he said, and I let him step in front of me.

Soon enough, we left the lava lake behind us, passed through the lava tube cavern, and then stepped outside into the fresh pre-dawn air. It was surprisingly chilly, and I started to see the need for these thick hemp robes, although they didn't quite keep the cold away as much as I'd have liked.

Now I didn't have any panthers I needed to conceal it from, I carried my golden hip flask in my hand. I kind of wish I'd had the hindsight to sew a pocket into the inside of my robe the previous night. I could have then concealed the flask quite easily and produced it at the last minute in the final battle against whatever Colas had in store for us. So far I'd only seen his crow and panther automatons, but I had a terrible feeling he had other tricks up his sleeve.

Now we were outside, we had changed our formation a little. The elder triplets took the lead, pushing themselves up the mountain with surprising agility on their bamboo canes. After a moment, the linguist raised his hand to signal for us to halt.

I looked at him in surprise. "I thought we were in a hurry?"

"I'm sure time can wait for you to get back your equipment, don't you think?"

"Our equipment?"

"Captain Colas ordered the tribespeople to bury it out of sight, so you wouldn't be able to find it. So they brought it up here and we offered to look after it. We planted it in a cave not far from here."

"So that's where Ratter found my pocket watch," Faso said.

The linguist nodded. "I'm surprised you didn't get him going after your rifles and other stuff as well."

"I assumed that would have remained at the base of the mountain," Faso said. "Much too far away for Ratter to retrieve and come back again in just a few hours. Meanwhile, I knew already that I'd dropped the watch out of the air somewhere around here."

"And it's quite lucky that the thing didn't break on impact."

"Yes, quite," Faso said. "It's a remarkably sturdy piece of equipment."

I smiled in amusement. I already had my hip flask, and we had one rifle. The tribespeople had allowed us to take both up the mountain and both had proven useful. All this time, the tribe had been on our side, and we hadn't even realised it at first.

But one thing still confused me. Why the wellies did they give me the Exalmpora? Did they know the effects it would have on me? And did they know I was going to have that vision? I wondered if I should tell the elders about what I'd seen down in the jungle, but I thought better of it.

It had shown me to be the conqueror of Alsie, the planter of the Tree Immortal, and the destroyer of the world. If word about this got back to Gerhaun, I'm not sure she'd let me back into the fortress.

"Dragonseer, you will become the most powerful being on the planet." That female voice came into my head again. The voice of an empress.

No, it had to be my imagination. I'd just spent a night sleeping through magma fumes. Whatever I was hearing was just delusions due to chemicals. Nothing else.

"Come," the anthropologist said. And he led us to a small crack in the ground. I wouldn't even call it a cave. And I couldn't quite see inside, because the shadows concealed its contents so well.

The elder rolled up his sleeve and reached inside with a bony arm. "Yes, here we are." And he threw back a pistol, which landed spinning on the ground.

"Dragonheats! Careful, old man," Faso shouted out and he jumped back in alarm.

But the elder wasn't listening. He threw out the other two pistols, which landed a lot more smoothly. My knives came next, secured within their sheaths. Somehow, he'd managed to stash two Pattersoni rifles in there as well, which he took out more gently and laid them out on the floor. They still had the bullets within the barrel, I noticed. Good enough for twenty-four shots and we hadn't used any of them.

After that, the anthropologist took out a bundle wrapped in brown paper, then tied in hemp rope. This was much bigger than anything else that had come out so far. "In there you'll find your clothes laundered and dried," the elder said.

"And what about our own hip flasks," Faso said. "Pontopa has hers, and what are Wiggea and I meant to do if we need to augment?"

"Didn't the tribespeople give you them?" the elder asked.

"Negative," Wiggea said. "Pontopa took a spare one from the armour on the dragon."

The old man smiled and his brother, this time the linguist, turned to the tribal chief to say something in his language. The tribal chief's expression fell away from its jovial norm and he bowed his head and shook it as if in shame. He turned to his own tribespeople, who now stood in a line with their rucksacks on their backs and he said something. In turn, they also lowered their heads, and their shoulders drooped.

"Hooooooooiiiiieeee," the tribal chief said. But this sound was much longer drawn out and deeper than any other of these calls had been. The tribespeople nodded, put their rucksacks down on the ground, and each of them began to rummage around in them, scattering things like bedsheets, pots and pans, various items of bone jewellery, and other paraphernalia on the floor. Eventually, three of them found the items in question. Three golden flasks, including my spare one. This was a blessing given my current hip flask was almost empty after spilling most of it on my face during the earthquake.

"Hooooooiiiieee," the tribal chief said again, this time returning to his former spirit. He spun around in a circle and then performed a backflip. Then he ran up to each of the three tribespeople in turn and slapped the hip flasks out of their hands. He returned to us with the acquired items in both of his hands and he dropped them on the floor.

"Thank you," I said.

"Welcome," the chief said. "You'll need."

Wiggea had already opened the package a little distance away from us, and now our clothes lay in a neatly stacked pile on a brown paper mat. I really was happy to see my jerkin, blouse, and three-quarter length breeches, which I loved to ride in, as well as my high socks and custom-built garters that I used for concealing my knives. They were much better than wearing this itchy robe.

I went over and took hold of my clothes. "Say, is there anywhere here I can get changed?" I asked the elders who were now clustered together in a circle mumbling to each other.

"We promise not to look," the anthropologist said. And he said something to the tribespeople to instruct them to turn away. Wiggea noticed what they were doing, and he also turned away from me like a true gentleman, although in all honesty, I wouldn't have minded him looking.

Faso was turning his head between all these people in confusion.

"You heard him," I said. "Turn away and let the lady here get changed."

I could swear his face went red then, although he turned away so quickly, I didn't see it change colour completely. His automaton sat on his shoulder, staring at me.

"And Ratter too. That thing freaks me out."

"Don't be stupid," Faso said. And he looked over his shoulder at me with what looked like an admonishing stare.

"You heard me. Show some respect, for wellies sake."

"Fine," Faso said. And he tapped Ratter on the back three times to turn him off then placed him on the floor facing away from me. "Happy?" The inventor turned away and folded his arms across his chest.

"Quite. Now, no peeking."

And quick as I could I took off my robe, catching sight of blackened welts from my previous tousle with the panther automaton. They had this unnatural colour to them that I wondered if they were also side-effects of the Exalmpora. But I didn't spend too long examining them before I was fully clothed.

"Right, you can look now," I said.

"Thank the wellies," Faso said, and he tapped Ratter three times again, before turning back to me. Ratter quickly ran up his body and onto the inventor's shoulder. It was as if Faso was keeping that thing on alert as a personal bodyguard. Well, admittedly, its presence also made me feel safer. That automaton had saved my life many times in the past and I had a feeling it would do so again on this little adventure.

The men didn't seem to mind so much if anyone was looking while they got changed. But I made sure I turned away to give them some time. Although I was almost tempted to take a quick peek at Wiggea, but I managed to restrain myself.

Soon enough, we were ready to set off again. I wondered, in many ways, if I could try going back down the mountain and also retrieving Velos. We'd already taken down one panther automaton, maybe with Ratter at our side, we could take down the other as well. But Colas' threats seemed genuine and he'd said we were running out of time. Whatever he was up to, we had to stop him.

The hike up was much harder on my legs than it had been the previous day. The volcano got steeper at the top, to such a point we had to scramble up the sharp volcanic rockface in places, and the scratchy surface made it hard to do this without drawing blood.

Still, these three old men seemed remarkably adept at getting up there, without seeming even to break a sweat. Maybe this was part of the male dragonseer blood in them. Although, admittedly, Faso didn't seem to share the same traits and had resumed his usual grumbling ways.

The air got thinner and colder as we got higher. Soon enough, the tribespeople saw me shivering, and one offered me the robe I'd been wearing previously, which I put on gratefully.

Eventually, myself much out of breath through the vigorous climb, we reached the rim of the volcano. Oddly, I couldn't see what lay inside the crater, as it had this massive green bladder stretched across it, almost like a drum. The wind whisked against this making an unsettling beating sound.

We could also see the hut there, the one that we were meant to meet Colas at. It looked just as insignificant as it had when we'd seen it on Velos. It was hard to believe anything other than that old man lived inside the thing.

Just shortly after that, I caught sight of something glinting in the sunlight, with a faint green glow, and a yellow tint. It didn't take long until I realised what it was.

"Dragonheats, not another panther. How many of those things has Colas got?"

It was the biologist who stepped forward to explain. "That one guards the entrance to Colas' base. As long as we don't all approach at once, it won't cause any danger. But here, I'm afraid we must leave you behind."

"What about our weaponry?" I asked. "I don't think it would let us go in fully armed. Why did you give us all this equipment if we'd have to give it back away again?"

The old man sighed. "I did it because I thought you should go inside guns blazing and teach the old man a lesson that you're not to be messed with. The tribespeople won't follow you past this point, though. They're still terrified of those panthers, and rightfully so."

I nodded. "Have any of you ever been in yourself?"

The three old men looked at each other and shook their heads in unison. "We tried to keep away from Colas' operations as much as possible," the biologist said.

I clenched my teeth and looked up at the thing. "But how do we defeat it?"

"How did you defeat the other one?" the linguist replied. "We heard from our friends here that you're quite accomplished at wrestling these beasts."

"Only because the earthquake helped me. And Wiggea... He shot it down, so it tumbled off the cliff."

"Then why not try taking a shot at this one and see what happens?"

"You've got to be kidding," Faso said. "It will eat us for breakfast. No, it's time to devise a plan. I'm not sure if you noticed, but I was observing as you fought the other panther, Pontopa. It has a battery hatch on its rear, just where, well you know what should normally be there."

"I noticed," I said, my arms folded. "Problem is that whenever we get close, it makes sure we stay in front of it."

"Which is exactly why one of us should distract it while another sneaks around the back."

"But as soon as a second person gets anywhere near its rear, it will turn on them and rip them to shreds,"

"I didn't say someone." Faso smirked and looked at the automaton sitting on his shoulder. "I made some modifications to Ratter overnight, and I changed his programming a little bit. He now knows how to disable these things."

Well, it seemed a good idea, I have to admit. Those panthers were probably much less likely to worry about a rat approaching them from behind than a human. "So who's going to fight it?" I said. And I looked at Faso, then Wiggea.

"I'll do it Maam," Wiggea said. Trust him to volunteer first.

"Not a chance," Faso said. "Lieutenant Wiggea, you are by far the best shot here, and we'll need that in case anything goes wrong. Pontopa already has the experience. Plus, I think it's a given that you need me back here to operate the automaton."

I put my hands on my hips. "Faso, who put you in charge all of a sudden?"

"I'm not giving orders. I'm just merely stating what would be good for everyone involved."

"Well, let me make the calls," I said. And I looked over at the panther. It had turned its head in our direction and glared at us with its red crystalline eyes. Probably, it would let us in without harm, and in one way we didn't need to fight it. But to go into the fray unarmed seemed as crazy as trying to bring down a Mammoth automaton with my bare hands. Especially given we didn't know what Colas would throw at us next.

"Fine," I said. "I'll distract the automaton, while Wiggea, you keep an eye on it through your sights and fire on it if you see a clear shot. And Faso, you stand back twiddling your thumbs while you watch Ratter doing his stuff."

"Glad to you're seeing sense, Pontopa," Faso said and gave a cocky grin.

I huffed and turned away from him. "Is Ratter ready? Because the sooner the better."

"Ready as can be," Faso said. "So let's get on with it then."

I swallowed hard and then drew the knives from my garters. I think I had better chance of beating it with blades than I had with my pistol. Bullets would probably just glance of the thing, and at least I could do things like jam a knife in its jaw to stop it tearing me to pieces with its teeth.

"On three," Faso said.

I glared daggers at Faso, lifted the robe off me and dropped it on the floor. I took a swig from my hip flask causing the world to glow in speckled green, and then I charged forwards. As I said, I didn't want Faso to start thinking he was in control all of a sudden.

The panther raised itself on its haunches and it turned its slender body to face me. I glanced over my shoulder to see Wiggea already had his rifle prepared and was watching the panther down the sights. Faso was crouched down on the floor, setting Ratter in place.

Meanwhile, the big cat automaton stalked forward and bared its sharp teeth, pulling back its mechanical mouth in a hauntingly realistic sneer. Its eyes glowed green in my augmented vision, and more green light emanated from its neck, head and legs as its internal mechanism pumped secicao to the essential parts.

"Come and get me, you bastard," I said. "I killed your brother."

And I sprinted forwards and then lunged in with one my knives. I hit the automaton on the head with the haft, a heavy blow that glanced off the creature, causing a pain to lance in my arm, all the way from my elbow to my hand. It growled and then raised its claws at me, and I rolled out of the way. This automaton didn't seem to have any qualms against taking my life.

I broke out of the roll early and pivoted around on my heel to face the beast. It had already entered into a crouch, ready to pounce upon its prey. Out of the corner of my eye, I noticed something small approaching fast, but I didn't turn to look at it. If anything, I didn't want to alert the cat that it had another adversary to deal with. But at the same time, Ratter wouldn't be able to work on a moving target. I had to somehow hold the panther still.

So, I let the mechanical cat leap forward, and this time I didn't try to pivot out of the way. Instead, I watched its front legs, so I could catch them with ease. Meanwhile, I braced myself, ready to take the impact, and I fell back under the panther's weight and let it flatten me to the floor.

Its legs felt cold and I pulled my head out of the way as its jaws snapped in towards me. "*Hurry up, Ratter,*" I thought. Then I watched in horror, as a spire came out of the automaton's mouth like a drill through a wall. From it, a small glowing ball started to grow, with lightning flashing out towards the circumference.

"Dragonheats," I said, and I flattened my head sideways on the ground. On one cheek I felt the hairs on my face getting pulled towards the static, while on the other the rock scraped sharply at my skin. I had no idea what the sphere would do to me. Maybe it would knock me unconscious. Or maybe it would melt my face or tear off my skin.

I turned my head to try and see where Ratter was, but I couldn't see anything behind the glowing blue light, which was getting intensely hot. I heard a bang then, and my mind automatically caused time to constrict. A bullet buried itself into the cheek of the automaton in slow motion, and I saw a green spark at the impact point. But it then squashed into a lead ball and bounced off onto the floor.

Dragonheats, these things were bulletproof. The previous panther had been knocked off the cliff due to the earthquake and the bullet's momentum. But there was no chance of that happening here.

The ball of energy had reached my eyebrows now, resulting in a burning sensation that made me want to open my mouth and scream. I struggled to push the thing off me. Ratter wouldn't get here in time and this whole plan had been a massively stupid idea. I shouldn't have listened to Faso.

And so I closed my eyes and prepared myself to enter the next world.

But all of a sudden, the crackling static sound died down, and I found myself a little lightheaded. The mechanical grasp that the automaton had on my shoulder went limp, and I dared to open my eyes.

The glowing ball had faded. And I saw spots in my eyes where I'd just been gazing into the intense light. I pushed the automaton off me, and I lifted myself up into a sitting position. My head started spinning and I leaned over toward the ground to retch. It took me a while to come to my senses, and then I glanced up to see Ratter sitting there like an obedient puppy. A long oblong battery rested just next to him. Next, I heard Faso's laughter from above me, where he stood pointing down at my face.

"Faso, you buffoon! That thing almost killed me."

"Oh, Pontopa. I had it under control. I'd made the calculations, and everything worked exactly as planned."

"And if you'd have made an error in your calculations, what then?"

Faso scoffed. "I never make mistakes. You should know that by now. It's other people's imbecilic nature that tends to get in my way."

"You know, why don't you get off your high horse and treat people like human beings once in a while."

"I treat people like they've always treated me," Faso said and he gazed off into space a moment.

Wiggea had just come over to join us. He looked down at me. "Are you okay, Maam? I let off a shot, but it didn't do any good."

I nodded. "You did well, Wiggea."

"Thank you," he looked over at the hut. "Well I guess now the coast is clear. We should probably get going before we have any more holdups."

I nodded. Behind me, the tribespeople and tribal chief stood back, gazing at us in awe as if we'd just performed some divine magic by disabling a panther automaton for the second time. The three elders stood with them, their foreheads wrinkled and their expressions calm.

I walked over to them, and I addressed the tribal chief first. "Thank you," I said. "For everything."

"Hoooiiieee," the tribal chief said. And he performed a backflip, almost kicking me in the chin. I took a step backwards.

"It okay," the chief said. "You strong woman. We respect."

He looked at the guides who all murmured their agreements. They then stepped back to make way for the three elders who fanned out in a line, their heads bowed as if in deference. "Dragonseer," the anthropologist said. "You serve Gerhaun and you embody everything that's good about this world. Don't let Finesia or secicao corrupt you."

I raised an eyebrow. "You believe in those things?"

"Of course," the biologist replied. "Just because we don't understand something yet, doesn't mean we can't make guesses based on the knowledge we have."

And I turned to Faso, expecting him to object to this in his usual characteristic way. But this time he simply nodded along. He looked as though he had something to add, so I let him speak.

"I'll think about what you said. You're right, there are things we don't understand, and I know nothing of my ancestry. But you have to understand, I'll need to verify the facts myself."

"When we meet again," the biologist said. "I can give you access to the data. And the sources, of course."

"Very well," Faso said. "I'll look forward to it."

The sun had now started to rise behind the cliff, and so Wiggea motioned us towards the hut. "Maam, we should really get in there."

"Yes, yes," I said. And I bowed again to the three elders, then to the tribal chief. I turned on my heel, walked over to pick up my knives off the floor where I'd dropped them by the panther, dusted off the dirt I'd gained on my clothes during the little tousle, and led the way towards the small hut at the top of the volcano.

18

There was no way you'd even suspect that the hut concealed a hidden base. It looked rickety up close – made of rotten wood, giving it the appearance that it was falling apart. Still, there were no gaps between the wooden beams, and closer inspection revealed them to be sealed by a black resinous substance.

A single wooden door led inside the hut, with a brass padlock over a bolt. Another grey cloud had now passed over us, covering the land in a fog so thick that we couldn't see the tribespeople and academics we'd left standing only several hundred yards away.

The padlock clicked open suprisingly as I touched it without the need for a key. Once again, a voice crackled from the air. Colas' voice came from no determinate location. "Now, now, Dragonseer. That's two of my glorious automatons you've taken down. Have you any idea how expensive those things are? I'm afraid you shall have to pay for them, but don't worry, I have a perfect way for you to cover the costs."

I wasn't sure if Colas would be able to hear me, but I figured now being so close to his base, he'd have something set up to listen to us. "We're coming for you, Colas," I said. "You will hand over the boy, and then you will answer for your crimes."

"Oh, and I've been looking forward to this moment so much. I even considered baking a cake, but then I realised I hadn't asked you about your dietary preferences."

"This is no time for joking."

"Indeed it isn't, Dragonseer Wells, come on in. And, you can leave your weapons on the floor outside."

Hah, there was fat chance of that. I pushed the door. It was heavier than it looked and creaked loudly as it opened to reveal a darkened room. On the wall opposite, a brass door stood closed, with cogs arranged around it in an intricate pattern. On the ceiling, a row of fluorescent lights kept turning on and then sputtering out again. But they remained lit long enough to reveal the way.

"Wait here, Maam," Wiggea said. And he stepped inside first.

"Oh, don't be like that, Lieutenant Wiggea." This time the voice came from a loudspeaker hanging above the brass door at the opposite end of the room. The voice had lost its robotic quality and now sounded like a frail old man. I guessed that Colas had no gullible tribespeople in here that he wanted to convert to his cause, and so he had no reason to masquerade as a god. "I won't open the door until the three of you have entered. You need to go through some vetting."

I turned to Faso. "Do you think we can trust him?"

"Does it look like we have a choice," Faso replied. And he tapped Ratter on the back several times. Apparently, there was a pattern to the way he tapped the automaton that told the mechanical ferret exactly what he wanted it to do.

Faso stepped inside. I shrugged then followed him, crossed my arms, and waited. For some reason, it felt incredibly hot in here, and I noticed a faint pattern of red light playing on the ceiling just above the side walls.

The cogs in front of us whirred into action, startling me, and the door opened just a crack. I half expected to see another panther automaton waiting for us on the other side with a great white ball of bolt-lightning growing out of its mouth. But instead, I saw only darkness.

From either side of us came a high-pitched whirring sound. I felt a tug on my garters, my hip and my back. Before I could even react, the weapons flew off me. The pistol and the knives left their holster and sheaths and stuck to the side walls. Faso's and Wiggea's pistols did the same thing. Meanwhile, my rifle pulled me towards the wall for a moment and I stumbled sideways. Ratter also seemed affected, but instead of being drawn to the wall, he started moving forwards incredibly slowly.

"Magnets," Faso said. "Colas, you…"

The pull stopped, and the weapons dropped into a hole in the floor just below the side walls. I ran to the edge of the room and saw that the gaps dropped down into a pool of lava. So that was where the heat was coming from.

"I guess you can keep your rifles," Colas said through the loudspeaker. "You won't be able to use them anyway. Oh, and Faso, I see that your automaton is non-magnetic. Very clever, I must say."

"I'm not stupid enough to fall for your traps, old man," Faso replied.

"Of course not. But let's see how you fare against everything else I've built in this base. One measly mechanical ferret can't defeat the world's greatest technology."

"Ratter is the world's greatest technology. There's never been an automaton like him."

A chuckle came from the speakers. "Haven't you seen my panthers, Mr Gordoni? I have you know that when you start to combine technology with Finesia's magic, you can create powerful things, indeed. You should try opening your mind sometimes. You'd achieve far much more that way."

The speakers cut out and the door in front opened. A line of floor lights turned on, displaying a short straight corridor leading ahead. At the back of this was a similar brass door. I looked behind me considering turning around, but I doubted we'd find another way in.

I turned to Wiggea and nodded. He stepped inside, scanning around for dangers. None of us dared take the rifles off our back, in case more magnets would rip them out of our hands. Fortunately, though we still had our hip flasks, since they were made of gold with not a trace of magnetic metal inside them.

As soon as we were inside, the doors slid shut. There came a hissing sound from the top of the room, and I looked up to see green gas spouting out of tiny vents at the top.

"Dragonheats," I said. "Another trap."

Faso looked up in alarm and immediately entered a crouch. "Get low," he ordered. Then he placed Ratter down on the ground and tapped ten times on the automaton's back.

Ratter scurried across the room, sniffing around the corners, presumably looking for a weakness. He examined the door and tried to climb up it with his short stubby legs. But every time he managed to get one of its six feet on the walls, he ended up sliding down it.

"Colas must have greased the thing," Faso said.

While Wiggea and I crouched watching him, Faso kept down low and went over to examine a hatch on the far door. But he had to stand up open it, which he managed quite easily. Inside, there was a complex arrangement of wires.

"Can you open it?" I asked. I was beginning to feel a little lightheaded.

"I don't know," Faso said. "Give me a moment. It's a little complicated." His voice had started to quaver and slur a little bit. Standing up there, he'd be getting a higher dosage of the gas than Wiggea and I on the ground.

"Hurry up," I said. "We've not got much time."

"I know... Let me... Wait, this one."

He pulled out a wire and turned to us his eyes wide. Then, he keeled over and collapsed on the floor.

"Ho, ho, ho, Faso Gordoni," the voice came again this time from somewhere above us. "Your genius is no good if you can't keep control of your constitution. Now, Dragonseer, you've got no brilliant mind left who can get you out of this tricky situation. What are you going to do?"

Wiggea was now standing up, banging at the far door. He kicked at it with his might. But the thing didn't budge. And it was no good because soon enough, my eyelids felt heavy and I lost consciousness.

WHEN I WOKE UP, I was lying down on a long sofa, facing towards its woven rattan back, which had depictions of panthers visible in the pattern work. I turned over on to my other side and then sat up to see an old man staring at me.

He wore thick glasses, and he was hunched over a wooden cane. On his head, he sported a tall top hat, and a tweed sports jacket hung loosely off his shoulders. He had deep wrinkles on his face, and he looked as if he should be teetering on the edge of death. But somehow, he also displayed a spry sense of animosity.

"Ah, welcome back to the real world, Dragonseer Wells. I didn't expect you to be the last to wake up of everyone. With your dragonseer blood, I expected you to be the hardiest of the three. Mind you, I can't blame you. You're probably absolutely exhausted after wrestling my panthers."

I heard a muffling sound from my right and turned to see Faso and Wiggea squirming in bounds, a cloth gag over their mouth. They were both tied around the waist to a stake that extended from a single four-wheeled wooden trolley. It was Faso making the absolute racket, of course, Wiggea stayed stock still and stared straight ahead.

Still, the lieutenant's fists were clenched tight by his side and the glare in his eyes displayed his anger. Both men had been tied so well that they couldn't move their heads. They had a rope around their foreheads, a rope around their chin, and another around their necks. On closer inspection, I noticed their gags were also tied into the stake. Wiggea looked at me out of the corner of his eyes. The whites of the eyes were bloodshot and there was a smattering of blood on his left cheek.

In front of Faso, Ratter lay sprawled out on the floor, flattened out by silver pins in each of its six feet. The thing looked like a rodent that had been sliced across the stomach and spread out for display in an anatomy museum, after being covered in gold paint.

"Colas, I presume..." I said. "What have you done to them?"

A growl came from behind Colas and another panther stalked out from behind him. This time, the automaton had a purple sheen to it underneath the green glow coming from its veins. I really didn't understand the purpose of these second colours. Perhaps they told of special abilities. But in all honesty, I didn't feel like asking.

"Oh, stop complaining, woman," Colas said. "All I hear is moan, moan, moan, moan, moan."

I clenched my fists hard. I wanted to wrestle down that panther and then go for this old man's throat. Instinctively, I felt at my hip. But there was no hip flask there I could use to augment. No rifle on my back either. And I already knew what had happened to my daggers and pistol.

We were on some kind of wooden deck, which seemed to sway slightly in mid-air. Around it ran a brass railing, reflecting the glow of what looked like firelight... Or lava... Indeed, this place smelled of rotten eggs and felt hot as hell, and I felt the clamminess clinging to my skin. Red light danced on the rubbery membrane that stretched out over the crater hole high above us. Ropes led up from the deck to the membrane, extending to its very edges at quite shallow angles. Colas stood next to a wooden staircase leading below the deck.

I regarded the panther as I stood up, slowly, and then I walked over to the railing. The automaton lowered itself on its haunches and growled at me. If I took any false steps, the thing would be upon me immediately. Colas watched me approach the edge.

"I hope you're not thinking of jumping, Dragonseer Wells, for its a long way down."

I glared at him and then touched the brass railing. Pain seared into my finger and I retracted my hand immediately. Dragonheats, the thing was hot. Far below, a pit of lava boiled and roared. Higher up a spaghetti network of cart tracks ran across the pit, arranged one over the other in no particular pattern. I couldn't see at what height they started, or how far down they went.

Around the inner walls of the craters, what looked like thousands of automatons on caterpillar tracks were working away at the walls with attached pickaxes. Panther automatons also stalked between them, as if supervising. It appeared that the old man had been mining here. Although for what, I had no idea.

I spun on Colas, who had an annoying rictus stretched out across his face that I wanted to thump off.

"What have you done with Taka, Colas? Untie my friends, give back the boy, then we can end this nonsense."

Colas let out a loud laugh. "Oh dear, oh dear. You're much more like Sukina than I'd expected. So headstrong. Making demands, even when you know that the ball is in my court. Let me tell you instead what we shall do."

I clenched my teeth. "I shall bend to none of your wishes."

To which Colas smiled. "We'll see about that." He turned his head so he could holler down the staircase. "Yarand," he called down. "Where are you when I need you?"

I heard a shuffling from beneath me, and the airship rocked a little. A massive man emerged at the top of the staircase. He had a long ginger beard, a bald head, and muscles so big that he looked like he could carry oil barrels for a living. He wore a white vest, stained green with what looked like secicao oil. "Captain?" he asked.

"Release the trolley."

My jaw dropped. "What the dragonheats are you planning, Colas?"

But the old man didn't reply. Meanwhile, the man he'd called Yarand strolled over to where Faso and Wiggea stood and he proceeded to turn a crank handle that jutted out from the floor between the two men. A square section around the trolley sank slowly beneath the deck, suspended by a rope from the centre.

I yelped out and lurched towards them. The panther automaton sprang forward and blocked my path and bared its teeth at me. A spire sprung out of its open mouth and glowed white for a moment, before dying down.

"Oh, I don't want you jumping on the platform too, Dragonseer," Colas said. "You, Finesia, and I all know already that your destiny lies elsewhere."

But I wasn't interested right now. I just couldn't help myself watching the abject terror in Wiggea's and Faso's eyes and Yarand continuing to turn the crank handle until the three of them vanished below the platform. "What have they ever done to you?" I said to the old man.

Colas shook his head. "Haven't you ever heard of collateral? The lives of your two comrades can make this world a better place. But don't worry, I won't kill them. So long as you do exactly what I say."

Tears flooded to my eyes. No, this couldn't be happening. Wiggea... Faso. I cared about them both in different ways. But I looked down into the glowing eyes of the panther automaton and I didn't fancy my chances wrestling this one after nearly having my neck snapped off by the previous two.

I needed to think of a plan and act fast. "What do you want Colas?" I asked.

Colas glared at me. "Your obedience, for starters." He hobbled forward and opened a thin steel case protruding out of the railing, next to the hole where Faso and Wiggea had previously stood. Inside there was a lever. The old man placed his hand over the handle of this and then turned his head to his lackey. "Now, Yarand. Release the latch." He then turned back to me. "Why not come over for the show, dragonseer?"

I stepped towards him, hoping that I could throw him off the deck. But the panther once again blocked my way.

"No, dear, not that way. I need you where you can't put my life in danger."

The panther nudged me towards the other side of the hole, away from Colas. I sighed and allowed the panther to push me to the opposite railing. Below me, the section that had split off from this platform now lay at a point on the cart tracks. I could see Yarand crouched on the floor, a crowbar in hand, which he'd stuck underneath the trolley that Faso and Wiggea were attached to.

"Hurry up, Yarand," Colas said. "We haven't got all day."

The burly man looked up sharply as if irritated. Then he pushed down hard on the crowbar. With an almighty creak, the trolley detached from Yarand's platform and trundled away. The momentum sent both

Faso and Wiggea downwards. And I watched in horror as the cart sped down the network of tracks towards the magma pit. Soon, it slowed a little and turned onto a trail that ended in a drop down into the abyss.

"No!"

"Oh, don't worry," Colas said. "Their life isn't over yet. You see, this is the fun part."

The trolley sped up for a moment as the track angled even more sharply downwards. It then reached the end of the line, and it fell off the edge. My breath caught in my throat.

But, instead of falling into the pit, the trolley all of a sudden was caught by the rope it hung from. It stopped with a jerk, which consequently sent Faso's and Wiggea's stakes tumbling off the edge of the trolley. Two more ropes caught them, leaving them hanging individually from a wooden beam which in turn hung from the tracks above. There they swung as the lava raged beneath them.

On the bottom of the beam they were suspended from, I noticed something glinting in the light. "Why don't you take a closer look?" Colas said, and he pushed a red button just next to the lever he was holding.

I jumped back as a short pole jumped out of the railing just in front of me and hit me on the bridge of the nose. A small section of this sprung out towards me, scraping against my chin. I now had a telescope in front of me that I could use to watch the action unfold.

I looked through the eyepiece and turned the device towards Faso and Wiggea. The thing that I'd seen glinting in the light was a straight blade, and it looked incredibly sharp. It was attached to a pivot at the bottom of the platform, at the same level as the two ropes from which the men hung.

They had now swung around, and I could see their faces. Wiggea looked straight ahead through squinted and bloodshot eyes, while Faso's were opened much wider and all the colour had drained out of his face.

I swallowed hard. "What do you want of me?" I turned to see that the annoying grin hadn't yet left Colas' face.

"You are the catalyst," he replied. "For the most momentous event in history. But first, let me tell you about my plans for this volcano."

"I'm not interested..." And at my defiance, the panther automaton bared its teeth at me and its red eyes glowed brightly.

"I would advise you not to rub me the wrong way," Colas said. "Because you see this lever here? Observe."

I looked again through the telescope, and I saw the blade turn slightly towards Wiggea.

"If I turn this one way," Colas said. "Your soldier will fall. If I turn it the other way, out goes the life of the brilliant inventor. Now, I'm curious. If you had to save one life, which of the two would you choose?"

"I won't play your stupid games."

"But what if you must? Otherwise, I may decide to make the decision for you."

"You can't..." I narrowed my eyes to slits.

"Why not? Surely the soldier should be the expendable one, should he not? After all, the inventor's technology is the best your base can afford, and honestly other than me, perhaps, there isn't a better scientist in this world. Although I have heard another brilliant young mind has emerged in Tow. But... Yes, I see you have feelings for the soldier. You're letting your emotions cloud your judgment. Oh, Finesia will work on you yet."

I shook my head. "Why does one of them have to die? Just tell me what you want me to do." I must have been almost in tears at this point. Sukina would have behaved differently, I'm sure. She would find some way to flatten Colas to the floor, and she would take his life before the panther could even stop her. I was hopeless in comparison.

I stepped away from the telescope and looked over to see if there was a way of reaching Colas. If I could use the railing to vault over the hole, maybe I could kick him away from the lever and into the abyss. But the panther tracked wherever I looked with watchful eyes. I had no way of augmenting, so I was sure the automaton could reach me much faster than I could get over the hole.

"Such an interesting specimen," Colas said. He cupped his hand over his mouth and called down to his lackey. "Yarand, are you back up yet? I need you here. And bring the Exalmpora solution."

I folded my arms beneath my chest and waited. All the while, my heart racing, trying to find a way out. "Exalmpora?" I asked meekly. And, all of a sudden, I found myself wanting it...

Yarand appeared at the top of the stairs carrying a glass yard filled with a silver liquid. I watched as he brought it forward, my eyes wide. The contents didn't act like an ordinary fluid should. Within its viscosity, patterns swirled creating depictions of an empress roving a barren land. Inside the swirls, I noticed two extra colours weaving their own paths. The first was green, the other red, much as they had been in the Exalmpora mix I'd taken with the tribespeople in the jungle. The green, I'd already guessed was secicao. But the red...

Down in the jungle, they'd taken my blood, the blood of dragon-seer. And it occurred to me, clear as the cleanest lake. That red was Taka's blood. That's why Colas had wanted the boy. Exalmpora was the blood of a dragon queen. And the blood of a dragonseer would make it more potent. And then with secicao added to the mix... No, I still couldn't quite work it out.

"Now, before you drink," Colas said. "I should tell you about the remarkable discovery I've made. For this, my name will go down in history." So maybe I didn't need to work it out. Not if Colas gave me the answer on a plate.

"You see, the collective unconscious is so much more than we've ever thought it to be. We imagined it as the construct of minds, but it actually thrums through everything in existence, from the cells that construct our body to the magma that rages beneath this earth. You, as a dragonseer, and dragon queens and dragonmen like Charth and Alsie have a remarkable ability to transcend this powerful force and connect to the makeup of other beings in seemingly magical ways.

"But when Finesia cut the bark of the tree immortal, she also learned how to harness this power. And so she catalysed the spread of secicao throughout the Southlands. And thus she lived within it forever.

"Here also, within this volcano, is an intense source of the collective unconscious. From the raging lava to the mesmerising cavern walls which write out its very essence. In fact, it connects to the magma at the heart of this earth, which is the most potent source in existence.

"Now, I was the first of my generation to discover Exalmpora, but I wasn't the first ever. But I was the initial discoverer of one thing. You see, you don't need to a dragonseer to create a dragonman or dragonwoman. Any person on this earth can become one. You only need the blood of a dragonseer mixed with Exalmpora and the blood of a dragon queen. Then once that dragonseer becomes a dragonman or dragonwoman, anyone who has drunk of the concoction can also join them in their transformation. So long as they first sacrifice themselves in the blood, or if you like magma, of the earth."

Colas knotted his fingers together and looked down at the volcano in glee. "Now," he continued, "with Finesia's aid, we shall cover the whole of East Cadigan Island in molten rock. And from it shall rise the most powerful race we've ever known."

Pah, I didn't care about this pseudoscience. I just wanted to feel the burn of the Exalmpora as it ran down my throat. I wanted to complete my conversion to dragonwoman. Then, I would hunt down Alsie and take my revenge for what she did to Sukina and Francoiso. And I would become more powerful than Sukina. More powerful than Alsie. The most powerful being on this planet.

"*Ah, now you feel it, my acolyte.*" The voice of a goddess again emerged in my head. "*Soon, you shall share my power and I shall gift you with everything you've ever wanted. You don't need to spend so much time and perseverance to become all-powerful. Acolyte, I can give you power in an instance.*"

"*No,*" I told myself. "*I have to resist.*" But another part of me didn't want to. The lure of the Exalmpora was too great.

"It's a type of magic, really," Colas continued. He paused long moments between paragraphs of speech, as if studying my actions and taking mental notes. "Our blood is the link. A drop of mine, a drop of yours, a drop of Taka's, and a dragon queen's, with additional secicao to help accelerate the process. We'll complete the conversion together. And you shall be our queen."

Colas got down on one knee and bowed his head to the ground. "Acolyte Wells, the catalyst. This is Finesia's will. On this island, we shall start a new race. A new society of immortals."

I stood still gobsmacked. I'd completely forgotten by this point about Wiggea and Faso. Just being here, the Exalmpora had taken control of my mind.

"Acolyte," Finesia said once again in my head. "You can have all this and more. You need to settle for no less."

Yarand now had got really close with his left arm wrapped around the yard and a long glass syringe in his right hand. He moved forward and jabbed the needle into my arm, and I let him take my blood. Then, he emptied the contents of the syringe into the Exalmpora, and I watched in glee as a third stream began to dance around the solution.

Colas' grin stretched even further across his face, and he opened his mouth to display two rows of rickety teeth. "Finesia was right, you are meant to be our leader. Patience is important now. The magic within the solution needs time to work." He took hold of a pocket watch hanging from his hip and held it up to his face. "Ten minutes should do it."

Dragonheats, I wanted to lurch out and take the Exalmpora down in one. But then I doubted that I'd have any chance of wrestling it out of that giant, Yarand's, hands.

"Hooooiiiieee," Colas said in mirth, "as our friends down in the jungle would say. Now, while we wait, let's get this show on the road."

He rushed over to the prow of the ship and pulled a huge lever on the floor there. A billowing roaring sound came from above and hot air swept downwards, adding to the heat rising up from the volcano. I looked up to see the bladder stretched over the crater bulging. It grew towards us and also lost some of its diameter. It wasn't long until I realised the whole thing was some kind of balloon.

Our deck bucked a little, and then it began to lift. We were on a gondola, rising up from the volcano fast into the air.

"What about my friends?" I asked. But still affected by the metallic fumes coming off the Exalmpora in front of me, this was merely a passing comment rather than one connected to any emotion.

"Once you're ready," Colas said. "You'll know what to do about them."

"And Taka? We came for Taka, didn't we?" And these words seemed distant – slurred slightly as if not spoken by my true self.

"All will be revealed in time. When Finesia chooses."

I noticed then for the first time how sparse this deck was. There was no steering wheel, no sophisticated rigging equipment. Nothing, in other words, that required manual control, and I guessed automatons ran the whole thing. If, that was, the airship had been designed to fly anywhere at all.

I looked back down into the shrinking crater below and the ever so distant lava lake within, the automatons scurrying around the inner rockface, the complex network of cart tracks, and Faso and Wiggea now looking like helpless ants. And I felt nothing other than excitement and a deep primal desire to take that yard of Exalmpora down in one.

19

We rose faster than an airship usually would, the balloon buoyed up by the heat currents coming off the volcano. Meanwhile, I watched through the telescope at Wiggea and Faso getting increasingly tinier, as they dangled tied to their wooden stakes, unable to do anything. And I felt strangely passive, with a thirst in my mouth for Exalmpora.

"Is this my dark side?" I thought. *"Do the lives of these men matter?"* No, there were other things far too important. Sukina would have told me that had she been alive. How I had to sometimes sacrifice the lives of only a few for a better world. A stronger race of dragonpeople. Or at least that's how I felt at the time.

"Yes, you understand it now," Finesia's voice came in my head. It was sweet and melodic and had undertones that almost made it sound like a dragonsong.

"Finesia tells me you're ready to meet the boy now," Colas said. He sat on a wooden stool, propped forward upon his cane and looking directly into my eyes. He turned to the burly man who was looking down over the side of the airship, plucking at his teeth with a toothpick while he still nursed the yard of Exalmpora against his chest. "Yarand. Bring Taka up. Her auntie wants to meet him."

I cocked my head. Yes, I was curious to see how Taka had evolved. Because something told me he was part of this too. He'd already been raised in King Cini's palace on a hefty dose of Exalmpora. Given his remarkable ancestry, it seemed that he'd be crucial for Finesia's plan.

Yarand entered a slouch, as if not wanting to follow Colas' orders at all. Still, he stomped below deck, at least half-obediently. The gondola rocked with each step the giant took. Strangely he took the yard of Exalmpora with him as if it wouldn't be safe to put it down anywhere. Presently, a door creaked open from below, and soon enough Yarand emerged from the bottom of the deck, still carrying the Exalmpora.

Taka followed him in tow. The boy had his head bowed low, and he'd lost much of the playfulness that he'd had when I'd last seen him in Fortress Gerhaun. His hair was a little greyer now and his eyes seemed to let out an ethereal white glow.

"Auntie Pontopa," he said in the collective unconscious. His voice was distant in my head, but definitely there, at the same volume as those empty thoughts that pass through the mind before sleeping. *"I thought I detected a source."*

"A source?" I asked. *"Is Charth nearby? Or Alsie?"* And I found myself suddenly on high alert looking around for any sign of my rival.

"It's not them," Taka said. His voice took a flat, lifeless tone. Like one of a child who'd already seen great pain. *"You're the source, Auntie Pontopa. You have the power within."*

"But how?"

"Can't you feel it? You're becoming a dragonwoman, auntie. Like Alsie."

I touched my hand to my face and felt how dry and cracked the skin felt. Something was changing within me, yes. And it was for the better. Surely it was for the better. Now, I didn't have Sukina around to stop me, to hold me back from the Exalmpora and Finesia.

"I'm still within you," Sukina's voice resonated in my head, much as it had in her shrine in Fortress Gerhaun, many days past. *"I'll always be here in the collective unconscious."* But I batted her words away as worthless. She was only a construct of my imagination, anyway. Gerhaun had pretty much told me that.

Colas waved his hands around in the air as if to attract my attention. "Oh, don't tell me you two are doing that telepathy thing. I bring you together and offer you great powers, and you don't think to include me in your conversations. Well, I'll soon be able to hear you there too, once the transformation is complete. Drink the solution, Dragonseer Wells, and all who have tasted the concoction will become just like you – your servants who'll together rule this world."

Taka's gaze was one of nonchalance. He stared straight ahead as he spoke out loud. "Auntie, is this right? It sounds great, but something... I don't know Auntie Pontopa..."

I smiled and rubbed him on the head. "We'll find a way, Taka. Now tell me, has Colas treated you well?" Despite the fact I wanted the Exalmpora and Colas was the man who would deliver it to me, I still didn't entirely trust him. What if he knew a way to take my power and rule the world alone? He knew a lot more about how Exalmpora worked than me, and he might be planning to usurp me as soon as he had the chance.

"The old man is part of the plan," the voice said in my head. *"Dragonseer, you will be the most powerful creature on this planet. This is my will."*

While the voice came in my head, both Taka and Colas stood stock still as if also listening to something. We'd all been exposed to Exalmpora, and so we could all hear Finesia. Although what she'd just said to the other two, I had no idea.

Finesia. How long had she been talking to Taka? Her voice may even had led the boy to Colas. Had this all been part of her grand scheme?

I raised my head to a sudden breeze that came from the sky. "So tell me your plan, Colas. I'm curious. Why is Taka so important? I think he should know his worth as well as I know mine."

I didn't just want to learn the final piece of the puzzle, I wanted Taka to discover it too. Because my destiny and the boy's destiny were intertwined. I knew this for a fact, even though he hadn't been part of my vision.

"Hah," Colas said. "Didn't you listen to what the elders told you? I heard every part, for my automatons have ears throughout this land."

Taka walked to the side of the airship and looked down slightly, his posture straight and his eyes fixated in the distance as if still entranced.

"Taka," Colas continued, "was the first time that the male offspring of dragonseers once again crossed with the true dragonseer bloodline. Which means that he's the only product of the union between dragonseers and normal humans." Colas turned to the burly man. "Yarand, take Taka below because the rest should not be for his ears."

"You better take care of the boy, mind," I said. "For he's my responsibility." And at the back of my mind, I could still hear the slur in my words. I didn't quite have the wits about me then to understand what that responsibility entailed, nor did I remember my promises to Sukina, General Sako and Gerhaun Forsi that I'd protect the boy at all costs.

Yarand nodded unenthusiastically, and he shepherded Taka back below deck, the yard of Exalmpora nestled against his massive chest. While the Taka I knew in Fortress Gerhaun would no doubt have a lot to say about this, this version of him didn't even mumble a complaint.

"So tell me," I said to Colas.

"Have you closed off your mind so the boy can't hear you?"

"Why are you giving me commands, Colas? I thought you said I would be the leader."

"As soon as I know that you've truly turned, you will be. But until it's time to drink the Exalmpora, you better heed my instructions."

So, there was a part of me that could still resist. A part of me that could refuse the Exalmpora and Colas knew it. But I had no idea where in my head that part of me resided.

"Very well. It's done." I said, and I closed off all channels in my mind.

"Good. So, Taka is the only creature in this world who will be able to mate with humans to create more dragonmen and dragonwomen, once he's metamorphosed into his true form, that is. You see, Exalmpora is a special substance that has the power to latch on to your DNA. Unlike no other person ever to have lived, Taka was born with

Finesia inside his head. With my help at Cini's palace, the empress has been moulding him into a powerful being since birth."

I nodded and folded my hands behind my back. "And that's why Alsie wants him so bad."

"Exactly," Colas said. "Alsie is barren. Charth is barren and so was his brother."

"But if Francoiso was barren, what was to be gained from my union with him."

Colas laughed. "Nothing," he said. "King Cini is a fool to have thought so. Now, Taka is Finesia's only hope to propagate our new race of immortals. With one exception."

"What's that?"

"We'll come to that later," Colas said, "once you've completed your transformation. But for now... Yarand!"

"What?" Colas' lackey called up from below deck, sounding ever so frustrated. It seemed he really didn't like to be ordered around.

"The Exalmpora should have mixed by now. Bring it." Colas turned to me. "From what I've seen through my panther's eyes and by my calculations." He reached forward and ran the back of his dry, wrinkly hand across my cheek. "Yes, it's as I expected. Now, you're ready to finally become Finesia's beloved."

The lackey came back up carrying the yard of Exalmpora. It had a different hue to it now. The river of red was much stronger in there and seemed to emanate a faint glow.

"Here you are," Yarand said. "Breakfast is served, I guess. Although why you'd want to drink this stuff." He walked over to stare over the edge of the airship at the jungle below and the great gaping maw of the volcano.

"Prop it down against the deck," Colas said. "I'm sure you've mixed it well by carrying it everywhere by now."

"Fine," Yarand said, and he plunked it down on the floor with such force, I half expected the glass to break.

"Very well Yarand," Colas said. "Your duty has now been served." And he clapped his hands.

From right next to me, the panther automaton stood up quickly. It pushed itself underneath the front of Yarand's legs and lifted its head to push them upwards. Yarand was sent tumbling over the edge, letting out a scream as he fell.

"What—" I began to ask, and the hackles rose on the back of my neck.

"That's the problem with hired hands," Colas said. "They're always wanting more, no matter how much you give them. Automatons are much more reliable, don't you think? Not to mention the primitive beings in this very jungle who once hailed me as a god. You caused them to lose faith in me, but I don't think it matters anymore. So long as you repay me in immortality for all you've done."

"Colas, what are you—" A sense of alarm started to rise in my chest, and I forgot about the Exalmpora for a moment.

"Do not worry, Dragonseer," Finesia said. "This old scientist is merely executing a well thought out plan. This is my will, and you will soon be part of it. Put your fears to rest."

There was something about that lilting melodic voice that calmed my spirits as soon as I heard it. I stared ahead at the horizon, into oblivion, not feeling anything for the death of this huge man, except that it was necessary. A part of my mind thought it was strange for me not to have any empathy whatsoever. But a stronger part of it didn't care one bit.

"Look through the telescope, Dragonseer," Colas said. "I can now reveal to you the rest of the plan."

I nodded and then walked up to the thin device that had hit me in the chin just a moment ago. I put the telescope to my eye, and I scanned the terrain below. Something inside me guided me towards what I was looking for. A panther automaton with a stick of dynamite in its teeth, moving down the inside of the crater. I angled the telescope up and to the right a little and found another one, again with dynamite in its teeth. Then another, then another, then another. How many of these things did Colas have?

"You see," Colas continued as I watched the graceful movements of the beasts, "I've been working on this place for a long, long time. So many tend to see volcanoes as just a lump of rocks, but really, they're just part of a larger phenomenon – a vent that connects to the centre of the planet, helping to circulate its blood. And so I've had my automatons chip away at this island, redirecting lava flows underground, loosening the rock at the edges, getting everything ready to create huge landslides, causing the whole underground reservoirs of molten rock to pop all at once."

"*Remarkable,*" I thought. And here I believed Faso to be the greatest scientist I'd ever known, even though I'd never say that to his face.

"You're going to create an eruption?" I asked.

The old man looked down towards the crater and nodded. "You know, it's no small feat. You can't just drill a hole in the earth and expect it to blow. You need to spend years of planning and know that you've got the variables just right. But fortunately, I've had Finesia in my head all this time to help. She knows how the collective unconscious flows through the earth, and so she knows how to spark this crater off. After its cooled, the earth will then become incredibly acidic, creating perfect conditions for the secicao I've planted here to grow. Soon enough, my dear, East Cadigan Island will be just like the Southlands. With a new race of dragonpeople to rule the land."

I nodded and looked over at the yard of Exalmpora again. I'd been so close to transforming back at King Cini's palace that I knew instinctively that the entire lot would be enough to tip me over the edge. And, because I was salivating for it so much, the lives that would be taken by the erupting volcano meant nothing to me. I simply wanted to be part of Finesia's plan.

"*No!*" I thought. There had to be a part of me that could resist. But even that sole thought drifted casually away.

"So, go on," Colas gestured towards the yard that Yarand had placed on the floor. "If you want to transform, you'll have to drink the whole thing. Much as Francoiso did. Your blood and Taka's blood will catalyse the process."

I smiled, and I picked up the yard of Exalmpora with both hands. It felt warm to the touch. Inside, the two red streams had now mixed together, creating one cloudy whole that glowed as I ran my hands over the glass. I raised the yard to my lips and started to tip it back.

"That's it, my child." Finesia said. *"We'll go far together."*

The liquid touched my lips and the metallic fumes seeped up my nostrils. Colas' eyes were affixed on me, as if in anticipation.

"It tastes good, doesn't it?" The voice of Finesia said in my head. *"Think of the power you'll have. The adulation your minions will give you. A people who'll look up to you as their god. With me, you'll never have to worry about death again."*

But then, and I don't know where it came from, a sudden flash of images came to my head.

My father raising me up in the air when I was six years old, me looking down into his sparkling eyes as he spun me around and around.

My mother untangling the knots from my hair. Her smile, as she told me that I was a special lady who'd go far in life.

Velos, when he was just a child, not much larger than an adult human, rubbing his nose into my hand and then tumbling across the floor.

Then came the darkness. The bareness of my farmhouse in the Five Hamlets burnt to shreds.

Alsie snapping Francoiso's neck as I watched it helpless from the air.

Sukina's wide eyes, when the dart thrown from Alsie's hand buried itself in her neck.

Watching Sukina die in Forsolano's sickbed.

And the promise I'd made to her that I'd look after Taka.

Sukina's body crumbling to ash under the flames at her first funeral, just outside Forsolano's cottage.

And then, finally, I saw myself growing out of the ground as the Tree Immortal. My roots burying into the soil and becoming the spirit of secicao. Me, the destroyer of worlds.

Worse than King Cini.

Worse than Alsie Fioreletta.

Worse than Finesia incarnate.

And all this terrified me so much that the righteous part of my mind surfaced once again.

"No!" I screamed out. And, with a strength that I didn't know I had, I launched the yard of Exalmpora over the deck.

Colas' jaw dropped.

And he reacted fast. He pushed himself forward on his cane, took hold of a hipflask from his hip and poured some liquid down his throat. I lurched forward to strangle him, but the panther rushed in front of the old man to protect him. The automaton tripped me and sent me stumbling towards the back of the airship. I caught myself against the railings and I spun around.

I found myself looking headfirst into the glaring red eyes of the panther. Its spire started to glow white and I backed away from it. It edged me towards the other side of the hole where the telescope was. Meanwhile, Colas lurched towards the lever and grasped it with one hand.

"I thought it might come to this, Pontopa Wells," Clearly, he'd decided to no longer address me as Dragonseer. "So, it's time to make your choice." His voice had raised in volume quite significantly, perhaps one of the side effects of his secicao blend. "It's either the soldier or the inventor. Which one is more important to you? Will you choose the future of science, an important heir to the dragonseer line? Or will you choose the man you care about, the one you have feelings for?"

"I won't—"

"You will choose," Colas cut in, bellowing at a volume that defied his age.

"No," I said, and I spat bile out of my mouth onto the floor. "I won't play your stupid games."

"Why? Are you telling me that you can't make the hard decisions? How will you lead thousands into battle against Alsie, if you can't sacrifice one insignificant life?"

For a moment, my breath caught in my throat. "Why's it so important to you Colas?" I said. "What do the lives of these men mean to you?"

"Absolutely nothing," Colas said. "Except Finesia is testing you. She wants to know that you have the capability to become her right-hand woman. Prove to her your true worth."

One name, that would be all it would take to end this. And part of me wanted to choose Faso, not so much out of malice, but because of how I felt for Wiggea. But that was a selfish reason and I had to push it away. "I said it once, and I'll say it again. I will not play your games."

Colas shook his head and looked genuinely disappointed. "I hoped it wouldn't come to this. But unfortunately, I'll have to choose for you." And before I could react, he pulled down on the lever. In the distance, I saw the blade swing to the right. Then the tiny ant, who I knew to be Wiggea, fell into the gaping maw of the volcano.

"No!" I muttered under my breath. "Colas, you bastard!" How could he? And the rage flared in my chest, like the lava pit Rastano Wiggea had just plummeted into.

I took one step towards Colas, but the panther automaton growled and gnashed its teeth at me, stopping me in my tracks. Colas pressed another button on the control panel next to the lever. The staircase at the back of the airship flipped into a ramp. There came a whirring sound from down below and up rolled an automaton on caterpillar tracks with an elongated oblong body and two stubby arms, carrying another yard full of liquid. This also contained Exalmpora.

"You know," the old man said. "The whole taking your blood thing was for show. I had the tribespeople deliver some up for me when you were down in the jungle and I took another ampule-full when you were unconscious here."

I could feel the pull of the Exalmpora. It was so enticing yet, at the same time, I knew I had to resist it.

Because the man who'd just kissed me the night before was now down there being eaten alive by the maw of the earth. Colas had not even given me a chance to say goodbye. He'd just snuffed out his life like a candle.

Is this what it means to be a servant of Finesia? To have everything that you love taken away...

I looked down at the husk of Ratter splayed out on the airship floor. If only I knew how to fix it. The automaton would do something, and I don't know what, to get me out of this situation.

"Dragonheats, Colas," I said through clenched teeth. "You deserve to die."

Colas shook his head and glared at me with renewed vigour in his eyes. "Now, will you drink the Exalmpora?"

I shook my head. "Whatever you do to me, you cannot force me to bend to Finesia's will."

"Then I shall kill Faso Gordoni as well." Colas clenched his hand on the lever.

"Then do it. I have nothing left…"

Colas shook his head hard. He clearly hadn't expected so much resistance. But maybe he'd just taken the wrong man. If I knew the life of Wiggea was at stake right now, he might have trapped me into fulfilling his wishes.

"Wench," Finesia's voice came in my mind. *"This is my will, and you shall obey my commands."* And I felt my muscles twitching, the empress' will pulling me towards the second yard of Exalmpora.

No, Charth had resisted. It was possible to have strength.

"I will not. You have no dominion over me, Finesia. I have my own will."

Colas raised his cane off the floor and pointed it at the staircase. "I will take the life of Taka Sako," he said.

"You said yourself that Taka is too important. You wouldn't dare kill the boy, and I shall not drink the Exalmpora, whatever you try."

Colas sighed. "Very well, you force me into my last resort."

He reached into his pocket with lightning speed. At the same time, I turned towards the railing and decided I would use it to vault over the hole and wrestle Colas down. I could take his life before the panther got to me. Then, at least Taka could live.

But, still augmented, Colas was too quick. He produced a pistol out of his pocket, and he pulled the trigger. Just as I started to launch myself off my feet, the bullet hit me hard and sent me stumbling backwards. An intense pain flared in my gut, and I looked down to see the hole there. Then came an excruciating throbbing in my back. I clutched my hands to my stomach as blood and acid frothed out of it. Then I looked back up at and the sneer on Colas' dry lips.

"Now, Dragonseer, you have a choice. You can either drink the Exalmpora and claim immortality, or you can lose the very life you hold dear."

"*Do it, my child,*" Finesia said in my head. "*Claim the power as your own. This is what you always wanted and it's much better than dying.*"

But I felt so weak I couldn't do anything. My head was spinning. My whole body was becoming numb. I felt ready to pass out.

But instead, I opened my mouth sung a song of harsh and grating notes. My voice lashed out and created shimmers in the air. I wasn't calling dragons but something else. I was singing with the voice of a goddess. Grey clouds started to take shape around us, and the gondola began to rock.

"What are you doing?" Colas said. "You can't heal yourself through singing."

But I wasn't trying to heal anything.

"*Take the Exalmpora, my darling. Taste the power of what you can do with secicao. Together, we can control storms and volcanoes. We can rule this world.*"

By this point, my senses had reduced to nothing, and I saw only blackness. Then, out of the darkness, I saw two paths, lit ever so faintly by torchlight. Finesia, the mad goddess, stood by one in ancient ceremonial robes of every colour. Her path led to a garden rich in fruit and flowers.

And by the other, Sukina stood in a simple floral dress. She beckoned me down a path that led back to darkness. I lifted myself onto my feet and I followed her down that path.

PART VII

CHARTH

"Free will is the most valuable thing that we possess. And to that, absolutely nothing can compare."

— CHARTH LAMFORD

20

I left Sukina behind at the cave just as my spirit floated out of the body of Pontopa Wells. And thus, I began my journey through the true form of the collective unconscious. An astral state where I could travel wherever I pleased. As long as, that was, Pontopa Wells still lived.

All around me, I no longer saw blackness, but sparkles of many colours, like sunlight gleaming off water. Glowing lines connected these sparkles together, forming an intricate network of brilliant light. They danced across the world proper, shooting out in every direction. And upon those myriad lines I could travel anywhere I pleased.

"You cannot control the power of a God," Finesia said to me. *"It isn't human."*

Because it hadn't been Colas who had called the storm on the Saye Explorer, but Finesia. She knew of magic to manipulate the world's essence. There were ways in the collective unconscious to higher powers, and Finesia had lived here long enough to know of them well.

But now, I wasn't in human form. I was something else. A wisp floating on the collective unconscious. One with the power to control more than merely muscles, songs, and words.

I could float over Colas without him even knowing of my presence. I could hover near to the panther automaton, and it wouldn't even turn its head.

I could dart into the clouds and disturb the currents there to throw out bright sparks of lightning. I could make the wind blow and rock the deck of Colas' airship and scare him to smithereens.

Colas had been right. The collective unconscious wasn't just about controlling minds. It connected the spirit and soul of every single thing on this earth.

"No," Finesia said in my mind. "You are not meant to do this." But even her voice was distant.

Because I had my own will, and I had my own spirit.

"Send me teetering over the abyss of death," I responded in kind, "and I will find myself. This is the will of the collective unconscious. And we will not let you hold dominion."

I darted down over the airship deck, following the slope of the volcano into the jungle canopy beneath. I ghosted through the canopy – I didn't have to worry about physical forms in this ethereal state, and I floated over to Velos. I felt the dragon's anxiety pushing away the collective unconscious, not letting it in.

So I, in my form in the collective unconscious, bid Pontopa Wells to sing a song that Velos could hear in his darkest hour. I watched Velos from my position above his back as he tossed his head to the sky and roared, and the panther that guarded him lifted itself up on its haunches in alarm.

The spire sticking out of the automatons mouth began to glow white, but Velos had renewed courage now. Unlike the panther he could fly, and that was to his advantage.

I floated even closer to Velos on the network of souls, until I was almost touching him. Tendrils of light spread out from my essence and kissed his skin. Then, I reached out further and found my way into his head. Now, I could watch the world through a dragon's eyes.

I didn't take control of Velos' will, as such. But I did enter his mind so at least I could help calm his anxiety. And in this ethereal form, I could understand the language he spoke in his head.

In short, he was terrified. Not just because of this beast of a panther that had shot him out of the sky, but because he felt that it could take his life. And Velos had not yet fulfilled his purpose. He hadn't fathered the egg of a dragon queen, which the whole of Fortress Gerhaun was relying upon him to do. He could die leaving nothing behind, he felt, and this is what he was so scared of. That and the fact his only friend in the whole world would soon lose her own life – he could sense that too. And I understood his pain. But, at the same time, I knew he had to face this fear.

So, as Pontopa's life slowly slipped away from her, I willed her to push through and sing out to the dragon, who once again tossed his head and roared out to the sky. Velos beat his wings, lifted himself up from the ground in one deft movement before the panther even had time to respond. The automaton turned its head to Velos, and the white ball began to grow out of its mouth. And Velos flew up into the sky and, instead of fleeing, he turned himself downwards again and covered the automaton in yellow flame.

It didn't do much, metal being metal, and that ball of blue light continued to glow, tracking Velos as he moved. It stopped him getting close to the panther, for Velos' most natural solution would be to take it up in his claws. But, just at the last minute, Velos turned away from the panther and circled around the branches in the forest. He kept his wings close to his body, while still wide enough that he could keep himself aloft. The dragon found a path through the trees as the panther made chase after him, that ball of blue light tracking every movement Velos made. Both Velos and the automaton gained speed, Velos' aerial acrobatics so impressive that he'd do a swallow proud. And as he did, the panther also sprinted with incredible pace, and one would think Velos wouldn't be able to outfly it.

But this was all part of the plan.

At the last minute, I willed Velos to steer upwards into a loop the loop. He crashed through the canopy above. A few branches slowed his ascent a little, but they didn't otherwise stop the gracefulness of the manoeuvre. The panther had too much momentum now that it couldn't slow down. It kept charging ahead, ducking its path through the trees, while Velos crashed back through the canopy and exited his stunt to approach the automaton from behind. He swept down and took the beast in its claws. Meanwhile, the automaton let out a vast thundering growl and released the ball of energy, which dissipated against a branch.

Velos lifted the automaton up towards the volcano. If he dropped it into the firepit, then it would trouble him no more. But the automaton also had more tricks up its sleeves, and it siphoned into its body the power it might have used to fuel its weapon, electrocuting the dragon. Velos' body shuddered, and his wings wanted to give out.

But here I was within Velos' head calming him. And I wouldn't let him give up. Meanwhile, Pontopa Wells, with pain still throbbing in her stomach where the bullet had pierced her, continued to sing. And Velos perked up his ears and latched on to the song, reminding him to be brave and that he had much more strength in his body than he thought. He closed his eyes to preserve energy and navigated using the scent of sulphur and the increasing heat.

As he climbed, his muscles continued to get increasingly numb, as the automaton increased the intensity of the electricity that pulsed through him.

He opened his eyes just briefly to see where the rim was, but he could see that it was still far above him. His will weakened for a moment, and the strength left his wings. He started to plummet to the floor.

"*No,*" I said in his mind. Not in Towese, but in the language of the collective unconscious that a dragon could understand. "*Velos, you're stronger than this.*"

And he tossed his head in agreement and let off a tremendous growl. His wings flurried into action, and he beat them as hard as he could. He climbed faster than I'd ever seen him climb and soon enough he was over the rim of the volcano. Meanwhile, the panther gnashed and snarled within his claws. Still sending volts outwards through Velos' body.

But Velos didn't need to flap his wings anymore, for he was high enough to soar. The electricity pulsing through his body made him want to contract his wings inwards, which would send both him and the panther into a dive towards the firepit. The panther automaton clearly didn't care if it died or not.

Velos tried to open his claws, but with the current passing through them, they remained fastened around the automaton's chest. *"Come on, Velos, you can do this,"* I reminded him, and the dragon opened his mouth to roar again. He opened his eyes, and, through a dragon's vision, I watched the waves of heat rising through the air, coming from the magma below.

It must have taken an intense amount of internal strength to do so. But, calmed by my presence and Pontopa Wells' song, Velos soon enough managed to open those claws.

The automaton tumbled into the magma pit and vanished beneath a wave of lava, letting out a dark plume of smoke.

"Faso," I said to Velos. *"We need to rescue him."* The dragon turned his head to the edge of the cart tracks where the inventor still dangled, the size of an ant from Velos' current location. He tucked in his wings and dived downwards. It was hot enough for Velos to feel it and so must have been searing for Faso. Dragonheats, there was a good chance the inventor wouldn't have survived the heat.

Velos approached Faso then, the inventor's face ashen and his skin looking blanched. He looked like he was on the verge of giving up. Faso looked up at the dragon approaching and, in his eyes, flashed a glimmer of hope. Yet with his mouth gagged and tied against the stake, he couldn't say anything.

Velos flew around the back of the stake and lashed at the rope with his claws, loosening some of it. He seared the rest of it off with a concentrated flame, taking great care not to also char the inventor. Then, Velos circled round once again and levelled himself in front of Faso.

I promptly left Velos' mind so I could see the rest of the action from a distance. Faso didn't hesitate to jump on Velos's armour, clutching on to the middle seat for dear life. As he did, Velos flapped his wings to get away from the sheer heat of the volcano, renewed energy coming from within. I followed them as I watched Faso clamber onto the back seat, find some footing, harness himself in, reach down and turn the spigot on Velos' flank.

A soft green light began to pulse through the brass tubing in the armour, then it pulsed even more faintly through Velos' veins. I found my way back into Velos' mind, for the next job was critical. We had bombs to disable. Even stopping just one of them might stop the eruption and save the island.

I could see through Velos' eyes now. The secicao the armour injected didn't have the same kind of benefit as Sukina's blend of secicao. Velos didn't see the world in speckled green and registered heat signatures but through a telescopic sight. He could zoom in on his targets with laser precision and watch them from afar. That would explain how Velos had been so accurate in his movements when augmented.

I willed Velos to use to search for the panthers with the dynamite on them. We found one, this time with a turquoise hue underneath its green glowing veins. Velos roared to the sky and dived down towards the panther, folding his wings and arms close to his body so he could spear through the rising waves of heat.

"What are you doing, Velos?" Faso objected from behind him. But Velos wasn't listening and wouldn't have understood Faso's words anyway.

The panther automaton noticed Velos approaching and turned its head upwards towards the dragon. But instead of creating a glowing white ball in its mouth, I could swear its mechanical lips curled upwards into a grin. I noticed the dynamite on its back then, the lit fuse and the spark travelling incredibly fast towards its target.

"Velos, it's going to blow," Faso screamed.

The dragon didn't need to be told twice. He opened his wings and jerked upwards into the air, just as the dynamite exploded. He shot out of the flames, super-fast due to the secicao pulsing through his veins. I could feel both exhilaration and fear in Velos at the same time. Faso screamed out from behind him.

But Pontopa Wells was fading, and I could feel the tug on my spirit back to her. It was time to become human again. Time to leave the collective unconscious to its own devices.

I dashed away from Velos and Faso, praying to the Gods Themselves that Velos and Faso would survive this explosion. Like a shooting star in reverse, I passed through the flames from the explosions that engulfed the volcano. Upwards and upwards, I went towards the airship. Over to Pontopa Wells, her face as white as a ghoul, her body on the edge of death.

Yes, it was time to become me again.

"So, I see you've chosen death," Colas said. "Very well, we shall all find our own path."

But I, Pontopa Wells, couldn't die yet. I stood up on shaky legs, trying not to expend any energy on screaming as the pain lanced through my stomach. The massive automaton on wheels tipped the flask as I approached it. I put my lips to the glass and I opened my mouth. The metallic liquid mixed with the taste of bile and blood in there.

"That's it, girl," Colas said. "I knew you'd come to your senses. I just hope it's not too late." And, through blurry eyes, I saw him rub his hands together.

Meanwhile, the Exalmpora trickled down my throat and for a moment, the pain left my stomach and my muscles became utterly numb. I would die here, and I knew it. This was the end of the road.

"Not now, my darling". Finesia's voice manifested itself in my head, clearer than ever. *"I can't let my most trusted acolyte just pass on. We have a long road to travel together, and this is just the start."*

The numbness left me, and the pain of being shot lanced through my stomach and the small of the back. I lifted my head to the sky to scream. But it wasn't an effeminate scream anymore. This was the roar of another kind of creature. The pain radiated from my stomach to my chest, to my neck and face and limbs and every nerve in my body. I felt my skin tear and stretch and writhe, as someone had just emptied a vat of boiling acid on me. I gnashed out at the sky and roared once again.

Clarity returned to my vision first, and I looked over at Colas, smiling at me. He said nothing, but his eyes were fixated on my arms. The skin there was twisting around black scales that had begun to grow out of it. I put my hand to my face and felt at the roughness, and then I looked at the leathery complexion on the palm of my hand. Blackened patterns swirled beneath the skin, like living tattoos.

"This is it, my darling. Your transformation will soon be complete, and then your minions will join you shortly after."

"Pontopa..." I heard Sukina's voice in my head then. *"You promised me..."*

Then I remembered Taka for a brief moment. What would happen to him now?

"It doesn't matter now, my dear," Finesia's voice came in my head. *"I've been working on the boy for a long time. Taka is part of this, he'll join our new race of immortals, and we'll rule together as one."*

I felt my strength returning and I felt more alive than I'd ever been. This wasn't the first time I'd started to transform like this. It had also happened back in the palace, just after I'd married Francoiso. I'd launched myself on Sukina then and almost strangled the life out of her. I'd wanted the power and she'd wanted to take it away from me.

"Pontopa, stop," Sukina's voice was there in my head. But no, it wasn't Sukina, this was the collective unconscious reaching out to me. But it couldn't quite find purchase inside my mind. Not while I had the spirit of Finesia thrumming through every vein and artery in my body.

"This is how it feels to have power," Finesia's voice was sweet and enticing," *and you can have everything you've ever wanted."*

I looked down at my arms and willed the scales to return to underneath the skin. I didn't need to become a dragon just yet. There'd be time for that later. Other scales had also grown on my body, my face, legs and breasts, and I also sent them back to from where they had grown. I walked over to the brass railing so I could examine my reflection, warped by the curve of the metal.

Yes, I was the same old Pontopa Wells, I still had her natural beauty. But now I had something else, an air of confidence and grace that could rival Alsie. Soon I could fight her. I could use the new powers which I could feel thrumming through me to take the wench down.

"Pontopa, this isn't you," Sukina said in the collective unconscious again. But I didn't want to listen to her anymore. I was sick of people telling me what to do. I'd been free before this had all started. Until Sukina Sako came to the Five Hamlets, told me I was a dragonseer and needed to join Gerhaun Forsi's cause, and thus snatched my free will away.

I took a deep breath and then raised my hands to my temples. Then, I pushed out with the will of my mind and let out a scream in the collective unconscious. That would shut Sukina's voice up for a while.

"Auntie Pontopa, that hurt..." Taka said after a moment.

"Taka," I said. *"I'll be down for you soon."*

"You've become a dragonwoman... Auntie Pontopa, is this right?"

I nodded and smiled. *"It is."* I felt sure of that fact at that moment.

"Auntie, can you hear the lady's voice in your head too? She calls herself an Empress and she scares me. She's always been there, Auntie."

"She's nothing to be scared of, Taka. Empress Finesia is our friend."

"If you say so, Auntie..." He didn't sound entirely convinced.

But I had nothing more to say to Taka, so I cut off the channel.

Then, I turned to Colas. He'd served Finesia now, but he no longer needed to be a part of this. "You deserve to die," I said.

Colas smirked. "Yes, I do. Then, I can join you, as Finesia has planned."

Then there came a roar from the sky and the deck rocked even more, and not from the wind. I heard a scuffle from behind me and turned to see a black dragon landing on the deck.

"Charth?" I said.

"Pontopa," he said. *"You're a dragonwoman. What did my father do to you?"*

"Oh, let's have this conversation out here for the benefit of us all. I'm sure your father would want to hear it too," I said, and I turned to Colas.

Colas was regarding the dragonman with wide eyes. "Charth, why don't you turn to human form so I can see you. I haven't seen you in years."

But Charth seemed even more different than he had done before. There was something wild about him now. Brooding. Intense. Passionate. And, somehow, I liked it.

"My father doesn't even deserve to hear my voice," Charth said in the collective unconscious. And he let out a huge roar to communicate the same to his father. He lifted himself up and shot towards the old man, grabbing him in his claws. He carried Colas off into the sky. The old man seemed to have accepted his fate, and he simply relaxed into the enormous black dragon's grasp. No struggling. No fighting for his life.

"We will all be reborn," he shouted out. "Oh Charth, you can't do anything to stop it now."

But Charth didn't seem to care. The dragonman dropped Colas into the volcano, and the old man fell like a ragdoll. He plopped into the lava just like Wiggea had, letting out a faint plume of smoke.

"Wiggea." I remembered what had happened to him and a tinge of sorrow rose up within me. *"How could I forget him?"*

But that brief feeling of sadness was soon settled by Finesia's soothing voice resonating through my mind.

"Oh, there's no need for sorrow now, my beloved immortal. Together we will rule this world and you shall not have to feel any kind of remorse or anger ever again."

Charth landed back on the deck and then he roared out to me. A plume of black dust rose around him. Soon, this subsided, and Charth appeared fully clothed in his human form. "Pontopa," he said and approached me fast. He took me by the collar of my jerkin. "Snap out of it."

"No," I said. "This is Finesia's will."

Charth didn't hesitate to react. He pulled back his hand and then slapped me across the face, stinging at the cheek. At first, I felt angry and wanted to turn to a dragon and tear out his throat.

But then my connection to the goddess snapped, and I remembered myself. I shook my head, and though Finesia was screaming out at me, I pushed her to the back of my mind.

Charth examined his hand as if the slap had hurt him more than it had hurt me. "I'm sorry. I really don't like to hit women. But Gerhaun had to do the same for me at one point."

I looked into Charth's grey, beautiful eyes then. Despite the plainness of his attire, he was handsome, just like his brother. And one of the most heroic men I'd ever known.

And yet he was livelier now. His voice less dour, as if he was on the edge of a transformation. But regardless, he'd saved me from stepping over the edge. He'd reminded me of what we were fighting.

"No," Finesia's voice came in my head. "You can't leave me. You've completed the transformation and I'll always be there."

"Not if I learn to ignore you."

"You can't just keep me out of your head."

"Yes, but I can choose not to listen." And I remembered Sukina's lessons about distancing my thoughts. How I'd managed to forget about the spider automaton crawling over me in the darkened room, how I'd transcended from fear to absolute calm.

"You won't win," Finesia said inside my head. "And Charth is already close to losing himself to me... You're one of the same you and him. You will bow to the will of Finesia eventually."

"We'll find a way to defeat you," I said. "Inside my mind or not, you are still my enemy."

And even though Finesia nattered at the back of my mind, I pushed her away and closed the door... at least for a while.

I took a deep breath.

"Charth... You're back?" I heard Taka say in the collective unconscious. "Are you here to stay?"

A sliver of regret graced the dragonman's face. "I can't stay forever, I'm afraid, Taka."

"Has the horrible old man gone? He said nasty things about me and he took my blood and then he made me drink this disgusting liquid. He said that I'd live forever, but I'm not sure I want to live forever."

I shook my head and looked down where the old man had plopped into the lava pit. He seemed to think that he'd return as a new creature, but I saw no sign of it. Hopefully, he was dead and gone for good. "*He won't bother us again... And Taka, I'm so sorry I forgot your birthday. I didn't intend to be mean to you.*"

"*It's okay...*" Taka said. "*But, Auntie Pontopa, that voice in my head, it won't go away.*"

I shook my head. "*Where are you?*"

"*I don't know, Auntie. The big man put me in a room down here and locked the door. He said it was a punishment for talking too much. I tried screaming, but I don't think anyone can hear me. I don't feel right Auntie, and I don't want to listen to the voice.*"

"*I'm coming down to get you, Taka,*" I said. And I looked around for the panther automaton, half expecting it to leap at me as soon as I took one step. But instead, it stayed in the corner by the deck, seemingly unwilling to move. It looked at me like a housecat would, squinted, and then turned its head away from me and yawned. Without Colas here, it seemed to have lost its fighting spirit, or maybe it had found its own type of free will.

"*Pontopa, there's something you should know,*" Charth said. "*I wanted to come straight here to finally get my revenge on my father, but I saw boats and airships on the horizon, so I went to investigate. Alsie has this place surrounded. The only escape is inland through Cadigan.*"

"*Then we'll go that way.*"

"*She gave me a message as well, and she told me she wouldn't tear me to pieces if you delivered it. Cini has a fleet stationed at Oahastin, just south of where your fleet is, cutting off any retreat. He was lying in wait all this time and knew you were coming.*"

"*Dragonheats,*" I said. "*We haven't got much time.*" I kind of hoped that I could turn to a dragonwoman and use my powers to turn the battle in our favour.

"*That's it, my acolyte. Use the powers I've granted you and bring yourself ever closer to your destiny.*" Something about those words caused me to latch on to them, despite having successfully kept Finesia's recent babble away. Much as I wanted to, I knew that if I turned into a dragon, I'd shift even further to Finesia's side. That's what she wanted me to do.

Was this why Gerhaun refused to let Charth back in? Because he'd turned into a dragon so much and called on Finesia's other powers. When I thought about it, it made a lot of sense.

"I won't do your bidding," I said to Finesia, and I shut her voice into a corner of my mind.

Charth was staring into my eyes as if he could look through them and see what was going on inside my head. "You must push her away," he said out loud this time. "I can't hold on much longer, but I think you're stronger Dragonseer Wells. Hold on for as long as you can."

"If only there were a way to reverse the process. If only you could become human again."

Charth looked out into the distance, as the volcano roared beneath us. "I've wished the same many times." And below us, came a massive crunching sound. I looked down to see dust rising from the volcano and earth sliding down the inner surface into the pit. The volcano hadn't erupted yet, but the gondola rocked even more as the rising heat created increasing waves of turbulence.

"We should go down and get Taka," I said, and I hurried towards the staircase, looking over my shoulder to ensure the panther automaton stayed in place. It no longer had that green light flowing through it now, nor did it have that purple sheen to it. In fact, its skin was black, like a normal panther. It had now fulfilled its purpose, I guessed and needed power no more.

I waltzed down the staircase and found myself in a corridor with several cabins on either side. Red light filled the space from the lava pit below. Most of the doors I passed were open, some with bunk beds in them and various mechanical bits and bobs such as radio equipment and piles of automaton parts. But one indeed was closed. It didn't even have a lock, just a metal bar over a latch. I lifted this and opened the door to see Taka over the other side, his eyes wide and reddened, as if he'd been crying. As soon as he saw me, he ran into my arms.

"Oh, Auntie Pontopa. You came. I was so scared. I thought I'd never see daylight again after Yarand shut me up for the last time."

I shook my head. "Do you still hear the voice inside your head?"

"Finesia's gone for now. She went away for a while when I left Cini's palace as well. But she comes back sometimes, Auntie. And she scares me."

I nodded. "She scares me too, dear. But we have to learn to ignore her."

"I'm trying Auntie. And I'm sorry I listened to her. I shouldn't have left Fortress Gerhaun. Finesia told me it would make me happy again, but she was wrong." He broke off the hug and took hold of my hand.

I went upstairs to see Velos hovering in the air just to the side of the deck. Faso sat on the backseat. The inventor had a pistol pointed at Charth. He must have had a spare one stashed in the backseat, maybe in a secret compartment that he hadn't told me about.

"Charth," he said. "I warn you, take one step closer, and I will shoot."

Charth had his hands up in the air. But I doubted Faso was a sure enough shot to take the dragonman down.

"Faso," I said. "Put the gun down. Charth means us no harm. And say hello to your son here."

Faso looked over at us. I snorted. He had been so focused on taking down his long-time rival that he hadn't even noticed us come up on deck. "Taka... A belated happy birthday, I guess."

"Thank you, Papo. Can we play dragons and automatons when we get home?"

"We certainly can. But, Pontopa, if I'm not going to shoot the drag-onman, then we need to get out of here. Did you see the landslide?"

I nodded. "It made a bit of a racket."

"Just a bit... Look, Colas set off some bombs in the volcano and I can tell from the way it's behaving, it's going to blow."

"But we're in the air," I said. "And this airship isn't showing any sign of sinking. Alsie has us surrounded and we need to take some time to work out our escape route. Why don't you come on deck?"

"No, you don't understand. If we get caught within the ash cloud, we're doomed. Not only will it tear at your lungs and cause permanent damage and dragonheats knows what else to Taka. Ash clouds fresh out of a volcano contains millions of shards of microscopic glass, not to mention massive amounts of superheated pumice. It will tear us and the airship balloon to pieces."

"Dragonheats," I said. "Then we need to fly west to Cadigan mainland. Alsie is waiting in ambush to the east."

"The wind's going west. We'll be drowned by the ash. Quick, Pontopa, before it's too late."

I heard a rumble from below and I rushed to the edge of the deck indeed to see the lava boiling and seeping up out of the crater below. Some incredibly dark smoke puffed out of the top. "Dragonheats," I said. And not just because I could see the black cloud starting to form. I also felt another presence shimmering in the collective unconscious.

The storm clouds had now shifted away from the volcano. They created a wall of grey on the eastern horizon, and from it, a black dragon emerged – a tiny speck on the horizon, but I knew who it was...

Alsie Fioreletta had come to greet me once again.

21

"Alsie," I said through clenched teeth as I stood on the airship deck, with Velos hovering beside it, and watched her approach. Behind her, a line of airships pushed out of the clouds, accompanied by swarms of green Hummingbird automatons. I didn't stand a chance... Maybe if I transformed into the form Finesia wanted me to, then I could fight Alsie. I could claim my prize and destroy her in aerial combat. I could avenge Sukina and punish the dragonwoman for every crime she'd committed to this age.

"Join me, Dragonseer," Finesia said. *"It's time to claim your destiny."*

No. I pushed the empress' voice away again. I wasn't going to taint my soul by tapping into these new powers. I wasn't going to risk losing myself in the darkness.

"Taka," I shouted. "Get on Velos, now."

Faso looked at me, astonished. "What are you planning, Pontopa? We need to surrender. There's nowhere we can run."

I looked down at the enveloping ash cloud rising from the crater. The volcano had begun to erupt, and it would spew out more of this stuff I was sure.

"We need to go through that," I said. And I followed Taka in a sprint towards Velos. The boy jumped at the seat with unbecoming agility and Faso's face twisted in alarm as he reached out to catch Taka. But he didn't have to because Taka grasped a ridge between two of Velos' armour plates like a monkey and then scrambled up to his place.

I launched myself forward as well, this time catching myself by hugging the seat that Taka had already strapped himself into. I clambered towards the front of the dragon, harnessed myself in and took hold of the spare gasmask I'd left in the compartment beneath. I had a feeling that the bit-and-plug wouldn't be enough, particularly if we had to fly through volcanic ash.

"Pontopa, we need to turn away from the ash," Faso said. "If you think shrapnel flak is bad, you haven't seen anything like this."

I didn't listen to him. Instead, I pushed down on Velos' steering fin to send him downwards through the cloud that had just started to spew up out of the volcano like a mushroom, with streaks of red lightning flaring within. Velos let off a growl – he didn't want to go through either. But I felt that we had a much better chance of surviving this than Alsie Fioreletta. Up above us, Charth had already launched himself into the sky and I saw the gigantic airship balloon straining as if it wanted to burst under the pressure of the rising heat. Soon, it would get ripped to shreds by the rising ash and pumice, and the gondola would come plummeting down.

Charth wheeled around once in the air, and then he sped towards Alsie and her forces. *"Find a way inland,"* he said. *"Towards Cadigan. I'll hold them off as long as I could."*

But really, Alsie wasn't going to send Cini's airships through the ash. That would be the stupidest thing in the world.

I checked behind me to ensure that Taka and Faso had their masks on, and then I entered Velos into a stall. I planned to pass so quickly through the ash cloud that it wouldn't be able to affect us.

And so, the wind tore against my face, tugged my hair back, almost out of its roots, and I screamed out in ecstasy. Yes, this was the joy of flying. Meanwhile, bits and pieces in the cloud scratched at my face, yet it couldn't tear the now hardened skin. I turned around to see Faso's eyes closed and his face scrunched up behind his gas mask as if expecting the worst. Taka, though, seemed to be rather enjoying himself and, like me, he was screaming in glee. He'd make a fine dragonseer yet.

We soon reached the bottom of the cloud and I levelled Velos out by pulling back on his steering fin to slow him a little. He spread out his wings and angled them backwards to help break the stall. Beneath us, streams of lava flowed down the mountain, and into the jungle below. The leaves had already browned and were curling up in the heat. I imagined the tribesmen on the ground would be huddling into corners away from the molten rock that would soon wash over them. Whole tribes destroyed by one madman and the will of a goddess.

And what had even happened to the elders?

A tinge of sorrow washed over me as I thought about their fate. They were meant to tell me more about my heritage, as well as Faso's and Taka's. Another opportunity lost to the void.

But I didn't have time to think about this now. Taka's future and the future of the dragons remained at stake. I decided not to take Velos down into the jungle but along the side of the volcano. Down there, it was probably a raging inferno, the heat of the lava trapped between the trees. So, I kept Velos as high as we could without entering the growing ceiling of black cloud and flashing red lightning above us. The whole land had now plummeted into such intense shadow that if it weren't for the glow of the lava, it would be difficult to see anything at all. Meanwhile, the volcano roared behind, and it took some skilful flying to keep Velos on course.

Suddenly, a landslide stopped us in our tracks – a layer of pyroclastic flow tumbling down the mountain.

"Pontopa not that way," Faso shouted out. "We'll be eaten alive."

But I didn't need to be told that this raging eddy of grey dust was dangerous. I pushed hard on Velos' steering fin and veered him down the slope away from the rim of the volcano. We missed the expanding pyroclastic flow by inches, and we had no choice but to enter the jungle below.

"Hold on to your seatbelts," I called. It was going to be a rough ride.

Velos folded in his wings as much as possible, and we ducked and pushed beneath the canopy. I'd hoped that we could get away from the pyroclastic flow, but it raced alongside us, covering the jungle in grey soot that might later preserve its remains for centuries.

Velos twisted and turned his body as we spun through the trees and I put my entire concentration in stopping us crashing into a bole. I sang a song to keep Velos steady and at the same time the armour pulsed green beneath my feet. Velos scratched his wings against the trees a few times, and I felt his pain lancing through my own arms. But the feeling wasn't as intense as it had been in the past. Was I losing my connection to him? Would the transformation lead me further and further away?

As we sped through the jungle, the earth opened up beneath us. A great chasm tore the ground asunder and columns of lava shot up into the air through fresh thermal vents. I had to steer Velos away from one raging fountain, and I felt the heat from it pluck at my skin.

I don't know how many smouldering trees we passed as their leaves wilted under the rising heat. I wanted to follow Charth's instructions and lead us inland. But the pyroclastic flow ran right the way to the coast then buried itself under the sea. There was no way through.

So, our only option was to head back to the ocean where the airships lay in wait. As we left the land behind, we could see the balloons spanning the horizon, as far as the eye could see. Alsie flew close to them, Charth hovering nearby. I felt a sudden dread rise up in my chest as soon as I saw them. Why weren't they in combat? Something didn't make sense.

"What do you want?" I said to Alsie in the collective unconscious. "You promised that you'd leave us alone."

"That, I did," Alsie said. "While you went in and successfully rescued the boy and, with Colas' aid, helped us execute Finesia's plan."

I kept the channel closed to Taka so he couldn't hear any of this, but who knows what Alsie was also saying to Taka in his own mind. Whatever it was, Taka didn't seem to want to listen, and he backed up in his seat as if wanting to get as far away from her as possible.

"Oh," Alsie continued. "*And I can see you finally completed your trans-formation. Which means that we're edging closer to our final battle, Dragon-seer, or should I call you Acolyte?*"

"No," I said. "*I shall not bend to Finesia's will.*"

"*We'll see about that,*" Alsie said, and there came an ear-splitting scream in the collective unconscious. Velos bucked underneath the pain and I clutched my hands to my ears, as did Taka.

Now, I had access to the innate ability, I was tempted to return the scream in kind, but that would be using Finesia's gifts and opening up a place for her.

It was then that it dawned on me. Charth had used the same scream to protect us in the secicao jungle from the pirate leader and his troop of automatons. That would have pushed him even further towards Finesia. How long would he last before he lost his mind completely? He already thought he was on the edge. Somehow, I doubted I could trust him anymore.

"*All your tricks in the world cannot hurt me, Alsie Fioreletta,*" I said.

"*Ah, but you have no choice but to surrender. You have no dragons around you to protect you, you're surrounded by a fleet of the king's best forces.*"

"*Then you'll have to kill me too.*"

"*Oh, you shan't die yet, Dragonseer. Finesia has many plans for you, and you don't even appreciate the abilities you've gained. Why don't you show us all what you're capable of and use Finesia's abilities to take down this fleet?*"

"*I'll do it without her,*" I said. I could at least try and escape without having to battle Alsie head-on. "*Charth, are you on my side or Alsie's?*"

"*Yours, of course,*" Charth said. But there seemed a lack of commitment in those words. As if Charth hadn't quite connected to the question.

Whatever, I didn't have time to worry about that now. I pulled back on Velos' steering fin and sang a dragonsong. In response, Velos let out a huge roar. He also didn't want to go down without a fight. And we flew towards the airships, as the Hummingbirds pushed forward to intercept us head-on.

"Pontopa, this is madness," Faso complained from behind me. He had his arms folded across his chest. "But no matter what I say, I'll never stop you. Why I always choose to travel with such an insane woman, I don't know."

I shook my head. "It's your choice, Faso."

"*Alsie Fioreletta,*" I then said in the collective unconscious. "*We will not go down without a fight.*"

"*Then you have consigned yourself to your own fate,*" Alsie said. She let out a huge roar.

"*Acolyte, it's time to claim your power,*" Finesia's voice once again came in my head. "*Change to your true form and claim the prize you deserve.*"

I tightened my grip around Velos' steering fin as I tracked the swarm of Hummingbirds approaching. A cloud of green enveloped them, meaning they were secicao-powered. But this time, Faso didn't complain that they'd stolen his technology. Probably because he now knew that what Colas had built was much more superior.

"*Auntie, I can use my scream again to take them down,*" Taka said. He'd done that two years ago when we'd encountered them at the Southern Barrier, just after escaping Cini's palace.

"*No,*" I said. "*Don't listen to what Finesia wants you to do, Taka, we'll find a way through without her.*"

And the Hummingbirds got so close to us that they almost engulfed us. The Gatling guns activated on Velos' armour and shot a few out of the sky, but the rest of them were fast enough to dodge the bullets.

"*Very well, I can see you're not ready yet,*" Alsie said. "*Such a waste of resources. Well, Charth, it's time to finally become a servant of Finesia.*"

"*Yes,*" he replied in an incredibly flat and distant tone.

He turned around towards the Hummingbirds, and out pitched that horrible screeching sound again in the collective unconscious, this time sending my head spinning so hard I wanted to throw up. One time had been bad enough, but twice in one row was enough to turn the brain to mush.

The Hummingbirds had only travelled several hundred metres

before they sputtered to inaction and dropped one by one into the water like a flock of seagulls that had just inhaled a noxious gas.

"*Charth*," I said in the collective unconscious, but I just spoke to emptiness. This time, the scream had disrupted my ability to communicate there and it would be a while until it returned.

"*Even when you can't reach the collective unconscious, you can still talk to me*," Finesia said. "*Transform, and I'll give you the power you want.*"

And, as I looked at the wall of airships edging even closer to us, I felt for a moment that we wouldn't have a choice. Then, I remembered how we'd escaped Cini's forces last time we'd encountered them in the ocean. A wall of shrapnel-flak in the air that would tear us apart if we flew through had blocked our escape. So instead, we dived beneath a battleship's hull and only barely made it out the other side. Hence, I appraised the churning sea and the vast waves that it sent up beneath us.

"Faso," I called back. "How much secicao do we have left in the armour."

"We've almost used it all up for dragonheats sake. We left the tap open when Velos was sitting there in the jungle by itself. But Pontopa, if you're thinking of going under, think again. The currents down there will swallow us whole."

Okay, so maybe going under was a bad idea.

There came another roar from the distance as we hovered over the ocean. Alsie Fioreletta sped towards Charth and I was half expecting him to raise his claws and try to take her down. But, instead of attacking the dragonman, the dragonwoman flew in a wide circle around him. "*Acolyte Charth*," she said. "*Embrace your destiny.*"

Charth lifted his head to the sky and roared, meanwhile wrestling with himself in mid-air as if exerting his very last ounce of will to resist something. But it was futile. All of a sudden, his body went stiff, and he curled up in a ball and began to fall towards the ocean, tumbling in the sky.

"*Goodbye, noble Charth*," Alsie said.

I watched in horror, expecting Charth to hit the sea and be swallowed up by the waves. But before he was even close, he spread out his wings and hovered there, as if pinned in place at the shoulders. Out of his chest emanated a ball of green light, streaks of white lightning flashing out to the circumference, much like the glowing sphere that Colas' panther had used to knock Velos out of the sky.

"*And hello, servant of Finesia,*" Alsie continued. "*You see, Dragonseer Wells, Charth was right. For only so long will you be able to resist Finesia's will. And Charth, my darling, did you really think that you could remain a traitor to Finesia's cause forever?*"

Charth tossed and turned in the invisible harness that had pinned him into place in the air. He gnashed and roared at the space around him but, as he did, the glowing ball grew, spreading a faint green oily light through the veins of his body.

I'd never seen anything like it. I mean, there were dragonsongs, which kind of made sense in a way and had their own rules to them. And the collective unconscious also had its own innate rules, and everything about it seemed to intuitively fit together, even if it hadn't yet been explained by science. But I had absolutely no idea where this ball was sucking its energy from. Indeed, I could only describe it as magic.

And as the ball of energy grew, Charth seemed to resist less and less, until eventually he just floated in the air, stock still.

"*What are you doing to him, Alsie?*" I said. "*Let him go...*"

"*This isn't my doing,*" Alsie replied, "*but Finesia's. Now, if you please, I'm quite enjoying the show. You can either comply or try to fly away and have your dragon shocked to death by Hummingbirds. The man you once knew as Charth is dead to you now.*"

"*He died long ago when he lost Sukina,*" I thought. But I didn't share that sentiment with Alsie.

"*Nothing to say?*" Alsie asked. "*Well, I never. Why don't you turn dragon yourself and fight Charth Lamford? He'd be a worthy adversary for you, I'm sure.*"

Dragonheats, Alsie had only sent that line of Hummingbirds forwards so Charth would use his ability. She knew that he was about to turn, and he'd pushed his limits far too far.

"No," I screamed out loud. "I won't sacrifice myself."

"We'll see about that," Alsie said.

She tossed her head to the sky and roared. In response, Charth, whom the green glow had now left behind, hovered in the air for a moment. He turned his head towards us and shot forwards.

"Charth," I said. *"What are you doing? Remember yourself…"*

But while his voice had sounded flat and dour before, now it was virtually monotone, a perfect representation of obsequiousness. *"This is Finesia's will,"* he said. And I knew right then that he'd also been lost to the void.

"You have no choice. My darling acolyte," Finesia said in my head. *"You must fight him. You and Charth were meant to be rivals."*

"No", I screamed out loud. And as Charth approached, Velos's Gatling cannons bucked into life. I pushed down hard on Velos' steering fin and we plummeted again towards the water. But no matter how much the cannons shot at Charth, they couldn't affect him. He was immortal after all. Unless, that was, they just happened to hit the weak spot at the throat.

"What's he doing?" Faso shouted out, craning his neck up at Charth.

"He's attacking us," I said.

"I thought he was on our side?"

I clenched my teeth. "Not now," I said, and I looked down once again at the ocean.

"You're not going under, are you?"

"Dragonheats, no. We'll hold off as long as we can." I decided not to tell him that I could probably get out of this by turning into a dragon myself.

I watched Charth come in for another pass and the voice of Finesia nagged in my head and told me that I had to fight him. But regardless, I wasn't going to draw on her powers. She wouldn't have dominion over me.

"I see you're not going to listen, wench." Alsie said in the collective unconscious, sounding very slightly irritated. *"Charth, return."*

And the dragonman obediently returned to Alsie's side.

"You see, Acolyte," Alsie continued. *"Finesia has decided to punish him*

for his long period of disobedience and relinquish control of his soul to me for a while. This is what will happen to you as well if you resist your destiny for too long."

I gritted my teeth. *"I will not succumb to the voice of Finesia. And I won't let Taka do so either."*

I heard a chuckle from Alsie in the collective conscious then, almost as if it came from the bottom of her being. *"Oh, we'll see about that soon enough."*

"Good shall prevail. Secicao shall not be allowed to rule this earth."

"That's what you think. But Colas has already prepared the ground for the secicao that the tribesmen have planted across the island." Alsie gestured towards East Cadigan Island and the ever-blooming clouds that enshrouded it. *"The sulphur of the earth will acidify the soil, creating the perfect conditions for secicao to grow. Colas has been working this island for Finesia for years and his efforts shall soon pay off in spades. Well, there's absolutely no point risking a dragonman when I have an entire air fleet at my disposal. Let's see how you survive the next wave."*

Alsie and Charth darted towards the line of airships and then she levelled so that she was flying perpendicularly to them. Hatches opened up on the side of the airships, and a colossal swarm of green secicao-powered Hummingbirds formed out of them. Alsie Fioreletta let out a huge roar and, as one, the Hummingbirds shot towards us.

Those things were so fast and light that Velos wouldn't be able to shake them off using aerobatics. And as they approached closer, I noticed something else about them. They had a faint red glow underneath the greenness. Just like Colas' panther automatons.

Flaming wellies. Colas hadn't just been working for Alsie, but he'd developed new technology for Cini. This had all been a ruse.

"Faso, fire up the guns," and I looked over my shoulder to see him turning the tap on the armour, while Ratter hung off the other side of Velos fiddling with a control panel on the other flank. Another modification, no doubt he'd failed to tell me about.

"There's very little secicao left," Faso complained. "So I hope you have a decent plan this time."

The armour was now hot under my feet, and I felt the Gatling cannons buck into overdrive. But, no matter how much they shot at the approaching automatons, the bullets never seemed able to hit their target.

"Dragonheats," Faso said. "What is this technology?"

"I don't know. It looks the same stuff that Colas used in the panthers."

"Impossible. How could Cini possibly have stolen their old man's inventions?"

But I didn't have time to explain my conspiracy theory as the Hummingbirds had now closed in. It was as if they wanted to toy with us. They'd spiral around us in a swarm, hovering nearby no matter where Velos flew. The Gatling cannons kept shooting out bullets, but none of them ever seemed to connect. Every so often, one Hummingbird would come close to us and send a jolt into Velos' unarmoured belly, causing him to enter a short stall.

"Turn the guns off," I shouted back at Faso, "You're just wasting ammo."

"I can't. Not without stopping the flow of secicao." A design flaw, I was sure.

"Auntie Pontopa," Taka shouted. "Finesia tells me I can use the scream."

"And you can too, Acolyte," her voice came in my head. "Claim your power and show us all what you can do."

I shook my head. "Don't listen to her," I said to Taka in the collective unconscious, pushing Finesia's voice away. "Close her out of your mind."

"Do we have a choice?" Taka asked.

"We'll think of something. But we have to do it the right way."

I tried entering Velos into a loop the loop, in an attempt to confuse the Hummingbirds. Faso screamed out as I did so – he hated these aerobatics. And still, the swarm stuck like bees after stolen honey. We just couldn't shake them.

"What are you going to do, Acolyte?" Alsie asked. "If you don't call for Finesia's help, we'll bring you down. It would be a shame to lose your dragon and the scientist so early, don't you think?"

"But you'll also kill the boy. I thought you wanted him alive."

"Oh, I won't let that happen," Alsie said. *"Well, I can see that I'm not going to convince you this way, it's time to take you down."*

She let out another roar, and the Hummingbirds swirling around us began to narrow their radius. The Gatling guns seemed to be running out of ammo now. And the swarm was moving so close and fast that I couldn't make out what was happening beyond them.

Sparks lashed out at us, stinging Velos and I felt his muscles weaken. I started to sing him a dragonsong to help him keep his strength, in the hope that a little dragonseer magic would at least get us through this. And he held his courage each time a stab of pain speared through his chest or his wings. But I knew this wouldn't last forever.

Then, I remembered all of a sudden. Sandao's fleet should be nearby with two hundred and fifty dragons at my disposal. Surely they could tip the tides of battle. But I listened out for them in the collective unconscious, and I could detect no sign of them. Instead, I felt only emptiness, as if hundreds of souls had simply been snuffed out. King Cini's fleet from Oahastin had already taken their lives perhaps. Or maybe my transformation had killed my connection to them. I tried singing out a dragonsong to call them into battle. But I got no reply from them.

But instead, I got a response from something else. A presence that felt more like electrical static pulling my soul towards it. It came from the direction of the volcano. I reached out to it. And as I did, I pulled it forward as magnets pull metal.

"Hoooooiiiieeee," came the first voice on the collective unconscious. *"Dragonseer finally found a way."* This was the voice of the tribesman manifesting itself in my mind. How was it possible?

"Maam, we're here to do your bidding," came another. *"Us and all you've summoned."* The voice of Lieutenant Wiggea on the collective unconscious. No, it couldn't be. I felt a stab of fear in my chest. I hadn't even had time to grieve Wiggea, and here he was emerging from the dead. This had to be my imagination.

"Yes, Dragonseer, you did it." Colas' voice came next. *"You've*

summoned your own army from the ashes, and you've created a new race of immortals. Upon this land, a superior civilisation shall rise."

Then came a scream on the collective unconscious, and this time it didn't come from one source, but from fifty or so dragonmen. I clutched my hands to my ears, once again, writhing in the pain. And then, all of a sudden, the Hummingbirds flew off in all directions as if they'd been launched out of random slingshots. Velos bundled through them, knocking some of them into the sea.

Finally, I could turn over my shoulder to see the black dragons. Dozens of them. They weren't quite as magnificent as Alsie or Charth. They were rather spindly, in fact, and around the same size as a grey. But still, I could sense their raw power, and also the same kind of immortality that Alsie, Charth, and now myself shared.

"Remarkable," Alsie said. *"So the old man did it. And there he is in the crowd."*

But none of them spoke back. They simply turned themselves towards the line of airships and speared towards them. They flew in a tight formation. The airships responded by firing with the heavy-duty cannons they had equipped at the front of their hull. But these weren't enough to even injure the dragons. These creatures were now invulnerable with their only weakness at their throat. The men on the airships would have to be terribly good shots to take them down.

Soon enough, I could see the little men running around on deck like ants. The king's redguards, with their rifles poised. They fired a volley. But still, the black dragons went forward unscathed.

"We are immortal," Colas said. *"And these men are buffoons not to flee."*

"We shall take them, Maam," Wiggea said next.

"Hooooiiiieeee..." This was a collective call of multiple tribesmen from the jungle, now in dragon form. A war cry, perhaps.

I decided it better not to reply to them. To even acknowledge their existence would be to heed Finesia's presence. And I could still hear her nattering at the back of my head, telling me to command them into battle. But I tried my best not to put importance to her words and to keep my cool.

The dragons soon were upon the airships. Out of their mouths spouted flames of unnatural green, setting the gondolas alight as the dragons raised their claws and slashed through the balloon linings that kept the airships afloat. And then the balloons sank, and I could see the horizon once again.

"Take control," Finesia said in my mind. *"Tell my minions what you want them to do next."*

But I kept pushing her away.

"Well, well, well," Alsie's voice came in my head. *"I see Finesia's still trying to grant you power, and you won't accept it. So I shall have to go in and claim the power myself."* She let out a huge roar and turned towards the volcano. Charth followed in her wake. They headed right into the volcanic ash cloud disappeared beneath it.

Meanwhile, I looked back in astonishment at the airships now strewn out across the churning water, balloons being thrown up upon the massive waves, and the gondolas getting even more torn apart by the power of the sea.

A whole aerial fleet destroyed by around what must have been fifty dragons. If the Greys had that kind of power, then Cini wouldn't even dare venture into the Southlands with his harvesting operations.

"No," I reminded myself. *"I can't think like that. This power comes with a considerable cost."*

"Oh," Alsie's voice came faintly over the collective unconscious. *"One more thing. You probably better use the dragons to exact vengeance over Cini's fleet. Your own measly flotilla has been reduced to floating shrapnel. I'd hurry south if I were you."*

And it pained me to realise that she was probably right.

I listened out for more signs of Alsie in the collective unconscious, but she remained silent after that. So, I turned back to Faso and Taka. "We need to go south. Our fleet is in trouble."

"What?" Faso's jaw dropped. "How do you know?"

But I didn't answer. Instead, I pulled up on Velos' steering fin. He let out a massive roar as if wanting at least to have a little rest. But, in all honesty, we had nowhere to land.

"Come on, Velos," I said. *"This is almost over, and your cousins are in danger."* I sang out a song to chide him a little.

He let out an even louder roar, and then he lowered his head a little and rocked it in shame. He then flapped his wings and started to head south.

The dragonmen and dragonwomen followed in our wake. There would be no shaking them now, I realised. But I refused to reach out and command them. And, if they turned against us, I'd find a way to take them down one by one.

Even if Wiggea was in there.

Wiggea. I wanted to reach out and tell him I was happy he was still alive. But I couldn't think of him like that. He was a servant of Finesia – a zombie risen from the dead. And the man responsible, Colas was amongst his ranks.

I shuddered and refused to think about Wiggea anymore.

And so we continued on into the distance as the volcano billowed out ash behind us and on the western horizon, the sun began to set. Who knew how many more men would rise from the dead and become dragons.

I didn't want to even entertain the thought.

PART VIII

PONTOPA

"I would not surrender my will, no matter how hard Finesia tried to take it from me."

— PONTOPA WELLS

22

Paradise Reef had completely changed colour since we'd last flown over it and had now lost the vibrance for which it was famous. Instead, the water below looked grey, with waves still churning out of it as the eruptions from the island roared into the sky. The sea also had a faint ghoul-like phosphorescence that ran across it in oily streaks. It had clearly now been tainted by the secicao blight. It was only a matter of time until secicao took over the massive East Cadigan Island and perhaps even spread into the larger Cadigan mainland – the largest landmass in the world.

This would be something I'd have to report to Gerhaun and she'd be furious. Mind, it had a strategic advantage in the fact that we could create another fortress with dragons, perhaps even send a dragon queen or two over there.

Dragonheats, I was thinking like Finesia and Alsie. This secicao wasn't right for the world, and we couldn't exploit it. But no doubt, King Cini would also take advantage of the extra resource and set up a special harvesting operation on East Cadigan Island. The Northern Continent's overuse of secicao was the sole reason that dragons sabotaged the king's secicao harvesting operations in the Southlands. In the north, people drank it like tea to help them get through the hard industrial working day. But secicao leached into the soil through urine, constantly acidifying it until it got to the point that no other plants could grow. Soon enough, as Gerhaun had explained in her book Dragons and Ecology, the conditions would be perfect for the secicao blight to spread into the Northern Continent, choking up all life there. Only the dragonmen and dragonwomen would remain.

Now, Colas – the man responsible for the fall of East Cadigan island – was behind us in a new form. I could recognise him out of the fifty or so dragons he flew with, even though the light was getting low. He lagged behind the rest of the flock a little and canted ever so slightly to one side. Wellies, I wanted to turn to a dragonwoman and rip the life out of his throat.

But, fortunately, I still had a cool head on my shoulders. I didn't want to use any of Finesia's abilities, nor did I want to put Velos' life in danger.

It was then that I realised, throughout this entire trip I hadn't had a chance to reconnect with Taka. Granted, he had been kidnapped and so out of reach for most of it. But even since rescuing him, I'd hardly said a word to him. Expected, I guess when you're in the heat of a battle against a mad goddess, her sociopathic minion, swarms of overpowered Hummingbirds, and a fleet of the king's best airships as far as the eye could see. Still, here was my chance to make amends.

"Taka," I said in the collective unconscious, and I turned around to him to check that he was still awake. He sat there, his eyes glued firmly ahead, staring into the distance with tears welling at the bottom of his eyes. Behind him, Faso had his head craned over his shoulder, watching the dragons with intent. Best, I thought not to include the inventor in the conversation, although I did hope that he'd reach out and also express his apologies to his birth son sometime soon.

"I'm here," Taka said, and his gaze met mine. *"Alsie, is she gone now?"*

I nodded. *"For now. Can you still hear Finesia?"*

Her voice was still nattering in my head, telling me to reach out to my minions who'd remain loyal to me until the end of time. But I kept that voice as distant as possible.

"*Yes...*" Taka said. "*What happened to Charth back there? One moment, I was talking to him. He was telling me never to trust Finesia. He kept telling me to never let her in. Then he just disappeared in my head.*"

"Charth," I asked. "*What did he want?*"

"*He always talked to me, Auntie. He kept telling me to keep the voice of that woman away, to never listen to her. And I wanted to leave Fortress Gerhaun because the voice told me to run away. I didn't listen to Charth when he told me it wasn't safe. I'm sorry, Auntie. I know what I did was wrong.*"

And then my heart dropped in my chest. Because all of a sudden, I realised why Charth had been hanging around Fortress Gerhaun all that time. Gerhaun had told me at one point that the dragonman had sworn to protect Taka. And none of us – even Gerhaun and Sukina – had realised what from.

Charth had stayed at the palace despite being banished because he'd wanted help keep Finesia out of Taka's head. To stop her pushing him over to the wrong side. And then later he kept vigil over Fortress Gerhaun, as Taka's guardian. Always keeping his promise to Sukina. Always communicating with Taka in the collective unconscious, making sure he stayed sane and kept his head around him. All this until Charth could hold on no longer. And he'd used his abilities to protect us all, despite knowing the costs.

"Taka," I said. "*Why did you run away?*" I just wanted to make sure.

"*Finesia told me it was a good idea. Charth was the only one who listened to me. And you and Papo never seemed to care about my birthday. But Finesia did...*"

"*I'm sorry, Taka,*" I said. "*I shouldn't have forgotten.*" And I'd have to be extra vigilant now. Finesia had been in Taka's head for a long time. I had underestimated the effects that the Exalmpora had had on the boy. Now, the empress wouldn't go away – from his mind or my own.

"*I'm sorry too, Auntie Pontopa,*" Taka said. "*But now, you're a drag-onwoman. You can do what Charth does, right?*"

"No," I said. "*I have to be careful. Finesia is dangerous, you have to understand that Taka. She's our enemy, and though she's in our minds, we can't let her control us."*

"I understand," Taka said. And in his eyes, I saw a sense of wisdom well past the child's age. Almost as if Sukina still lived inside him. As I felt she lived inside me sometimes – there to keep us both sane.

"We'll get through this together," I said.

"I'm sure we will. You protect me and I'll protect you."

I smiled. *"Something like that. But in future, make sure you listen to Gerhaun and me. We tell you things for a reason."*

"I know. It's just the voice was so strong."

"We'll work on it," I said. Unfortunately, I'd have to put the poor child in the dark room with the spider automaton and teach him how to control his mind much earlier than I'd hoped. But Finesia had left me with no other choice.

"Don't tell me you two are doing that meditation thing again," Faso said. He had woken up to us and had stopped staring at the V-shaped line of dragons following us now.

"I'm merely having a heart to heart with your son," I said. "And Faso, it's about time you had one too."

"But we don't even know if we'll survive today," Faso said. Then he lowered his head in shame as he noticed my hard stare. "Okay," he said like a scorned child. "You're right. Taka, I'm sorry, I shouldn't have forgotten your birthday."

Taka turned around to face him enthusiastically. "Is that all?"

"No," Faso kept his head bowed down low as if afraid of his own son. "I'm sorry I didn't let you in when you wanted me too. I wanted you to learn the technology and how to become a great inventor, but maybe you're not ready yet. I guess you need time to discover yourself before you discover science."

I shook my head. *"That's not it, Faso, when will you ever learn?"* But Taka seemed to take this as a satisfactory apology.

"Apology accepted," he said, and he turned back to me.

Faso's jaw dropped in shock. He shook his head hard, and he looked unsure if he should chide Taka for insolence or laugh along with him. After a couple of seconds, he went with the latter and let out a nervous chuckle. "Right then, so I guess we have an hour or so to go."

Darkness was almost upon us now and either there was no moon in the sky or it was concealed by the wall of volcanic ash behind us. Beneath it, I could see the red glow of lava streaking across the island. And the green phosphorescence of the sea seemed even brighter as night came closer. There was now a coolness to the air, unexpected in this part of the world, no doubt a side-effect of the eruption.

Taka, Faso and I spent the rest of the journey in silence, making no noise except the occasional rustle of clothing as we shifted in our hard metal seats trying to find a little comfort. Meanwhile, the roar of the volcano diminished with each furlong we flew, until all that could be heard was the howl of the wind and the flapping of the dragons wings behind.

Dragons, who were now invisible to the night. What they'd do when we reached our fleet, and the ambush that Alsie had told lay in wait for us, was anyone's guess. They might act as our allies, but there was no way I would reach out to them and ask for their help in battle. There was no way I'd call on any of Finesia's gifts.

Alongside the voice of Finesia, every so often I heard Colas' voice, or one of the tribespeople's, the tribal chief's, or sometimes even Wiggea's. They babbled nonsense now as if afflicted by madness. They certainly didn't have the eloquence of myself, Charth, and Alsie.

"Ah, but that will change," Finesia nattered at the back of my mind, *"once this land becomes rich in secicao. The more they can draw from and twist the nature of the collective unconscious, the stronger their human form will become."*

"No," I said. *"These men are dead. They'll never be human."*

"But if Dragonseer Sako was there among them. You'd maybe listen to her."

I gritted my teeth. Why was I even letting the empress in? *"Sukina would never succumb to your will, Finesia,"* I said. And with those words, I shut her out of my head.

And that was the last I listened to anything other than the sounds of nature until another light came into view. The flashes of war accompanied by the roars of gunfire and cannon fire.

We had arrived at the end of what would become known as The Final Battle of Cadigan. And my stomach tightened as I realised that we'd got here too late.

23

I didn't have to travel much further to taste the death on the collective unconscious. And then closer still, I caught sight of the husks of the sinking dragon carriers, and the corpses of dragons on the water, and The Saye Explorer still floating yet battered. All this I saw in speckled green after taking a swig of secicao oil from my hipflask.

We'd arrived just after the battle and all was calm. But it didn't seem that the Saye Explorer had been raided yet, because I could see General Sako and Admiral Sandao standing in the centre of the lower deck, their backs to each other.

"We haven't got a chance," Faso said. Because of the heat signatures, I couldn't quite see his facial features or the expression on his face.

"We've been through worse."

"You've got to be kidding. Have you even seen those things?"

On closer examination, I noticed Faso was holding a telescope to his eye. I turned back and squinted into the distance to try and make out what he was looking at. Lo and behold, amidst the fading cloud of shrapnel flak, massive Hummingbird carriers, airships, and swarms of Hummingbirds, there was something else.

Not one but three of them...

Automatons large enough to be mammoths. Except they weren't on the land or floating on the water, yet flying, lifted up by slow beating wings with a span three times the length of their body. They had long beaks with sharp ends that looked like they could pierce an ironclad's hull. And even from this distance, it wasn't hard to make out their evil glowing eyes – green in my augmented vision, but which I'm sure would have been red otherwise. Behind those eyes, the rest of their bulk also emitted a faint green glow.

"How much secicao is left in the armour?" I asked Faso.

"Why, I only brought enough for one resupply, and we used that. I hadn't expected us to have many chances to refuel."

I shook my head. So it was just Velos against what the king probably saw as his finest technology. Though we did have allies. I looked back at the black dragons who were taking a backseat. I could use them. I could reach out Finesia and call them into battle.

"No, Auntie," Taka said in the collective unconscious as if reading my intent. *"You said we mustn't. There's got to be a better way."*

"But what else can we do?" And it seemed for a moment I wasn't talking to a young boy, but Sukina inside his head.

"We fly up to them and find out what the king wants," he replied.

But Faso had other ideas. "We have to surrender," he said. "This is it. King Cini has won."

I bit my tongue to stop myself screaming at him for his negativity. I'd had quite enough of it. There was no way we were going to go down without a fight, not after everything we'd been through. "What are those automatons, anyway?" I asked, making sure we focused on the important stuff.

"Beasts of the sky," Faso replied. "I had no idea the king had completed them. Years ago, I gave him the blueprints for an automaton I called the Roc. If he's created them to my specifications, they'll have more armour than a Mammoth and enough weaponry to sink three battleships at once."

Fortunately, nothing seemed to have noticed us yet, or at least regarded us as dangerous. Then it occurred to me, the king was probably out there somewhere waiting for us to land on the Saye Explorer so he could finally come in and claim his prize. Dragonheats, he probably had an automaton on deck somewhere with a gun pointed at General Sako's and Admiral Sandao's head.

And indeed, as we got closer, I noticed that General Sako and Admiral Sandao were in fetters that had been welded into the floor of the ship. Their hands were free, and they were throwing them up in the air and gesturing towards the front of the vessel. But they remained silent, presumably because they didn't want to wake any guards.

I looked over the prow of the Saye Explorer, and I didn't notice anything unusual, other than a bowsprit with a white flag handing off it, that I could swear hadn't been there before.

"The cannon," Faso said. "Dragonheats, I'd forgotten about it. Maybe, after all, we'll stand a chance of taking one of the Rocs down."

"Keep it down, Faso," I snapped. We were still fortunately far enough away from the ship that nothing would be able to hear us. But we wouldn't be for long. "And where's the cannon? I can't see it."

"That's because they disguised it as a flagpole," Faso said a little quieter this time. "Whoever's idea it was, I'll have to commend them for their quick thinking."

Indeed, now Faso had mentioned it, I recognised it. Our crew had simply pushed the trolley towards the front of the ship, angled the cannon upwards a little, and hung a white surrender flag off the gun to make it look as if it was part of the construction. It was ingenious.

I saluted General Sako and Admiral Sandao and pointed to the cannon to let them know we'd noticed it. Once they realised they'd got the message across, they stopped flailing their arms about and stood stock still on the deck as if nothing was happening. I couldn't see any sign of any other guards, neither ours nor King Cini's. But as we got closer, I noticed war automatons sitting dormant against the ship's railing, as well as a crisscross latticework of green lines of light that stretched across the floor of the deck.

Probably, these were infrared, and I could only see them because of my augmented vision. And, no doubt, if we touched them, we'd trigger an alarm, waking up the war automatons. Then King Cini could come in, reclaim Taka, and order the public execution of Faso and myself. Giving us no choice but to get the cannon and try shooting the automatons down.

Fortunately, I recalled a while back how someone had told me that the cannon could be equipped from the air. But Velos would need to be incredibly accurate to pick it up, and we only had one shot at doing so.

Then I smiled because I remembered something. "Faso... Last time we were facing off against the king's fleet, you told me Velos has a reserve tank. Have we used that yet?"

He paused a moment.

"Faso?"

"No," he said. "But we might need it. And it only gives us five minutes."

"Do it," I said. "Faso, power on the reserve tank, and then Velos can pick up the cannon, shoot down one of those legendary Roc automatons, and after we've scared the king a little, we make our escape."

"And then what?" Faso said.

I looked down at the Saye Explorer and Admiral Sandao and General Sako onboard. They would already know that they had nothing left, and both men would want us to take Taka to safety. I swallowed hard. "We'll leave them if we have to."

"Grandpa," Taka said...

"He'll be okay," I said. And I immediately hated those words. I'd also told him the same about Sukina just before she'd died. If I were Taka, I wouldn't trust me right now.

"Very well," Faso said. "You're the boss, but after this, we have absolutely no secicao left in the armour."

I nodded. "Faso, I want you to use everything."

"Everything?"

"Down to the last drop. We mustn't fail at this."

And so, he reached down to the spigot on Velos' flank and turned it. The armour suddenly ghosted green and a little strength returned to Velos.

"Don't roar," I told him. And I sang a song to make sure he stayed calm. I flew him around in a circle and readied him to descend towards the faux flagpole at the Saye Explorer's prow.

"We'll need speed for this," Faso said. "It takes a good bit of oomph to get that cannon on Velos."

"Good thing he's augmented," I thought. And I took another swig from my hip flask as the see-in-the-dark effect had begun to fade a little. We only had one chance, and I could feel the power surging through my veins, a side-effect of my connection to Velos. I pushed down on his steering fin and urged him to edge a little closer to the ship. Meanwhile, I kept my eye on the cannon, or should I say bowsprit. I didn't want to attempt equipping it yet. Instead, I wanted to fly over the Saye Explorer and see what we were up against.

As we passed overhead, I saw the worried expression on General Sako's face as he looked up at me. It was as if he was saying, "I hope you know what you're doing," but of course he didn't utter a word. I don't know if he even saw Taka then, but hopefully, he'd at least catch a glance of him to know he was safe.

As well as the war automatons hiding on deck, several of the king's redguards had been posted there too. They were propped up against the railings and all of them were asleep. The buffoons – they were so reliant on the technology that they didn't even think to put a single man on watch.

I flew around in a circle once more and then I pushed on Velos' steering fin to move him down towards the ship. He hurtled downwards at an intense speed, fueled by the secicao in his armour. The wind rushed passed us, and I wanted to scream out to express my joy of flying. But, of course, I didn't want to attract attention to ourselves.

"Easy," Faso said. "You need to be a little off to the left."

"I know what I'm doing," I said. This time, I hadn't been hit by Alsie's glamour spell or whatever she'd thrown at me all those days back in the Southlands. I could see perfectly. Plus, the secicao that I'd augmented with allowed me to compress time in my own mind.

Soon enough, we connected with the cannon, and I heard the clanking of machinery. If Velos' claws even touched the deck, then the

war automatons would wake up and King Cini would be alerted to our presence.

I pulled up as soon as Velos' armour bucked, praying that he didn't touch a single line of light the crisscrossed the floor. One swept ever so close to Velos' feet, but he missed it by inches.

Then, we were up and back into the cool night. I looked over my shoulder, half expecting that the cannon would still be on the ship. We'd have failed and Velos wouldn't have enough secicao left in his armour to have any chance of another successful pass. A guard stirred on deck, probably awoken by the noise, but I knew by the time he came to, we'd be long gone.

"You did it," Faso shouted out. "First time, I'd never have expected."

I snorted. "Well, I guess it's time to go and deliver our message to King Cini." He probably would expect us to emerge bruised and battered, and not in any state at all to fight back.

"That's right," Faso said. "And remember, we only have three shots."

I nodded. Three shots. Three Roc automatons. Hopefully, I'd only have to use one before we made our escape. The king's boat would try and stop us with shrapnel flak, of course. But by that time, we'd be long on our way to the Southlands. And we were so far from the volcano and the dangerous currents it had created, I could probably try taking Velos underneath the ships.

I pulled Velos over to the side and we flew towards the line of airships that I saw in the distance. They had their searchlights ready, watching the water. No doubt keeping watch if any of the captive crew of the Saye Explorer tried to escape in a lifeboat.

I could now see the flying automatons' massive heads, turning from side to side and scanning the horizon. Their beaks were the most monstrous thing I'd ever seen on a bird or anything that resembled one. Their upper and lower beak had two sharp inner edges flecked with razors that looked like they would dash apart anything that got in their way.

Ratter now sat on Faso's shoulder watching what I imagined the ferret automaton regarded as his nemeses. Now we'd destroyed the panthers on Colas' island, the Rocs were perhaps the most impressive automaton known to mankind. Although Faso would claim they weren't as intelligent as Ratter, I'm sure. And who knows what the inventor had in mind for his dragon automaton.

One of the Rocs turned its head to us as we approached. It let out a caw to the sky, just like a crow's but a thousand times the volume. So loud, in fact, it seemed to rock the waves in front of it.

All of a sudden, some airship propellers began to hum in unison and a searchlight swung around to focus on us from the airship behind the Roc. Not long after that, King Cini's voice emanated out of a loudspeaker. "Well, I never. Pontopa Wells, and indeed Alsie was right, you brought the boy. Taka... Long time no see, aye."

"Dragonheats," I said back to Faso. "I wish you'd brought along a loudspeaker so I could tell that idiot king to stuff his felt crown up his behind."

"Pontopa... There's a child present."

"Yes, you're right," I said. "Taka don't try that at home..."

And he smiled as if getting my joke. This boy, in many ways, was years past his age.

"Is the cannon ready?" I asked Faso. "We have a better way of showing the king our contempt." I glanced over my shoulder at the two great hulking aerial automatons now following us. Under each wing, they had three massive guns all lined up next to each other, again with that faint secicao gleam running across the length of each one. While we flew ahead, the automatons tracked us with remarkable precision, their wings adjusting automatically to match any change in direction. Despite their size, they seemed quite mobile, although I guessed they weren't quite equipped for aerobatics like Velos was capable of.

"Ready," Faso said. "You won't miss this time, will you?"

"Of course not." I took another swig of my secicao oil just to make sure.

Ratter launched itself off Faso's shoulder and onto the side of Velos where the special control panel was. I felt the armour thrum again, but this time it didn't glow or emit heat. It wasn't being powered by secicao, but rather the cannon beneath was gaining power. Meanwhile, I kept Velos steady and on course. We had about thirty seconds now before we'd pass the Roc, which I could see clearly now. It had a Gatling cannon on the top of its head, pointed right at us. Then, there was another much larger machine gun on its under-belly, connected to a long bandolier that coiled around its chest and tail, from where it hung off at the tip.

"Fire," I said.

"Aye aye," Faso said.

For a moment, nothing happened. And I worried that we'd either pass the bird automaton or it would fire on us before we'd even had a chance.

"Faso?"

"Give it time."

And just as we were almost upon the Roc automaton, a tremen-dous white beam of light erupted from Velos' underbelly. It passed right through the Roc, searing through the metal. It lasted only a moment and then fizzled out. And we were about to collide with the thing.

"Dragonheats," I said. And I pushed down hard on Velos' steering fin. The dragon entered a sharp dive, and this time the immediate effect of the gravity made me almost want to throw up.

And then, I levelled Velos out, and everything was silent for a moment. I turned back to see a trail of smoke in my green augmented vision coming up off the Roc. Then, the great beast plummeted. It hit the water, sending up a huge wave out in all directions, rocking the Saye Explorer.

"Dragonheats, Faso Gordoni," the voice came out from King Cini's airship. "I didn't know you had those tricks up your sleeve and you now will pay. This time, I'm not even going to give you the option of surrender. Oh, and before you think of going under Lady Wells, I'll have to know that I've modified my entire fleet to also eject shrapnel flak into the water. And I don't care about any of your passengers, including the boy. Now I've sacked my consort, my single objective is to take you down."

You know this king liked the sound of his voice far too much. His father would have just killed us by now and had done with it. But sacked his consort, or in other words Alsie Fioreletta? Now that was news. Which meant that Alsie and King Cini probably weren't allied when I bumped into her at the volcano. Which meant...

I didn't have much time to think about it, because almost immediately after he cut himself off from the loudspeaker systems, the Roc automatons behind fired on us. Green smoke erupted from the three long launchers on their wings and out screamed three missiles. They were heading straight towards us and so I pulled Velos upwards in a loop the loop. But I grimaced as soon as I saw the missiles start to follow us.

"Homing missiles," Faso said. "Be careful."

"You what?" I asked. But my voice was cut off by the scream of the wind cutting against my face.

Faso shouted out something else, but I couldn't hear a word of what he was saying.

"*Auntie,*" Taka said. "*They're secicao powered, I can use my scream.*"

"No," I said. "*Don't listen to Finesia. Velos can get through this one with sheer agility.*"

And no doubt Faso was probably screaming out how crazy he thought I was. I was now upside down in the air and I looked at the ocean below us to see the missiles heading upwards straight at us. Taka was right – they had a green trail to them. Although, admittedly, with my augmented vision, everything was green.

If I could just get in front of them, then Velos could shoot them down with fire. That gave me an idea. Fire. If they sought heat, maybe we could redirect them.

I quickly sang a staccato-tipped song and Velos latched on and spewed out a column of flame. While the missiles had been heading towards our heads, they suddenly began to veer off in a new direction. Right into Velos' flight path. Not good.

I turned Velos sharply to the right and entered him into a half barrel roll so we could get upright again. Meanwhile, the explosion rocked us in the air, and I felt the heat prickle against my arm. I pushed downwards to get Velos as far away as possible. Faso would have the worst of it, but then he had Ratter to administer first aid. I looked over my shoulder to check that Faso and Taka were okay. They looked a little shocked but not injured. Behind them, Velos' flame had now mixed with the explosions to create a magnificent blossoming display of light.

And we'd got away from it.

Somehow, we'd survived.

Conveniently, our movements had sent us heading towards a second Roc automaton.

"Faso," I said, "can you fire it up?"

"I need a minute."

"We don't have a minute."

"Very well, I'll put it into overdrive, but it might backfire…"

"Just do what you can," and I turned to see Ratter already fiddling at the controls while Faso leant towards him and tapped commands onto the little automaton's back in a strange rhythmic pattern that only the inventor understood.

"I hope this works," Faso said. And the armour began to rock underneath me again.

"Taka, you okay back there?" I asked.

"I feel a bit sick… But this is so cool."

For some reason, that made me smile.

I readied Velos and pointed him at the Roc automaton. It opened its beak and let out a huge roar. The sound entered my bones and sent a cold shiver down my spine. Part of me wanted to back away.

Yet, I wouldn't let Velos' aim waiver.

"Ready?" I asked.

"Ready," Faso shouted back, and a blinding white light came again from Velos' underbelly for a split second. Then came a huge crashing sound as the beam seared through the Roc automaton's armour. The hideous mechanical beast opened its mouth again, but no sound emerged. Shortly after, it plopped into the ocean below, this time letting out a splash so high, it looked almost like an erupting volcano.

"Two down, one to go."

And there came a laughing over the loudspeaker from King Cini's airship. "This is quite a show you're putting on for my men here, Lady Wells. Apparently, a lot of cash has changed hands amongst my men of bets placed against you winning this. But two Rocs down, bravo. I didn't expect you to get this far, I must admit."

I clenched my teeth. Once this was over, I'd head straight towards Cini's airship and douse his head in flames, despite all the Hummingbirds and protection he'd have surrounding him.

As soon as the loudspeaker sounds crackled out, the remaining Roc launched another slew of missiles at us. This time, they came at us from the side with such speed and proximity that Velos' flame wouldn't be able to lead them out of the way. The Gatling cannon on the Roc also bucked into life, and Velos' guns responded in kind by returning fire.

"Everyone augment," I shouted. And I took a swig from my hipflask again. I sloshed my flask to test how much secicao was left in it. Almost nothing. Then, I pushed Velos down, just in time for the missiles to come screaming over our heads.

I kind of hoped they'd then continue into the distance, but instead, they corrected their course, did a one-eighty in the air, and sped back towards us. I reacted by singing a song to instruct Velos to let out another flame. But this time, the missiles didn't change course.

"Dragonheats," I said. "They're learning."

"Fascinating," Faso said. "And now we're dead."

"Auntie, I'll use the scream." Taka said.

"No," I said. If anything, I'd be the one to use it and risk going further over to Finesia's side. But we had to try and evade these things first.

Then, I had another idea. "We're going under," I shouted. Even though King Cini had warned us about the shrapnel flak underneath, the boats were so far away that we shouldn't encounter any here.

"Not again," Faso said. And he jerked his head around to look at the approaching missiles. "Okay, you're right. No choice."

Finally, he was starting to understand these things. "Hold your breaths," I shouted.

I pushed up hard on Velos' steering fin and sent him diving. We hit the waves with such a speed that the splash of impact stung my face and arms. Down we sank, so far that we could see the little luminous fishes and other creatures. The weight of the water started to press against my ears, and I worried for a moment that Taka wouldn't be able to take it.

But then, the boy was a dragonseer. It would be Faso who'd have problems if anything. I jerked my head to the right to see the missiles still following us, swimming like minnows. Dragonheats, if this didn't work.

I pulled back on Velos' steering fin to take him back up again. Meanwhile, I sang a song in my mind, because there would be no way I could blubber the notes through the water. Velos speared upwards, keeping his wings folded back for momentum. Then, we broke the surface and I immediately switched to an audible song that instructed Velos to spew out his flames. He created a column there that lingered for a moment, heating the sea up. And I then steered Velos sharply away.

The missiles exploded before they even emerged from the sea. They sent up a huge wave that threatened to pull us back under again. But I kept Velos as steady as possible and soon we broke through gasping for breath.

I took a moment to recover, and I scanned around for the Roc so we could at least make our move. But this wasn't a board game and we didn't take it in turns. While we'd been busy underwater evading the missiles, the Roc had tracked our movements. Now it was behind us and close on our tail. So close, in fact, I could see the shimmering green of secicao washing over it.

The larger cannon on the Roc's underside let off a barrage of bullets. I entered Velos into a barrel roll to evade. Meanwhile, the Roc got even closer with its beak. Dragonheats, it wanted to spear us out of the sky.

I pulled back on Velos' steering fin again to enter Velos into a loop the loop. As I did, I kept track of the Roc's position. Although it couldn't do what we did aerobatically, it could match our speed. And if it slowed whenever we slowed, Velos wouldn't be able to get behind it, and the Roc could impale Velos on the way down.

And it flew with utmost precision, never letting us fall behind. As we came down, it found its way underneath us and raised its beak at Velos, who sent an orange flame over it, but that only made the metal red hot. And then I tried to swerve Velos out of the way to avoid collision with its beak.

We almost made it...

But we were jerked to a halt. The harness dug into my shoulders as the momentum threw me forward. Velos let out an intense, low-pitched growl and I felt a terrible pain lancing in my tailbone. I screamed and writhed in my seat.

I could see nothing but the churning sea beneath me. We were hanging, and I looked up to see Velos suspended from the meat of his tail, the Roc's beak speared through it. The dragon let out another roar and kicked and tossed to try and free himself. But as he struggled, the Roc opened its beak to hold him in place. Then, to add to the cruelty, the front parts of the Roc's beak pivoted outwards on hinges to create two hooks. There was no way Velos could escape that without tearing his tail in two.

"Dragonheats, we're dead," Faso said.

I shook my head. He didn't need to repeat it for the thousandth time.

"Well, well, well," Cini's voice crackled over the loudspeaker. As pompous as ever. Looks like I can take the boy back as a prize after all. Artua, how we'll need to discipline you once you return to the palace. But first, Lady Wells and Faso Gordoni, we shall execute you right here.

The airship propellers hummed into action again and from the horizon came the faint green glow of Hummingbirds. Meanwhile, I looked up into the glowing red crystal eyes of the Roc automaton, staring down at me as if the machine wanted to be the one to perform the execution.

I had no option but to wait, short of unbuckling the harness and dropping into the water.

Meanwhile, Ratter had disappeared from Faso' shoulder. Hopefully, it was up on the automaton somewhere trying to find a way to get us out of this. Velos had stopped roaring and instead kept letting out these long, rumbling moans that sent shivers down my spine as I watched the airships approach, their faint green outlines getting even brighter.

"This is your chance," Finesia's voice came. The temptation was so intense that I had stopped closing the door on her. *"Send my minions forwards and become a leader yourself."*

Yes, the black dragons. Finesia's minions. They were still hovering far in the distance, waiting for my order. I couldn't hear their voices in the collective unconscious anymore, just strange sounds that could almost be described as static white noise – the kind you hear when trying to tune a radio.

The king's airship was soon upon us. In the light that shone out of the gondola of the airship, I could see the bowsprit and the red flag on it with the four white sabres radiating out in a circle, arranged like propeller blades. The king's redguards milled around on the deck of the gondola. King Cini III stood between them in his white fur overcoat and tall felt crown, his hands behind his straight back, watching out with discerning eyes.

Soon enough, he was within speaking distance, and four guards had flanked him. All four of them had their rifles pointed at my head, clearly, after deciding I was much more dangerous than the other two in the party.

"So, Dragonseer Wells," King Cini said, putting an extra sarcastic undertone on the title, "how are you going to sing your way out of this one?" He lifted a pocket watch hanging from his hip. "You know, I'm a generous soul. So I'll give you exactly one minute to make any last requests before I fire."

"Auntie Pontopa," Taka said in the collective unconscious, and I could hear the fear in his voice. *"You can't let him shoot you. Finesia tells me you can stop this. Please, you must listen to her."*

"We're not going to bend to her will. No matter what happens Taka, you can't let her in."

"Fifty seconds," the king looked at a pocket watch dangling from his waist. "Oh, please don't tell me you have no tricks left up your sleeve... How disappointing."

I could feel the blood rushing to my head. And meanwhile, power began to surge through my arms and legs. It would only take a moment to transform, and I wanted to so much. If only the king knew how easy this would be. I could turn to a dragonwoman and rip off his head.

"That's it, my acolyte," Finesia's voice came in my head. *"All this power could be yours. That's what you've always wanted, isn't it? To be the best. Better than Sukina. As great as one of the Gods Themselves."*

"No," I replied to her. And I pushed her away.

"Thirty seconds," King Cini said. "Don't you have any last requests? I can even ship your remains to Fortress Gerhaun if you just tell me its location..." He let out a dry laugh.

I had no choice. My life. Velos' life. Taka's life. The whole of Fortress Gerhaun depended on it. I closed my eyes and willed the scales to grow out of me.

"No," this time I heard Sukina's voice in my head. *"There's always another way. Don't take the easy way out, Pontopa. Remember the vision."*

Her words brought me back to the present. Destroying Alsie. Becoming the source of the Tree Immortal and the growth of secicao. No, this life would turn me into a destroyer of this world. If I had to make a sacrifice, so be it...

And I stopped the transformation before it even started.

"Ten seconds left," King Cini said. "Actually, I've changed my mind. Guards shoot her."

And I heard the rifles click into place.

"I'm sorry, Taka," I said in the collective unconscious. *"Whatever you do, be patient, and be strong."* And I closed my eyes and prepared to die.

For a moment, everything went silent and I got ready to enter the next world.

Then, instead of the boom of rifle fire, came the screams of a thousand dragonmen. It resonated over the collective unconscious, so strong that every man and woman present clutched their hands to their ears, including King Cini and me. Rifles dropped on the deck. The king reeled forwards and looked as if he wanted to throw up.

"You are a fool, Dragonseer Wells." It was now Alsie Fioreletta who now spoke in the collective unconscious. *"A complete disappointment to Finesia. I've known all along that you would never claim her power, and so I've decided to do so myself."*

I turned around to see a flock of dark dragons come into view in speckled green, many more now than had escorted me here. And I felt their presence, but they were no longer calling out to me. Wiggea had left me. Colas had left me. And in their centre, I recognised the largest of them all. Alsie Fioreletta at their centre, her loyal minion Charth flying beside her.

"And you, King Cini. This is how the collective unconscious sounds, you know. You've never believed in it, which is why I've always thought you a complete waste of time. But now, out of the ashen soils of East Cadigan Island, your old servant Captain Colas created a source loud enough for any human to hear my voice. Yes, Faso Gordoni, the youngest male heir of Dragonseers, that includes you too."

"Dragonheats," Cini shouted to his men, still on the ground clutching his ears. "What is this? Shoot them all."

But the men on deck were slow to respond if they could even hear him at all, and the dragons came in fast and strong.

"Auntie Pontopa, I'm scared," Taka said in the collective unconscious.

"Hold on, Taka," I said. *"Just hold on."*

And soon enough, Alsie's troop of dragonmen ripped Cini's airships to shreds, the gondolas crashing into the ocean. The Hummingbirds that had surrounded us had already plummeted under the weight of the scream. And still, we just hung there, with no choice but to await our fates.

"Ratter did it," Faso shouted out suddenly.

I craned my head upwards to see what he was talking about. The speckled green effect of the secicao oil was now beginning to fade in my vision. But still, above me, Ratter stood on the Roc's beak, looking triumphant. Fortunately, the colossal scream hadn't downed the massive flying automaton, like it had downed the Hummingbirds, perhaps due to the beast's enormous scale.

Now, the two parts of the beak that had sloped outwards lay in line with the rest of the beak. Velos roared again in pain, but it seemed Ratter had loosened something on the beak and the dragon was now sliding off it.

I reacted by singing a song to give Velos strength.

"Wait," Faso said, "if we leak the remaining reserve from the cannon into the armour…"

"What?"

"We didn't take our last shot," Faso said, and he reached down to the spigot while Ratter jumped over and began to work at the control panel on the other side. Velos then reached the end of the beak and he dropped headfirst towards the ocean.

But the dragon opened his wings so we could glide down a little slower. Yet he had no strength left in him to fly.

"I thought you said there was no secicao left in the armour?" I asked.

"It wasn't in the armour, but in the cannon. And if we'd taken a third shot, we would have used it all up."

Dragonheats, I hated that man for withholding valuable information from me. But I didn't have time to express my anger at that present moment. Instead, I pulled up on Velos' steering fin. *"Dragonheats, Velos, fly,"* I willed. But his muscles were weak, I could feel it. And he'd lost the will to survive.

But Faso's plan worked. The armour beneath us began to glow green. Strength rushed to Velos' wings, and just as his head crashed into the water, he slapped the waves away with a massive flap and lifted us back up into the air.

"That's it Velos," I said.

"Up, up and away," Faso shouted.

"Hoooooiiiiieeeee," Taka called out, and I looked back at him in surprise.

Then, I turned Velos back towards the Saye Explorer. Meanwhile, gondolas and balloons floated on the water and I could see them burning as thousands of Finesia's dragons coated them in flame. I caught sight of Cini's flagship and the king who raised a flask of secicao oil to his lips and then jumped into the water.

I didn't see what happened to him after that.

The Saye Explorer wasn't far away and our crew had already returned it to operation. The war automatons had been turned over deck, and the redguards who were asleep there had now been tied to the railings. Meanwhile, the admiral and general stood on the edge of the quarterdeck, watching the battle unfold in front of them.

The men had returned the trolley designed for landing Velos when he was equipped with the cannon. I landed him there and I promptly leapt off the dragon and rushed over to join them.

"We need to make our escape," I said.

"But the dragons," General Sako said, "they'll come after us once they're finished with Cini. What are those things? I thought it was just Charth and Alsie."

I shook my head. "I'll explain later. And somehow, I don't think we're their target. Admiral Sandao, head east. I think Alsie Fioreletta will let us go."

He saluted and scurried off to give the orders. Meanwhile, General Sako turned to me, then looked up to Velos where Taka still sat strapped into his harness.

"You made it... And you brought my grandson back."

Grandson... Hopefully, he'd finally learned to accept the boy's changed gender.

I nodded. "Yes, but at what cost?"

General Sako stared out into the distance.

"Did you hear it? Before our men mutinied and overturned the automatons, everyone said they heard a woman's voice in their head. Then, the automatons holding our men hostage below went dead and we managed to reclaim the ship."

I nodded. "That was Alsie Fioreletta in the collective unconscious. She created a strong enough source for everyone to hear her, it seems."

General Sako's jaw dropped. "What? Impossible."

"We need to call a meeting with Gerhaun as soon as we get home – whether she's sleeping or not. Alsie Fioreletta is no longer loyal to King Cini and the world is about to change."

And on that note, we thus crept away from a churning sea as Alsie's dragonmen and dragonwomen tore up the last of King Cini's fleet.

"Escape, for now," Alsie said in my mind once we were out of sight. *"But Finesia will continue to work on you and Taka and you both will join our side."*

"Not if I can help it," I replied. And I shut Alsie Fioreletta and Finesia out of my mind.

Or, at least for the time being...

After the battle, Faso applied some special balm made of secicao and aloe vera to Velos' tail, which seemed to have magical healing abilities. And as soon as he was fit to fly again, we decided to take Velos ahead so we could report to Gerhaun as soon as possible. Of course, Velos didn't carry the cannon all the way to the Southlands. Everyone agreed that there would unlikely be any need for it on the journey.

General Sako insisted on coming with Faso, Taka and I, and he sat in the middle with his grandson seated on his lap. Somehow, despite the heavy turbulence, both Taka and his grandfather slept most of the journey, and General Sako's snores were quite audible, even above the roar of the wind. Of course, we had to wake them to remind them to put their gas masks on just before we hit the secicao clouds in the Southlands. Then, they both just moaned, reached down for the masks, placed them over their faces, and were very shortly afterwards fast asleep again.

Faso was also incredibly quiet on his journey. Probably musing over what the old academics had told him about his heritage. I hadn't sensed them in the covey of dragons that Alsie had brought over from the volcano or the ones that had followed me to the Saye

Explorer. So, I had a feeling that they'd perished during the eruption.

The first people to greet us when we arrived were my parents. They waited in the courtyard and, just as we were about to land, I caught sight of their pale faces and the enormous bags they sported underneath their eyes. They looked as if they hadn't slept for a month. We touched down quickly and Velos let out a light roar to greet my parents. I immediately scrambled down Velos' ladder and ran into my father's arms.

"Pontopa," he said. "You look like you aged years."

I laughed. "Such a sweet thing to say to your daughter."

"I'm sorry, it's just. I can't get over how much you've grown in the last few years. And there's something different about you. In your eyes…"

I smiled and then I embraced my mother with a hug. "What happened out there, dear?" she asked. "You seem like you've endured a lot."

Wellies, why did parents have to be so perceptive. "I'll explain later. For now, I need to talk to Gerhaun. Is she awake?"

Papo smiled. "I believe so… And she has news."

So it appeared East Cadigan Island wasn't the only place things had happened. "What?" I asked.

"I think she'll like to explain this herself." Mamo looked up at Velos. "But it's quite exciting."

"Dragonheats," I said. And I stormed through the corridors so fast that neither my parents nor General Sako would be able to keep up with me. The double doors to Gerhaun's treasure chamber were open and it looked sparkling clean.

"You didn't announce your visit," Gerhaun said in the collective unconscious.

But I ignored her slight objection. *"Gerhaun,"* I said instead. *"My parents tell me you have the news."*

"Later Dragonseer… There's something different about you." Gerhaun furrowed her massive golden brow. *"Finesia… You took Exalmpora."*

I felt my heart leap in my chest, and I wanted to cry. *"It was forced upon me. Colas shot me in the stomach, and I had no choice but to take it otherwise I'd die."*

And then, it all came out it a flurry of tears and words. I told Gerhaun about the storm, and the tribespeople we'd met in the jungle and how Colas had converted them to his cause. I told her about the academics and their theories – something which Gerhaun admitted to already knowing a lot about. I then told her about Colas and how he'd incited a volcanic eruption, and how his nefarious plan had managed to birth thousands of dragonmen and dragonwomen from the soil. And how he'd shot me in the stomach and I'd almost died. And when teetering over the abyss of death, I'd managed to transcend the collective unconscious and had become something else entirely. And thus I'd had no choice but to take the Exalmpora down my throat, as Taka still needed saving and it wasn't time to die. And how I'd then almost become a dragonwoman and I started hearing the voice of Finesia inside my head. Finally, I told her about Charth. How he'd lost himself to Finesia. That, it seemed, he'd never help us again.

There was only one thing that I held back telling her, and that was about the vision I'd had in the jungle when I'd become the Tree Immortal and destroyed the world. It terrified me, and I was also terrified of how Gerhaun would react if she knew about it. She might cast me out or worse, once she learned what a threat I was to this world, tear me to shreds on the spot.

After I'd finished speaking, there was a long pause as I waited for Gerhaun to digest the words. Eventually, she nodded and looked down upon me with her wise eyes. *"If you kept Finesia out, then you've not lost yourself yet."*

I looked over at the gleaming pile of treasures. *"But I'm a dragonwoman,"* I said. *"Just like Charth."*

"No," Gerhaun replied. *"You're not like Charth at all."*

I shook my head. *"Gerhaun, what happened to Charth? Why did you throw him out?"*

And that caused her to sink her head and let out a low and sad growl. *"First, I need to know, Pontopa. Did you ever call on Finesia, or use her powers?"*

"Never," I said. *"And I told Taka not to let her in."*

Gerhaun nodded. *"Then keep it that way. You see, Charth turned on us when we least expected it. He returned to us after what his father had done to him in the palace and continued to work for us, while his brother travelled the world wooing women and Alsie decided to try and create a life of her own in the palace. But King Cini II kept sending automatons to the Southlands and Charth felt he needed to use his abilities to destroy the king's operations. I told him he shouldn't call on Finesia. That the power she gave him was dangerous, but he wouldn't listen.*

"One day, he went out with a task force and he turned into a black dragon to fight the king's airships. But in doing so, he lost his will and he ended up massacring our own men. After that, I had no option but to cast him out.

"He said he was sorry. He vouched never to turn again. But I could see that it was only a matter of time until he became lost to Finesia's will. He didn't have the strength inside to resist."

I felt a tear well at the corner of my eye. *"Charth works for Alsie now."*

"Yes," Gerhaun replied. *"Because, Finesia kept exploiting that weakness, much as she'll try to exploit your own."*

I clenched my fists by my sides. *"I won't let her. I'll be strong."*

"You need more than strength." Gerhaun said, and she looked down at me with her yellow knowing eyes. *"You need patience, Dragonseer Wells. You need to accept you can't have everything at once. It will take time to become who you want to be."*

And with those words, a tear dropped from my cheek. That's what I'd found so hard to accept. *"We lost so much out there. The dragons. The fleet. East Cadigan island is now a wasteland and Alsie tells me that secicao will grow there soon."*

"The world is changing," Gerhaun said. *"And we must be strong to face it."*

A gust of wind came from the chimney and I smelt the egginess of the secicao fumes trying to close in through the collective unconscious.

"Gerhaun," I said. *"There's something else."*

"Tell me."

I took a deep breath. I had to tell Gerhaun. Maybe she'd help me understand. Or at least, perhaps she could give me the courage to face up to what I was becoming.

"I had a vision," I explained. *"The first time Exalmpora was forced on me in the jungle, I saw myself in battle against Alsie. I beat her and I became the Tree Immortal, Gerhaun, and I... I caused secicao to grow across the world, and I couldn't stop it. I was the catalyst, Gerhaun... I destroyed this world."*

Gerhaun's lips folded downwards. Her response wasn't one of anger or fear as I'd feared, but instead compassion. *"Do not let Finesia in,"* she said. *"She wants you to believe that you're not in control of your own destiny. She wants you to think that you're a servant to her will."*

"But you said there's a prophecy."

"Yes, one where we'll rise with free will and decide what the fate of this world will be. You have to believe, Dragonseer Wells. And you have to have the patience to hold on to those beliefs, even in the darkest of times."

"I see that now," I said. *"Thank you, Gerhaun."*

"No, thank you," she said. *"You've done great things for us all."*

I nodded. *"What about Lieutenant Wiggea?"* I asked. *"Will he have a funeral?"* And, again, a tinge of sadness rose up to me as I remembered him holding my chin and the warm kiss he placed upon my lips.

Rastano Wiggea had done nothing to deserve this. He'd been a humble servant of dragonseers all his life and had already witnessed the death of two of them, the first being his wife. And now, he'd been forced to join the side that he'd fought so hard to protect the dragonseers from.

And that thought caused me to hate Finesia even more.

"But Lieutenant Wiggea's not dead yet, is he?" Gerhaun said.

"We lost him to Finesia."

"No", Gerhaun said. *"We must believe there's a way back for him, just as there is for you. But for the rest of the men and the dragons who died, there will be a long period of mourning. And then we'll need to rally the dragon queens. We've not had to call a council since the dragonheats. Yet times are getting dark once again."*

"I understand," I said. *"But tell me... I need to hear the good news amidst all this darkness."*

"Very well," Gerhaun said. *"There is something you'll be pleased to hear."*

"Go on..."

"Well, something good has come out of all of this. I had to sleep long before you went because I was about to give birth."

"Another egg?"

"Not just any egg. But the next dragon queen."

And for the first time in a while, elation rose in my chest. And, as if Velos also felt my feelings and knew what had happened, he let out a distant roar. This roar, I imagined, passed across the courtyard and the through corridors of Fortress Gerhaun and over the parapets.

I imagined it even reached out into the secicao cloud and over the thorny secicao from where Finesia could hear its intent.

"No," Velos' roar seemed to say. *"We have a will. And, Finesia, you shall not have dominion. For the good and the collective unconscious shall prevail overall."*

SUKINA'S STORY

WANT TO LEARN MORE ABOUT Sukina? You can download a full-length novel about how she came to be a dragonseer by signing up to my email list.

I send emails approximately twice a month. You can subscribe at http://chrisbehrsin.com/sukina/.

If, at any time, you want to shoot me an email, you can reach me at: author@chrisbehrsin.com.

DRAGONSEERS AND AUTOMATONS

The story continues in Dragonseers and Automatons, where Pontopa battles hordes of automatons, while Finesia gets stronger in her head.

Start reading it today at: mybook.to/dragonseersautomatons.

ACKNOWLEDGMENTS

Firstly, I'd like to thank my good friend, Patch Willis for all the writing sessions and motivation. And a big shout out for all the members of NaNoWriMo Vietnam this month (November 2019). I'll start sprinting with you guys soon.

And to all the fantastic people at Miblart for your wonderful cover.

A big thanks to Wayne Scace for his incredible generosity in helping me find those niggling typos.

Also, to my father, who has read a lot of my work and given me the verbal encouragement I needed to keep going. And to my mother, for giving me emotional support through those difficult career times.

And finally, thank you most of all to my dear wife, Ola, for the best support a husband and writer can ask for.

ABOUT THE AUTHOR

Chris Behrsin is a British fiction writer who is pursuing the digital nomad lifestyle, hopping from pond to pond and working remotely he goes. Fiction-wise, he writes in multiple genres, but mainly science fiction and fantasy.

He's also a working freelance copywriter and he co-runs the Being a Nomad (beinganomad.com) travel blog with his wife. In his spare time, he enjoys reading and playing the piano, whenever he has access to one.

He's travelled extensively, having lived in France, South Korea, Poland, China, Spain, and Vietnam. He has a passion for exploring off-the-beaten-path destinations and infusing pieces of them in his work.

CPSIA information can be obtained
at www.ICGtesting.com
Printed in the USA
FSHW010444070821
83853FS